Sacrifices

J.P. Grider

Published by J.P. Grider, 2018.

Sacrifices

(A reimagined, rewritten version of The Honor Trilogy)
Published by
Fated Hearts Publishing
Jefferson Township, New Jersey 07438

PROLOGUE

The woods are unfamiliar.

Yet I know I need to be here.

They're calling to me.

Something is.

I feel it everywhere—my gut, my head. Like I'm being punched.

Naked.

Bare.

Violated.

Frightened. Very frightened.

When I stop running, it's worse, so I keep my feet moving, pounding the ground as I follow the silent call deep into these woods.

To where?

I've no idea.

But I run. And I run. And I run.

And I pant, breathless. Because I am so out of shape.

But when the call is no longer silent, I stop.

"Tamlin?" I yell when I see her scrambling on the ground, fighting off two guys while she screams into the air.

When they hear me shout, three sets of eyes look my way. All three shocked, but only one set relieved.

The one holding her down grunts in frustration before he flees, while the other stands there clueless. Fortunately, this gives Tamlin time to get up and straighten up what's left of her tattered clothes before she runs to me and grabs my hands. "Let's get outta here," she says, pulling me along the path back to civilization.

PART ONE
HONOR
Chapter One

Do you know those things they crush cars with? A hydraulic press, or something like that? Well my head may as well be sitting beneath one, because it couldn't feel any worse than it does right now.

But even though my eyes are closed, and I'm willing the crushing pain to leave me alone, I can still feel *his* stare burning behind me. The teachers call him Ethan. So do the girls who ogle him. I've never had any conversations with him to call him anything, but I haven't been oblivious to his presence either. I mean, maybe I wouldn't be all that aware of his flawless beauty if he didn't stare all the time. At first, I thought maybe he was into me or something, and I was kind of flattered, because yeah, he's adorable. But when I smiled at him, he'd narrowed his eyes like *I* was the one out of line. Yet, he continued to stare after that and still does. I don't know if he does it to anyone else, or just to me, but right now, he's staring at me, and I want to punch him. And I'm not a violent girl, so you know he's pissing me off right now. Especially because my head hurts so much that I can see Christmas lights flickering through my head.

The end of Algebra class can't come soon enough. I hate it. And not only because I have trouble with it. As soon as I walk through this particular classroom, I am paralyzed with intense agony. I can be having an okay day, but then I walk into this class and bam, instant migraine. Christmas tree lights, stars, whatever you want to call it, that's what I see when I feel the pain. Mom says it's anxiety about using numbers that causes it, but I don't think so. I don't ever get a headache when I'm doing my algebra homework.

I wish Ethan would just stop staring at me. His violet eyes are so intense when they meet mine. *Wait. Violet eyes?*

I can't take it any longer, though—the migraine, his staring, the new found realization that his eyes are the same exact shade of violet as mine. This unnerves me most. So, instead of catching glimpses of him by straining my neck, I slam my hands on the desk, jerk my head around and shout, "What? What is it? Why do you keep looking at me like that?" I'm not one to lose my cool, God knows, but he just pushed the wrong buttons at the wrong time.

"Honor Stevens," the teacher exclaims. "What was that outburst all about?"

I turn around, back towards the front of the classroom, before even getting any type of reaction from Ethan. "I'm sorry, Miss James," I apologize, my face burning beneath my skin. "May I be excused?"

Miss James lets out a huge sigh, but turns to retrieve a laminated hall pass from a hook next to the smart board. She stands there holding the pass; I stand from my seat to get it.

"You have five minutes, Miss Stevens."

Before I even have a chance to take the pass from her hand, Ethan races up and grabs it. "I'll make sure she gets there, Miss James," he says.

"No, Ethan, that's okay," Miss James says as Ethan's face goes white.

I take the pass from him and walk out. From behind me, I hear Miss James say, "Ethan, honey, are you all right? You look like you've seen a ghost."

But I am too wrapped up in my own migraine problems to worry about him. As I'm walking to the girls' room to splash water on my face to calm down, I realize my headache is gone. Before I can contemplate why that may be, I feel a hand on my shoulder as I'm opening up the girls' room door. It's Ethan. When I turn to face him, his violet eyes grip mine, and I jump back a foot.

"Honor," he rasps, as if he hasn't spoken a word in days.

"Ethan, is it?"

He nods.

"What is it you want from me?" I am beginning to feel fear rise up in my throat.

"I want to be sure you're okay," he says to me softly.

"Really? You've been watching me and following me in the hallways...and...and to the library after school these past two days just to be sure I'm okay?" I, who usually remains collected, just had my second outburst today.

His head drops in shame. "You saw me...at the library?"

"Yes, I did," I clip.

"And...you didn't report me for following you?" he asks, looking back up with a smile pasted on his face.

"Well," I say and think to myself, *why not*? I know he's being sarcastic, but I really should have. "No, I didn't think of it." With my hand still holding open the bathroom door, I'm thinking, I need to hurry him along. "Could we, like, discuss this, um, later? Miss James only gave me five minutes."

He nods. His eyes are peering through mine again. I avert mine to avoid his stare.

"Meet me by the back parking lot after school," he tentatively demands.

Hoping this is not going to be a big mistake, I agree to meet him. I really am curious to find out why he keeps staring at me the way he does. I get the feeling that it's not because he's interested in dating me or anything like that.

I go about my business in the girls' room, but when I return to math class and hang up the hall pass, I see lights. Like, a million bright LED Christmas lights. Stars. The planets. Whatever. The migraine is back in full force, and I nearly pass out. Miss James pulls out her chair, and Ethan comes flying over to place me in it. *What is with this guy*?

"Ethan," Miss James says. "Why don't you go get the nurse?"

"Miss James, with all due respect, ma'am, I'd rather you send someone else."

I peer at Ethan through my hand, which is covering my face, wondering why he would disobey.

"Fine,." She resigns. "Tamlin, will you go get the nurse?"

Tamlin, my new best friend who is right near the desk making sure I am all right, straightens her back and opens her mouth. "Certainly, Miss James." She darts out the door, willing and ready to save the day.

With my elbow resting on the arm of the chair and my hand still covering my face, I see Miss James through my spread-out fingers reaching for my shoulder. But before she actually rests her hand on me, Ethan comes between us, practically pushing the teacher away.

"Ethan," Miss James snaps.

I hear him take a deep breath. "Miss James," he says weakly. "I'm sorry. I uh, kinda lost my balance."

"You're all white again," she says.

"I'm fine, Miss James," Ethan replies. "Let's just focus on Honor here." He pats my shoulders.

"Miss James?" I hear the nurse walk in with Tamlin.

"Honor's not feeling well. I didn't want her to walk to your office until you checked on her." Miss James whispers. "She was about to pass out."

The school nurse crouches down before me. "Honor," she says, and I take my hand from my face. "Tell me what's happening, dear."

"I have a really bad headache. Really bad." I am getting embarrassed, sitting here with the whole class watching. "Can I go to your office and lie down?"

"Sure." She and Ethan help me up.

"Ethan," Miss James calls, "you don't need to go."

He looks at me.

"Fine, but Miss James," I hear Ethan once again as I'm walking out of the classroom. "Why don't you get an MRI on your head? I'm sensing you need one," he trails off as I walk further down the hallway.

"Ethan Sutherland, sit down," Miss James' raised-voice response echoes through the hallway.

In the nurse's office, while I rest on one of the cots, Nurse Wentick phones my mother at the library. My poor mother. She has taken so much time away from her job to either pick me up from school, or chauffeur me from doctor to doctor, and all in vain. Test after test, scan after scan, nothing is ever found. Doctors are at a loss, unable to figure out what is wrong with me. The pain travels, which is peculiar in itself, so a couple doctors have diagnosed me with fibromyalgia, but others say that diagnosis doesn't fit. And, oddly, nothing ever hurts when I'm alone. When I'm by myself, away from people, I feel no pain.

"Your mother will be here soon," Nurse Wentick tells me. "She's alone at the library; she's just waiting for coverage."

I nod. "I feel all right now. I really can go back to class."

Nurse Wentick tilts her head to the side. "I'm sorry, Honor. You don't look well, and I suggested your mom take you to the doctor."

"Mrs. Wentick, really, that won't do anything. It's just a migraine." I plead to go back to class.

"Honor, you've been looking really pale lately. Very fatigued and run-down." She touches the back of her hand to my forehead. "You don't feel warm or anything," she tsks. "I'd feel better if you got checked out."

"Mmm." I lay my head back on the pillow, dropping my forearm over my forehead. I do feel run-down, and it does feel good to lay here and close my eyes. I guess I won't be meeting Ethan in the back parking lot after school. I'll have to find out what all his staring is about another day.

Chapter Two

Today when I walk into Algebra, I'm amazed. Flabbergasted. For the first time since the beginning of the school year, I have no sudden attack of a migraine. No Christmas lights illuminating my brain. No stars or planets. Just peace inside my head.

"Hey, Honor," one of my classmates calls out to me. "How you feeling today?"

"I'm good, thanks."

"What's with that new guy? He's so into you...in that creepy, stalker way," she mocks.

I let her comment hang there, not knowing if she is trying to be friendly or making fun of me. But it doesn't matter, because I am concentrating on avoiding Ethan's gaze. As usual, he is watching me. This time he stares surreptitiously, averting his eyes every now and then instead of overtly gaping right at me.

As soon as I sit at my desk, the class bell rings. A second later, Mrs. Johnson, a substitute teacher, enters the classroom and welcomes us. "Hello students." Mrs. Johnson is a regular sub and very familiar with all of us. "Obviously, Miss James is not here today, but she did leave assignments. Please open your books to page 104."

Though algebra is still Greek to me, it's refreshing to have a clear head through the entire period.

"Honor," Ethan calls, approaching me after class. "You look good today. Your color's back."

I gather my books from my desk and fit them into my backpack. "Thanks." Glancing at him quickly, I continue packing up.

"Can you meet me today after school?" His head is down, his eyes staring at the polished concrete floor.

Shaking my head, I offer a negative answer. "Sorry, I can't. My mom's picking me up on her way to work. Maybe tomorrow?" I ask, blurting it out without even thinking first.

"Sure." He nods and walks away, but the straightening of his posture tells me he is trying really hard to restrain himself from looking back.

Today is going by almost pain-free. Sure, I have sudden twinges here and there walking through the halls, but for the most part, I feel good.

"Hey there, Honor." Tamlin catches up with me. "You're looking happy today."

I smile, practically skipping alongside her.

"What're you all smiles for?"

Still smiling, and yes, still hovering between a walk and a skip, I shrug. "I dunno. Just feel good, I guess."

"Nothing hurts?" she inquires.

"Barely," I smirk, yet retain my smile.

"What else?"

"Whaddya mean, what else? That's enough. For nearly— " Quickly, I try to do the math in my head, with a little help from my fingers, "—seven months—" I think, yes, it's almost April now, "—yeah, for nearly seven months, I've had a splitting headache every freakin' school day. Today, nothing. That should be enough to make me happy, don'tcha think?" I nudge her with my arm. "Shouldn't it?"

She gives me this huge grin. "Sure it should. I'm happy for you."

"Hey, Tamlin." My tone turns serious. "How've you been?" I raise my eyebrows, concerned that I haven't even brought up her attack in weeks. Maybe she's been hurting, and I've been too involved in my own misery to even notice.

She nudges me back, "Oh, Honor, you know I'm fine." Her arm slips around my shoulders, which is no easy feat for her, since, at 5'2", she's a whole seven inches shorter than I am. "You know I'm just grateful you were there." Suddenly it's silent, and I know we're both thinking the same thing. *How in the world did I know she was in the woods, behind the school, being attacked by two delinquents?*

Tamlin interrupts the silence. "I just don't understand how you knew."

My heart races a bit. "I told you Tamlin, I don't know. I felt afraid ...I told you that...but not for me. I...I can't explain it."

She opens the door that leads to the parent pick-up lot and stops, holding up a slew of rowdy teens behind us. "But you said you felt like you were being punched and...and," she lowers her voice, "you felt like you were about to be raped." Her voice raises, "it's like you were there with me...and then...you were."

"Hey, move it up there," an impatient teenager yells.

Tamlin looks back. "Oops, sorry." And continues walking...and talking.

"I wish I knew how you knew I was in trouble."

Tired of trying to find an explanation, I respond, "Maybe we just have a really strong bond." I sigh.

"Yeah. That'd be true...if we were friends then. We barely even knew each other a month ago."

Closing my eyes, I try to calm myself from my sudden irritability. I love that Tamlin and I have become instant friends, but I am getting tired of her wondering what I can't answer. It frustrates me as well, but I try never to dwell on the things that just waste my time. Figuring out why I always hurt so much takes up most of my time anyway.

Finally, I say, "Tamlin, maybe there is no definitive answer. Maybe God just led me to you. Some things are just inexplicable. Be thankful and...be glad we got a friendship out of the deal."

She hugs me one of those tight bear hugs. "You're right, Honor. You're the best friend anyone could ever have. Even if you have only been my best friend for, like, a month."

I laugh and peer over her shoulder to see my mom pulling up. "Tam, wanna go to the library with me? Mom's here now."

"Aw, no thanks Honor, I'm going home to dye my hair."

"Again?" Every week she seems to come in with a different vibrant color; today it is Katy Perry blue.

"Yeah, I was thinking violet. Like your eyes." She winks and kisses me on the cheek.

"You're crazy, Tam. Your hair's gonna fall out," I yell as I run towards Mom's car. "You're going to be bald one day," I bellow before shutting myself inside Mom's Volkswagon Passat.

"Hey, Mom."

"Hi, Honor." She leans over to kiss my cheek. "Good day?"

"Yeah, Mom, it was."

"No pain?" she asks, her eyes wide in surprise.

Shaking my head, I say, "No, Mom, no pain, but it's weird. When it usually hits me bad, in Algebra, nothing happened. The really odd thing is, Miss James wasn't in today."

Mom pulls into the library parking lot, which is only half a mile up the road.

"That's significant how?" Mom wonders.

My bottom lip juts out a little as I shake my head. "I don't know. Maybe it's not, but...maybe it is."

"Is she mean, dear? Maybe she makes you nervous." Mom grabs her bag and gets out of the car. I follow.

"Nah, she's really nice." I hold the library door for Mom. "Don't worry about it, Mom." I kiss her goodbye as she heads to her desk, and I head for the computers.

"I always worry, Honey."

The library is crowded as usual after school, with students taking advantage of the free Wi-Fi. At least there is a computer available. I'm one of the unlucky ones who does not own her own laptop. We don't even have a computer at home. Mom says since she is at the library every day working, there is no reason I can't come see her and do my homework there. I tell her it'd be nice to have one at home for late at night when the library is closed and I'm still lying awake bored. She tells me to read a book if I'm so bored. But really, that's all I do—read. I know I prefer separating myself from people, but sometimes, it'd be nice to have a life—even if it is just a virtual one.

So I'm working on my paper for Global Issues, which is ironically about the desensitizing of America due to the vast amount of violence on the Internet and television, when I feel someone watching me. I think, *it couldn't be, could it?* Apprehensively, moving my eyes from the computer screen to the opposite end of the room where I sense his presence, I catch him. Looking right at me. Again.

Why is he following me? I hesitate to look back up, but I do. He's gone. What the heck? Furtively scanning the room, I jump and nearly fall off my seat when I find him directly behind me.

"Careful there." He smirks.

"Ethan," I exclaim with my hand pressed hard against my chest. "God, you're gonna give me a heart attack."

He muffles a laugh. "Sorry, Honor. You have a minute?" His tone is more serious. He reminds me of a little boy with his hands stuck in his pockets, his feet shifting from one to the other. A 6'5" little boy. I hadn't realized before how tall he is.

I roll my seat back from the computer to stand and face him, still feeling diminutive at 5'9". He is just so...ginormous.

Suddenly there is a warm sensation flowing up my spine, and I realize Ethan has his hand on the middle of my back, leading me towards the library's vestibule. Though I enjoy the feel of his hand on my back, I'm still uneasy about him, so I lengthen my gait to pull away. Because his legs are so long, he reaches the door before I do and holds it open.

"What's this about, Ethan? I have a ton of homework to finish," I press.

He paces the small room, trying to think of what to say. I can tell, because his eyes keep darting up to the left, as if the words will somehow appear in mid-air. After an abrupt end to his pacing, Ethan looks directly into my eyes, which by now I'm getting uncomfortably used to, and opens his mouth. "Would you go on a date with me?" he blurts out.

I blink. This feels somewhat anticlimactic, considering all the spying and eyeballing he's done since he's moved here. Subconsciously, I back away while he does the same.

"Um...no," I answer, almost regretfully. Aside from the persistent staring, I do find him uncommonly beautiful. But I don't date. Never have. And the staring...it's just strange.

"Oh," he murmurs, his hands dipping back into his pockets. "Ok." Still looking me right in the eyes, as if he is trying to read something in them, I avert mine, feeling way too weirded-out.

"Ethan," I pause. Not sure how to say this without insulting him, I try the direct approach. "If you're trying to, you know, get a girl's attention...well, gawking at her isn't exactly the most effective way of going about it."

He says nothing.

"Y'know, it can be kinda...creepy," I shrug.

His head nods once. "Yeah, sorry." He walks out the library door without uttering another word. I watch *him* now. He's getting into one of those new Mercedes C-class styles. A black one. Boy, my parents won't even *think* of buying me a car yet. And I turned seventeen six months ago. They say that since I'm only a junior in high school and have no job, there's no reason to have a car. The bus will get me where I need to go. If *it* won't, *they* will. Still, a car would be nice. Ethan's folks probably have none of those conservative rules that mine have.

When I return inside the library, three Jefferson cheerleaders are gaping at me, mouths wide open, face contorted in disgust. "You *know* him?" One tiny brunette asks, a disparaging tone way too apparent in her voice.

"Who? Ethan?" Playing dumb was probably the smartest way to go.

They cover their mouths with their hands as if they are twelve, and they pretend to whisper.

Attempting to ignore them, I return to my computer. From a distance, I can still hear them whispering.

"She is such a freak," the short one ridicules. "What could he see in *her?*"

"Oh, you know," a taller girl responds. "Her ridiculously long blond hair and her huge boobs," she continues mocking. "He's new. Once he gets to know her, he'll figure out she's a loser," she reassures herself.

This is one of the reasons I prefer being home schooled as opposed to being subjected to petty gossip and ridiculing. But Mom thought once I'd reached high school age, I should enter the public school system to socialize more. I really hate socializing. Not that I'm above it or anything, but it makes me anxious. Of course, my anti-anxiety meds don't help. I still get all those aches and pains too. It's just an overall unpleasant experience.

Since I can't stand gossip, especially when it's directed at me, I try really hard to ignore the three cheerleaders. Though the tiny one is giving off some horrible vibe that makes my bones hurt. But I just chalk it up to my anxiety...and a delusional mind.

Picking up where I left off on my essay is not an easy task. Once distracted, I can't easily jump back into what I was doing. Besides, I'm thinking about Ethan now. The warm sensation of his hand on my back still tingles where he touched. Which is ridiculous. Just yesterday, he pissed me off with all his weird staring. Today, however, I feel bad for him. The boy really needs to learn how to approach girls.

Chapter Three

The heaviness surrounding Miss James' classroom the following morning is unmistakable. Something is wrong. The principal is talking somberly with Mrs. Johnson, the substitute, when the bell rings. Though we aren't told to do so, the class sits silently for Mrs. Johnson to begin the curriculum. Instead, she starts with a grave announcement. Miss James would be out indefinitely. She has what the doctor thinks is an inoperable brain tumor and is taking time off to see specialists for second and third opinions.

The sinking feeling I had in my chest when I first walked into the classroom now feels like a lead weight pressing against it. My hand is instinctively drawn to my chest, where I hold it for the remainder of the period. Since Miss James is well-liked, the class remains pretty silent for the whole forty-eight minutes, absorbing this horrific news. I cannot help but think of Ethan's insolent comment two days ago to Miss James about getting an MRI on her head. He sounded so rude, but could she have taken him seriously and actually gotten one? Could Ethan have known about Miss James' brain tumor? Or was his flippant remark some kind of divine intervention? Maybe it was just a coincidence. *I* do not believe in coincidences myself. To every thing there is a purpose, right? Isn't that how the song goes? Or the Bible for that matter?

No, it isn't just a coincidence. Of that, I am certain.

What could have possessed Ethan, though, to point Miss James in the right direction...and possibly have saved her life?

I am so absorbed in my own thoughts, that I do not hear the period bell ring. Not until Ethan taps me on the shoulder do I even realize the room is empty—except for him and me.

"Hey, Honor, you okay?" Sincerity is entirely present in his voice.

I stand from my desk and grab my books, not bothering to put them in my bag. "Hey," I say, my voice shaky and showing unexpected nervousness. All of a sudden, I am strangely aware of Ethan's presence. Not just him being near me, but like some electric force is emanating from him. I can *feel* him.. "Yeah, I'm all right," I say, ignoring the strange tingling inside of me. "Just sad for Miss James." My eyes stay fixed straight ahead of me while we walk to the next class. I am too self-conscious to look at Ethan right now. I can't understand the pull he is having on me. It's not attraction, it can't be. There's something entirely different going on. But I can't look him in the eyes. I'm afraid of what I'll see if I do. "You really liked Miss James?" he asks, genuinely concerned.

"She was okay," I say, but I want to divulge so much more. *How every day when I'd walk into her class my head would throb, and I'd get this overwhelming sadness for her.* It is so hard to explain, I don't even know if I could. But in hindsight, I think I knew Miss James was sick. My heart keeps racing as I think about this, and my emotions are just so overwhelming that I cry. *What a baby.* Outside of class, Ethan pushes me into an alcove on the other side of the hall.

I yank my arm from his grasp and say, "Stop."

As I attempt to pull myself together, I turn and walk away from Ethan. Instead of getting the hint, he follows me.

"Why are you here? Why do you keep attaching yourself to me?"

"I like you. " He shrugs.

"You don't even know me."

"I'd like to get to know you."

I stop and turn to him. "Why?"

"Do I have to have a reason?"

"Uh, yeah."

"Maybe I think you're nice."

Shaking my head, I start for my next class. "Doubtful."

"Why doubtful?" His eyebrows knit together.

"First of all, I'm not even being nice to you. Second of all, I'm not the most popular girl in the school. I'll certainly ruin any reputation you might want."

He smirks, then smiles. "I'm not too concerned about my reputation. Or my popularity."

"That's not how everyone else seems to think."

Ethan puts his hand on my shoulder to stop me from walking and purposely turns me with his other hand to look him in the eye. One pair of violet eyes peering deep into another set. "Well...I am not like everyone else," he enunciates each word slowly.

That's for sure, I think with a smirk. "What?" he asks, apparently catching the smirk on my face.

"Nothing." As if he is holding me prisoner with his eyes, I am unable to look away.

We remain like that for several seconds before a hall monitor interrupts, "You two should be in class, no?" she reprimands.

"Yes, Ma'am," Ethan answers. "Sorry. We had a little...thing, and we were...sorting it out. We'll get to class." He takes my hand and walks with me to my next class, but I come to my senses and pull my hand free before I get there.

"How did you know I have English Lit?" I ask when he stops right in front of the classroom door.

He laughs. "Didn't you just ask me, like, yesterday, in so many words, to stop *watching* you?"

Red blotches must be covering my face, because I feel flush. "Well, not...exactly, I just meant..."

"I know what you meant." He stops me. "And...," he looks down momentarily, "you were right, I shouldn't have been staring at you like that...and following you everywhere," Ethan admits.

"Good. Thanks."

"Anytime. I'll catch you later." Then he watches me walk into English. I know, because I turn and see him following me with his violet eyes. I'm not as weirded out as I had been by him, but he's still an oddity. More so than I am. And that's pretty odd.

After school, Ethan is standing at the bottom of the stairs outside the building and he's smiling. Slowly, I make my way down, not sure if he's waiting there for me or waiting for someone else. Though, I'm pretty sure I know the answer. "Hey," I say, as I finally make it down the steep steps.

"I was wondering if I could drive you home...or to the library...if that's where you're going?" he asks.

"Um, well, my mom should be here any minute. And I thought we talked yesterday?"

"Yeah, we did, but...I thought you'd give me another chance, plus I kinda thought we could talk...again."

"Oh."

"Is that a no?"

"Um." Yes? No? "I guess."

"Don't sound so excited," he jokes. "How 'bout tomorrow after school? Can I drive you home tomorrow?"

I nod just as my mom pulls up. "Sure," I tell him before hopping in Mom's car. As we drive away, I watch him watching me...and wonder if I made a mistake in agreeing to have him drive me home.

Chapter Four

After school the next day, Ethan is at the bottom of the stairs waiting at the exact spot he stood the day before. Only this time, I expect him. "Hey," Ethan says as I meet him down the stairs.

"Hey."

"Y'goin' home or to the library today?" he asks.

"Library."

"Y'need to get there right away?" He tilts his head to the side. "Or can we take a detour?"

"I have time, I guess." Fortunately, since I knew he wanted to talk and not just drive me home, I told my mom, I'd be late.

"Awesome." He takes my backpack, then my hand.

There's an unfamiliar tingling inching up my limbs before I yank my hand from his. He opens his car door, throws our backpacks in the back seat and motions for me to get in. His car has that new car smell, and the seats are crazy comfortable.

Not sure of what to say, I'm relieved when Ethan puts his iPod on. Plain White T's, *Killer,* is in mid-song. He must have been listening to it on the ride in this morning. We're not driving more than five minutes when he turns into Mahlon Dickerson Reservation.

"Mahlon Dickerson?" I wonder out loud why he's taking me to a hiking trail.

"Yeah, ever been?" His eyes stay on the dirt road.

I shake my head, then realize he may not see me shake it. "No."

"No? You've lived here all your life and you've never been here?"

"Uh, and how did you know I've lived here all my life?"

"Um, I just assumed?" he asks, so obviously he didn't just assume.

Ethan pulls into a lot and shuts off the car. "C'mon, I'll show you around."

His little lie leaves me even more apprehensive.

He circles the car and reaches for my hand again, but I stick them in my pockets. He shrugs it off and says, "C'mon, I wanna show ya somethin.'"

He leads me up a long path where chipmunks and squirrels scurry past. In the distance, I can hear crickets and tree frogs. It's quiet here. Serene. And I realize that I am feeling no pain at all. Not even an ache.

As we continue on, the woods open up to a small glistening lake.

"Wow," I mutter more to myself than to Ethan.

"I thought you'd like it here. It's quiet."

"I do." I whisper, wondering how he'd know I'd like it when he doesn't even know me.

"I found this place my second day here."

Ethan climbs up a huge rock, motioning me to follow. When we reach the top, Ethan sits.

"How long have you been here?" I ask, sitting several inches away from him.

"About two weeks."

"Where do you live?"

"An apartment on Berkshire Valley."

"Oh."

"I come here almost every day...to be alone."

"Really?" I ask, surprised he'd want to be alone. I thought that I was the only teenager who sought solitude.

"Yeah," he says, turning to look directly into my eyes.

Since it makes me feel uncomfortable, I avert my eyes and peer out at the lake. The funny thing is, earlier, his actions made me feel uneasy, but right now, I've never felt more calm.

"I like to be by myself," he admits, when I don't respond to him. "That's when I'm most comfortable." I turn to look at him this time, and again, his violet eyes search mine for some kind of reaction.

"Do you like to be alone, Honor?" His tone is serious, and I wonder what he is trying to get out of me. It's odd, but he's searching for something from me. I can feel it.

I swallow my suspicions and nod.

"Being a loner is a way of life for some; nothing to be embarrassed about."

He knows it embarrasses me? "What are you talking about?"

"What's the matter? Did I offend you? I'm sorry if I did."

I take in the beauty of the lake and ignore Ethan.

"Honor," he persists. "Look at me." His fingertips touch my chin, but I back away.

"Ethan. Boundaries." He's too touchy-feely for me. For a girl who's rarely around people, his touches are unnerving. His hand falls to his lap, but he keeps talking.

"Sorry. I'll keep my hands to myself."

"What is it you want to know about me, Ethan, because obviously, it's something specific."

"How do you figure?"

"All this talk about being alone, or being a loner...I know you're referring to me. You've only been here two weeks. How do you know this about me?"

"It's not really hard to figure out."

"Yeah, well, then you're paying too close attention to me. Stop it." I bring my knees to my chest and hug them.

"You hurt too, right?" Snapping my head in his direction, I drop my legs and jump down from the rock.

"Did you ever figure out *why* you hurt?" He jumps down and follows me back up the path.

"You know, this was a mistake. I wanna go home."

"Honor. I do have a reason for being here. You're right."

I stop and let him continue.

"Let me tell you about me first...then I'll be able to tell you why. 'Kay?"

Thinking about this for several seconds, I wrap my arms in front of me and say, "Fine. But you better have a point to all this."

"I do. I'm from Pennsylvania...I'm a loner too, as you already know. My family is...everywhere. None of us stick together and we all go our separate ways...brothers, cousins, everyone."

"What about your parents...you live with them?" I ask with a chip on my shoulder.

Ethan's eyes dart to the ground. "They're dead."

"Oh. Sorry."

"It's fine. It's been years."

I ignore the sudden pain in my chest. There's no way I could be feeling anything for this guy. I barely know him. "Who do you live with?"

With a raise of his blonde brow, he says, "Myself."

"Yeah, right. No, really."

"Really, Honor. I live by myself." He shrugs. "Besides, I'm eighteen; I'm old enough."

The pain in my chest grows stronger, but I don't know why. "How do you afford it? I mean, your car. It's, like, a Mercedes."

Ethan laughs. "It *is* a Mercedes...and my parents left my brothers and me a huge amount of money. They had some huge life insurance policy."

"Your brothers don't live with you?"

"Nope. Like I said, they live all over the place."

"How many brothers do you have?"

He holds up three fingers.

"Why don't you live together?"

He sighs, and I wonder if I'm asking too many questions. Maybe I should stop, but really, he needs to get to the point.

"We're close, we just prefer to live alone."

"Oh."

When I look into Ethan's eyes, the pain in my chest intensifies, and I want to throw up. That's when I realize Ethan is holding his stomach. "Are you, like, feeling nauseous or something?"

"Thinking about my family tends to do that? Why? Are *you* feeling the urge to throw up?"

"What? No. Why would I?"

He steps toward me, and touches my arm. "Tell me something, Honor. Do you always feel sick or in pain or anything?"

I instinctively pull away from him.

"You do, don't you."

"Stop."

"You ever see a doctor about it all? "

How does he know this? "Okay. I gotta go. This is...this is too strange." I start the walk up the path, and again, he follows.

"You know deep down there's something different about you, don't you?"

What the heck? Now, I not only have chest pains and an upset stomach, but I'm getting really angry as well.

As I speed up in front of him, I hear his cellphone ring. Behind me, he says, "Yeah?"

I continue heading toward his car, but it's not hard to overhear him.

"Lead them out west," he says. "California. Out of the country. Just get them far from here." There's a pause before he says, "Yeah. Call ya later."

Ethan catches up to me and pockets his phone. "Sorry, 'bout that. " he says, but his whole demeanor changes. He's anxious. Worried.

"What's wrong?"

"Nothing. C'mon. I'll take you to the library."

Chapter Five

The car ride to the library is somber. Ethan even shuts his music off, making the silence that much louder. While he is driving, I notice him biting his lip, and I assume he is thinking about the phone call. Yet...he says nothing.

When he drops me off, he reaches over and squeezes my knee. The boy really has boundaries issues. "Thanks for letting me drive you today, Honor. I'll see you tomorrow at school."

"Sure." I said goodbye and started up the steps to the library. "Honor. Honor." Cindy, the library aide, in all hysteria, bolts towards me. "We tried to..." she's out of breath, "call you. Oh, Honor...your mother."

I clutch my chest. There's that pain again. I scan the library. "Where?" My voice cracks. "Where is she?" Where's my mother?"

"The ambulance." The aide slams both her hands on my shoulders. "They took her to Saint Clare's...in Denville."

"Oh my god. Oh my god." I'm now wearing out a three foot path in the library's rug with my back and forth pacing. "I need to see her. Oh...I don't even know how...how I'll get there."

"Honor." Cindy is not doing well at calming me, since not only is she just a year older than I am, she's always so helplessly neurotic. Especially now. "They called your dad. Oh my goodness, he's going straight from work to the hospital. Oh my god, Honor, where were you? You shoulda been here." In the meantime, while I pace, I remember that I had threw my cellphone in my backpack when we were at the reservation. "You coulda gone in the ambulance. Now what're you gonna do?"

"Cindy. Stop." I hold up both my hands as if I'm stopping traffic, which metaphorically I am, since her words pour out of her mouth at breakneck speed. I'm barely able to get a thought in. "Just stop. Please." I need to think. I reach for my backpack and retrieve my phone. Flipping through my contacts, I see Tamlin's name. She'll help. I'm sure of it. With trembling fingers, I press her name. No reception. Damn. I run outside hoping...just hoping to get reception. Nothing. I tear down the handicap ramp, eyeing the reception bars on my phone while I run. Stopping at the end of the ramp, I try her number again. My hand shakes so much that I drop my phone. When I bend to pick it up, a hand lands on my shoulder. There's no need to look to see who it is. I already know.

"Ethan." I turn to him. In his metallic, violet eyes, I search for sanity.

"Honor?" He tries to hold me.

But I push him away. "Ethan." I huff and I puff. "I need a ride...St. Clare's...Denville." My words come out in breathy whispers. "Oh my god, I just realized...I don't even know what happened." I turn and take off back into the library, feeling Ethan right behind me.

"Cindy." I call to the aide. "What happened to my mom?"

Still in tears, Cindy cries, "Heart attack."

I nearly collapse, but Ethan, lately, always near, catches me in his arms and helps me to his car.

He does not follow speed limits. We arrive in Denville in a record twenty minutes,. For that, I am grateful. For the whole ride, I'd wanted to jump out of my seat. At the emergency room desk, I give my mother's name, and they immediately direct us to her bed. At about the same time we reach it, a bunch of scrub-adorned medical staff rip open her curtain and start commanding technical directives. A man in green hovers over my mother, while a flat line displays across the screen next to her bed, sounding an unforgettable, deafening noise. My father is in the corner, in shock.

I'm ordered to leave immediately, by another woman dressed in green, but I stand there, like my father, in a state of shock. Ethan grasps the back of my arm and whispers, "Go to her, Honor. Touch her." I faintly hear him but not well enough to respond. "Go by your mother, Honor," he demands again. Allowing what he asks of me to sink in a bit, I realize he's not making any sense. They won't allow me anywhere near her, why in the world would he want me to touch her?

"She can't come in here." The scrub commands, obviously overhearing Ethan.

Oh god, I hold my chest. I look at Dad, still standing in the corner. His eyes are as wide as quarters, and he hasn't moved an inch.

"Honor," Ethan presses. "Go." This time his command is stern. "Touch her. I'll explain later, but you have the power to heal her."

"What?" I turn in his direction as he pushes me toward my mother.

"Go. It's been inside you all your life. I'll explain later, but right now, you have to put your hand on your mother's chest."

He's speaking gibberish, but I do as he says and reach my hand out toward her as I step between two scrubs. When I look back at him, he's nodding for me to continue.

"Hey. Get her out of here." I hear from behind me.

"No," Ethan barks. "It's her mother."

"Mom." Resting my hand on her chest, I plead with her. "Mommy, please." I cry harder than I've ever cried before. "Mommy, please, please, please, don't die. I need you. I need you, Mom. Please." I close my eyes and lean my head on her arm. I feel the tickle of my tears on my cheek when in the near distance, I hear the start of a machine—a beeping sound. The flat line noise is gone. I jerk my head up just as the nurses race toward her again.

"Mom?"

The beeping steadies, and I look at my mom. Her eyelashes flutter, as her lids open and close. "Mom?"

Her chest rises and falls. Such a beautiful thing. My mother is breathing. She's alive.

My breathing, however, becomes laborious. Heavy. And suddenly, it is me who can't get in enough air. My mom is there, and then she's not.

Chapter Six

"Oh. Ew." I startle. The scent is horribly potent. My eyes flash open. Then they shut. I just want to sleep. But...that smell.

"Honor. Open your eyes. You can't sleep." the faint voice orders.

The pungent smell stuns me awake again.

"It's smelling salts, Honor, now stay awake," she orders.

I force my eyelids up to my eyebrows, but they want to shut. Lead weights must be pulling them down.

"Honor, c'mon, you need to stay awake."

Closing my eyes, I mutter, "I just...wanna...sleep."

"No. Honor. You can't." Ethan's voice is now near. Soft but firm. I feel his breath on my hair. Smell his sweet and spicy scent near my face. He smells like ...spearmint? Maybe. Wood? Something...sexy. "Honor, please." I hear him again. "This is important. You need to stay awake." Ethan's voice sounds far away.

I try with all my might to open my eyes. I try with all my might to hold them open. Ethan's arm is cradling my head. It feels just right beneath my neck. "Good girl," he says, smiling.

"Honor." The female, a nurse, I think, hands me a cup. "It's cola, hun. I put some table sugar in it. Drink it up."

Gross. I take the cup. Put it to my lips. My eyes are still fighting me, but I think I'm winning. I sip the soda. Though it's way too sweet, I manage to get it down. As the lead weights lift from my eyes, I remember.

"Mom. My mother. What..."

"She's fine," Ethan and the nurse reply at the same exact time.

"It was a miracle." The nurse continues. "Her heart had stopped. She'd died." Ethan is holding me, caressing my arm while the nurse still goes on. "She was dead...for several minutes, but you," she shakes her head in disbelief, "she must really love you...all you did was *touch* her, and..."

Ethan cuts her off. "Yes, and Honor really loves her, too." Then suddenly, I know he's trying to hide something. Something about me.

The nurse drops it, as does Ethan, but my mind is now racing, trying to put two and two together.

"Can I see her?" I ask, desperately needing to see for myself that my mother is still alive.

"In a little bit. We'd like you to stay here a while. Get your bearings. You passed out; we need to know you won't do it again."

"Where is she?"

"They're bringing her to ICU right now."

The nurse starts typing things into her laptop, then walks out of the room.

Ethan tries to read something in my eyes. "You okay, Honor?"

Sighing and chuckling at the same time, I feel lost in a strange land. I know I'm here in the hospital, but I have no idea where I stand at this time. What happened? Mom stopped breathing. I reached out to her and just like that, she's alive...and I feel like I've been hit by a train. "I don't know, Ethan." I take in a whole bunch of air; I'm just so winded. "I know my mom just... almost died, but why...am I so...tired?

A tender smile slowly spreads across his face, and he blinks one of those slow blinks. You know, the kind that's almost like closing your eyes, but not really. "It's very draining...to do what you did," he says.

"What'd I do?" I'm so utterly confused. It's my turn to do one of those closey-eyed, blinky-things, only I'm too tired to open them back up, so I just keep my eyes closed. I feel Ethan's warm lips on my forehead and smell his sweet breath on my face. I'm too drained to even pull away, and besides, this boy is growing on me.

"I guess you need an explanation." There's a catch in his voice. Almost like he doesn't want to tell me something.

My eyes find strength enough to open. I blink once, in lieu of a nod.

"When you're outta here. I don't want to talk here...not about this." The deep purple cloud that emanates from his pupils alerts me to just how serious he is. I am not capable of changing his mind; I'll have to wait until I'm out of here to find out what the heck is going on.

With a sincere smile on her face, the nurse returns, asking me how I'm feeling.

I lie and tell her I'm much better. Because if I tell her my chest is still on fire, my head is in a fog, and I'm just plain exhausted, she'll never let me up to see my mom. And above all else, I need to see my mom.

"Well," she says to me, "let me check your blood pressure." Wrapping the squeezie thing around my arm, we wait. I look at Ethan, and he winks, despite the pensive scowl on his face. "Ok," the nurse says when she's done tugging at my arm. "You're good. Let me just get your release papers."

When the nurse leaves the room, Ethan returns to my side. "Honor," he cries, empathy strong in his voice. Something is clearly on his mind. "I know you deserve an explanation and...I promise, you'll get one." He runs his hand through his blond hair and closes his eyes. "But not here. Not now." He hesitates, but it's clear there is more. "Please don't ask me why, but until I explain everything, please *don't* touch anyone." He takes both my hands and peers into my eyes. I see something behind those worried violet eyes of his. Pain. "Promise?" he asks again.

Taking a moment to think that over, wondering what the heck he is talking about, I answer. "Promise." Then I pull my hands out of his.

**

My mother is wide awake when, finally, I make it to her room. Machines and tubes are popping out of her every which way, but besides that, she has a glow on her cheeks and a sparkle in her eye. She looks better than I feel. It's strange, but I feel so weak. My left arm tingles, and the gnawing in my chest is so present that I feel as if *I* suffered from the heart attack instead of my mom.

"Honor," Mom says, smiling so broadly it makes me smile. "Oh, sweetheart, come here." She holds her hand out to me. Ethan stands back unseen, unsure if Mom would be comfortable with a strange boy in her room.

"Oh, Mom," I cry, my voice weak. "I was so scared. I thought..." I just start bawling right there. Bending over her to hug her, I think I might drown her in my tears. She smoothes my hair down with her velvet hand. "Shh, baby, it's all right. Everything is just fine." I squeeze myself into the edge of Mom's hospital bed and spread out next to her, letting her hold me in her arms. Letting *her* comfort *me*. Even though she is the one who just died on the table and came back to life...what seemed to be from the touch of my own hand.

Chapter Seven

After spending about an hour with my mother, Ethan sitting in the waiting area, the nurse tells me my mom needs her rest. I need to go. Giving my mom the tightest hug I can, considering all the tubes entering and exiting her body, I kiss her goodnight and whisper in her ear that I love her. Of course, she loves me too.

With all the resolve I can rally, I wait until Ethan pulls into the library parking lot to inquire about what seemed to be my supernatural ability to bring my mom back to life.

He shakes his head no. "Go get the keys to your mother's car." He watches me look right at him, unmoving. Sighing, he says, "I've a feeling this conversation will take a long time...and I don't want the library to close before you grab your mom's purse...and then her car stays here all night."

"Fine," I whine. "But I'm not dropping this," I say as I hop out of the car.

Spending about ten minutes inside, relating the story to Cindy, I anxiously return to Ethan, who has parked his Mercedes and is sitting on its hood. "Put the purse in her car."

I do.

"Let's take a walk," he commands, again, but his soft tone conveys compassion. He takes hold of my hand, and we proceed to the wooden playground area off to the side of the library. A maze of playthings built from wood will serve as the background to, I suspect, a life-changing turn of events.

We ascend the wooden...plank, I think to myself, though it is really a wooden ramp. But *"walkin' the plank"* seems so much more appropriate at this time. Since, unfortunately, I intuit a death sentence on the horizon.

"Honor," Ethan starts, sitting down on one of the built-in benches. Of course, I follow. "I've been having this conversation with myself all afternoon," he drops his head back against the seat's wall and shuts his eyes. "Yet I *still* don't know where to begin." He opens his eyes and raises his head. Looking straight at me, right into my own violet eyes, he blurts out, "You're adopted. You do know that, right?"

Now if I had not been aware of this fact already, I'd be quite traumatized right now. In fact, I'd have become just a bit unhinged at the moment. Come to think of it, I am anyway. "How do you know this?" I ask, astounded that he is aware of something so personal.

"Oh my God, Honor," he puts his hand on my knee, "you didn't know?" he asks, shocked.

Pulling my knee out from under his hand, I slide as far over as possible. But when I turn to face him, I swear...there's a tear falling down his cheek. This tempers my anger...a little. "Yes," I answer, hearing the sardonic tone in my voice. "I knew. I know..."

Ethan moves toward me.

"But...how do *you* know? We've kept this a secret. *No one* knows." Tingly chills run up my spine. I am suddenly afraid.

"Your mother's name was Hanna. Your father...Daniel. Your last name was Robinson." Ethan ceases to talk, probably surmising, correctly, my need to absorb this new piece of intelligence about my own life.

Too dumb-stricken for words, I remain silently in awe.

"They gave you up for adoption...because they were dying," Ethan resumes. "They were only in their early twenties."

Hearing this makes me sadder than I've ever been. My body goes slack, and my eyes begin to burn. My mom, the one who raised me, had told me that my mother, the biological one, was dying when she gave me up. But I'd no idea she was so young. And no one had ever mentioned a father. There is a hollowness in my chest that I'd never known. A vacant home that had been hidden away, not knowing my true identity, now manifests into a cavernous canyon, because now I do know.

"You are from a special breed of people, Honor." Unaware of the current turmoil taking place in my mind...and my heart, Ethan keeps on talking. "The violet eyes?" He pauses for a reaction from me, which he gets in the form of a blank stare. "They're characteristic of your true nature."

There is just no voice in me. All my thoughts are actually knotted into one mess of a ball in the pit of my stomach, where I can feel it trying to find its way up my esophagus. I want to vomit.

"Honor?" Ethan probes, as if I'm not listening. "All that pain you feel...day in and day out," he pauses and is intent on looking me directly in the eyes. "And *healing* your mother. You know...you did do that. You know that, don't you?"

I shake my head slowly, hand over my mouth.

"Honor Nicole *Robinson* Stevens."

My head moves back and forth quickly now, unable to grasp this. My hand is still covering my mouth.

Ethan will not stop.

"You feel people's pain, Honor." Ethan shakes his head now. "It is...a horrible existence, I'm not going to lie." Tears roll down his face again. "But you *are* special." He smiles through his tears.

"You..." His head drops in a slight bow. "You can heal people...you are an empath, Honor. You take on the hurt and the pain of others...and you can take them away."

It's out. Whatever was tangled up in my stomach is now spewed...in a muted mass of colors, all over the wooden ground of a children's playground.

"Oh, Honor." Ethan puts his hand on my back and rubs. "Oh, I am so sorry. I...I should have, I guess, been more sensitive about it."

"No." I've found my voice. The huge knot falling out of my stomach may have affected that. "I don't...understand this. At all!" I scream. I stand, taking care not to step in my mess. "Why? Why are you here, Ethan? I mean, really? You obviously didn't move here for no particular reason. So...why?"

"Fair enough." Ethan nods and pats the bench next to where he sits. I sit back down. "Yes, Honor, I came here for you."

"But...how did you know where to find me? Or how do you even know all this stuff about me? If it's even...true." I cover my mouth with my hand, wishing I had a mint to put in it.

"I saw you on the news. When you saved Tamlin." Ethan waits. He wants it to sink in.

It does.

"Tamlin. Was that...because..."

He nods. "Yes. You most likely found her because you felt her pain. You felt what she was going through. It happens a lot with empaths."

Still not believing all this, I shake my head. "But...how do you know *me*?"

"Well until recently," he smiles, "I only knew *of* you. You were," he looks up to the left, trying to remember something, "a legend, I guess you can say. Or at least your parents were. Hanna and Daniel."

He takes a deep breath. Sweat falls from his brow. He pats my thigh. "Listen, Honor, this is so much to take in in one night. It's getting dark; your dad will be home from the hospital soon. You should be getting home."

Fatigue has taken over, but curiosity is killing me. "There's so much I want to know though."

He squeezes my hand. "In time, Honor. In time. In the meantime, touching people when you're in a lot of pain should be kept to a minimum. If at all." He stands, still holding my hand, and leads us out of the playground. Back to our cars.

"Why can't I touch people?" This sounds too silly.

"Well for one...it drains you." And I think, yeah, today I nearly crashed. Come to think of it, the afternoon I had found Tamlin, I couldn't even go to school the next day. "And two...I really didn't want to say this yet." We stop at my mother's car and Ethan takes my other hand. We are now facing each other. "Honor." He breathes in deeply and lets it out slowly. "For every life you potentially save by healing them, you *shorten* your life by several years."

While continuing to hold my hands, Ethan draws me closer to him. We are now almost nose to nose. "Your parents died before they were twenty-five years old, because they couldn't resist taking the suffering away from other people."

"And that's bad?" I wonder out loud, Clearly not understanding.

Ethan chuckles. "Nooo. It's not bad for the one they're healing...but...unlike you, most of us grow up on our own, because our parents are dead." His tone turns flat. And then I think, yeah, now I get it. I couldn't be raised by my birth parents, because they didn't live long enough to do it.

Then I catch something he just said. "Wait a minute. Us? You?"

"Yes, Honor. Me. I'm an empath too."

Chapter Eight

Sitting at my kitchen table with me, Ethan is now trying to be more sensitive with feeding me information about myself. Like how I can control the pain and emotions that are not mine. It's possible to *choose* to ignore them, as long as a conscious effort on my part is made. But that's easier said than done. Plus, now that I know I can help someone, how do I choose to ignore them? Doesn't that go against my very grain?

Ethan agrees that, yes, it does go against the very nature of who we are. And because of our deep ability to feel, the guilt of *not* helping is most often worse.

"So what am I supposed to do? If my mom has another heart attack or my Dad...I don't know...gets hurt in a car crash or something, am I not supposed to try and save them? Now that I know I can?" Which I still can't fathom, because it's like I have superpowers, and supernatural things don't exist. Not in my world anyway.

"No, Honor," Ethan says quietly. "Your mother and father are different. Of course you'll want to save them when you can." His hand runs through his hair as he sips the water I got him when we first got home. "But...you need to be careful who you touch. You can very easily, inadvertently, heal someone, without even realizing it." He snickers a little. "Though, now that you know how draining it can be, I'm sure you'll know when you are absorbing someone else's pain." He takes my two hands, which are cupped around my tea mug (I didn't want water, I had gotten myself a cup of tea instead) and holds them, almost lovingly, in his own. I begin to pull away, but his hands feel kind of nice wrapped around mine. "Then...you'll be taking away your own precious years." He sighs. "That's why I tried to keep you from making contact with Miss James."

Snapping back my hands from his, I push back my chair, jolting out of my seat. "Oh my goodness. Miss James. I knew it. I knew I felt something from her," I cry out, pacing the kitchen floor, while Ethan quietly taps his thumbs on the kitchen table. My hand automatically goes to my head, which is now throbbing just thinking about her. I stop pacing and sit back down, bracing myself, palms flat, on the kitchen table. "Ethan. You knew." This fact just sinking in.

"Yes, I knew."

"So...you felt it too?" I ask, amazed.

He nods, obviously waiting for more revelations from me.

"But...you...you...never looked like you were in pain."

"I ignored it. Remember I told you we can train ourselves to do that," he said, almost mockingly. Almost. Not quite. His voice held a little empathy as well. Which, now that I think of it, I guess is natural for him.

"Yeah." Then I realize. "Ethan. She might die. We can save her."

He covers my hands with his. "Yes, Honor, we can." His voice is soft, as is his touch on my hands. I close my eyes for a second to absorb the joy in his running his thumb across mine. "But at what cost to us?" he asks.

"But isn't that selfish? And doesn't that go against our nature?" I hear the whine in my voice.

Tilting his head to the side, indicating the compassion he possesses, he says, "It is selfish, I guess." Then his tone changes slightly. "But I always thought it was selfish of my parents to keep on saving others with no regard for their sons' futures. Futures spent alone without parental supervision or love, because they couldn't keep from saving the world." And that's the first time I hear vinegar in his voice, the stimulus that makes it easier for him to push aside the suffering of others.

Sighing out loud, I realize that the pain I feel in my chest, right this minute, is his—his hurt—caused by the betrayal of his parents' love and empathy for mankind.

Is it possible for one empath to take away the pain of another? I lay my hand flat against his heart.

He smiles. "It won't work, Honor." he says, aware of my intent to take away the pain in his heart. "We would just keep absorbing each other's emotions. A painful, endless cycle."

"Oh." Ethan stands and pulls me from my chair. Wrapping his arms around me, I fear he'll feel my heart racing. It's then that I realize my feelings are much more intense when I'm with him. Is it because I'm feeling double the pain and emotions? Both of us empathizing with a beaten human race? Or could I be feeling emotions I've never felt before? Could I be *attracted* to Ethan?

A soft flutter taps the top of my head. Ethan's lips. "It's not going to be easy. You know that, right?" His chin rests on my head, and I like the feeling it produces—little tingles beneath my scalp. "But if you can control your emotions, you'll at least make it to see *your* kid grow up." The sharp pang of resentment strikes both our chests.

Kid? Kids! I've always dreamed of having lots of children. The loneliness of being an only child was a miserable existence, especially being home-schooled. I want children. And I want to see them grow up. If what Ethan says is true, then I will make it my business to handle my inner emotions and ignore everyone else's. Learning to decipher between the two will also be top on my priority list.

"Ethan?" Pulling away, just far enough to see his face (I don't want our embrace to break just yet) I ask, "How do I tell the difference? What's my pain and what's not?"

He strokes my hair while still holding me, and I want so badly to kiss him. "It's not easy," he laments, "but you need to feel the connection...between the pain, your brain...and your heart."

Nodding my head, I lean my head against him, embracing the thundering heart beneath his chest, wondering - is it *his* feelings for *me?*

Or a reflection of mine?

Chapter Nine

The next morning, I don't get ready for school. Instead, I ready myself to go to the hospital and see my mom. While I am there, I will test my new, or at least new in knowledge, superpowers. Healing is not my intention. No. My intent is to be cognizant of any new aches or pains, anything I don't have now but suddenly inherit as I walk the hospital halls.

While I am still home and alone (Dad is already at the hospital), I do a mental body check. I am in absolutely no pain. This is good. It will make it easier to distinguish any new pain that comes my way. I grab Mom's car keys off the table. Her little green Passat is fun to drive. Of course, I wish I had my own, but this will do for now.

The time it takes for me to get to Saint Clare's is quite a bit longer than it took Ethan yesterday, but I'm there in about forty-minutes. I am a slow driver. Plus, getting lost along the way doesn't help.

Entering the hospital is uneventful, but as I precede further inside, I feel less energetic. Lethargy kicks in, as does smarting pain in several areas of my body. I get to mom's room and I feel somewhat better. The pain feels distant. There is nothing emanating from my mother. Good. Sitting up in her bed, Dad seated beside her, Mom shows all thirty-two of her teeth in her smile.

"Mom. How are you?" I ask as I lean forward to kiss her on the cheek.

"Oh, Honor." She cups her palm on my cheek, her eyes tearing while she's looking at me longingly and lovingly. "I feel wonderful. I am so sorry to have scared you."

"Oh, Mom, stop." Then, timidly, I tell her, "I'm just so happy that you're here."

With her top teeth biting her bottom lip, Mom removes her hand from my face and leans back on her pillow. "Honor...it's..." Mom puts her smile back on. "It's like a miracle," she whispers. "They said I was having a heart attack. I'd even died for four minutes." She makes a soft tsking sound to herself. "Now...not one sign of ever having the attack. Nothing." She tsks a bit louder. So does Dad. It's true, there aren't words for this kind of thing.

Mom begins to cry, and I feel myself tear up. Funny, but they're not my tears. They're hers. I am actually crying someone else's tears. It occurs to me then, that all those times in my life when I thought I was sad for no reason, I must have been sad for someone else. Now I can decipher the difference. Ethan was right. There's a remoteness to the sensation. Something faraway about it. Yet, I feel the bittersweet joy my mother is feeling, nonetheless.

My little family relishes in the moment a few more minutes before Dad breaks it up. "Honor, I'm going for coffee, would you like me to get you something?"

"Oh, sure. A chai latte would be nice. If they have it. Otherwise, tea with milk and honey is good."

Dad leaves, and I sit on the edge of Mom's bed. She takes my hand.

"Mom," I begin slowly, "do you remember anything about...my birth mom?"

The look on Mom's face nearly breaks my heart. Suddenly I feel...threatened. And I realize, my goodness, Mom must feel threatened by my birth mother. Immediately, I am sad for my mother.

She is silent for a few seconds before her lips seem to move without any sound coming out of her mouth. "Your birth mom?" Her head shakes a little. "But...why? Why now?"

I kiss her on the cheek. "It's nothing. Never mind."

She caresses my face. "No, Honor, don't be silly. You have a right to ask. I was just wondering why now, while I'm here?"

"Oh, Mom, it has nothing to do with your being here. Really. I just, well..." I am at a loss as to what to say first. My breathing picks up the pace. Mentally, I try to calm myself down. "Well, Ethan knew her. Or rather, knew *of* her."

My mother's eyes jump wide, while her mouth drops open. "Ethan? The boy who was here?"

I nod. "Yes. His mother was best friends with her. My birth mom."

"With Hanna?" Mom is astonished.

"Yes. With Hanna. He said she was in her early twenties when she..." This is very hard for me to say out loud. "When she, um, gave me..." After a long pause, I muster it. "Away."

"Hanna? No. Couldn't be. She was close to forty or fifty, I think. So sick. So fragile." Mom closes her eyes. "I remember feeling sorry for her. I mean, I knew I should have gone through proper channels to adopt you, but..." Mom shakes her head. "She was so desperate. *Begged* me to take you, no questions asked."

I'm speechless. It never occurred to me whether I was adopted legally or not.

"You know," Mom adds. "That's why I home-schooled you."

"I thought it was because I was sick all the time."

She half-smiles. "Yes. Home-schooling was a convenient choice due to all of your illnesses, but...I was afraid. I was afraid I'd be questioned. I mean, I still had to register you and all. And after Hanna gave you to me, a few weeks later, she'd sent me an envelope with a birth certificate and some other stuff, so I had legitimate papers. I was just scared that in a public school, more people would ask questions."

"Did she say why, Mom? Why she gave me up?" I know my mother had already told me this, but I need to hear it now, now that I know what I know.

Another audible sigh escapes her. "All she said was that she and her husband were terminally ill. They had no family members they could trust and well," Mom hesitates, clearly uneasy. "They said you'd be in danger if they kept you with friends."

This surprises me. "In danger of what?"

Mom shakes her head. "She never said. I got the feeling I shouldn't ask, so I didn't." Mom gives me this strange look. "I know I should have, Honor. I'm usually very prudent, but one look at your precious face, with those huge violet eyes." My mother smiles when she sighs. "I fell in love with you, Honor. I couldn't let you go."

We sit there in silence for a while, not sure where to go with the conversation from here. I want to tell her I'm an empath, but I don't believe it myself. Believe it? Heck, I don't even understand it. But Mom needs to know. Who else could help me through this?

Dad walks in and puts a kibosh on my news.

"Thanks," I say to Dad when he hands me my tea.

He nods. "Leanne, everything okay?

"Sure, Jack. Honor and I had a nice little chat."

Dad smiles at me, then at Mom, "Good. Couldn't live without you two."

My father states his declaration casually, but a heavy heart is dragging it down. I feel it. Deep within my own heart, I know my dad is scared. He'd never come so close to losing his wife. His world has been shaken. And I feel his torment.

Knowing what I did to not only save my mother from death but my father from heartache, maybe I could embrace this empathy thing and find a way to live with it after all.

Chapter Ten

Pulling into the high school parking lot in my mother's VW, I spot this awesome looking bright orange Challenger in a front spot. I'm not one for noticing cars much, but this one is crazy cool with its black stripes on the hood and black rims on the tires. I know I would have noticed it before. Either someone got a new car, or someone new has come to school.

But the Challenger conveniently slips my mind when I walk into school. Through the glass windows of the main office, I spot the most handsome boy I think I've ever laid eyes on. Even better looking than Ethan (though I feel really bad for thinking that). This boy's hair is a beautiful yellow blonde and his skin, flawlessly pale with a deep dimple that graces his cheek. At the angle I am standing, it's difficult to see the color of his eyes, but I'm sure they are as exquisite as the rest of him.

The first period bell rings, and I'm so caught up in gazing at this wonderful piece of Heaven that I am now late for class and nowhere near my locker to get my things. This, come to think of it, is now a fortunate coincidence, because now I have to enter the main office to get a late pass. As I'm opening the door, the six foot god slips his sunglasses on and turns to walk out the door. But not before he pauses in front of me and smiles. "Hey, Angel," he says, before floating away.

I can barely remember my name when the receptionist asks if she can help me. "Oh. Yes. Um, who was that boy?" I ask instead of requesting my pass.

"A new student." She's annoyed. "Do you need a pass?"

A new student? Wow. He just seems too together to be a student.

"Honor. Isn't it?" The secretary attempts to pull me from my daydreaming. "Do. You. Need. A. Pass?"

"Oh. Yes. Please. Thank you." I shake my head back to the present.

In my first period class, French, I find myself too distracted to pay attention. Yesterday, I was falling for Ethan, and today, I cannot get that new guy out of my head. Incidentally, I find it hard to concentrate all morning. Not only am I pining over some beautiful boy I don't even know, I am still trying to wrap my head around the idea of having the ability to heal people. Such a huge responsibility. One that doesn't come without huge repercussions.

At lunch, Ethan is in a horrid mood. My own mood makes me aware of this. God bless him, though. He is actually trying to hide it. My emotions inform me of that, as does the plastic smile he's wearing on his face.

"Hey beautiful," he says, sending tiny tingles through my body. *New guy from the office who?* Seeing Ethan sitting across the table from me reminds me of how much I was starting to like Ethan. "How's your mother doing?"

"She's better. The doctor wants to run a few more tests, but she should be coming home in a couple days."

"Great," he says to me, though his mind is elsewhere.

"Ethan. What's bothering you?" I reach across the table and put my hand on his, realizing this kind of behavior is new for me.

He squeezes my hand. "Nothing, Honor. Nothing I can't handle." But I still feel his apprehension. Ethan is brooding over something. "Honor?" I'm asked after several silent seconds—seconds I use to take a bite of my sandwich. "Can we go up to the reservation again after school?"

With my mouth full of turkey and Swiss on rye, I mumble, "Sure."

My heart feels heavy for Ethan. I'm not loving being able to feel his emotions. I just hope his anguish is a result of someone else's, and not his own.

"Everything'll be fine, Honor." But it isn't fine. Ethan is alone with his thoughts the rest of lunch period, while I chat with Tamlin about nothing in particular.

Walking into seventh period Math, my breath catches. The beautiful boy from the main office is talking with the teacher. His back is to the door, but I know it's him. There is no mistaking the blonde mass of beauty. For a high school kid, he is abnormally tall, having probably three inches over Ethan, who, according to Ethan, already towers at six-feet two-inches tall (even though I thought he was taller than that).

I advance slowly to my desk, not paying too much attention to what I'm doing when I walk into a desk, dropping my books and splaying them across the floor, *grabbing hold of everyone's attention in the meantime*—something I am not particularly fond of. Hustling to the floor to pick up my mess, a long pale arm slips around me and reaches for my fallen books. When I turn to see who my Samaritan is, I am staring right into another set of violet eyes. And they burn right. Through. Mine.

Suddenly, I don't know what I am feeling. But I get a funny taste in my mouth, and my chest begins to burn. The intensity of his gaze does not lessen. It heightens. And as it does, the burning in my chest deepens until it feels as if it were burning a hole right through my chest.

The violet eyes holding me in fiery shackles are not Ethan's.

They are his.

The beautiful god from the main office.

Chapter Eleven

After he tears his gaze away from mine, he stands and hands me my books. "Ya gotta watch where you're going there, love," his deep, velvet voice instructs.

Motionless and unable to speak a single word, I nod.

I cannot stop looking at him.

Until Ethan walks in.

And his face turns stone-cold.

"Class. I'd like to introduce to you, our newest classmate," Mrs. Johnson announces, "Storm Sutherland. Ethan's brother."

Ethan's searing expression, directed at Storm, is unnerving. But the callous smirk on Storm's face is actually blood-chillingly disturbing. I am suddenly afraid for Ethan.

The rest of the students ooh and aah at the realization that Ethan and Storm are related, while the female gender of our class already begins darting coquettish glances at the new addition to our class. Mrs. Johnson finally demands the class focus on their math assignments, but I notice Ethan doesn't appear to be paying attention at all. He seems to be stewing over something big. Something so disconcerting that I immediately run to the garbage can and throw up.

I end my day in the nurse's office, where Ethan shows up to walk me out. He's still stone-faced.

"You okay?" he asks, but his thoughts are on something entirely different.

"Yes." He reaches for my hand, and I wonder if he thinks we're an item already. I squeeze his hand, then let it go, staying close to him while we walk to his car.

I know better than to inquire about Storm. When Ethan is ready, he will talk about it. Maybe that's why he asked me to go to the reservation today.

"I'll drive," he says out in the lot. "I can bring you back to get your car." He opens my door to let me in, then circles around to his side.

The short ride is quiet.

On the same rock at Mahlon Dickerson, Ethan nervously taps his fingers on his leg. "This is bad, Honor. He's bad news."

I don't need to ask. Of course I know he's referring to Storm Sutherland. "Is he really your brother?" I really don't know what else to say.

"We share the same biological father, but that's where it ends."

"What's he done that's so bad?" I figure he brought it up, it should be okay to ask, right?

Ethan drops his shoulders and sighs. "He's evil, Honor." I watch him shake his head and close his eyes. "He kills..." Okay, I actually feel my eyes reach my hairline. "Just because they make him hurt. They don't ask him to feel their pain, no one ever asks. But he hates them so much...he kills them."

"Who? Who does he hate?"

Ethan turns and stares at me. Violet eyes to violet eyes—for what feels like a whole minute. "He's an empath too. And he kills the very people whose pain he absorbs." Ethan drops his head. "It's all a game to him."

I sit horrified at what I've just heard.

"It's not good that he's here, Honor," Ethan continues. "Not good at all—," he trails off into another world.

But I need to understand this. "Ethan," I nudge. "Are you saying he kills *everyone*? I mean, wouldn't he have been caught by now?"

Ethan jumps off the rock and paces the ground beneath me. "No. Not everyone. And maybe he hasn't killed a whole heck of a lot of people." Ethan paces before sitting back down on the rock. "But isn't one or two enough?"

"Yes, of course." Murder is murder, whether it's one or twenty, but I need to know what is really on Ethan's mind.

"She was so special," he whispers.

"Who?"

"The girl he killed." Ethan drops his head again. This time a tear falls from his eye. "My sister."

"Oh my goodness, Ethan, I am so sorry." I put my hand on his back and rub it up and down, trying to calm him and absorb his pain at the same time.

"She was only eight." He squeezes the bridge of his nose. I think he's trying to stop the tears. "Summer was my father's pride and joy. I think Storm was jealous of her."

"That's horrible. He just *killed* her? How?" I am trying so hard to ease his hurt but it isn't working, so I take his hand instead of rubbing his back. I'm new at this. I don't exactly know what I'm doing.

"With his bare hand." His eyes closed, Ethan is inhaling what I think is courage to say whatever he's about to say out loud. "I think he just...crushed her heart." Ethan winces. "I walked into the room, and he was leaning over her. There was an indent of a hand burned on her chest. When he saw me, he fled. Haven't seen him since. He was only fifteen, yet capable of murder. But we heard he had murdered others. Before Summer. I didn't know that then."

"Oh my gosh. Can't you call the cops now? It's not too late, is it?"

"It was seven years ago. There was never any case. Our family tended to live under the radar." Ethan shakes his head. "My parents didn't want anyone to find out about us. Being empaths and all."

"That's terrible."

"We heard he became really mean and powerful after that. I also found out that once empaths kill, they gain strength. And if we kill another empath, we can live forever."

"How is that possible?"

The belief is that since we can absorb a person's pain, if they die at our hands, we gain their lives as well. I'm not a hundred percent sure, but that's what we've been taught.

"Wait. So, Storm is immortal?"

"We don't know. Summer hadn't shown any signs of being an empath yet, so I'm not sure."

"And wait. If it was seven years ago and he was fifteen, he's, like, twenty-two years old. What's he doing in high school?"

"Yeah, he probably made up false records or something."

A faraway expression shadows Ethan's face. "You know, it's funny," Ethan says. "We thought Summer was the *only* one Storm was fond of." A tsk escapes his mouth. Then an angry chuckle. "He hated us, Honor. Especially me. I'm what caused his parents' divorce. My mother got pregnant with me when my dad was still married to his mother." Ethan takes my hand and gives it a tender tug. "I guess I can't blame him for that. But...it was such a shock what he did to Summer. We thought he really loved her. I just don't understand it." He shakes his head in devastation. I want so much to hold him, but I don't know if I should.

I stop thinking about it, though, and just do it. I take my hand from his and wrap both my arms around his neck. He turns in my direction and lets me.

We hold each other like that for God knows how long when we hear something move behind the trees.

"It's probably a bear," Ethan remarks as he steps down from the rock to check things out.

I jump down and follow him.

"Honor, you should stay where you are. Bears can be dangerous."

"I'll be fine."

A resigned "all right" forces its way out of Ethan's mouth.

We follow the noise but find no bear.

What we *hear*, however, is the roar of an engine, and the squeal of spinning tires crunching across the gravel parking lot.

What we *see*, is a bright orange Challenger hightailing it out of the park.

Storm.

Chapter Twelve

"Hi, Honor." A deep voice calls from behind me in the cafeteria.

I come to a halt, knowing who it is before I turn. "Storm."

"That's me. Trip over any desks lately?" His joke falls flat on my ears, but my face grows hot.

"Just joking, sweetheart." He places his lunch tray next to mine on the table and slides in on the bench. Smack dab next to me. Arm touching very large arm. I move as indiscreetly as I can without hurting any feelings. Then I think, why should I care if I hurt his feelings? He's a murderer. "Don't worry. I put my deodorant on this morning," he says in response to my sliding away.

"I wasn't worried." My defensive tone betrays my words.

"Did I do something to offend you, honey?" Though he sounds sarcastic, something in his tone is off.

"No."

"So, Honor. I like your name."

He's waiting for a response from me, but I don't give him one.

"I've been asking around about you."

Still no response from me.

"You're shy?"

Why does he keep talking to me? I bow my head and break apart my sandwich, unable to actually eat it.

A sharp pain stabs at my chest. Heartache. But it's not mine.

"Honor?" Storm's face drops, as does his mood. "Would you like me to take my tray somewhere else?" he asks, and I literally feel his hurt deep in my heart. Storm is hurting, and I don't want to make it worse, but I can't explain why.

"No. You can stay," I answer quietly, forcing myself to look him in the eyes - his beautiful violet eyes which are so dark right now. "I'm sorry."

"No need to apologize. It's all good."

"Yeah." I smile and then see Ethan walking toward the table. Now I begin to worry.

Jumping from my seat, I wave Ethan over, feeling guilty for being so near Storm.

Storm stands and holds out his hand. "Long time, no see."

But Ethan just stares at Storm, and I watch his eye twitch and his face contort. And I think, *wow, this guy really repulses Ethan.*

Storm drops his hand. "Suit yourself, little brother." Storm sits back down and dives into his lunch.

Picking up my purse and tray, I follow Ethan to another table, but not without feeling bad for Storm that I did so.

"I don't like that he was talking to you, Honor. He's up to something." Ethan's hand runs along my lower back while I sit down. He straddles the bench next to me, his hand still warm on my back.

"He seemed okay, Ethan. He was just making small talk."

With Ethan's right hand still on my lower back, he lays his left hand on my thigh. "He worries me. I can't tell you why. I really can't put a finger on it, aside from the fact that he murdered my baby sister, but," he pauses a minute. "I still think he's bad news."

My emotions are torn. I feel Ethan's suspicions, literally. But my own feelings just don't match up. When in Storm's presence, the burning in my chest I experienced yesterday is still there, but...so is a sharp pain. Deep down in my soul I can feel the breaking heart of Storm Sutherland.

Nodding my head, I silently agree with Ethan. How could I tell him that I feel sorry for his eight-year old sister's murderer?

Ethan removes his hand from my leg and instead squeezes the bridge of his nose again.

"Are you all right, Ethan? You shouldn't let him get to you, really." I turn and straddle the bench to face him. Taking his hands in both of mine, I close my eyes and try my hardest to remove his hurt.

Unfortunately, he is on to what I'm doing and pulls his hands from my grasp. "Honor. Stop that. I told you what healing people will do to you. Please stop. I'd like you to live a while. If that's all right with you."

He makes me smile. My face grows warm, and I'm wondering if maybe he likes me romantically, since he intends for me to be around a while. We never did qualify our relationship, so I've been having my doubts as to whether he likes me or is just hanging with me because I'm some sort of legend in the empath world - because I'm the one that got away from it all. Though thanks to Ethan, I've now been found. Not sure if I am happy about that or not.

"What's the matter? I didn't mean to hurt your feelings..."

"No. No," I jump in."You didn't hurt me at all." In an attempt to hide my smile, I bite the inside of my mouth. Which hurts.

His fingers touch beneath my chin, gently lifting my face to look at him. "What is it, Honor?"

His smile is so beautiful. His perfect white teeth are just the right size - not too big; not too small. For several minutes (or what seems like several minutes), we gaze at each other, assessing what the other is thinking...or feeling, rather. My stomach gets that butterfly effect right in the pit of it, chased by a bunch of tingles that run up and down my limbs. Though I'm sitting, I feel my knees go weak. Ethan's face is closer. He leans in, nose to nose. The cafeteria disappears around us until it's just us. My head tilts to one side, his to the other, when he sets his lips to mine and I close my eyes. His arms wrap around me and I move in closer, allowing the embrace. His sweet lips part just a bit and I feel his tongue separating mine. Parting my own lips, I meet his tongue with mine, and I melt in his kiss. *My* first kiss. *Ever.* Time passes, and who knows how long it's been, but nothing else matters but Ethan's kiss.

Until Storm interrupts us with a blatant cough. "Honor. I was wondering if I could talk to you after school about something?" Ethan and I stop kissing, but he keeps his hands on my thighs. Storm's grin is unreadable; I can't tell whether he is mocking or serious. But he continues talking to us, though Ethan's own expression doesn't welcome any other comments from his half-brother. I know this, because Ethan is only looking at me. Trying hard to ignore the elephant at our lunch table. "So, the thing is," Storm keeps going, "since brother-dear deems it appropriate to not acknowledge me, I would like to get to know *someone* here at school and, well, I was wondering if I could get to know you."

"That's it." Ethan tears his gaze away from me to stand and face Storm. "Get the hell outta here." Brother to brother, they stare each other down.

"How 'bout it, Honor?" Storm still persists with talking to me, though his gaze hasn't left Ethan's. "Ya wanna hang after school...with me?" The evil that escapes Storm's lop-sided grin is apparent, but I can tell it's only skin deep. The boy is hurting inside. And I hurt for him.

Ethan continues the stare-down. "She has plans with me."

Storm is first to break the stare. But only to look at me. "'zat true, Honor? You have plans with this loser after school?"

"Yes." I nod, but look only at Ethan. Afraid to feel anything else for Storm if I look at him.

"Very well. Maybe another time, sweetheart." He strides away all boss-like, but I see the real Storm beneath his deceptive arrogance.

Ethan sits back down, straddling the bench so we're facing each other again. "You can't let him befriend you, Honor...you just can't. He's dangerous, and I don't know his intentions right now."

Looking down, I bite my lip before I speak. "I get that, I do. It's just," I hesitate, not sure of Ethan's reaction to my feelings for Storm. "I don't think he's as dangerous as he lets on."

I regret it as soon as the words are out of my mouth. Ethan's eyes shoot up in disbelief. "How can you say that after what he did to my sister?"

"I'm sorry, Ethan." Rage begins to fill me unexpectedly, and I realize it's Ethan's rage I'm feeling. "Please, Ethan. Stay calm..."

"Stay calm? I tell you he murdered my baby sister and you tell me he's not dangerous?"

With the palm of my hand, I attempt to soothe Ethan by rubbing his arm up and down. To which I receive his jerking away from my touch. I still say what I need to say. "Listen, Ethan, I didn't say he was good or anything. I just meant, I don't think he means me any harm. I think he's in pain," I say quietly. "Emotional pain. And because of it, I, like, think he's..." Because of my determination not to anger Ethan, I stop talking.

"He's what?"

"I think, well, I think his heart is breaking, that's all."

Ethan takes a step back, scorn displayed in the contemptuous way he holds his mouth. "You have feelings for him." The throbbing vein in his neck causes an ice-cold chill to seep up my spine. I knew he wouldn't understand.

"No. No, Ethan. That's not it at all," I plead, trying to make him understand. "My feelings are not *for* him. They *are* his. I feel what *he* is feeling. That's all."

"Then it's only a matter of time," he whispers, then turns and walks out of the cafeteria.

So much for my first kiss. I guess it didn't end too well. I drop to the bench, slide my legs under the table and hold my face in my palms, sobbing into my healing hands. Which, ironically, do nothing to heal my own pain.

Chapter Thirteen

The clang of the period bell clashes with the cursing in my head. Mentally kicking myself for letting Ethan in on my feelings about Storm, I let the bell's indication slip by me.

"Honor?" Tamlin's voice is as soft as her hand is on my shoulder. I'm embarrassed to look at her, aware that my face is a wet mess. "Honey, are you okay?"

Nodding into my own palm of tears, Tamlin hands me a cloth to wipe my tears. I look at it when I take it from her and start cracking up in between sobs. It's her gym shirt. "You're crazy." My half-hearted laugh makes her chuckle.

Tamlin straddles the bench alongside me. "What is it, honey?"

She wraps both her arms around me and hugs me. I don't know whether to laugh or cry, because not twenty minutes ago Ethan was hugging me on this same bench, where we shared our first kiss. Now my best friend is hugging me, because I'm crying over him. "Oh, Tamlin," I sob into her shoulder. "I messed things up horribly."

"Girls." We glance up at the assistant principal. "You need to get to class."

"Oh." I scramble for my stuff and slap my purse over my shoulder.

"We're sorry," Tamlin offers, taking me by the elbow and scurrying us out of there. "Listen, sweetie. I'll come to your house after school. K?"

"K."

She hugs me and we get to class.

Seventh period math is challenging. Ethan and Storm are both in class with me. I contemplate going to the nurse, but I've been spending too much time in there as it is. Instead, I walk in with my head down and focus only on getting to my desk. Once there, my eyes remain on my books and I try to keep them there while Mrs. Johnson gives her lesson.

Acquiring any type of knowledge this period is a moot point, because I'm too busy taking on the emotions of the two boys I'm trying to avoid. The two gorgeous blondes who are causing this moment of despair for me - one who is hurt and angry because I succeeded in unintentionally making him jealous, and the other who is hurt and bemused because he knows he caused this whole ordeal. Sort of. I guess I'm to blame as well, since I can't help but wonder why Storm is hurting so bad and that's really the reason Ethan is upset. Crawling in a hole and dying would be better right now. Yeah, I know, it's just teenage drama, but really, up until these past couple of months, I had zero drama in my life, being a recluse and all. So, yeah, I deserve to be a little melodramatic right now.

I try hard not to look at Ethan, but being strong-willed is just not my strong suit. With my head down, eyelids up, eyes peering out of their corners, I see Ethan brooding. It doesn't take an empath to know that. Even Mrs. Johnson takes a double-look at him every once in awhile, and it makes me wonder what *she's* thinking.

Forgetting my eye focus is supposed to remain on my desk, I inadvertently glance at Storm. He winks, catching me mid-glance. Wishing I felt nothing when Storm stares at me, I curse myself again. If he didn't seem to be hurting so much, I probably wouldn't be thinking about him. Well, he *is* gorgeous, so I might be thinking about *that*. But I digress. What is he hiding behind his haughty façade? And why am I so concerned with Storm, when I'm heartbroken over the boy with whom I shared my first kiss? I know, melodramatic. I'm not really heartbroken, but I do hate conflict, even if it's inner-conflict.

The period flies by. It's already over, and I don't recall Mrs. Johnson teaching us anything. Absorbed in my own thoughts, I hadn't paid any attention to math. Certainly, I'm going to be lost tomorrow. But I can't think about that. More important matters persist. My new love-life, for one. Or at least my lame excuse for a love-life, anyway.

Tamlin pushes me into my bedroom, playfully, of course. As she'd promised, she came ringing my doorbell mere seconds after I got home from school.

"So, tell me what happened to cause you to bawl your eyes out?" she begins, jumping on the edge of my bed with her bum.

Sitting *my* bum on my white beanbag chair across from her, I whine (I can't help it, I get whiny when I'm depressed), "Oh, Tam. I made such a mess of things with Ethan."

She raises an eyebrow at me. "Does this have anything to do with that new Sutherland boy...the *really* hot one?"

"Um...yeah. How'd you know that?"

"I see the way he looks at you. He practically gawks at you."

"No he doesn't."

"Uh, yeah, he does. Anyway, so what about Storm was it that ruined things for you and Ethan?"

What could I possibly say to Tamlin? She doesn't need to know about my new-found abilities. I'm not ready to divulge that to anyone.

"I don't know," I finally say. "Storm kinda asked me to hang with him after school, and he asked me right in front of Ethan."

"Aah. But unless you said yes to Storm, why would Ethan be mad at you? Unless, o.m.g., did you say yes?"

"No. No, of course not." I lean back on my bean bag and fidget with a string that had come loose from it. "Ethan got jealous anyway." I sort of sigh, thinking how sad that makes me.

"So that's good, right?" Tamlin reassures me. "If he's jealous, that means he likes you."

I yank at the string and make a big hole in my bean bag chair. "No. Not right. He got mad, and now he's not talking to me."

Tamlin plops down on the floor and leans against the bed. "But what's he mad at? I mean, why? You said no."

"Mmm. But I...kinda told him, well, that Storm's not as bad as he wants everyone to think he is."

"Honor, you like Storm, don'tcha?"

"No. No, not at all. I don't know." I really couldn't answer that question honestly. Not even to myself.

Stretching her crossed-at-the-ankle legs atop my bean bag, she whacks her heels right onto the hole I'd just made. Thousands of foam pellets fly up in a puffy white cloud.

Tam slaps her hand over her mouth in apology. I crack up at the surprised look on her face.

"Tam, it's okay." I giggle. "I'm the one who made the hole. Thanks for making me laugh though."

"Glad I could help."

Both of us have a good chuckle while cleaning up the mess.

After we calm down, Tamlin puts on her serious face. Though, how can someone with bright blue hair *ever* look serious. "You going to see your mom today?" she asks, dumping a handful of pellets into my waste basket.

"Nah. Mom said stay home and study. I'll call her later. She's doing well, so Dad's just gonna go see her," I tell Tam while I pick up the last of the pellets and throw them away.

"Cool. We can do homework together if you want."

"Sure. Want a soda?"

"Sure."

Grabbing our backpacks off the floor, we dart for the kitchen. Tamlin takes a stool at the counter, while I get two sodas out of the fridge.

"Honor?" Tam asks, snapping open her can of soda and taking a sip.

"Yes?" I take a sip of my soda and sit down on a stool across from her.

"You gonna be okay? I mean with Ethan and all?"

Shrugging one of my shoulders, I answer as best I can. "I think so. I guess I just have to prove to him that it's *him* I like..." I trail off, not sure if I believe that myself. I mean, I really like Ethan. He's terrific. And sensitive. But there's something about Storm that sets my heart to flutter. Maybe it's just his bad-boy image, or maybe it's just my empathetic feelings. I wish it were easier to tell.

"Yeah," Tam says. "Good luck with that. Boys are thick."

"Yeah," I whisper so low she probably doesn't hear me, but I'm having a problem agreeing with her. Ethan will not be hard to get through to. He's pretty reasonable. What will be hard is hiding feelings from him. Recognizing emotions are something I'm guessing he's very good at. I'll just have to try extra hard to convince him I have absolutely no feelings for Storm.

But like Tamlin said, good luck with that. I can't even convince myself.

Chapter Fourteen

Though my bed is warm and cozy, my mood is cool. Hurt from Ethan's cold shoulder yesterday and today, I can't seem to find my smile. I don't understand why he is so mad. It's not like I can help it if Storm's emotions enter my body. Ethan should never have told me what I was. It only makes me too aware of the people around me. Damn him for telling me.

And damn him for being so upset with me. He didn't even say hello to me today. At lunch, he was nowhere to be found, and in class, he just kept his frowny face down. With my empathic awareness, I pick up sadness along with the anger or worry he carried over from yesterday. Anger should be an easy emotion to figure out, but because I'm not accustomed to bouts of it, I'm not sure if that's exactly what he's feeling. If he'd only open up and talk to me, I'm sure we'd both feel better. But since I'm also not accustomed to being in a boy-girl relationship, I'm too nervous to approach him first.

If only I hadn't felt anything from Storm. *For Storm?* I wish I knew for sure.

"Go" from Boys Like Girls is playing on my iPod. I close my eyes and let Martin Johnson's voice pacify the hollowness in my chest. My rising anxiety.

Sleep must have found me after all, because when I wake to a tapping at my window, Red Jumpsuit Apparatus is playing "Cat and Mouse", which is near the end of my playlist.

The tapping continues, and as I make my way across the room, it gets louder. In spite of the trembling, I still push aside my curtain. A rejected Ethan sits on a tree branch outside my window.

"Ethan," I say, surprised to find him there.

He escalades the window sill and enters my bedroom—in the middle of the night.

"What are you doing here?"

Ethan sits on my bed. "Is this okay?" He motions with his finger to the mattress he's already sitting on. I close the window and turn back towards him.

"Yeah, it's fine. Why are you here? It's late." I don't want to sound callous, but all day I got the silent treatment, and now he shows up outside my window. Though I'm thrilled to see him, I don't want him to think I'm some kind of pushover.

He falls back on my bed and rests the crook of his elbow across his forehead. "Oh, Honor. He worries me." Ethan drops his arm to his side and looks at the ceiling. "And I'm scared for you." He sits up again and holds his hand out for me to go to him. At first, I only allow my fingertips to graze his, but he grabs my hand and pulls me between his legs at the edge of the bed. He stands to embrace me. "I'm sorry, Honor," he whispers in my ear. "I'm so sorry I've been ignoring you. It was so immature of me."

"Why *did* you?"

Ethan moves me to arm's length to look me in the eye. "Because I was upset about what you told me."

"That I feel his pain?" I ask, though I know exactly what he means.

"Yes. You feel his pain, and soon enough, it will affect your feelings for him. *That* scares me."

He's perceptive. "Do you have feelings for everyone you take on? I mean, do you...." I trail off, unable to form the sentences properly.

Ethan runs his hand through my hair, sending a tingle through my body. "Not in the way you think, but yes, when I'm not ignoring the pain, there's no way to *not* build a bond with them."

"So, what? You think I will *like* him?"

Both his hands slip through my hair when he holds my head, his pinkies grazing my neck. "I sure hope not." He pauses. "Because *I'm* falling for you."

Not only does my blood trickle through my veins like droplets of hot lava, but my knees are weak and unable to hold me up for long. Fortunately, Ethan pulls me close and presses his lips to mine. Warm and velvety, his mouth feels wonderful on mine, and after making his way down my neck with his lips, he pulls me down to my bed, sits me on his lap, and stops kissing me. "Oh, Honor. I never expected this. When I came here looking for you, I never intended to start liking you like this. It just makes things so much more complicated. Y'know what I mean?"

"No. Not exactly. What do you mean? How does that complicate things?"

"Because we're empaths. We take on too many bad things. When an empath falls in love with another empath, nothing good happens. They die. They do good for everyone else, and then...for each other...they die." His explanation stops short.

Fall in love? "Why do we have to die?"

Ethan's eyes pop out of his head. "Have you listened to *anything* I've said about being an empath, Honor?"

"Yes, of course, but didn't you say that we can *ignore* the pain?"

He springs up from the bed and begins pacing my room. His hands run through his hair in some nervous attempt to think things through. "That's just it. The pain, the aches, the hurt. It'll all be too much." He stops pacing and kneels down in front of me, placing his hands on my knees. "I'll absorb someone's hurt, you'll absorb someone's hurt, and then we'll feel each other's pain. And not just our own heartaches and illnesses, everyone else's too." Ethan tilts his head to the side and continues speaking softly. "It'll be too much to bear. We could never ignore it. It's getting hard already." He takes a deep breath, kisses my left hand, and continues. "Our only choice would be to heal everyone. Then we'd die within five, ten years. Just like our parents did." A guttural sound escapes his lungs. He's crying.

"That's why they kill," I whisper.

"Yes...that's why they kill."

By the weirded-out expression on Ethan's face, he appears to have recalled something. "They were killing people. That's what my brother Hunter told me the day he called. I forgot about that. It wasn't just to tell me to watch out for Storm. They're after something." He stands now and leans back against my bureau. "If they were *with* Storm, then we're all in danger," he realizes. "They'll follow him out here. What if he's part of this group? We could be in danger."

"You know, Eeth. The other day at the hospital, my mother told me that Hanna and Daniel had told them that if I had stayed with them, I'd be in danger." A dire expression shadows Ethan's face, but I ask anyway. "Could this be related?"

Ethan slides down to the floor and slams the back of his head against the bureau. "Oh shit. I'm so friggin' stupid for coming here to find you. Now I've dragged you into something; after all your parents did to get you away from us."

"Ethan, stop." I go over and sit next to him. "I'm *glad* you're here." I *think*. Since I really have no idea what I'm in for anymore.

Chapter Fifteen

"Honor?" Ethan asks after several minutes of silence. "Would you be willing to leave New Jersey? Leave your parents? To come with me?"

"Oh my God, Ethan, no. First of all, I just met you; I barely know you. Second of all, I can't just leave my parents. You're crazy." I chuckle at the thought.

"Just thought I'd ask." Ethan gives a hopeless shrug and stands up, lending his hand to aid me up.

"We'll deal with it, Ethan." I tell him at last. "And I'll watch out for Storm." Then I had a thought. "Hey, can you teach me *how* to ignore someone else's feelings? Like Storm's?"

Ethan touches his lips to my forehead. "There's not much to teach, Honor. You just force yourself to shut everyone out. That's why I prefer living where no one else is. Most empaths prefer to be alone. But I don't want to talk about that right now."

I step back. "Why?"

"Because. I wanna talk about something else."

"Like what?"

"Like...I want you to be my girlfriend." His smile spreads across his face as he says this.

"Oh." I hesitate to answer. I never had a boyfriend, so I'm kind of curious to see what it would be like, and I do like Ethan. He's sweet. Protective. "Okay," I blurt, not really thinking it through.

He cups the back of my neck with his hand and brushes my lips with his, sending those little electric fuzzies throughout my entire body. Maybe I did make the right decision.

Ethan's tongue is now in my mouth, and all of a sudden I am too aware that we are in my bedroom. Late at night. Reminding myself that this is much too tempting, since kissing Ethan is really nice, I force myself out of his arms.

"What's wrong," he asks, clearly surprised that I've pulled back.

"I'm sorry." I look down at my fuzzy-socked feet. "I'm not, I, mean, I don't think this is a good idea. To be in my room, I mean."

Ethan chuckles and kisses me on the nose. "You're cute. It's no problem. I don't want you to feel uncomfortable..."

I stop him short of finishing his sentence. "No, that's not it at all. I'm enjoying it, I just don't want it to, y'know, go any further. I'm not ready for that."

"Don't worry about it." He smiles. "We'll go as slow as you want it to go. I should leave anyway. Your father doesn't need any more trouble on his hands, with your mom recovering and all."

I nod. "You're not mad?"

"Of course not." He taps my lips with his. "I'll see you at school in the morning."

Ethan springs back down the tree, and this time when I lay my head to rest on my pillow, I feel my smile reach from one ear to the other as I drift off into a peaceful slumber.

***

Walking up the stairs to school the next morning, Storm catches me by the elbow. "Honor, I really need to talk with you," he whispers in my ear.

In his tone, I hear regret. In my heart, I feel his sorrow. Storm is hurting. There is no mistaking the hollow-heart aching in my chest. While his hand is still clasped around my arm, whatever is troubling him is now being passed on to me. Whether he is doing this purposely or unconsciously, I know I need to break contact immediately.

Pulling my arm from his desperate grasp, I act as annoyed as I can. "What is it, Storm?"

"I need a friend, Honor," he pleads. "Please just give me a minute. One minute. That's all I ask."

Not sure if his plea is a façade, I agree to let him talk anyway. "Fine. One minute. I can't be late for homeroom."

He turns and starts walking, motioning for me to follow. We stop at his car.

"Storm, we can't leave campus. School starts in ten minutes."

"Shush, Honor. We're just sitting inside. We're not going anywhere." He opens the passenger side door to let me in, then practically hops over the hood of his beautiful car and gets in on the driver's side. Adjusting his seat as far back as it can go, he gives an awkward turn towards me and exhales. "Honor," he begins. "Um, you're in, I mean, I'm in, well, we're all in a bit of trouble right now." Storm looks down at my lap. No way does he look like the arrogant smartass he paraded around as yesterday.

"Who? Who's we?" I keep the edge in my voice to avoid absorbing all this guy's emotions. His lower jaw moves just slightly, and I think to myself that it makes him look so vulnerable right now. But also on my mind is the fact that I'm afraid Ethan may see me sitting in Storm's car. I'm very torn at the moment. And very agitated.

"You, and, uh, me, Ethan, his brothers." He's obviously reading my expression, but I don't even know what to say. "There are some dangerous empaths out there, Honor. They're after something that, well, I don't really know at the moment, but they know I followed Ethan out here and it's only a matter of time..." he trails off, quirking that lower jaw again. "They also know Ethan found you."

"Wait a minute. Back up. I don't even know what you're talking about. *Why* are they following us? What makes us so special?"

"Ethan didn't tell you?"

"Tell me what, Storm?" I start rubbing my thighs with my hands. Storm is making me nervous now, and he's sending mixed signals. Mixed emotions. And I'm understanding none of it.

"Well, the fact that he wants you to stay away from me means he must have told you about our," he hesitates, "sister." It's very subtle, but that glazed-over look of grief flits through Storm's violet eyes.

"Yes. Summer. He told me."

"Then," he pauses again, "he told you what I did to her."

I only nod. Words were definitely failing me at the moment.

"Well, what I did, well it makes me somewhat *attractive* to empaths who want to reach immortality." Storm squeezes the back of his neck, leaving his hand there for a few moments.

"I don't understand."

The corner of his mouth involuntarily quirks. Storm tries to stifle it by tucking in his lips.

"Talk to me, Storm. What are you trying to say?"

"Did Ethan tell you that if an empath kills another empath, he becomes immortal?"

I stare wide-eyed at Storm, still unable to comprehend this paranormal life I am part of, but I find myself able to speak despite my shock. "I don't get how that's possible."

"Since we can absorb their pain, we can absorb their souls, if we kill them...no matter *how* we kill them. I don't really understand it myself, but...anyway, each empath is at risk of being killed by another empath for solely that reason—gaining immortality. But if an empath has already killed an empath, then he's of more value because he has taken on the soul of the person he's already murdered. The more souls collected, the more powerful he is. And since I, well, y'know, anyway, I'm going off course. There are other real reasons why they are looking for you."

"For me?" I jump in quickly. "Why me? I haven't killed anyone."

"Honor, I really don't know. It's everything. All I want you to know is that you and Ethan need to be careful."

Something Storm said just sunk in.. "So, if a soul goes into the person who killed it, then..."

"Yes, Honor. Summer did not go to Heaven and find eternal bliss. She's right here. Living inside me. Her own infernal Hell." The regret in Storm's eyes mimic the remorse

I have brewing in my own soul. Remorse for a murder I didn't even commit. There's a deep contrition emanating from Storm, and it takes all I have not to lean forward and hug him.

But I refuse to believe this paranormal stuff. "No, I don't believe you," I stammer.

He grabs my arm and is aggressive in his attempt to pull me close. To feel his self-hatred. Resisting him is too much. He is strong, yes, but my emotions for him, *from* him, whatever they are, won't let me tear away. It is dangerous, yes, to allow him to touch me for so long. His pain, his guilt, his loathing will all become mine, but there is something so sincere, so profound about him, that I can't pull myself away.

"Listen to me, Honor." His grasp is tight. "It's true. All of it. And Summer is not the only one I've killed."

The lump that sits in my throat while he touches me finally lets loose when Storm abruptly drops his hold on me. "Why are you telling me this? This has nothing to do with me."

"Oh, but it does. It *so* does."

"No, I can't listen to this anymore. I gotta go." I already have my door open when he reaches across me to lay his hand on my arm, blocking me from stepping out of his car.

"I'm not done, Honor. You need to find time to talk to me again. I'm telling you, you need to listen to me. There's more. Your grandfather..."

Nothing comes out. I'm speechless, but I manage to push him away and get out of his car. I can't be near him like this. Ethan is right. Storm *is* dangerous. But Ethan has

no idea just how dangerous Storm is. To *me*. And my relationship with Ethan.

Chapter Sixteen

Today's headache is all my own. Caused by my conversation with Storm this morning. I know I should have stayed and let him finish what he had to say, but trying to decipher which emotions were his, which were mine, and the fact that he just told me he'd not only killed Summer but someone else—well, it was just all a bit too much for me to handle. To top it all off, he says *I* have something to do with the impending danger that we're in. Was it not only last month that my life was relatively normal? Was it not only last school year that I had barely *anyone* in my life at all? How did I all of sudden fall into this inconceivable life? It has to all be a dream. It has to be.

Ever since Ethan showed up, my peaceful world has been disrupted. I'm glad he did. I enjoy being with Ethan. But this whole empath community stuff frightens me. And I don't even understand my own emotions anymore. Whether I'm *with* Ethan or not, I know I like him. The thing with Storm is, I think I'm only attracted to him when I'm with him. So are they his feelings or mine? It all just drives me crazy.

By lunchtime, I realize Ethan isn't in school, and he hasn't even texted me. Though my head is still reeling from Storm's declaration, I am now concerned with Ethan's absence.

"So, the freaky Honor Stevens doesn't have her pretty boy to hang with today." I turn to see that tiny brunette of a cheerleader standing behind me. "What's the matter? He finally figured out what a freak you are?" With her hands on her hips, three cookie-cutter cheerleaders to her side, she tries to intimidate me with her sneer. "What's the matter? Loser's cat got her tongue? You're such a weirdo, Honor, it's no wonder Ethan dropped you like yesterday's news."

Writhing in pain, I nearly buckle over, my bones hurt so bad. The cheerleaders see me flinch and taunt me because of it. The little one can't keep her mouth shut. She keeps rambling on how scared of them I am and that weirdoes like me don't even know how to defend ourselves. She pushes me, and my tray goes flying as I land ass first on the floor. Without warning, I am propelled back up to standing position. Ethan is behind me, holding me around the waist.

"Ethan, where've you been?"

"Get outta here, you slut." Ethan addresses the tiny bully, but before he finishes his command, she turns and heads back to her table. Now he gives me his attention. "What was that all about?" Ethan's whole face is twisted in disgust.

"It was nothing."

When I bend down to pick up the contents of my tray, Ethan grabs my hand.

"Stay away from her, Honor," Ethan says quietly, but his voice is stern.

This causes me to chuckle, because I was staying away from her. She had approached me.

"I'm serious, Honor. She's bad news." *Like Storm?* Everybody's bad news to Ethan.

I gather my ruined lunch and toss it in the garbage. "Well I wasn't planning on being her BFF," I mock.

Ethan takes my hand and walks me out of the cafeteria and into the school foyer. I get a chill and I'm sensing we're not alone, but when I glance around the hall, I don't see anyone. But now I have that heavy feeling in my chest—as if I'm being burdened with something. I try to ignore it, though and focus on Ethan.

"By the way," I ask him. "Where were you this morning?"

Ethan's violet eyes take on a deep purple. "My brother Brad was killed last night." He tries to say with a straight face, but I can see the pain in his eyes. I can feel the pain.

"Oh, Ethan, I'm sorry." I wrap my arm around his waist. I feel his silent cry deep in my heart. After letting him release his sadness into me, I pull away, trying to hide the despair *I* now own. "How?"

"Another empath."

"An empath?" This whole thing is crazy. Aren't empaths, by nature, supposed to be compassionate? "Why?"

Ethan's deep purple eyes have now turned almost black. Ethan's mouth is moving, but I barely hear him say, "Storm had something to do with this."

Then it registers. Storm said he'd killed someone else. Could this be what he was talking about? But that's impossible. Storm was with me this morning. "Ethan, where was he killed?"

"They found him at a rest stop off of 95. He was in New Jersey."

So, if he did it last night or something, then Storm *could have* killed. No, I don't believe it. Those are not the vibes I get from Storm. "Why do you think Storm did this?"

"It's just too much of a coincidence," he says.

"Was Storm after him for something?"

"Hunter says Storm was looking for all of us Sutherlands."

"But why?" The Storm I am getting to know may be arrogant, but I do not see him as a cold-blooded killer. He carries around too much remorse. I know. I feel it whenever I'm near him.

"I don't know, Honor. I just don't know."

Ethan's eyes are slowly fading back to violet. His anger is subsiding. The fact that emotions play a part in the color of our eyes is something I never knew about our violet eyes, since anger had never been one of my regular emotions. Plus, if I ever were angry, I wouldn't have been looking in the mirror to watch it happen.

"My brother Hunter is on his way from wherever he is. I'm not even sure where all my brothers live anymore. I do know that each of them lives with a different relative." Ethan makes a hmmph sound and I see a tear bubble in the corner of his eye. "Well, except for Brad. He's in Heaven now. I hope."

Which makes me wonder about what Storm said—empaths who kill are now the owners of their victims' souls. So if an empath killed Brad, his soul is *not* in Heaven, it is being held captive within his murderer's body. Poor Brad.

"You know, Honor, I better go before someone sees me. I'm ditchin' again. I have to meet Hunter and my uncle at the airport later. I'll knock on your window when I get back." He gives me a sweet kiss on the mouth and heads toward the door.

"Well look who it is?" I cringe when Storm's voice stops Ethan in his tracks. He steps out from an alcove on the other side of the foyer. "Shouldn't you be trying to find your brother's killer or something?"

"Why you..." In a blur, Ethan is at the other end of the foyer flying at Storm and tackling him to the floor. "You've been listening? What the hell..."

Storm kicks up both feet, slams them against Ethan's gut and sends him flying across the hall. Ethan again attempts to attack Storm, but in one smooth movement, Storm wrestles Ethan to the ground and thrusts his knee in Ethan's throat, keeping it there and rendering Ethan unable to move.

"You know I could if I wanted to," Storm sneers. "Kill you, I mean. Right now." He pauses, leaving his knee in the crook of Ethan's neck. "But you're not worth my time. You or your loser brothers." Then he laughs. "You better watch yourself, brother," he cracks. Removing his knee from Ethan's throat, Storm stands, his foot now positioned on Ethan's stomach. "Someone's out there looking for your precious Honor. You better keep her safe."

Ethan swats Storms foot away and jumps to his feet. Storm chuckles to himself as he walks away, his laughter echoing through the halls.

All I get from Ethan is another short kiss before he storms out the door. Understandable. Storm angered him.

Probably embarrassed him too. How different Storm is with Ethan than he is with me.

"So, were they fighting over you, princess?" The tiny cheerleader berates me as I walk back to my table in the cafeteria.

Can't she tell I am already in a bad mood and in a lot of pain? I need her comments now, too? "You know, I don't even know your name, yet you choose me as your firing target." I say, tired of saying nothing. "You know what, cheerleader? Get a life." I finally speak up, and it feels good.

But as I am strutting back to my table, I feel her hand grab my shoulder. She spins me around so hard I almost fall.

"Fight, fight." I hear our immature classmates in the distance.

Cheerleader grabs me by the shirt, places her hands on my chest and pushes me to the floor. I gasp in pain. It's not the fall. When she touches me, something flows from her to me. She must feel it too, because I see it in her eyes and in the frightened expression on her face. She jumps back, spews "whatever" and leaves the cafeteria.

My ass is still planted on the floor, and I am stunned by what just occurred. Something is wrong. Terribly so.

Chapter Seventeen

Still hunkered down on the lunchroom floor, I see Tamlin heading my way. I force myself to get up and quiet the streams of fire burning through my bones.

"What was Shelby's problem?" she asks, a little late for rescuing me. "I'm sorry. I just realized it was you she was fighting with. I usually stay out of those things. I'm so sorry, Honor."

"It's fine. Shelby? That's her name?" I ask, sitting back down at my table. I rub my forearms, trying to alleviate the pain that still resonates after Shelby touched me.

Tamlin laughs and sits down across on the bench across from me. "Yeah. What was that all about?"

"I have no idea. I guess she just chose me to hate." I take a double look at Tamlin. "What the heck did you do to your hair now?"

"What? You don't like pink? Anyway, who could hate you? You're so sweet. Plus you barely speak to anyone; you're always keeping to yourself."

"Because I'm a freak." I laugh. Tamlin chuckles with me, not realizing that I really am a freak. "I think Shelby's really sick or something." I whisper.

Tam scrunches her face up. "What? You're crazy. What makes you say that?"

I want so badly to tell Tamlin. I hate keeping this to myself, but I know Ethan wants me to keep quiet about it. "Just a hunch I guess." The time to tell Tamlin about my *empathic* abilities is not now. "Like an intuition or something."

Tamlin continues knitting her eyebrows, probably deciding for herself, finally, that I am indeed a freak. "Don't give her a second thought, Honor. She's a bully."

I only nod. She *is* a bully, but why? Bullies always have a reason for bullying. Low self-esteem, bad family life, a terminal illness. I do believe that whatever it is that I felt when Shelby touched me is fatal and is the catalyst for her bullying. Down deep in my bones, I know it. Down deep in my bones, I feel it.

***

Hurrying to Mom's car in the lot, Storm catches me, just as he had this morning. "I was serious y'know, Honor," he remarks, despite my attempt to ignore him by opening my car door and getting in. "They are after y'all. I told you that earlier. I wasn't lying." He blocks me from shutting my door by standing in front of it.

"Storm, if you're so concerned about Ethan, why do you treat him the way you do?"

By the startled look on his face, he is surprised by my comment, but his words come out icy cold, "Just warnin' the wimp." Though Storm appears to want to say something else, he turns on his heel and walks away.

After spending some time having tea with my mom, I lock myself in my room for the rest of the night to wait for Ethan and do homework. I still feel guilty not telling Mom about my abilities, but it just never feels like the right time. I don't think she'd believe it anyway. Paranormal stuff is just fictional, not real life drama in her only daughter's life. The whole idea of my empathic nature reaching beyond the normal is still an uncomfortable thought. That I have the power to heal is even scarier—a big responsibility, I am sure. Healing my mother was easy. Who wouldn't save their own mother if given the choice?

Though I can't stop thinking that something is wrong with bully cheerleader Shelby, she is in pain and I have the power to take that away. But at what cost to me? Several years off my life? I'd already shortened it saving my mom and Tamlin. What if there are others to come? How do I choose who to heal and who to let fate decide its course? That type of decision goes far beyond my scope of reasoning for sure. Who am I to play God?

I now understand why Ethan and his brothers live alone, with nary a neighbor. It isn't just the pain they are escaping. It's the unfair burden of weighing life against life—a worthy existence versus an expendable one. How can a mere human decide that?

It is all too much and now my head pounds from overthinking this. Figuring out how to live this way is something I need to do quickly. But with a headache this huge, today is not that day.

My homework is far from complete, because my thoughts keep wandering back to Ethan and his poor brother to Shelby and whatever she is suffering from to Storm and the whole mystery that surrounds him. How can I possibly concentrate on my algebra and chemistry homework? Not that it matters, because seconds later I see Ethan sitting on the tree limb outside my window.

"Ethan," I scold, while lifting the window jam. "You could use the front door you know. It's not even dark yet."

He gracefully hops into my room in all his gorgeous glory. "I know." He shrugs, pulling me in for a hug and a kiss. "But I told you I'd meet you at your window, and I never break my word." He winks.

At least he's smiling. "Did you pick up your brother Hunter?" We mosey over to my bed where we sit crossed-legged, facing each other—Ethan leaning against the headboard, me, at the foot of the bed.

"Yeah. He and my uncle are at my apartment. Sorry about that fight with Storm before, he just, I can't figure him out, that's all. And with Summer and all—"

I playfully tap him on the leg. "You don't need to explain." Ethan pulls me close and I turn to sit between his legs. My back against his chest, his chin on my head, I let him hold me, knowing he needs it as much as I do.

"So was everyone talking about how Storm kicked my ass today?"

"Actually," I let a sideways glance prelude my own ass-beating tale, "they were discussing another fight that happened right after you left."

"What? Who?"

"Umm, me."

He pushes me away just enough to turn me and look me in the eyes. "Honor, who did you get in a fight with?"

"That little cheerleader who's been harassing..."

"Honor," Ethan interrupts. "I asked you to stay away from her."

"Yes, you did. Do you think *I* approached *her*?" I ask, a little annoyed at the tone he takes with me.

"No. I guess not. But tell me what happened? Did she hurt you?"

"Well, she did kick my butt, but no, I wasn't really hurt; not the way you think."

"Oh, Honor." He sighs. "She touched you long enough, didn't she?"

"You know?"

Ethan glides his hand down my back, catching his fingers in my hair.

"That's why you wanted me to stay away from her?"

"Yes, she's sick. It's terminal."

"How do you know?"

"I've been an empath all my life. You get to know the different levels of pain. Like Miss James, for instance; I almost felt her tumor in my own brain."

"Then can't you warn Shelby?"

"The little bitch?"

"Yeah."

"Listen, Honor, I know your inclinations are to help her, but you can't." He grabs my face with both his hands. "You'll take a lot of time off your own life if you do."

"But, my mom, I saved her."

"Exactly. That's already knocked years off. Honor, listen. Shelby is it? She's sick. It's her bones. I think it's cancer. It has to be. She's gotta know; her pain is intense. You know it, you feel it just like I do."

"But maybe she doesn't know. We can warn her. Tell her to see a doctor or something, like you did for Miss James."

"How do you think that'll turn out, Honor? She can't stand you. She's gonna let you tell her she's dying?"

"I have to try, Ethan."

"Run away with me."

"What? Where'd that come from?"

Ethan pulls me onto his lap again. "We can live somewhere remote. Alone. Then you won't have to worry about Shelby's pain or anyone else's."

His shoulder is strong, I think, as I lean my head on it. "I didn't even graduate high school yet. I want to go to college, and I don't want to leave my parents." *I don't even know how much I really like Ethan - definitely not enough to run away with him.*

His head nods above mine. "I know that. Just wishing, I guess."

"I can't just let her live like that, Ethan. When she touched me, it was *so* bad. Like a hundred times worse than I ever felt anything."

"Why do you care? She's not even nice to you."

"Maybe that's why though. Maybe she's nasty because she hurts so much. I can take away her pain, Ethan. How can I choose not to?" *Even though she is a little bitch.*

"You are not God, Honor." Ethan is adamant. "You can't save everyone; not without killing yourself."

We are at a stalemate, and nothing we say right now is going to change that. Not tonight.

"Listen, let's forget Shelby tonight." Ethan pats his hand on the bed next to him.

Anxious and apprehensive at the same time, I crawl off his lap and sit next to him as close as possible without actually sitting back down *on* his lap. He drapes his arm around me, turns my face toward him and with his fingers makes little butterfly tingles along my cheek. My breathing picks up its pace along with my heartbeat. Ethan tilts my head towards his and presses his lips to mine. His hand on the back of my neck sweeps through my hair, sending a feeling of warm liquid trickling through my veins. He holds me closer, deepening his kiss. I open up just a bit to allow his tongue to invade my mouth. It feels silky and warm. Kissing Ethan wakes up every nerve ending in my body, while turning me to putty at the same time. *Are these his feelings or mine?*

As his tongue circles mine, I get lost in his embrace. And though he is the first person who has ever kissed me, I cannot help but wonder if we're going to take it any further right now. I don't want him to stop, but in the back of my mind I begin to worry that we might go further than we should. I continue to melt in his kiss and stop thinking at all. *His emotions or mine?*

Ethan's hand slips under my t-shirt, and it feels hot on my back. Softly, he caresses my skin with his fingertips, skimming over my bra strap as he does. Soon, he starts playfully snapping the back of my bra. His flirting makes me smile while he's kissing me. *Maybe my feelings?*

With one hand still on my back, his other hand cups the back of my neck again, and he gently slides me down on the bed. Ethan is now lying next to me with one of his legs draped over both of mine. His mouth is still on mine, his tongue still probing inside. Ethan's hand slides down the front of my shirt, stopping at my chest. It feels like nothing I've ever felt before. The stroke of his hand sends an unfamiliar sensation right to the pit of my belly.

"Oh, Honor," Ethan rasps. "I love kissing you."

"Mmm." I'm so aroused I can barely talk. *Who cares who's emotions these are.*

He slips his hand under my shirt now but over my bra. Though this feels amazing, I gently squeeze his forearm and pull his hand away. "Eeth," I whisper, turning from his kiss.

"Too fast?" he whispers back, kissing me on the tip of the nose.

"A little." I wrap my arms around his neck. "I'm sorry."

"Honor, please, it's okay. We don't have to do anything you don't want to do," he says, rolling me on top of him.

"Well, I *want* to. I, just not yet. Not today."

"Did you think we were going to *do it* today?" He chuckles. "I don't move *that* fast." He squeezes me and rolls on top of me. His lips meet mine again, and he slips his tongue back inside my mouth.

After several more minutes of making out on my bed, Ethan lifts off of me, yanks me up and says, "C'mon. Let me take you to the diner. I've worked up an appetite."

"Ethan." I stop him. "You didn't even tell me what you found out about your brother. Don't you wanna talk about that?"

"No. Not really." He sighs. "I haven't found out anything yet. Hunter and my uncle are at my apartment, and we just don't know where to start. My uncle's making some phone calls. So, c'mon, I'm hungry."

We get into Ethan's Mercedes and head up Weldon Road to the Jefferson Diner. I'm all excited, because I've never gone there with friends, only my parents. I'm a seventeen year-old geek, but I feel cool going there with a boyfriend. But nervous as hell.

I notice Ethan's hand on the steering wheel. At first, I think he is tapping his fingers to the beat of the Neon Trees song playing on the radio, but at closer inspection, I notice his fingers are shaking just a bit. Maybe he's just as nervous as I am going out together. This *is* kind of like our first date. Thinking about this makes my stomach even more of a mess, because now it occurs to me that I have to eat in front of him. It seems different than just eating in the cafeteria at lunch time. What if I get food stuck in my teeth? Crap, I wish I hadn't thought of that.

"Whatcha thinkin' about?" Ethan asks. His voice sounds smooth and easy, not at all jumpy or jittery like I feel.

"Nothing. Just listening to the music," I lie, trying to sound calmer than I am.

"Oh. You nervous?"

"What? No. Why would I be?"

"'Cause it's our first time out together." He puts his hand on my thigh and gives it a little squeeze. "I'm a little nervous."

Wow. That just relaxed me so much. "Yeah. I guess I am."

Ethan laughs and squeezes my leg again. "Well, don't be. It'll be fun."

The headrest is comfortable as I lean back against it, finally feeling at ease. A few moments later we're at the diner. We get out of the car and Ethan takes my hand, opening the diner door for me as we walk in.

"Two, please," Ethan tells the hostess, and those twitters in my stomach start flipping all around. I'm actually on my first date—*ever*. I know it's a lame diner date, but to me it is so exciting to feel like an *almost* normal teenager.

My eyes begin to hurt while I look at the menu. Leaning my elbow on the table, I press my fingertips to my brow line.

"Honor, you okay?" Ethan asks, reaching for my free hand.

"Yeah. It's just a headache," I say, ashamed to be in pain on our first date. As I sit there, I notice other parts of my body beginning to hurt.

"It sucks," he says.

"What?"

"Feeling everybody else's pain."

"That's what this is?"

Ethan gives me one of his sideways smirks. "Yes," he says slowly. "I thought you're able to recognize the difference?"

"I thought so. Maybe not." I shrug.

"Do you wanna leave?"

Shaking my head, I blush. How could I want to leave our first date before it even begins? "No. I'm good. I'll try to ignore it."

"Good girl," he praises and kisses my hand from across the table.

I'm not sure I'm loving the whole romantic hand-kissing gesture.

"You guys ready to order?" the waiter walks up and asks.

"Yeah. I'll have the tuna melt. Can I have a side of sweet potato fries instead of the regular?" I just love sweet potato fries.

"Sure, and for you?" The waiter looks at Ethan.

"I'll have a cheeseburger and regular fries and a coke please. Thanks."

We hand our menus back and look at each other.

"I'm glad I found you, Honor. I mean, I know I've invited trouble into your life, but I'm really glad I'm with you." Ethan begins talking at a regular voice level, but he ends in a whisper. It's almost like he is nervous to tell me this.

"I'm glad too." I shrug, not sure what I should say next.

"I still want you to run away with me," he says.

"Eeth," I sigh. "I can't. My parents would be so upset. I couldn't do that to them."

I hear him make that "tsking" sound.

"Besides," I continue, "wouldn't it be safer to just stay put until we know who's after us?"

"Hmm." He raises his eyebrows and smirks. "When did you get so smart?"

He takes my hands again.

"You're right." He looks me directly in the eyes. "We'll get through this. I promise."

"I know." *I hope.*

All of a sudden Ethan's eyes go to the front of the diner, and his expression shifts. His lips tighten while his eyes turn a deeper shade of purple.

"Eeth...what is it?" I ask, simultaneously turning toward the door. The sudden stinging in my bones is almost intolerable. They burn. My body is on fire, and its source just walked through the diner's front door.

Shelby is here.

"Honor," Ethan whispers. "Turn around and ignore her. Please," he says, sterner than I'd ever heard him.

Reacting to the pain, I fold my arms and squeeze my biceps really hard. Attempting to further alleviate the burn, I close my eyes and take in a deep breath.

Before my eyes open, I hear a mean cackle nearby. I open them to see the tiny dark-haired bully standing next to our table.

"Well, looky here, it seems the loser somehow got pretty boy's attention again."

Ethan opens his mouth, but I hold up my hand to stop him. "Shelby," I start, timidly at first, but I swallow my fear and keep on. "I know somewhere deep inside you is a nice girl screaming to get out, and I know whatever it is you're suffering from must be terrible. But really, trying to bring me down is *not* going to help your situation." I smile, despite the fact that her eyes tell me she is seeing red at the moment.

I look to Ethan, and he's rolling his eyes and shaking his head. I shoot him a puzzled look and shrug, wondering why he looks embarrassed.

When I turn my attention back to Shelby, her face is bright red, and I see her chest rising quite rapidly. Her cheerleading minions are standing there wide-eyed and speechless. Shelby—speechless herself—storms toward their table, and her followers do the same.

Ethan still looks annoyed.

"What?" I ask him.

"I told you *not* to talk to her."

"No," I say very slowly. "You said *ignore her*, but she stopped at our table. I wasn't just gonna cower to her."

"I didn't want you to cower, I just don't want you touching her."

"Well, I didn't." I hesitate, but I need to say it. "I do *want* to touch her. I want to help her."

Ethan tightens his lips again. "Why? She doesn't even like you!"

"I know, but maybe it's just 'cause she's sick."

"She doesn't like *you*, because *she's* sick? Honor, that's crazy."

"I mean maybe she's mean *because* she's sick."

"I think she was mean *before* she got sick," he remarks.

"Regardless, Eeth...if my pain is any indication, she's got to feel miserable. And it'd be better for me, if I heal her. I won't feel this every time she comes near me. Don't you feel it?"

Ethan closes his eyes for a few long moments. "Yes. I do. But I'm not going to risk ending my life to help her. Nor will I allow you to risk yours."

Hmm. I hadn't seen this side of Ethan before. "Excuse me. Allow me?"

"I just mean, I didn't mean that I won't allow you, but what is it with you and these bullies anyway?" he asks.

"Bullies? Plural?"

"Yeah. Storm too. You have this thing for people who are cruel."

"No, I don't. Maybe I just see someone else beneath their mean facades."

The waiter comes with our food, but Ethan pushes his plate away. "I'm not hungry anymore."

"Look, Ethan," I say, trying to salvage our first date. "You've had your whole lifetime to learn to block out everyone's pain. This is all new to me. I'm only figuring all this out. You have to give me time. Please."

"I get that, Honor, I do. But I just know you're gonna go and do something stupid, and you're not going to be able to reverse the effects. Once it's done, it's done."

Stupid? Stupid? Did he just call me stupid? "I am *not* stupid, Ethan, and you have nerve saying that."

"No. I didn't say you were stupid. Oh geez, really, Honor, are we gonna do this tonight?"

I push my plate away. I'm not hungry anymore either. "Take me home. I want to go home."

"Fine."

Ethan throws a ten on the table then leaves the cashier with two twenty dollar bills. I turn back to look at Shelby. She's sneering at me.

Chapter Eighteen

Resolving not to cry over our first real argument, I attempt to close my heart and shut down my mind. The entire ride back is completely silent. Only the sound of angered breathing can be heard—Ethan's *and* mine. He's upset that I won't give up on Shelby, and I can't fathom how a boy whose innate abilities are to absorb the sufferings of others can be so cold-hearted. Plus...he called me stupid.

When we reach my house, I open the car door and walk swiftly to get inside. Behind me, I hear Ethan's long stride, his angry steps pounding the pavement to reach me before I go in.

"Honor, please wait."

I reach for my key and unlock the front door. His hand falls on top of mine before I pull the key out of the lock. "Leave me alone," I say to the front door, afraid if I turn around I'll lose my resolve and the tears will tumble out.

"Honor, please." He gently lifts my hand off the door and turns me around. "I am so sorry. If I told you it's my own selfish fear of losing you that makes me so mad, would it make a difference?"

With an unaffected expression and a make-believe hardened heart, I look him in the eyes. "No. It doesn't make a difference. You can't just command me to do what you want, nor can you call me stupid and get away with it." *And lose me? He just* found *me.*

"Stupid? Oh, no, you're blowing this all out of proportion."

"Oh. I am?" I pull my hand from his grasp. "Leave me alone." I try again to open the door.

He tries again to turn me around.

"Ethan, I'm serious. Leave me alone."

His shoulders drop with his resigned sigh. I open the door and close it behind me. When I move to the window and peek outside, he's still standing there frozen in place. My heart sinks. I don't want to fight about this, but it aggravates me that he thinks he can tell me what to do. I've never been in a relationship before, but I'm pretty sure that's not how it works.

"Honor," my mom says, turning on the living room light. "You okay?"

"Yeah, I'm fine." I go to the kitchen, get myself a bottle of water, and hole up in my room for the rest of the night.

Seeking solace, I grab my purple fuzzy pillow, hug it to my chest and plop face down on my bed. But only for a few minutes. Music will make me feel much better, so I reach for my iPod. That's when I see my wicker trunk standing lonely in the corner of my room. During my lonely years of homeschooling, that white woven trunk held all my extra-curricular activities—scrapbooking stuff, my sewing basket, and my yarn and crochet needles. Some extra-curricular activities; I was living in a nursing home, not a teenager's room. I shuffle to the corner and open the lid. My solitary past comes back to me, leaving a bittersweet taste in my mouth. I take out a few skeins of sapphire silk and my letter J needle then close the trunk.

Holding the soft silk in my hands brings back a comfort I forgot I had gotten used to. Not skipping a beat, I make a slip knot on the hook and chain four single stitches and begin working in rounds, creating what? I have no idea.

Before long, it's four in the morning, and I have finished crocheting myself a new scarf and hat—in sapphire blue. Pleased with myself for adding antique jewelry to my scarf and designing my own newsboy cap with some old buttons I had in my dresser drawer, I put it aside to wear to school today. Since it is senseless to go to sleep now, I draw a hot bath and soak in it for a while, wondering how things will play out with Ethan later.

My classes go by quickly enough this morning, but when I enter the cafeteria at lunchtime, Ethan's not there. Nor do I see Shelby or Storm—the two bones of contention between Ethan and me. I spot Tamlin getting off the lunch line and wave her over.

"Hey, Honor, what's up?" she asks, sitting down across from me.

"Hey."

"What's the matter?"

"We had a fight." I sigh.

"You and Ethan?"

"Mmm."

"Oh, honey, what happened?"

How can I explain this without giving our secret away? "He's mad at me." I shrug. "Because I feel sorry for Shelby."

"Why in God's name would you feel sorry for *her*?" Tamlin's floored. "She treats you like dog poo, Honor!"

Holding up my hand to stop her from repeating what I'd already heard from Ethan, I see her mouth the words, "I'm sorry."

"It's okay. But, anyway, that's why he's upset with me. He can't understand why either."

"Can I ask *why* you feel sorry for her?" she asks, trying to understand—so unlike Ethan.

"I think there's something going on with her."

"Like what?"

Taking a courage-inducing breath in, I tell Tamlin. She is my best-friend after all. "I...can feel pain...and emotions," I whisper. "That's how I knew *you* were in trouble and that's how I know Shelby is sick."

"Seriously?" Tamlin seems impressed but not surprised.

"Seriously. You don't think that's weird?"

"No, not really. Lots of people feel empathy for others."

"Yeah," I say, looking around to make sure no one is within earshot. "But can they heal?"

"What?" Now she raises her brows.

"I can heal," I whisper. "I healed my mom from her heart attack...just by *touching* her." Then I realize, I shouldn't be boasting. It's way too freaky a capability to be proud of.

"Really?"

"Please don't tell a soul, Tam. Please."

She crosses her heart and hopes to die, then gives me the two-finger scout's honor.

"Evidently, I've always been this way, but I didn't know it."

"When did you find out?"

I tell her the whole sordid story, and she comes around the table and hugs me. "Oh, Honor, I always knew you were special." She beamed.

"You mean a freak."

Tamlin cracks up. "Not. At. All. You're special, Honor. That's why you're my bff."

"Thanks, Tam."

She gives me a big bear hug, and the bell rings.

In science class, which I usually find boring, we are treated with a nice surprise. Standing in front of the class is the most magnificent man I've ever seen. With hair the color of melted butter and eyes that matched the sapphire scarf and hat I spent all night crocheting, this man is stunning. It's like the Sun god Apollo had just come to life and decided to stand here in Jefferson High's eighth period chemistry class.

"Hello class," he calls in a voice so deep and hot he can turn solids into liquids just by the sound of him. He sounds like golden honey pouring over my ear drums. Thick. Smooth. Sweet. And by the blank stares I see on the girls' faces, I'm not the only female in the class mesmerized by him. "I'm Mr. Moore. I'm your new chem teacher."

"Where's Mrs. Bello?" A silly boy asks. Who cares?

"She took an unexpected leave; now you have me."

When I finally turn my attention away from the hunky teacher, I recall that not only have I not seen Ethan in school today, but Storm hasn't been around either. Now I'm wondering what's going on with them, which will keep me from paying attention to anything the rest of the day.

Adrift somewhere in my own mind, I lament over my lost home-schooled days. Sure they were lonely, but learning from my mother was much less complicated...and much less dramatic.

After school, pelting through the parking lot is Ethan's black Mercedes. He zips into a space, gets out, and slams his door. I stay right where I am—next to the school steps. He spots me and runs towards me.

"Honor," he yells. Not sure whether he is mad or excited, I nod without saying a word. Of course, *I'm* still upset with *him*.

When he reaches me, Ethan takes my wrists and sighs. "First, I'm sorry. Really. I wasn't saying you were stupid. I just didn't want you to do something you'd regret. Saving someone's life may seem like the right thing to do, but when you're playing with your own mortality, well...it's just something you need to think about." He pauses, waiting for a reaction from me.

"I get it," I finally say. "But I don't like being told what to do."

"And I get that. I'll never do that again, but we have a situation here we need to deal with."

"I forgive you, Ethan."

His sideways smile appears for a fraction of a second. "Thanks, but that's not what I'm talking about."

"Then what?"

"Effin' Storm." Ethan drops his hands from my wrists. "He flippin' took my credit card and my license."

"What? Why would he do that?"

"I don't know." Eeth shakes his head. "But I checked; he's nowhere around."

"How would you know? You weren't even in school today."

"Yeah, I was. But I waited for him to show up in the parking lot this morning. He never did. When I went to his house, his car wasn't there." Ethan's pacing slightly.

"How do you know it was him? Maybe you just misplaced them."

"No, Honor. The credit card people called. They'd suspected suspicious activity. Two one-way tickets leaving from Newark to Nevada were purchased under my name and yours. I drove to the airport. His car was there."

"Wait. My name?"

"Yeah, check your wallet. Is your license there?"

My suspicions aroused, I pull my wristlet out of my backpack. "Oh my goodness," I say when I search through it. "It's gone."

"See."

"Still, why would he do this? What could his intentions be?"

Ethan squeezes the back of his neck. "With Storm, it's just plain evil intentions."

I can't help myself, but a chuckle escapes my mouth.

"You think it's funny?" Ethan grunts.

"Well, I think it's comical that you're so quick to jump to conclusions about him."

"Damn it, Honor. You don't get it, do you?" He fumes. "He's dangerous."

Stifling my laughter, I try to understand his point of view. "Okay, well, what's your brother Hunter say about it? Does he think Storm has some evil plan?"

"Let's go to the rock, Honor. I don't wanna keep talking here." He takes my hand and starts leading me to his car.

"Eeth, I have my mom's car."

"Leave it here. We'll get it later."

"I don't want to leave it here. I want to take it."

He stops short and looks at me. "Why?" he asks with a twisted face and puzzled expression.

Only because of what happened at the diner am I doing this, but he just doesn't get it—I don't want him expecting me to jump just because he tells me to. "I don't want to, that's all. I'd like a cup of tea, and I'd rather go home."

His eyes get even wider before he frowns. "Well, can I follow you over? I'd still like to talk to you."

"With me. You'd like to talk *with* me not *to* me."

"I'd still like to talk *with* you, Honor. Please."

Hesitating, I say, "Yeah. See you in a few." Walking away from him, I can feel his eyes on me, but I keep my own eyes straight ahead and don't look back. It's merely a matter of principle.

****

The whistling of the kettle sounds at the same time the doorbell rings.

"It's Ethan, Mom," I yell to her in the living room.

"Come in, Ethan," she calls.

"What was that about?" Ethan asks when he sees me.

"You want a cup?" I hold up the kettle.

"No thanks...Honor...what's up? Why'd you walk away like that?"

Taking my cup with me, I head to my room, knowing Ethan will follow me.

"What the heck?" he asks.

When I put my tea down on my nightstand, Ethan wraps his hand around my arm and turns me. "Honor, talk to me."

Resorting to relationship games is not my strong suit, and I cave. "I'm sorry, Eeth. I guess I'm still not over what happened at the diner."

"Man, Honor. I said I was sorry." He drops to the bed and sits with sulking shoulders.

My heart feels like it has claws tightening around it. He's sad. "Ethan. I'm sorry." Sitting down next to him on the bed, I lay my hand on his leg. "This can't be easy for you. You just lost your brother; we never even talked about it. Now something big is going on, and I'm only concerned with girly teenage stuff. Really, I am sorry."

He wraps his arm around my waist and closes his eyes. "I haven't even had time to mourn Brad. I'm really worried about this Nevada thing. Hunter told me there's someone sinister involved. There may be a connection to Brad's murder. Plus, he may be after..." Ethan stops abruptly.

"After who?"

"Never mind. We just have to be careful. Be on our guard."

"No, Ethan. Who? They're after you and me, aren't they?"

"Please, Honor, it's nothing."

"Storm told me..."

"Storm told you what? What did he tell you?" Ethan jumps in, in one breath, not allowing me to finish my sentence—though he would have gotten the answer he was searching for, had he let me continue my sentence.

"As I was about to say, Storm told me he knew the guy, or guys, who were after us—us, empaths."

Ethan breathes a sigh of relief, though I do not know why. "Yeah, but Storm said he knew the guy? So he *is* involved."

"I don't think so. It didn't sound that way to me. He actually seemed worried about it."

"Yeah, right. He's probably just worried about his own ass."

"Whatever, whoever, it is, we need to figure it out. If someone's out there killing people, we can't have him coming to Jefferson. We can't let him, Ethan."

"I know, Honor. I just wish...wait, I *do* know who it is." Ethan says. "I don't know him personally, but I know *of* him, if it *is* him." Ethan starts mumbling, but I think he says, "Boy, I just wish I knew what Storm had to do with this."

"Why are you so hard-pressed to believe Storm is involved?"

"You like him don't you?" Ethan pulls away from me and stands up.

Not again. "Of course not. I just don't think he is as bad as you believe he is."

"Did you forget about Summer?" Ethan is annoyed and probably not going to drop this jealousy thing anytime soon.

"No, I didn't forget her, but I think Storm feels, I don't know, but I don't think he meant it."

"Did he tell you that?" Ethan snaps.

"No, he didn't, but I felt it." I cringe, knowing Ethan wouldn't like that, but it's the truth.

"He stole our stuff, Honor. Or do you *feel* that he didn't?"

"That was uncalled for, and no, I have no clue, but if he did steal our id, then why?"

"That's what I wanna know." Ethan sighs. "Listen, Honor, I'm sorry I'm so touchy when it comes to Storm." He takes my hands and pulls me off the bed. "I trust your feelings," he resigns. "An empath's feelings are strong, and as far as I know, extremely accurate. For some reason, I get nothing when I'm around Storm, but I'll take your word for it and..." Ethan pauses, probably trying to swallow the words caught in his throat. Admitting a lifelong nemesis may not be the evil being he always assumed is never an easy task. "I'll try to give Storm the benefit of the doubt."

"It's just my intuition. You may be right about him. I don't know," I admit.

"Mmm." Ethan shakes his head. "So did Shelby bother you much today?"

"Not today, she wasn't in."

"You know, I'm this close to saying something to her myself. I hate the way she treats you."

"You think I can't stand up for myself?"

"You're not doing a very good job of it."

"I'm *choosing* to ignore her. It's a choice. Her words don't hurt me. Her situation does."

"You amaze me. How can you care about someone who's so nasty to you?"

"We're empaths. You don't?"

He shakes his head. "I've had eighteen years to get over that. You're just realizing what you're feeling—you'll learn to close your heart eventually."

"Close my heart? That's so sad. I feel sorry for you if that's what you've done."

Ethan sits back on the bed and pulls me to his lap. When he looks at me, his eyes flash a deep purple, and the creepy crawly feeling climbing up my spine indicates his intense indignation. "Don't judge me, Honor. When the pain gets too much, you'll see. It's either close your heart or live in total isolation." He turns his gaze at the wall, and when he speaks again his voice is much softer. "Which is what I was doing until I came looking for you."

"What? I never asked you to come looking for me. I never asked to know about my past or whatever. Why are you here then? Go. Go back to your isolated life. I was fine before you came along." I get up and go to the window.

I hear his footsteps behind me. "Honor, please. I'm sorry." He stands next to me and peers out the window too. "I'm sorry I hurt your feelings, I'm glad I found you."

I keep my eyes out the window; it's easier to ignore him that way. Once I get a glimpse of his face, I know I'll cave. And I am not ready yet. Maybe in a minute or two.

"I shouldn't have come. I realize that now. But when I saw you on the news...I..."

Now I look at him. "You what?"

"I was afraid someone would find you." Ethan shakes his head again. "They obviously didn't. They would have been here by now, but I saw you. I'd heard your story all my life."

"Ethan, you're rambling. What are you talking about?"

"Never mind."

"No. I want. To know. Now," I demand.

He drops his head and looks back up to meet me in the eyes. "When you were three, your grandfather was murdered right in front of you."

"What?"

"Your great-great-great-something-or-other grandfather." Ethan holds my hand and walks me back towards the bed.

"I had a great-great-great grandfather? Who was alive in my lifetime? How is that even possible?"

"Your great times three or four grandfather was an empath who'd killed several times. With his *bare* hands."

That sounds harsh. And mean.

"Legend has it he wasn't a very *nice* man but an extremely intelligent one. A scientist. From what my parents had told me, he took you out for a walk through some woods one day, and someone murdered him right in front of you. They found you kneeling over him." Ethan rubs my arms, aware that I have goose bumps sprouting out all over them. "They think you were trying to save him. It was so long ago, but this was how the story was passed on. You had both hands on his chest, and I think, from what I've heard, whoever found you scared you away and you ran."

Ethan cuddles me from behind and holds me tight. He continues telling me about my past. "Your parents were warned that whoever murdered your granddad was on the lookout for you. He must've seen you and realized you were an empath. And well, it was right after your parents were approached that they gave you up and disappeared."

"Wait. Disappeared? I thought they died."

"Yeah, well, we assumed they died; they were so frail and weak. They'd reached their limit in healing people. Once you were gone, the community figured they'd left to die. I'm sorry."

What could I say? I never knew them anyway. Then it hit me. "Wait. So this guy is still after me?"

His frozen stare says it all.

"Oh, Ethan, what am I gonna do? Why didn't you tell me sooner?"

"I didn't want to scare you. We are still not sure who he is. There's a group who hang with him, but Hunter says they call him Gaffer."

"Like a TV lighting guy?"

"No. I think it's an old term for old man or boss or something. I don't know anyone who knows what this guy looks like. I'll tell you one thing, he's about as old as that granddad of yours, but he may not look it. It all depends on when he made his first kill."

"Whattya mean?"

"When an empath kills, he stays the age he was when he first killed. Nice, huh?"

"So we don't even know what type of guy to look for?"

Ethan shakes his head. "His followers may not even know. They do what he asks, though. He contacts them through messenger or phone calls." Ethan shrugs. "I'm sure it's easier now that cell phones are around, but he's an extremely powerful man. And he's after you for something. But..."

"But what?" Ethan's scaring me.

"Maybe just 'cause you witnessed the murder, but there's a rumor your granddad left you something ancient."

"How's that possible? My parents gave me up when I was not even four years old."

Ethan's shoulders drop. "I don't know, Honor. I just don't know."

"Will Storm know?" Now more than ever I need to find Storm.

"He may. I'm not sure. He could be working with this group. But I told you, I'll give him the benefit of the doubt."

"Can't we just talk to him?"

"No. Not you. I will. When he gets back from wherever he is. If he gets back. And of course, when his guard is down, maybe."

"Hmmm." But I think - *Storm's guard is never down.*

Chapter Nineteen

Since Ethan is worried for my welfare, he talks my mom and dad into letting him stay over for a while—claiming it is too crowded in his studio apartment for three grown men—his uncle and brother who are staying with him for a while. Mom and Dad agree that Ethan can stay as long as he needs...provided he inhabits the guest room. My stomach begins its usual fluttering just thinking about Ethan staying overnight. I never even had a girl sleep over...no slumber parties...nothing. Now I have a boy, whom I like, staying in the room right next to mine. I'm not your usual excitable teenage girl, but having Ethan as an overnight guest makes me giddy, God help me.

With only the four of us in the house this weekend, Ethan's and my pain are at a minimum. It's reminiscent of when I was home schooled and not going out much. Only now I am not suffering from loneliness. I have Ethan. And he has me—just the way I like it right now. The entire weekend we barely talk about evil empaths and murders and...Storm. We just enjoy each other like normal boyfriend and girlfriend. After playing a game of Scrabble and a several-hour game of Monopoly, we turn on my iPod and share ear buds. I cuddle close, enjoying his musky scent and root beer breath. Later, my parents go to bed, and we decide to raid the kitchen. Together we bake double chocolate brownies with chocolate chunks that mom has hidden in the cupboard. I am in Heaven right here in my own home. My fluttering stomach had subsided sometime during the weekend, and I am now comfortably relishing in Ethan's company.

Though Ethan is staying with us for the duration of his family's visit, I am sad to see Monday arrive. I am already looking forward to another quiet weekend at home with my boyfriend (and not thinking about Storm).

***

When I walk into homeroom, I feel something amiss. The principal is whispering to the teacher, and I am filled with despair. The sadness overcomes me and I am afraid to know the reason. My body becomes chilled, and though I try to stay still, I am shaking so hard everyone is staring at me. The clicking in the room is the sound of my own teeth chattering.

When the teacher excuses the principal, and quietly asks for her attention, she says, "I have some terrible news."

My heart drops to the bottom of my already jumbled stomach.

"Shelby Marten's illness took a turn for the worse," the teacher continues. "It looks like the doctors have given her only days to live."

This is why my feelings of hopelessness feel so personal. Shelby really is ill.

"Her cancer has spread through her bones and organs, and there is nothing more they can do." I hear Ms. Williams speaking, but it sounds like she's talking through the other end of a tunnel. "I just ask of the class to give a moment of silence for your prayers or your positive thoughts that Shelby is in as little pain as possible these last few days."

The class remains silent, and though my eyes are closed to try and contain my tears, I feel their prayers. Each and every one of them.

But prayers are not enough.

I can take away her pain.

I can cure her.

How could I just sit here praying when I am capable of *really* helping her?

I pack up my stuff and stand from my desk. "I'm sorry, Ms. Williams," I say through a crackling voice and teary eyes. "I need to leave." I don't wait for her response...or her permission. I just flee.

Luckily Mom isn't back to work yet, and I still have her car.

One problem—I have no idea where Shelby Marten lives.

I pull into the library parking lot hoping for a chance at some help. Since Mom is the head librarian, maybe someone there would help me right away.

"Honor." I hear when I walk through the door. "How come you're not in school? Is your mother all right?"

"Yes, Marge. She's well, actually. I'm just not feeling great today." I hesitate, knowing I shouldn't be asking this. "I don't know if you've heard about Shelby Marten."

"Oh yes, that poor dear. Her parents must be beside themselves."

"I agree. I feel so bad for them. Especially Shelby." I take a breath, for courage. "I want to send her some balloons or something, but I don't know her address. Do you happen to know where she lives?"

"Hmm. Not personally, but she does have a card here. I'm not really supposed to do this, but since you're Leanne's daughter, it should be okay. It's not like your mother wouldn't give it to you if she were here."

A huge sigh of relief escapes me, and I blush, embarrassed by my display of emotion. "Thanks, Marge. I appreciate it."

She writes the address on a piece of paper and slides it across the desk. Wow. Shelby lives right near my house. Mom had kept me so sheltered growing up that I wasn't even aware of who my neighbors were.

When I pull in front of Shelby's house, my nerves are frayed. I am anxious, scared and beginning to feel that familiar ache in my bones, but I focus on why I'm here then head to the door.

"Hello, Ms. Marten?" I offer when a red-eyed woman opens the door.

"Yes, may I help you?"

"I...I'm...a...classmate of Shelby's. I was wondering if I...could see her...if she's up for it."

Her tears fall, and I'm guessing this isn't the first time today that she's cried. "Well, she's probably sleeping," she says between sobs. "She's on a high dose of morphine, but I guess it'll be all right." She opens the door wider to let me in.

Following her to the back room, we pass a myriad of photographs of Shelby hanging on the walls and adorning the furniture along the way. The room we enter is a bright yellow sunroom with skylights and windows everywhere. Towards the back of the room, under a pale cream canopy, Shelby Marten lies feeble and tomblike—her eyelids purple and sunken, her skin the color of ash. She is so not like the blustering bully I'd met with in the cafeteria.

I inch closer, holding out an apprehensive arm. The pain is near intolerable. I brace myself mentally before making contact. Reminding myself of poor Shelby's horrific suffering helps.

I start slowly. As soon as my fingers touch her forearm, I nearly buckle over in pain. The fluxion of stinging pain from her body to mine is fierce. Though my instinct is to pull away, I squeeze her arm with my whole palm, willing myself to ignore how excruciating it is. My slow shift over her body to place my hand on her heart aids in lessening my already wanting confidence in healing her. If I'm going to do this, it has to be straightaway. Faltering no more, my hand hovers gently over her heart, feeling an exaggerated stinging, before laying it flat against her chest. Heat builds until my hand is scorched. Like a swarm of bees moving en masse over their prey, the color scarlet rapidly streams up my arm until I can no longer see the natural color of my flesh. My arm is on fire and my bones feel like they are going to crumble under the intense heat. It is impossible to remain focused anymore, and I slowly begin sliding into unconsciousness. As I fade, Shelby's eyes open...and I know I have done my job.

The next thing I am aware of is two medical people hovering over me, fading in and out of my vision. The blare of the sirens pierces my eardrums.

"Honor?" I hear repeatedly. It may be Shelby.

"Honor?" I hear it again. It's not Shelby.

"Honor?"

"Huh?" My voice. I hear it, but I don't. I'm in some kind of daze.

"Honor? Honey. You're in an ambulance. Your parents are in their car behind us. They're going to meet us at the hospital." Her image gets clearer. Louder.

"Honor? You fell unconscious sweetie. We just want to make sure everything is okay. You scared everyone, honey." It's the paramedic. She smiles.

"Shelby?" I manage in a broken whisper.

"Shelby? Oh, the sick girl you were visiting? She's fine sweetheart. A little confused as to why you were there and...well...a little confused as to why she is feeling so well. Her mother said she was pretty much hours away from dying. With all this going on, they think maybe her adrenaline sparked some energy. Anyway, don't you go worrying about her right now. We gotta tend to you at the moment."

I'm slowly returning to a state of full consciousness. I'm drained but cognizant of my surroundings. In minutes, we are at the hospital, and they are transporting me through the emergency room.

"Honor, sweetie, what happened?" my dad asks.

"Oh, Honor, we're so glad you're okay," Mom states almost simultaneously.

"What were you doing at Shelby's house?" Dad's voice is weak, and I think, *he just got Mom out of health's danger, now he's here with me.*

I am too exhausted to explain. "Just...I don't...know." I trail off a bit at the end, not having enough energy to finish.

"Oh, Honor. Look at you. You look so tired." Mom cries. "What happened in there? I know you're too tired to talk, but Shelby said you were holding her? Honey, I didn't know you were even friends with her."

"Actually, I hear she's not even nice to you," Dad quips.

"How?" I ask. How does he know? I never told him that.

"We texted Ethan on our way in. He called us back. He's very upset. He'll be here soon. We told him not to leave school, but he insisted."

Speak of the devil.

"Honor, goddammit, what did you do?" Ethan reprimands.

I see my father's eyes shoot up to his receding hairline. Mom's brows furrow. I'm sure they're wondering why he's so upset with me.

Ethan walks toward me shaking his head. "What the hell, Honor?" he asks before kissing me on the tip of my nose. "Was it worth it?"

"What's he talking about?" Mom and Dad ask, clearly annoyed at the tone Ethan is taking with me.

Ethan and I look at each other. After letting out an audible sigh, Ethan responds, "Mr. and Mrs. Stevens."

I hold my breath for fear of my parents' reaction to what Ethan is about to tell them.

"Shelby does nothing but bully Honor. She's even gone so far as pushing her. I just don't see why Honor had to go there in the first place, that's all," he says, lying through his teeth.

I could have sworn he was going to tell them about my empathic abilities, but then, he wouldn't. That would just turn everything upside down.

"Is that all you're upset with, boy?" My dad throws up his hands in exasperation. "Honor's a forgiver. She doesn't hold grudges. And from what we were just told, that girl was on her deathbed. What harm could it have done Honor by going there?"

I hear Ethan let out a cynical chuckle as he holds up his palms in my direction. As if to say, *hello, your daughter ended up in the hospital because of her forgiving nature*. But not having a reasonable nor believable explanation, Ethan holds his tongue.

"I just don't like her to set herself up for rejection, Mr. Stevens." Ethan turns to me and takes my hand, looking at it while he slides his hand up and down my arm. "These are delicate hands, Honor," he whispers, almost mouthing the words so only I can hear. "You need to be careful who they touch."

Chapter Twenty

After checking all my vitals and running tests, the ER doctor releases me with a request for me to see my regular physician. *Yeah. I know that already. It's the same thing every time.* It's well past dinner by the time the four of us get home. Mom and Dad don't mind me riding with Ethan...but I sure do. I am not in the mood for a scolding from my boyfriend.

"Honor," he begins, literally a tenth of a second after he sits in the car. Not even shutting his door before he starts on me. "What in the world were you thinking going over there?"

"Please don't start, Ethan. I'm so tired."

"Exactly. You don't know how this is going to affect you. You don't just heal someone like it's magic and then, voila, everything's ok. This could affect you for a very long time." Ethan's voice rises. "She was dying, damn it. Your mother died. You saved them both within, what, a month or two of each other? Honor, you're killing yourself!"

"Oh stop."

"Oh stop? Stop? Are you serious?" he yells. "My parents died young just healing regular stuff. You practically brought your mother back from the dead, and Shelby was so close herself. I don't know what ramifications this is going to have." He runs his hand through his hair, while he squeezes the steering wheel with his other hand so hard his knuckles are white.

"Why do you even care?" I mutter, too tired to discuss the whole thing.

"You just don't get it, do you?" He's looking at me and not the road. While my eyes are glued to what is beyond the windshield, his attention is on me. "I care about you, Honor. You can't do this."

"Ethan, the road." It's making me nervous to know he's driving with no eyes on the road.

"Forget the road, Honor." He pulls over to the side. "You're not God," he screams again. "What if He meant for Shelby to die today? What if she wasn't meant to live a longer life? You just messed with God."

"What if God meant for me to save her, Ethan?" I rebut. "What if that's why He put me here near Shelby? You can't tell me you know for sure that He *didn't* want me to save her life. Right, Ethan?"

He closes his eyes and lets out a long, tormented breath. "I care about you," he takes a breath. "I even think I love you. Do you understand that? I've never loved anyone before. Even my parents. I'd never felt this intensely emotional about anyone. From the moment I saw you in person, I wanted to be near you. I know I'm only eighteen, but jeez, Honor, I...think... well, I really think I love you... so much." His voice cracks. His heart pounds. I feel it.

Ethan takes my face in his hands, and I must say it hurts. My skin hurts. My jaw hurts. Everything hurts. He holds my aching face in his hands and looks me in the eyes. "You cannot take that away from me. Please." He keeps my face in his hands and kisses my nose. "Let's get you home." Putting the car in drive, we head home.

"After pulling into the driveway, Ethan swings around to get me and walks me up the stairs.

"Where'd you guys go?" Mom asks from our front step as Ethan helps me into the house.

"We just stopped to talk for a while, Mom."

"Oh. Well come on now. You need to rest. I got some pillows and blankets out for you. I set them on the couch. C'mon, Ethan, bring her over here." As if he didn't already know where the couch is, we follow her.

"Mrs. Stevens. You go sit, I'll take care of Honor," Ethan insists. "You're supposed to be resting yourself."

"Oh I'm fine, but you cover her up, I'll put on water for tea."

"Thanks, Mom." I look desperately at Ethan. "What am I gonna do? I have to tell her. She's going to be calling all these doctors again and going through all this money. I can't let her do that."

"It's your call, Honor. As long as you make it clear they have to keep this a secret, I would try and explain. I'll be here when you do, if you want."

"Of course. Of course I want." I rest my head back on my pillow. "They'll never believe it."

"Well, they have no choice. You are what you are." Ethan taps the end of my nose with the tip of his finger.

"Maybe tomorrow. I'm exhausted tonight."

Ethan lifts my head, pillow and all, and sits on the couch, allowing my head and pillow to rest on his lap. He reclines his seat and caresses my face. Until we drift off to sleep.

**

I wake the following morning, head still resting on Ethan's lap, weak and fatigued. My body feels like it is being held down by an elephant. I cannot lift myself off the couch. I can't even lift my head off Ethan's lap.

"Honor?" Ethan runs a concerned hand through my hair. "What's going on?"

"I, uh, I can't move."

I'm sure he doesn't mean for me to hear him, but a low "tsk" escapes Ethan's lips before he sighs. "Oh, Honor. I wish I knew how this was going to affect you. Hopefully it's just temporary."

"I need to get up though. I have to try, otherwise I'm gonna pee my pants."

Ethan groans as he lifts me up from the couch.

"Hey. You implying I'm heavy?"

He doesn't even crack a grin, and he ignores my question. "Honor, do your joints hurt?"

"Everything hurts," I joke.

"Your joints, Honor. Do *they* specifically hurt?"

"Yes, but..."

"Like arthritis hurt?"

"Well I'm not sure what arthritis feels like, but I guess so." I shrug and wince. Even my shoulders hurt.

He helps me over to the bathroom. Before I go in, I have to ask. "Why?"

The expression on my boyfriend's face is grim. His jaw tightens as he pulls his lips in. After a quiet second he murmurs, "I think it's starting already."

"What?"

"Go pee, Honor. I'll wait right here."

Since I really can't hold my bladder any longer, I have no choice but wait for his answer. When I come out of the bathroom, Mom is up. Ethan holds his arm behind my back to steady me.

"Good morning," Mom chirps. then frowns. "You two look ill. What's the matter?"

"I'm still feeling weak, Mom, but I'm actually getting better." I realize I'm feeling better as I answer my mother.

"But what about you, Ethan? You don't look so well either. Are you getting sick?"

"I'm fine, Mrs. Stevens. Just worried about Honor."

It occurs to me then—Ethan not only has his one arm around my back. His other arm is reaching across me to hold my hand. It isn't an indolent hold he has on my hand either. He is squeezing my hand—not so it hurts, but so it heals. With a jolt, I pull my hand from him and glare as sternly as I can to let him know he shouldn't be doing that. His eyes close for a moment, and he shakes his head in disappointment. No wonder he isn't feeling well; all night I'd been lying on his lap, and he's been holding me all morning. Ethan is absorbing my pain.

"What's going on, you two?" My mother finds our behavior suspect.

"Nothing, Mom. It's just something between us." Her sudden frown indicates that I've hurt her feelings. Mom has always been my confidant, until Ethan had divulged my past. Now Mom knows nothing about me. That saddens her...and me. I *want* to be able to talk with her. I'm just so unsure.

"Well, come on, I'll get you some tea. Ethan, do you drink coffee or tea? I've a pot made." My mom resigns to dropping the subject, yet I still see the hurt in her eyes.

"I'd love a cup of coffee, Mrs. Stevens."

We sit at the breakfast bar while Mom makes my favorite—banana pancakes.

I watch the color return to Ethan's face now that he isn't in physical contact with me. He's still annoyed though.

"Ethan," I whisper. "Thank you for trying."

He turns his head from me, ignoring my gratitude.

I tug on his sleeve. "Ethan..."

"Not now, Honor." He doesn't even bother to keep his voice down. I see Mom look at us from the corner of her eye. I know she is trying to surmise what's going on between him and me.

Ethan's phone rings. "Hello," he answers. "No, not going today...mmm...it's on Weldon Road...yeah, just go to the front office...Sure. I'll stop by later...yeah...bye."

"Who was that?" I ask, curious to know.

"My uncle. He's registering Hunter for school today."

"I thought you guys were all emancipated?"

"We are, but Uncle Tom just wants to make sure it all runs smoothly. He likes to look after us, and Hunter's the only one that lets him." Ethan sighs.

"You don't?"

He shakes his head. "I moved out a long time ago. I need to live on my own."

"I thought Hunter lived on his own too?"

"He does. He did...until he came here. He stays close with Uncle Tom. He never leaves him for too long."

"What about your other..." I stop, realizing Brad had just been killed.

"Brad and Elijah left with my mom's sister. Aunt Kim. Though, I don't know why Brad was in Jersey. Last I heard they were all in Florida." Ethan puts his head on the counter.

"You better lift your head, honey, here are your pancakes." Mom slides our plates on the counter. I wonder what she thinks of our conversation. She remains quiet, obviously still hurt that I won't confide in her anymore.

"Thanks, Mrs. Stevens."

"Thanks, Mom."

After breakfast, Ethan and I go back to the couch. Mom brings us the Scrabble board, so we put it between us on the couch and play a few games until we get bored. Ethan stays pretty quiet himself.

"Ethan," I finally offer. "I know you are upset I pulled away, but I don't want you to always rescue me from my pain. What I did for Shelby I did because I wanted to. I knew the repercussions. You don't need to protect me."

Ethan glares at me, but I don't look away. I watch his eyes turn from angry to concerned.

"Don't you know I *need* to protect you," he says. "Because I *want* to? You are already starting the aging process, Honor. I can't watch you do this."

"But it's okay to watch you grow old?" I snap.

He sighs. "I don't have the answers, Honor. I wish I did."

I put my hand on his. "It'll be okay, Ethan. Really." My voice struggles, not really convinced of my declaration at all. Will it all be all right? By saving Shelby, had I committed myself to an early death?

Chapter Twenty-One

Ethan and I pretty much veg on the couch all day. After Scrabble, I rest my head on his lap, and we share earphones and listen to *A Day to Remember* and *Blink 182* from Ethan's iPod. Dad comes home from work at five, and Mom fixes dinner.

"Hey Honor, how ya feeling, kiddo?" Dad asks before kissing me on the top of the forehead.

"I'm fine, Dad. Feeling much better."

"Thanks to Ethan here." Dad points his chin in Ethan's direction. "He's been takin' good care of you?"

"Yes, Mr. Stevens, but Mrs. Stevens has been doing most of it. She's been waiting on both of us all day."

"Yeah, she's great like that...though she should be resting herself." Dad walks into the kitchen to see Mom. I hear them talking softly while Dad rummages through the day's mail like he always does. He reappears, holding out a yellow padded envelope. "This one's for you, honey." Dad hands me the envelope and returns to the kitchen.

"No return address," I note before opening it. "Hmm." I pull out three small cards—mine and Ethan's driver's licenses and Ethan's credit card.

Ethan takes the envelope and its contents from me, investigating them closely. "It's post-marked from Nevada. Why am I not surprised?"

"Whattya think?" I whisper so Mom and Dad don't hear me from the kitchen.

"I think...Storm is done with them for now." Ethan steals a dramatic pause. "And I think...I won't be surprised if he's back in town soon."

**

Sure enough, when we return to school the following Monday, Storm is present...not a word spoken by him about where he'd been. Of course Ethan tries to prod it out of him, but Storm remains adamant that he knows nothing about the disappearance and/or reappearance of Ethan's credit card and identification. Storm also reassures Ethan that he would help him get the sucker who tried to pull one over on his dear sweet younger brother—Storm's words; not mine. Naturally, this annoys Ethan while simultaneously entertaining Storm.

Hunter has the same lunch hour as we do, so he sits with Ethan, Tamlin and me. Ethan's brother Hunter is just as gorgeous as Ethan and Storm, only his hair has more auburn-coppery tones dispersed through his platinum hair. His skin is just as fair, and yes, his eyes are violet. Tamlin is making googly eyes at him the whole time, but it doesn't look like it fazes Hunter. Then again, he and Ethan are engrossed in whispered conversation and aren't paying attention to much else. Every once in a while, I'll get a little squeeze on my thigh from Ethan, letting me know he is still there.

It's unnerving to know they are talking about something so dangerous, yet I am not privy to the details. The anxiety inside of me is building just knowing that sometime in the near future, whoever is after us will inevitably find us.

Tamlin and I leave Ethan and Hunter at the lunch table when the bell rings. Ethan turns his attention away from Hunter briefly to kiss me goodbye then goes right back to his conversation...disregarding the signaling bell.

After school, Hunter comes with us to my house. Sitting at the breakfast bar with my mother when we walk in is Shelby...sipping a cup of tea.

"Shelby?" My voice quakes as I am suddenly very aware of the events that had passed between us a week ago.

"Honor." Shelby's voice is soft, and I hear an equally unsettling rattle in her voice as well.

"Ethan, is this your brother you've been talking about?" Mom walks from behind the bar to the dining room.

"Yes, Mrs. Stevens, this is Hunter."

"Hello." Hunter holds out his hand to greet my mom. "It's nice to meet you."

"Why don't I get you two a glass of iced tea and I'll bring it into the living room. Ethan, show Hunter to the couch." My mom gives her sweet command. It makes me chuckle.

"Honor, honey." Mom addresses me now, after the boys leave the room. "I poured you a cup of tea." She puts it down on the bar next to Shelby's. "Shelby would like to talk with you, so I'll leave you two alone and see how Ethan's doing." Mom leaves with two glasses of iced tea in her hand.

"How are you?" My nerves are tangled in knots in my stomach as I sit on the stool next to Shelby. Both of us look at our cups of tea and fidget with our saucers.

Shelby nods her head. "I'm good." She chokes out.

"Good, I'm gl..."

"Listen, Honor." She finally turns towards me, but my focus is still on my tea. "I'm really sorry about the way I've been treating you."

"It's fine." I attempt to look at her but then quickly avert her stare.

"No. It's not fine. I was angry and mad at the world and...I took it out on you. That was so not cool." Her voice is getting stronger; her confidence is building.

With my stomach settling just a bit, I turn to face her. "I understand though," I say softly.

She nods. "How? How did you know, and *how* did you...cure me?"

Okay, forget the settling. My nerves are now firing full throttle. "I...I didn't..."

"Don't lie to me. I felt it. I felt all my pain leave me...and..." She taps her fingers rapidly on the counter. "I know you were taking it away, Honor. I just want to know how."

"I...I don't know what you're..."

"Stop. Honor. Don't. I know you did." Her voice is loud.

"What's going on here?" Ethan walks in, and I feel his hand on my lower back. My anxiety calms at his touch. Because I'm so extremely distraught, I am not about to stop him from using his *powers* this time.

Shelby swivels on her stool to address him. "Your girl-friend cured my cancer. I am very grateful for that. I owe her my life...I just want to know *how* she did it."

Ethan looks to me and then back to Shelby. Opening his mouth to speak, he doesn't. Shelby stops him.

"Look, Ethan. Honor." Her eyes dance back and forth from me to Ethan. "You have my word I will not say any-thing to anyone. As far as the doctors and my parents are concerned, God performed another of His little miracles," she says sarcastically. "But I know better. It was you...It's go-ing to drive me crazy if I don't know how the hell you did it."

"Shelby..." I speak before Ethan can. "It *was* one of God's miracles." That's not a lie, not really. Whatever I can do is most certainly a gift from God—a gift for those I can heal, anyway. To me, it feels more like a curse.

Shelby sighs. "Look. I need to know. What if it comes back? I need to understand...this, this...whatever it was that made me get rid of my cancer. I was *dying*, Honor. On my way...out. Then you...you touch me and I'm fine. No more pain. No more fatigue. No more friggin' *cancer*. Honor. Is it going to come back?" There is such desperation in her voice I want to cry.

"Ethan?" My eyes plead with him. He knows what I am asking of him. A slight nod of his head signals his permis-sion to divulge our secret to Shelby.

I place my hand on her thigh just above her knee. "You're right," I whisper, not wanting my mom to hear. "I did heal you...but..." A guttural sigh escapes from some-where in my gut. "I still don't understand how." Removing my hand from her leg, I now hold my own head in my hands—elbows perched on the bar. Hearing my own words leave a sour taste in my mouth. I still cannot fathom the idea that I have the capability of healing someone from the crippling effects of cancer. It just makes no sense to me whatsoever. My response to Shelby sounds ludicrous. Finishing my thoughts is impossible. I am getting too depressed over it. Trying to understand all this is just too overwhelming.

Ethan's hand is on my back...warm and comforting. Slowly, my dismay leaves my body. Ethan is taking over again.

"Shelby." Ethan's other hand rubs my arm when he speaks Shelby's name. "Honor is just finding this all out herself."

"Finding what out?" Shelby's impatient with this whole subject, and I don't blame her.

"She is what we call an empath. She and I both are."

Shelby's head shakes in confusion. "An empath?"

"We feel other people's pain." Ethan explained. "And if we touch that person, we actually absorb it and take it away from them. If we touch them long enough and focus on their pain, we can take it all away...for good...like Honor did for you."

A couple of tears escape Shelby's eyes.

"It's a painful process," Ethan continues, his face tight and unexpressive, "*for us*. And it doesn't come without dire consequences. I begged Honor *not* to do it." His tone is unyielding; he will not find compassion for Shelby, though he should be naturally feeling it for her.

Shelby's wide eyes signal her shock at Ethan's honesty.

It doesn't faze Ethan. "By saving *your* life, she began digging an early grave for herself."

"Ethan." I snap. He does not need to tell her that.

"What does that mean?" Shelby asks, clearly confused by Ethan's resentment.

"It means...for every life she saves...or every person she heals, her years are cut drastically. Most empaths who focus on healing others die shortly after their teenage years...so yeah, you're here," Ethan snarls. "But in a few years, Honor may not be."

"Ethan." I sigh.

"Sorry, Honor. She needs to know what you sacrificed for her...your personal bully."

"Ethan, stop." I cry.

"No, Honor. He's right." Shelby interrupts. "I *was* a bully to you, but I promise, I will *never* mistreat you again." She steps off her stool and hugs me. "You are such a special person to have done that for me...I owe you my life. I hope you can forgive me..." She pulls away and sits back down. "And be my friend...I need more people like you in my life."

"So every time you get hurt or sick she can make it all go away?" Ethan scoffs.

Now it's getting too much. Why on earth won't Ethan stop?

"No, Ethan." Shelby responds in a calm voice while she looks him in the eye. "So I can learn to be a better person." Shelby turns toward me. "You were never the freak, Honor. I was."

An involuntary chuckle slips out from somewhere inside me. "Well...no...I am a freak. I'm the one who's not so normal anymore."

Shelby laughs and I suddenly feel a new type of bond form between us.

"Yeah," she says. "I guess you're right...but you're a nice freak."

"Don't hurt her again, Shelby," a weary Ethan warns. " And *please* do not share this secret. It'd be detrimental to all of us...especially Honor."

Right away Shelby promises, "Of course. I promise. I'll never tell. And Honor, thank you so much...again."

"You're welcome. Do you like Scrabble?"

"Scrabble?" Ethan and Shelby answer in unison.

"Yeah, there are four of us. Wanna play?"

"Okay," a jubilant Shelby answers, while a resigned Ethan groans, "Again?"

We all laugh and go in the living room by Hunter, who is watching a Netflix episode of *Switched at Birth*.

"Did you turn into a girl while living with Uncle Tom?" Ethan mocks Hunter. "Since when did you start watching chick flicks?"

"Don't mock it; the chicks in it are hot."

Ethan just shakes his head and sets up the Scrabble game.

Scrabble is interesting with Ethan and Hunter. Their use of the English language is colorful to the say the least. It feels good to laugh the way the four of us do. It's comforting...and I'm feeling good about my decision to help Shelby recover from her cancer. Unlike Ethan, I can't just let someone suffer, knowing I can cure them.

Chapter Twenty-Two

Lunch period the next day is interesting. Shelby walks into the cafeteria with her clique. As expected, energy is high. With Jefferson High School's most popular cheerleader returned and in good health, the cheers and well-wishes are loud and spirited. Shelby looks genuinely touched. What's interesting is - after Shelby gets her lunch, she carries her lunch tray to *my* table and sits down. The dropped jaws and surprised expressions are comical. When Shelby's one side-kick finally closes her mouth, what comes out is an expletive towards me.

"Honor's my friend now. If you don't like it, leave." Shelby tells her entourage.

"Uggh," says cheerleader number two. Shelby is, of course, number one. "What happened to you, Shel? You hated that freak."

"No...I didn't. I just never knew her. *I* was the freak."

"Oh gimme a break." Number two laughs. "This is a joke, right? You're going to dump her food all over her lap or something I bet."

"No." There is no expression on Shelby's face. "I'm not." Shelby picks up her fork, turns to me and smiles. "Hey, Honor."

"Hey, Shelby."

Number two and the gang let out an audible "hmmph" and walk away...to eat their lunch...without their leader.

Fiddling with the food on my tray, I try to think of something to talk about with Shelby—small talk, girl talk, anything. But being I'm not the most socially-forward teenager, I fall short on coming up with any topics at all. Though Shelby is the number one popular girl in school, and therefore socially adept, the fact that she's poking at her mashed potatoes makes me wonder if maybe we aren't really meant to be close friends and lunch buddies. I mean, I appreciate the effort she's making, but she belongs with her own friends—as inconsiderate as they are. Maybe the new Shelby can lead her old friends on the road to kindness and compassion.

There's no time like the present for being straight-for-ward.

"Shelby," I begin, startling my tiny friend. "You know...you don't have to sit with me, and you don't have to alienate your friends to be nice to me."

Casting her eyes downward, Shelby looks embarrassed.

"Shelby, they're your friends. It's okay."

"Yeah, but...I'm sorry the way they talked before. I started their...dislike towards you. I'm so sorry. I can't believe the kind of person I am." Shelby's eyes glisten and fill with tears.

Not knowing what to say, I feel ashamed, and I know those are not my emotions. They're hers. "Shelby, you're a good person." If she's feeling shame, she must have a compassionate heart. "You were angry before. You had all this pain, the knowledge that you were going to die. It's hard to be kind when you're going through that."

Chuckling beneath her frown, Shelby shakes her head. "What was my excuse *before* I had cancer?"

My hand naturally drifts over her tiny one, which is now skimming the edge of her tray. It is an inherent reaction of mine to touch a person who is hurting. The realization as to why has just sunk in. My natural inclination, now that I know what I am capable of, is to take away her hurt, but I don't concentrate on that. My intention now is to show her kindness and compassion...so that she may learn to do the same.

"Shelby, don't define yourself by your past behavior." Her tiny hand quivers a bit beneath mine. "Now that you know better, be the person you want to be *now*."

She takes her free hand and rubs her eye. I feel her other hand reposition under my hand. She squeezes it. "Thank you, Honor. You're a good person."

"You're welcome."

The atmosphere between us becomes strained again, but fortunately, or maybe unfortunately—I haven't made up my mind on that yet—Storm sits on the bench alongside of me and erases any awkwardness between Shelby and me. Of course Storm brings along his own thorny climate.

"Ladies." Storm so arrogantly takes my fork and helps himself to my mashed potatoes.

"Excuse me," I say, my eyes darting from him to my food.

Dropping the fork back on my tray, the corners of Storm's face curl up in one of his evil—or charming, I haven't decided that either—grins. "Sorry, princess, didn't mean to touch your food."

I shake my head in exasperation. I'm still not sure what to make of Storm and it frustrates me. But when I look at him, I see a not-so confident boy beneath his cool-as-a-cucumber façade.

"But seriously, Honor...I need a few moments of your time." He's staring directly at me. I feel him, even though I am looking down at my tray. "Can you take a walk with me?"

"No...she can't." Ethan's voice from behind startles all three of us.

"Hey there, little brother." Storm plays it cool with his greeting. "You're looking rather joyful today," he mocks, clearly reading the total lack of joy on Ethan's face.

Ethan ignores him. "Honor." He motions to the three inch space between Storm's knees, as he's straddled on the bench, and my legs, as I sit correctly at the lunch table.

I move as close to Shelby as I can to let him in, but Ethan doesn't need to squeeze next to me. Storm gets the hint and gets up.

"I know when I'm not wanted." He laughs, then taps me on top of the head. "Remember, Honor," he says much too loudly as he walks away.

"What? What're you supposed to remember?" Ethan interrogates.

Quietly I tell him that Storm needs to tell me something.

Ethan rolls his eyes. "Geez, Honor. I wish he'd stay away from you. Why can't he just confront me?"

"I have no idea." My phone buzzes in my purse. It's a text...from Storm. How he got my number, I have no idea. Wondering why it should surprise me, I chuckle. He did steal our identification without our knowledge, after all.

"What's so funny?" Shelby and Ethan ask at the same time.

Still looking at my phone, trying to delete the message, I say, "My mom. Her attempt at a joke." I lie.

Luckily Ethan isn't too concerned about mom and her joke; he's still brooding over Storm.

"Listen, Ethan." I try to talk some sense into him. "You said yourself that you'd give Storm a chance..."

"Yeah," he interrupts, ready to bite my head off. "That was before he stole our stuff and ran away with it."

"Well," I muster as calmly as I can. "Maybe if I see what he has to say, I can find out what he's up to."

"No. You are not to see him. If he's involved with those people, he can be dangerous. What if he kidnaps you or something?"

"On school property?" I laugh. "I don't think so. Really, Ethan, think about it. Besides, I don't think he's a threat...not to me, anyway."

Ethan grunts just as the bell rings. "C'mon, I'll walk ya to class."

"Oh don't worry about it. I need to go to my locker first. I forgot my notes." I lie. I don't want to tell Ethan, but Storm's text said to skip my next class and meet him in his car in the parking lot. It read, **yes, it's that important**. Cutting classes is not my thing, but I'm pretty sure Storm's right when he says it's important.

Ethan lifts his right brow, "Okay, Honor. See you after school." He pats me on the butt and kisses me quick on the lips.

I walk in the direction of my locker then take the back door out of the school. My brow is sweating, my stomach churning. Breaking the rules intimidates me. I fear authority and despise anarchy. Bile rises up in my throat as I try to nonchalantly search for Storm's bright orange Charger. Like someone is *not* going to see us in that car.

Storm is parked behind a tree and a side wall that separates two lots. *Convenient,* I think. I'm not sure if he had planned it that way, but knowing Storm, he did. Maybe he parks there every day. Maybe he cuts class every day and sits in his car. Who knows? Storm is a challenging guy to figure out.

The window on the passenger side of his car slides open. "Get in, princess."

Rolling my eyes, I open the door and get in. "So...what's so important you have me cutting class?"

Storm laughs. "I thought you'd be happy to be pulled out. No?"

"No. Now what's this about?"

All at once, Storm's devilish grin is gone, replaced by one of Ethan's stone-cold expressions—eyes narrowed, lips pierced, nostrils tight. And now I see the brotherly resemblance between him and Ethan.

I narrow my own eyes. "What is it?" I ask, wondering if I really want to know the answer.

"Remember I said *they* were after us? You said you didn't believe me, but...I know you really did."

My mouth opens to object, but he puts his finger over my lips. "Let me talk, Honor."

He waits...making sure I'm really listening.

"Your grandfather. He left you something."

"Yes, Ethan told me..."

This time four of his fingers cover my mouth. "Shush. Let me finish."

"Sorry," I mumble through his fingers.

"Your great-great-times-something grandfather left you something very valuable. I hadn't known this before. I found out on my little trip to throw you and Ethan off their track."

I open my eyes wide, as well as my mouth, but I quickly shut it when Storm runs his finger across his own neck, begging me to stop talking before I start.

"Your great-great...you get it...grandfather was a scientist. A self-proclaimed alchemist, if you will. I'm not sure how long he'd been alive, but along the way he found ways to...lengthen...a person's life. He found it through empaths' blood. I don't know too many particulars. Asking too many questions would have made them suspicious of me, and I did *not* want that. But this *elixir* he made can turn someone into an empath...plus make him immortal."

"What? Who are *they*?"

"Oh, Honor, will you just let me..."

"Finish, I know. Sorry, go on."

"They are a group of men who follow some man called *The Gaffer*. He's about as old as your dear-old gramps would be...roaming this world for centuries. I hear they were friends, but then your dear-old grammpie ran off...*with* the elixir...that they *both* had developed. This elixir...this liquid highway to immortality...it was left to you, Honor."

I feel the blood drain from my face. My eyes are on top of my forehead, I'm almost sure. Shaking my head and unable to speak, I'm at a loss. I don't know what to say, what to think. Plus...I have no clue where any sort of elixir is. "I don't...have..." I stammer.

"You don't have it." Storm reinforces. "I didn't think so. But *they* think you do. And that means you're in danger."

"Oh my goodness." My eyes tear.

"Don't worry, princess. We have some time. They think you left for Mexico."

"Mexico?" My voice comes out in a rasp.

"Before I left Nevada, I bought two tickets to Mexico." I shake my head.

"Yeah, I'm the one who took your ID. Anyway, I got a one-way ticket to Mexico, figuring that would buy us some time. Then...I used some random guy's ID and headed back here."

The corner of Storm's mouth quirks, almost like a quiver. He's scared too. My fear or his own, I have no idea. But it really doesn't matter, does it? Something like an elixir that can grant immortality along with the ability to heal is certainly something to kill for. I swallow hard. If they think *I* have it...and I don't...what will they do to me to find out where it is?

I tremble...like I've never trembled before.

And I cry.

Storm reaches over and pulls me close. His hold is tight, and I feel safe.

Then...I can no longer breathe.

I hit him rapidly on the back, attempting to get him to loosen his grip.

He holds me tighter...his hand pressing hard on my arm, as if he were trying to take away my fear.

But...it's not working. I'm more than afraid.

I pound ferociously with both my hands.

Pounding.

Pounding.

Pounding.

He pulls away and looks at me with notched brows. "Honor. You're white as a ghost...almost blue...and...so...cold."

Chapter Twenty-Three

A dark cloud envelops me. The size of the car has been reduced to the size of a Dixie cup. I need to get out. Remove myself from Storm immediately. Opening the car door and not bothering to shut it, I run straight for the building, pausing at the top of the stairs. Ethan is standing there with his hands deep in his pockets. A scowl taints his pretty face.

Realizing he saw me with Storm and aware that he is angry, I ignore it and leap into his arms. Like the hot sun that forces its way out after a storm, Ethan wraps his arms around me and takes away the darkness - my sunshine after the thunderstorm that is Storm Sutherland.

I am not quite sure what to make of Storm. He pulls me in. He almost demands it of me without saying a word. Yet...he frightens me now. There is something dark. Almost evil. And I'm not even sure he realizes it.

"Honor." Ethan says so seriously. "What did he do to you?" His question is asked above my head, his chin resting on it.

"I don't wanna talk about it yet." I mumble into his shirt.

Ethan squeezes me tight, all the while rubbing my back with firm strokes. I know he's trying to absorb some of my fear, but it's a pointless endeavor. Ethan will take on my emotions, then I'll take on his, and like he once told me, it would just be an endless cycle...with benefit to no one.

Glancing up into Ethan's dark purple eyes, I affirm that I will let him in on Storm's revelation. Just not at school.

"Right now, Ethan, I want to go to the nurse and lie down. Maybe even go home."

"Okay, I'll take you."

I hear the defeat in his tone. It's killing him to not know what Storm and I were talking about. But I've a headache so huge now—a headache resulting from my own turmoil, no one else's—that closing my eyes and going to sleep is the only thing on my mind.

**

A warm hand on my forehead nudges me awake.

"Honor." It's Ethan. "How ya feelin'?"

I sit up to determine what I'm feeling before I answer. "Better."

"So...ya gonna tell me?" Ethan asks, sitting down across from me on my bed.

The knot of worry in my stomach reaches my throat. Ethan must sense it, because he comments. "That bad, huh?"

"Oh, Eeth, they're after me."

"What? Who?"

"Those people. That Gaffer guy."

Steam comes out of Ethan's ears. Of course not literally, but his narrowed eyes, his deep purple irises, and his pursed lips indicate a severe agitation.

But I continue. "Apparently, my great, great, great something or other grandfather had developed an elixir that can make a person an empath...and immortal."

"What? Storm told you that shit?"

"Ethan...I'm pretty sure he was serious. You said yourself...my great times something grandfather was a scientist. Storm said he thought himself more of an alchemist than a scientist. He'd taken the blood of some...empaths...and I guess combined it with something to make the elixir."

"Crap." Ethan squeezes the bridge of his nose.

"Ethan. I'm scared. What're we gonna do?" My bottom lip quivers, but I want to be strong and not cry. Being strong is not one of my strengths.

Tears fall from my eyes, and Ethan moves closer, pulling me into his arms. "It'll be okay, sweetheart. But I think it's time I talk to Storm."

My head snaps back so I can look at him. "What're you gonna say?" I wonder if he's going to start a fight or something with Storm.

"I don't know...but we need to get to the bottom of this. I'll have Uncle Tom and Hunter come with me. They need to know what's going on." Ethan squeezes me and kisses me lightly on the head. "I need to go, Honor."

"Right now? Can't I come?"

Ethan utters a low growl. "Honor, I don't want you getting involved."

"Involved? I'm the whole reason we're in trouble."

"Yeah, yeah. I *mean*...I'd like to keep you safe."

I jump off the bed, stomp my foot, and, hands on my hips, say, "Well, I don't wanna be safe if it means sitting here playing with my thumbs while you go searching for some murderer."

Ethan moves to the edge of the bed in front of me. Staying seated, he reaches for both my hands. "C'mere, Honor."

My hands stay where they are, on my hips. "No, because I won't let you change my mind."

Ethan's tongue clicks in his mouth when he inhales. Sighing as he exhales, he relents, "Fine. Come with me." He stands up and hugs me again. "I just don't want you getting hurt...I love you too much." *That's the second time he's told me he loves me. I feel bad that I can't say it back.*

**

Before searching for Storm, Ethan and I stop off at Ethan's apartment to see Hunter and their Uncle Tom. Parked outside the apartment, however, a bright orange Challenger mocks my boyfriend.

"Dammit." Ethan grumbles under his breath.

Placing my hand on his forearm, I make an effort to transfer Ethan's hostility from him to me. The abrupt snatching back of his arm backfires when his hand slams against the steering wheel. "Fu..mmm," he snaps, successfully stopping himself from cursing by pursing his lips. "*Don't* try to take away my emotions, Honor. I *hate* when you do that."

Ethan's mad that Storm beat him to his brother's, I get that, but *hate* is such a strong word. It upsets me that he used it towards me. Yelling and stuff is not something I'm used to, since I've never had any real friends before this year. But I'm inclined to snap back at him. Instead, the dashboard serves as my focus while my mood simmers.

"Listen, Honor." Ethan strokes my hair. "I'm sorry. I'm taking my anger out on the wrong person. Please don't be mad."

I let him apologize and drop it for now. We have much more important things to take care of than worrying over the way Ethan just talked to me. Helping me out of the car by taking my hand, Ethan and I walk quite briskly up the apartment stairs—the apartment being a one bedroom suite on top of a yoga studio, the stairs run up the outside of the building.

Flinging open the door and slamming it against whatever stands perpendicular to it, Ethan barrels in, still attached to my hand. "Get the hell out of my house," he demands in a voice so loud it stuns me.

"Hey there, little bro," Storm's derisive sneer infuriates Ethan even more. I see it in his deep purple eyes, rigid jaw, and clenched fists. The bones in my fingers crack and hurt when Ethan clutches my hand in a death grip because he's so incensed.

"*You* are *not* my brother." My hand and its crackling knuckles are set free. Ethan's hands have other things to do—like grabbing Storm in a chokehold to threaten an explanation out of him. "What the hell do you have to do with my brother's murder...and the rest of this effin' bullshit I'm hearing about?"

Storm pushes Ethan away like he's brushing a fly from his face. Storm's strength still impresses me. But I feel bad for Ethan. He wants so inherently to protect me. Protection from Storm is not what I need, though. I'm sure of that. Ethan needs to get over these issues he has with his half-brother and get to the bottom of whoever is after us...whoever is after me.

Stumbling into the countertop, Ethan closes his eyes, gathering composure and strength.

"Yo, bro," Storm snarls. "I have nothing to do with the murder *or* your effin' bullshit," he mocks. "But you better sit down and listen to me if you know what's good for ya."

With both his hands clenched tight in front of him, Ethan leaps for Storm, but his half-brother's brute strength allows him to hold up one arm in defense and stop Ethan's punch.

"Yo, Ethan," Uncle Tom breaks in, jumping in between the estranged brothers. "Just stop. Storm isn't involved...but he does know something about it."

Ethan throws his elbow out wide to push back his uncle and storms away.

Uncle Tom follows Ethan to the living room couch. Ethan reluctantly sits on its edge.

"Ethan." Uncle Tom sighs and then looks at me. "You're Honor?" He holds out his hand. "I'm Tom. Uncle Tom."

"Nice to meet you...Uncle Tom." I say, a little embarrassed to use such a familiar term with someone I just met.

"Hi, Honor. It's good to see you again." Hunter chimes in and shakes my hand also.

"Okay, now that we have the pleasantries done with, can we explain to my moron little brother what's going on?" Storm offers, digging the knife a little deeper into Ethan's psyche.

A sharp pang strikes my chest when I approach Ethan, whose eyes are closed again. Brushing off Storm's caustic remarks demands a concentrated effort on Ethan's part. It's killing him to do so—I'm feeling his residual pain deep in my own chest. I know it is important to Ethan for me to keep from taking away his pain, but I love him so much. I cannot help but want his heartache to disappear. Rubbing his back will not whisk away his pain, but I'm sure it will ease some of his tension...while hopefully avoiding a reprimand from him for doing so.

It must be working, because his breathing returns to normal.

"Eeth," Hunter informs. "Storm says he knows what that Gaffer guy and his men want."

Ethan casts a quick glance in my direction before turning to Storm. "Yeah. Tell me, Storm. What is it that you know?" He scoffs. "And tell me...exactly *how* do you know what you know... if you're not involved."

"Some things, dear brother, I keep to myself." I know Storm is doing this just to goad Ethan, and it's getting irritating. "But what you *do* need to know is that they're after your *lovely* over there." Storm juts his chin in my direction. "Her great granddaddy had some secret empath elixir he made...This elixir can make anyone an empath...and because he'd used the blood of several...how can I say this...murderous empaths, it can also make one immortal. It's been used before. But from what I hear...dear-old-grandpappy ran away with it...just took it from the one person who helped him create it. The Gaffer. Now he and his men are after it." Storm smirks at Ethan, but then when he catches my eye, I see a slight frown form on his face. And if I'm not mistaken, I see sadness in his eyes.

But he continues. "They're not going to quit until they've got it in their hands." Storm looks at me again, frowns, and says, "And they think Honor here has it."

"How d'ya know this?" Ethan demands to know. Though he's trying to stay calm, his breathing is quick and his jaw is tight.

"I just do," Storm says with an arrogant sneer.

"Storm, stop," I command, getting totally tired of his attitude with Ethan. Everyone in the room turns their wild eyes on me. I ignore them and glare at Storm. "Stop harassing him and just tell us what we need to do. Do we need to run, what?" Clearly, I'm exasperated...and frightened. I can hear the quiver in my voice; I can feel it in my chest.

Storm bites his lip and tilts his head as he looks me in the eyes. His violet eyes turn a light lavender—a color I've never seen in his eyes before.

Noticing the look in Storm's eyes, Ethan extends his arm and wraps it possessively around my waist. "Okay, Storm. I'll listen." Ethan resigns. "Who are these people, and how do we stop them?"

I'm just about to snap at Storm, because that obnoxious grin returns to his face. But just as quickly, it disappears. "Well, running's not going to help. It'll only prolong the inevitable. What we need to do is *find* the elixir that Honor's grandfather left her." Storm looks directly at me.

"Honor, did Hanna and Daniel leave you or your parents anything when they gave you away?"

A light bulb flickers on in my head. "An envelope. My mom said they sent her a birth-certificate and some other things in an envelope." I pause, trying to remember. "She never said what those other things were, but...maybe there'll be some kind of explanation."

"Good," Storm says, and I hear the others murmuring amongst themselves.

"I'll fly back to Nevada in the morning, find more information out. You guys search the envelope, and for goodness sake, try to find a clue or something."

"Whoa. Stop right there," Ethan says. "Why the nice guy act all of a sudden?"

"Ethan," I snap, annoyed that he'd start this again.

"No, no, pretty lady, it's okay." Storm reaches out and runs the back of his fingers down my cheek, sending hot tingles down my neck.

Storm looks at Ethan and further explains. "'Cause then *your* pretty little girlfriend will see *me* as her knight in shining armor." Storm turns to me and winks. And again, I feel that trickle of warmth slide down my skin.

Rising from the edge of the couch, Ethan leaps toward Storm. Uncle Tom breaks in again, placing his palms on both their chests—like a referee holding back two boxers in the ring. "Guys. Focus. Deal with your personal issues later, when we've defeated the Gaffer and his boys."

Chapter Twenty-Four

Creeping into the house slowly, unsure of how to ask Mom for that envelope, my stomach assaults me. I clench my middle and will it to settle down—a futile effort. Continuing into the house anyway, I hope for the best.

"Honor, what's the matter?" Mom looks up from her novel and asks. "You're white as a ghost. Are you all right, honey?" She leaps off the couch and puts her hand on my forehead.

"Mom. Stop." Swatting her hand away, I move to the couch. "I'm sorry, Mom. I just...I'm fine."

"You look pale."

"Mrs. Stevens," Ethan butts in even though I'm not ready for this. Asking Mom for that envelope is definitely going to include me telling her I'm an empath. "Can we sit?" he asks my mom, motioning for her to sit back down on the couch while he remains standing.

Suddenly I'm wishing I could just disappear.

"What's up?" Mom asks, her pitch an octave too high.

"Mom." And though I try very hard not to, I cry.

"Honor, honey, what is it?" My mom takes my hand. "What happened?"

Ethan sits next to me and places his hand on my thigh.

"That envelope...you told me about." I hesitate to take a moment to catch my breath.

My mother's eyebrows are knitted and she looks totally confused.

"The one...with my...my birth certificate."

Mom's head bobs up and down. "Right, right." Then she shakes her head back and forth a couple times. "What about it?"

I take a second or two to clear the imaginary tickle in my throat. "You said there were other...things in there."

"Oh." Mom takes a moment to remember. "Yes. Um, yeah there were other papers in there, but...why, Honor?"

"Mrs. Stevens." Damn Ethan for rushing me. He squeezes my thigh gently then releases it. "Honor's birth parents were what you call empaths. They could take on other people's pain."

My mom cringes. Her shoulders hunch and she starts moving her jaw back and forth. "Oh...that...sounds...painful."

"It is, Mrs. Stevens." Ethan exhales loudly. "They were also able to...take that pain away."

"Whose pain?" she asks.

"The people whose pain they felt." Ethan answers. In the meantime, I want to throw up.

"Oh." Mom brings her hand to her mouth. "Oh." Realization sets in. Her eyes widen and her hand tightens over her mouth. Mom begins looking pale herself.

"Mom?" My hand goes to her arm. "Are you okay?"

"Honor," she whispers. "You." She nods her head. "You healed...me? You...did...that?"

I nod very, very slowly...afraid to say the word.

She pulls me into her arms, and I'm amazed that she accepts this knowledge without doubt. I expected her to not believe it possible...like I did when Ethan told me.

"Mrs. Stevens." Damn that Ethan again. He's too anxious for my own good. "These papers Honor is asking you about. Where are they?"

Mom unclasps her hold on me. "Oh. They're in my lock box. Why?"

"We need to know what they are. We're hoping we find some unanswered questions in them," Ethan comments.

"What...like what kind of questions?"

"Well," Ethan continues while I fidget with my thumbs. I'm so not ready to let Mom know someone is after me. "Evidently, Honor had a very old grandfather. Centuries old in fact." Ethan ignores Mom's look of disbelief and keeps on talking. "He was some sort of scientist. The kind that...plays around with things and comes up with...well...immortal type elixirs. Like an alchemist." There. He said it.

But he has to stop talking now, because Mom looks almost green. I guess we've reached her believability threshold. I grasp Mom's hand. "It's okay, Mom. I still can't fathom this either...but, look, I can actually...*heal* people. If that's possible...well, maybe other things are possible too, right?"

Mom just nods. My stomach churns for her.

"Anyway...her grandfather made this elixir and well, we think he may have left it with Honor."

After several minutes of Mom gazing at Ethan, her eyes register sanity again. "No. There was nothing in it but documents. No bottles or anything."

"Right...but maybe these documents hold some type of clue or something."

"Oh," she whispers. Clearing her throat, she says, "Sure. Let me go get them."

While we sit waiting for my mother to get the envelope, I silently thank God that my Dad is working late tonight. I don't know if Mom will fill him in or not, but Dad would have been a much harder sell.

"Honor." Ethan wraps his arm around me. "How you holdin' up?"

I shrug.

Both his arms come around me, and he holds me tight. Kissing me on the top of my head, he breathes, "It'll all be all right, I promise."

Now I know Ethan can't possibly keep a promise like that. After all, how does he know if it will all be all right? But I accept the sentiment just the same.

I have no choice.

The alternative sucks.

Chapter Twenty-Five

Mom reenters with a large yellow envelope gripped in her hands. If I'm not mistaken, I see the envelope shaking in her hands—a sure sign this is throwing my mother for a loop. As if I needed a sign. The anxiety playing havoc with my nerves is sign enough. I'm convinced it's not only my nerves I'm feeling, but Mom's as well.

Ethan hops off the couch and takes the envelope from my mother. Splaying the contents across the coffee table, he angles himself over it, like a miner digging for gold. Slowly he slides his fingers over each piece of paper as he carefully inspects each word. My body stills as I watch him pick up an old yellowed photo. His eyes widen, and his heart picks up speed. I feel it in my own heart. A cold tickle crawls up my spine the moment I realize he's found something. Ethan sits back on his heels as he stares at the photograph. Leaning over his shoulder, I try to see what he is seeing. He points at a particular spot in the photo and hands it to me.

It's an old photograph of a one-room brick schoolhouse. There are three windows and one door that I can see from the image. The adults and children in the photo appear to be posing for the photographer. Nothing distinct strikes my attention. There is, however, a small black smudge above the building's foundation in the back left corner of the photo. I only notice it because Ethan points to it. To me it looks like part of the aging of the photograph.

"What do you think that is?" I ask, still unsure why he pays any attention to it at all. Mom moves in closer to get a better look.

"I think," he starts slowly. "It's our clue."

"But why would you think that? It's just a smudge."

"Because it looks like it was put there purposely...it was made with black ink...I'm pretty sure."

"Oh," Mom and I both say.

"We just have to figure out where and if this school still stands," Ethan muses.

"That's the Old Monroe School," Mom remarks.

With mouths dropped, Ethan and I turn towards my mother.

Mom offers a nervous chuckle. "It's in Hardyston...twenty minutes from here."

"What?" Ethan asks. "This building is in New Jersey?"

"Yup. On Route Ninety-Four."

Ethan drops his shoulders. "Great. We can go search it."

"Not now," Mom says. "It's dark. There are no lights up there. Besides, the building is still tended to. It's an historical landmark. They only open it in July and August. I'm sure there will be alarms."

"Mrs. Stevens, with all due respect, we are not going to wait until July to get in there. We need to get this...elixir stuff now."

"But why? Why is it so important that you get it?" Mom asks. I close my eyes and tense up, hoping Ethan doesn't tell my mother that there are dangerous men after me.

"Because, Mrs. Stevens." While Ethan continues, my body stiffens and my insides are running amok. "We don't want it getting into the wrong hands," he finishes.

Allowing my body to relax, I silently thank God that Ethan didn't tell Mom the truth. Well...the other truth. We certainly do not want the elixir falling into the wrong hands either.

"Okay," she says. "But do you need to go tonight? In the dark?"

Ethan shakes his head. "No. We can wait until tomorrow."

"Tomorrow after school," my mom corrects.

"Yes, Mrs. Stevens. After school."

"Oh, goodness. Please don't get caught breaking in," she cries.

"Mom. We'll be all right." I get up and hug her...thanking God I have such an understanding mother.

My mom gets up and goes into the kitchen, leaving Ethan and me alone.

"Honor," Ethan whispers, getting up and pulling me aside. "You go to school tomorrow. I'm going to check out the school with Uncle Tom and Hunter."

"You don't want me coming with you?" I sulk.

"There's really no need, sweetheart. Besides, if we do get caught, why should you get in trouble? I'm emancipated, remember? No one's around to punish me."

"No...just law enforcement," I whine.

Ethan laughs and kisses me on the forehead. "We'll be fine." Then my oh-so-handsome boyfriend gazes into my eyes and whispers, "I love you, Honor Nicole Stevens." His soft lips graze my own and then he presses them more firmly against mine and deepens the kiss.

And again I feel guilty for not saying I love him too.

**

The next morning, Ethan leaves for his apartment, and my mother drives me to school. Since she's back at work, I have to give her car back. It was nice while it lasted.

I kiss Mom goodbye and enter the school. Feeling nervous about what Ethan is setting out to do today, I seek out Tamlin and find her at her locker.

"Hey, kiddo." Tamlin greets me with a smile.

"Hey, Tam." I respond with a trepid voice.

"What's up, hon?"

"I told my mom...about being able to...you know."

"That you're an..."

"Shhh." I cut her off, not wanting anyone to overhear her. "Yes, I told her that."

"O-M-G, what did she say?"

"She took it rather well, I suppose. She didn't think I was making it up or anything...she was cool."

"Wow. I bet that's a relief," she comments.

"Yeah, but..."

"But what?"

"We kinda had to tell her...there are some people looking for me."

"*What?*"

"I'll tell you about it later. I don't want to be late for class."

"Okay, hon. But I'm here for you. You know that, don't you?"

"Of course."

**

For forty minutes at least, I can forget about Ethan and whatever he's doing right now. It's Chemistry time...and I just love looking at Mr. Moore.

While I'm daydreaming about his beautiful sapphire eyes gazing into mine, Tamlin slides a folded piece of paper across my desk. I tear myself away from gawking at our fine Chemistry teacher to surreptitiously unfold her note.

**So why did you
have to tell your
mom about your
being an empath?
T.**

I close my eyes and shake my head. Why does she have to ask me this now? I wanted to forget the drama in my life for a few brief moments.

I quickly write her back.

**There are some dangerous men
after me. I'll tell you about it
later.
H.**

I fold up the note and pass it back to her. After she opens it, I watch her eyes bug out of her head. She frantically scribbles something down and returns the note.

What?

What kind of dangerous men?
Aren't you scared?
T.

Shaking my head to alert her that I cannot keep passing this note back in forth, I make sure she sees me fold up the note and set it aside.

"Miss Stevens," I hear Mr. Moore call from the front of the class.

God, please don't let him ask me about the note.

"Do you have something you'd like to share with the class?"

"No, Sir," I answer, feeling like I'm going to throw up.

"Hand me the note, Miss Stevens." He is standing in front of the room with his hands on his hips—intimidating as all hell.

God no. "Um, Mr. Moore, really it wasn't..."

"*Now*, Miss Stevens."

Damn. I close my eyes and take a deep breath, bracing myself to give him my tell-tale note. The chair screeches across the terrazzo floor when I stand, sending penetrating shivers throughout my body. The classroom disappears around me as I walk the plank to my demise—well...at least life as I know it. Once Mr. Moore gets a hold of this note, there is no way the empath species is staying a secret.

Then there's no telling what will become of us.

Chapter Twenty-Six

With a trembling hand, I place the note in Mr. Moore's hand and turn in a dither to go back to my seat. As I sit at my desk, I see Mr. Moore read the note and without a second glance at me, he sticks it in his front pocket. He returns to his lesson as if he hadn't just read the most peculiar exchange between two people.

What is he thinking? He's probably going to show the note to the principal, and then they'll want to talk to me. What will I say? Ethan is going to be so mad. The government is going to find out, and they'll want to do all sorts of tests on us. Just like Ethan said—we'll be reduced to nothing more than lab rats.

After the bell signals the end of class, Tamlin strides over to my desk. "Honey, I'm *so* sorry. I didn't think we'd get caught."

"It's okay," I murmur, lurching down the aisle...dizzy as all hell. I've made such a blunder by telling Tamlin, I can't even get my bearings. We walk out of class together, but I tell her I'll see her later.

Too distraught to finish the school day, I slip out the back door and head for the reservation...seeking solace in the big rock that Ethan and I occasionally share. All I can think about is what Ethan is going to say when he finds out what happened...and what *I* will say when Mr. Moore and the principal call me down to the office to explain the note.

Mahlon Dickerson is serene right now. The sky is gray, and the air feels damp—like it's going to rain soon. For me, it is comforting—the weather matches my mood. If it were sunny, I'd just feel like it was mocking me. Instead, Mother Nature is down along with me.

I guess because I am lost in thought, I don't hear anyone approaching until I feel a hand on my shoulder. "Ethan," I utter under my breath.

But quickly, another hand wraps around my mouth before I am lifted and pinned with my back against a hard, large body. Mumbling is all that comes out as I try to scream against his hand. Another person dressed in all black sticks a piece of duct tape across my mouth then grabs my legs as the man already holding me straps a band around my arms so I can't move them. I am overpowered with terror as these two masked men barely struggle to carry me to their black SUV. Just like in the movies, they throw me in the trunk and shut the lid. *Oh my god, I'm going to die.*

It is an understatement to say that panic has set in. I am beyond frightened. For the first time in my short life, I believe I have seen my last day on earth. The car jounces beneath me while the thunder rumbles above me. I can feel the shortage of air and space. My heart races with anxiety, pounding furiously to get out my chest—my arms unable to do the same to get me out of this trunk. Sometime during the ride I fall asleep...or pass out...I'm not really sure. But I know I was out, because suddenly I wake up in a cold, dark, cinderblock room...alone...still tied to myself and unable to move from my sitting position.

No one comes in for several hours. At least that's what it feels like. There is no way to tell, since my purse is somewhere by the rock at Mahlon Dickerson. The tape is still over my mouth, so I can't yell to get anyone's attention...but inside my mind, a sharp piercing shriek is screaming to get out.

Footsteps are creaking on the floor above me, causing my heart to race so rapidly I really think I'm going to have a heart attack. The huge door that sits atop the stone stairs to my right screeches open. I scream as loud as my bound mouth allows me to, but what good will it do? Only a muffled whine comes out. My tears *pour* down my face. Two sets of feet step down the stairs. When I finally get a good look, I see their faces are still covered with ski masks.

"We thought you might be hungry," the one man says before placing a McDonald's Happy Meal in front of me. "My friend here is going to feed you. I'll be standing outside waiting for more instructions. Now when he pulls off that tape, you better not scream." Then he laughs. "Not that it's going to help. You're in an icehouse. No one will hear you from down here." He walks away laughing.

The other man touches my face to get hold of the tape's edge. The strangest feeling runs through me, but I can't put a finger on what it is. Gently, the man begins tearing the tape from my mouth. When he's done, I open my mouth to scream, but he puts his gloved fingers to my lips and says, "Shhh."

He opens my hamburger and presses it to my lips. Though I'm hungry, I'm too scared and upset to eat. I keep my lips pursed so he can't force the hamburger in. My kidnapper drops his head to the side in a show of hurt feelings.

"Please let me go," I sob. "Please."

He closes his eyes, and that's when it occurs to me that his eyes are violet. I was so scared that I hadn't noticed. *This man is an empath. He must be feeling my pain.*

"Please, let me go," I cry again, only this time a bit more soberly. I realize that if he can feel my pain, he might have some empathy for me and release me. "Please, I don't know what you want, but you can have it...if I have it."

The violet-eyed abductor looks around and appears to be trying to listen for something. When he's satisfied, he slowly pulls off his mask.

My eyes widen in disbelief. Too shocked to say anything, the room starts fading away and I head backwards through my own envisioned tunnel. My eyes close. Once again, I've slipped into unconsciousness.

I awake lying sideways across someone's lap, my arms and legs now free from their ties. I'm afraid to turn to see whose lap it is, so I take a look around the room. Realizing I'm still inside the icehouse, the knowledge of whose lap I'm resting on becomes clear. I spring up to standing position much too aware of my tight limbs.

Touching my mouth to be sure it's not duct taped again, I shriek, "He was right. You *are* on their side. How could you?" I get to my feet and scurry backwards to the other side of the room.

"Honor. Stop. Let me explain."

I shake my head, staring in disbelief.

Storm.

My abductor.

For some reason... my heart is broken.

Chapter Twenty-Seven

"Honor," Storm says softly, standing still and not taking any steps to come closer to me. "I am not going to hurt you, so please don't be scared."

I just look at him. Disappointment settling deep in my chest.

"I had to pretend to be on their side to find out information. I was going to make all the arrangements last night to go to Nevada...like we'd planned." Storm pauses a second to close his eyes and run a hand through his hair. "They came to me first. Honor, they suspect that I'm trying to gather information from them...they're making me prove that...I'm not."

Still standing there dumbfounded, I feel a couple tears run down my cheek.

Now Storm approaches me. "Oh sweetheart, please don't cry." He takes me in his arms and holds me tight.

As much as I want to pull away, there is some force keeping me there.

"I swear to you, Honor, I do *not* want to hurt you. Feel me. I know you can. You're the only one who has ever been able to feel what I'm feeling. I know you can. Just do it. Concentrate...and you'll see...I am not lying to you."

Since I have no other choice, I do as he says.

He's right.

All I feel from him is...hurt and pain and love...I feel no evil coming from Storm. But I do feel drained all of a sudden...and find it hard to breathe.

But I sigh into his neck.

"See. I would never harm you. But I do need to explain what's going on...I don't have much time; I'm not sure when someone will be visiting with us."

More than curious to hear what Storm has to say, I pull away from him and look him in the eyes. "Okay. Explain."

His hand feels warm on my shoulder as he drapes his arm around me and leads me to the wall where we were sitting before.

"I still don't know who Gaffer is, but he's definitely the one instructing us." Storm shuts his eyes when he takes a deep breath. Letting it back out slowly, he continues. "Obviously...they want *you*," he says as a matter of fact, but I sense his compassion behind the statement.

I remain quiet, encouraging him to continue—begging him to explain this horror to me.

"They realize you don't have the elixir. However...they also realize that Ethan will go to any length to find it...in order to find you. They've made him aware that if he doesn't find the elixir, he doesn't get you."

"Oh my god, Storm, why can't you just tell Ethan where I am and what's going on?" I plead.

"It's not as simple as that, princess. They want that elixir. They know that Ethan is more likely to find it based on any clues he may have found...plus his anxiety in finding you. This way, Gaffer gets to sit back, stay anonymous, and still get what he's after. They were watching you, y'know. They followed Ethan too...two days ago. They followed him to the school."

"Two days ago? How long have I been here?"

"About a day and a half."

"Oh my god...my parents."

"Ethan asked them not to go to the cops. He said that if they found out about us, well then, we'd be at risk of becoming...well...government property."

"This is ludicrous." My forehead starts sweating, and my stomach feels warm. I'm getting that nauseous-going-to-pass-out feeling. I rest my head against the wall to keep from swaying. "Does Ethan know you're involved?" My insides are screaming to get out of my skin. I get up and pace around the room, staying next to the walls because I'm dizzy. But staying still is out of the question. *I. Want. To. Scream.*

Storm stands up and walks next to me without touching me. "I'm *not* involved, Honor," he insists. "I'm just trying to get as close as I can to them so I can stop them from hurting you."

A guttural sound rises from my belly and escapes my lips. "Yeah. You really did a *good* job at that," I mock, taking a look around the dank icehouse.

"Are you hurt?" he says sarcastically.

"Not physically, no, but my parents are probably going crazy with worry right now."

"Yeah. Ethan says they're a mess, but he's assuring them that he will find the elixir and get you back."

"This is nuts, Storm. Why can't you just get me outta here, and we can all help Ethan find it?"

"We're all taking instructions from a very dangerous man...a man, I might add, who finds pleasure in killing people for his own benefit."

"What does he need the elixir for if he's killing empaths and getting the same results?"

"Because he was wronged...by *your* grandfather. He wants revenge as well." Storm pauses and drops his head, the look of guilt painted across his face. "Your birth parents were smart to give you away. You were safe for so long." A sideways smirk stains his face now. "Until Ethan came looking for you, that is." Storm shakes his head. "Such a loser, that boy."

"Stop. He had no way of knowing he'd put me in danger by finding me." I walk back to the wall and sit down...further away from Storm than I was before.

The sadness in Storm's eyes betrays his cool exterior. He tears his gaze from me, choosing the floor as his focal point instead. Since he has his head down, I'm unable to read his expression, but the energy I'm getting from him is filled with sorrow and guilt. I have that tears-stuck-in-my-throat feeling, but I know it's not coming from me. Inching closer to Storm, I lay a trepid hand on his leg. He doesn't turn to look at me, but I see the corner of his mouth quirk, and I feel comforted. So I know that he does too.

Finally, Storm looks at me. His violet eyes are now an intense plum color, and he stares right into *my* violet eyes...which I assume appear just as intense. My face warms, and the heat ignites throughout me. Suddenly I'm on fire with desire. Storm leans in just a hair...it's almost imperceptible, but I know his intention. Leaning in towards him myself, I lick my lips and slightly part them. I close my eyes. His soft lips feel hot on my mouth, and my breathing picks up. Moving in closer, he reaches his hand behind my neck, and pulls me closer. Storm's tongue feels moist as he runs it between my lips.

Just then he pulls away and jumps to his feet. "Well, princess, it's been a hoot." Storm says, all sincerity gone. I try to catch the soul behind his eyes, but he won't have it. He will not look me in the eye. "Gotta go, sweetheart. Be good. I'll be back."

He two-steps the stairs and he's gone, leaving me breathless...and alone...in the dank, dark, old icehouse.

Chapter Twenty-Eight

The chill in the air becomes more prevalent now that Storm is gone. The warm tingle my body had enjoyed just moments ago has been replaced with a cold shiver. I'm alone and I'm afraid. Can I really trust Storm? He runs so hot and cold; maybe he isn't really trying to help us. What if he's just leading me on to *believe* he's trying to help so that I don't cause a ruckus while I'm down here?

Wringing my hands together because I'm so nervous, I realize I can't sit still. I get up and start screaming. Someone *has* to be out there who will hear me. My scream echoes, but I alone here it. Not knowing much about icehouses, I'm sure if they were built solid enough to keep ice cold. they'd effectively keep sounds from escaping. That means no matter how loud I strain my voice, it'll be in vain.

Resigned to save my voice since it won't do any good to scream, I sit back against the wall, close my eyes, and pray for sleep. But it's impossible, I'm too wound up. Repositioning myself to somehow get comfortable, my hand lands upon something small and cool. A black iPod Shuffle...one of those old small square things. White ear buds are attached to it. After inspecting them for cleanliness, I put them in my ears and press play.

The first two songs are two of my favorites from Ed Sheeran. I let out a sigh and silently thank Storm for at least leaving me with some music to keep me calm.

**

When the playlist starts all over, I figure several hours have passed. I don't know if that means it's another day or if it is still the same day, but I'm really worried about my parents. How are they handling this? They are not going to understand all this empath danger stuff. God, I don't even understand it, and I've had a little more time to adjust to the idea. I feel my eyes begin to water, but I hold back the tears. Now they just feel as if they're stuck in my throat.

Footsteps creak above me, getting louder as they approach the door at the top of the steps. Storm is coming back. Though I'm not sure what to believe, I can't wait to see him. The footfall on the steps is much heavier than Storm's. Crawling up the wall with my back, I sidestep the wall to get further away. Those feet do not belong to Storm.

"Looking for your boyfriend?" the masked man asks. "Or should I say...your boyfriend's brother?"

I can see his smirk through the mouth hole on his mask.

"Your little friend got caught."

Oh my goodness. Storm.

"Yup. Shame on him trying to pull one over on the old Gaffer." The man laughs. "Yup." He nods his head. "Let me tell ya'...your other little boy-toy better come up with that elixir, otherwise the old man is going to be concocting a new one with you alls blood." He guffaws again.

Those tears that were caught in my throat are forcing themselves out from my eyes. My bottom lip hurts from the intensity at which I'm biting it. Storm is dead. Ethan'll be next. Oh my God. I drop down to the floor against the far wall. Sinking my head in my hands, I cry and cry and cry. My parents will never see me again.

"I got instructions to leave you some water and a roll. Make it last. It'll be a while before I come back." The big bad wolf turns and walks up the stairs, laughing all the way up...before the door locks shut.

So many thoughts are running through my mind right now. Aside from my poor mom and dad, I can't help but feel bad that I doubted Storm. I know he's gruff on the outside, but his insides are all mush. I should have known he was only helping us. Clutching my heart, I sob all over again. The cement wall is unforgiving when I drop my head back in a crying fit. Stars circle my head in a cartoonish manner before I fall to the floor...not unconscious but dizzy. My tears continue to drop to the floor, and curling up into the fetal position, I pray for someone to save me...from my pain.

I don't want to be an empath anymore—it hurts too much. Whether I'm hurting for someone else or hurting because these stupid empaths are in danger, I just don't want to *hurt* anymore. Besides, what good comes out of it? I can heal people, but then I'm out of commission for like days. Ethan says I'm going to die anyway. So really, what good does being an empath do me? I'm not a selfish, narcissistic human being, but how much torture and pain can one person endure? Praying that God takes my abilities away is the last thing I remember before falling into a deep, pitying sleep.

**

An unfamiliar anxiety jolts me awake. Like a snake coiling its limbless length around and around my gut, this strong sense of imminent danger is new to me. This is not my anxiety. Someone is near. Closing my eyes to concentrate, I take a deep breath in and hold it—allowing the outsider's emotions to take residence inside me. Not so I can take their impending doom away but to try to gather whose emotions they are. He's afraid—more so than I am. If my feelings are correct, Ethan is nearby.

Running for the stairs, I fall up the first step...my body is tight from lack of movement. I pick myself up and take one step at a time. I bang on the door at the top. Banging. Banging. Banging. "Ethan," I yell as loud as I can. "Ethan...Ethan...Help...Help." I take a deep breath and bang harder—so hard I know there will be a bruise on the outside of my hands later. "Ethan.....Help me...Ethan...It's me...It's Honor."

I yell and bang like that for I don't know how long, but suddenly I hear muffled voices. "Ethan...I'm down here...Ethan...Help...I'm here." I keep banging until I hear the clang of a latch being open. I push hard on the door. "Oh, Ethan." I fall into his arms and cry.

"Oh my god, Honor. Are you hurt? Oh my god, oh my god, baby...I was so," he's breathing heavy and can't finish.

"I'm all right, Ethan...I'm just...so...scared. They killed Storm..."

He holds me at arm's length. "What?"

"They killed Storm. Someone with a mask...he said they caught him...they knew he was helping us."

Ethan closes his eyes and sighs, pulling me back to his chest. "I'm just so glad they didn't hurt you."

Out of the corner of my eye I see a figure, so I turn. "Oh, Hunter..."

"Hey. You good?" Ethan's younger brother asks.

"Yeah." Turning my attention back to Ethan, Hunter walks away. "How'd you find me?" I cry, looking into Ethan's violet eyes.

"I was actually looking for the elixir. I had no idea you'd be anywhere near here."

"Where's here?"

"The school. The one in the picture."

Standing back from Ethan, I look around. I'm inside some small building. I walk to the door that leads outside and there it is. To my right stands an old stone building—the old Monroe school. "I had no idea," I muse.

"Give me a hug, babe. Don't let me let you go ever again." Ethan pulls me so tight, he feels like that snake that held my gut. It's not a good feeling...and I don't understand why.

"Ethan," I mumble into his neck.

"Yeah," he says above my head.

"You're scared."

He chuckles. "Uh, yeah."

"Fill me in." I pull away again. "Tell me what's happening."

"Not here, Honor. Let me get you home. I'll come back later to look for the stuff. Your parents are so worried."

"No," I demand. "I mean, yes, I wanna go home, but we need to end this thing. We need to go to the police...something. I can't live afraid the rest of my life."

"Honor. We're *not* going to the police. I've explained why. Either they'll think we're crazy or they'll keep us, report us, and do whatever testing they want on us. No. We can't trust the cops. Your parents know what's going on. Let me bring you to them. They'll take you to some hotel somewhere and hide you while we find this stuff...and hand it over."

"What?" I'm stunned. "You want to hand the elixir to that Gaffer? He'll use it for evil."

"Better that than him killing you. No, I can't take the chance, Honor."

"But how do you know he won't want to kill us anyway? We can dump the elixir...if it even exists...and be gone with it forever."

"Oh, Honor. I just don't know. But we gotta get you outta here. If they hid you here, they'll be back. Please let's get the heck home. I'll come back on my own." He wraps his one arm around my waist and bends to put his other arm behind my knees. Ethan carries me away.

"Oh geez, Eeth. Please. Put me down."

"Nope. I want a guarantee I'm getting you outta here."

"Ethan. Put her down." Hunter comes back from around the corner in a frenzy. "Send her back down."

"No..." I beg.

"Yes, hurry. *Now.* One of his men is coming. Now, Honor. Go back," Hunter demands.

Ethan, still carrying me, walks me back down the dank and dreary icehouse.

"No, Ethan. Please. You don't know what it's like down there."

Ethan takes off his coat. "Here. Take this. I'll be back when they're gone. Don't let them know we were here."

He gives me a quick kiss on the lips, and just like that...he's gone. The lock latches, and I'm alone again.

Disappointment spurts through my body like venom...destroying all hope. They'll hurt Ethan...like they did Storm. There is no way they didn't see Ethan leaving the icehouse. Impending doom slithers across the floor and up the walls, and it's getting stronger with every stubborn breath I take. Closing my eyes, I think...*for the first time in my life, I wish I were already dead. What's to come seems far worse.*

Chapter Twenty-Nine

Footsteps approach above me again, but I keep my eyes closed. Any energy I had had to fight is lost. The snake inside me tightens its grip, causing an intense nausea to overcome me. If I'd eaten anything in the last few days, I'm sure it would be splattered across the floor any minute. Two sets of feet stomp down the stairs, but my eyes are still shut, so I can't see who they belong to. If it were Ethan, I'm sure he'd have let me know already.

My heartbeat races, defying my resolve to keep calm and not care, but with that and my stomach's contents reaching my throat, calm is something I will not be achieving this night.

"Get over there." I hear a familiar but unsettling man's voice say before I hear a thump and a moan. "Don't go anywhere near her. You stay there on that side and she stays on her side."

Curiosity has gotten the best of me, so I open my eyes. "Storm?"

"You," the now familiar masked man says. "You stay where you are, y'here?"

Holding duct tape and rope in his hands, he strides over to me. Paralysis sets in, and I am now unable to move even if I wanted to. The man slaps the duct tape over my mouth then proceeds to tie my wrists together and then my ankles. I am now tied up in the same position as Storm is across the room.

"Now, because your boyfriend here acted as a spy on your account, he gets to end his short life down here in the dark with you. Now be good. I'll be right upstairs on the other side of that door. My instructions are not to leave the premises, since the boy can't be trusted." The man laughs that evil laugh he has and leaves us alone.

Storm bangs the back of his head against the wall and leaves it there, his gaze to the ceiling as he realizes he's been defeated. He sits across the room, but still, his frustration seeps into me. His hackles are up though, so I know he's not finished fighting.

I rest my head against the wall and close my eyes again, trying to let go of any emotions I have...including Storm's. It is *not* reassuring to be both scared *and* angry. Forcing air slowly into my lungs through my nose, I let it out even more gradually—collecting myself more and more with each breath. As my deep breathing continues subconsciously, I contemplate recent events with a bit more objectivity than before. Storm is not dead. This is good. That means Ethan is most likely okay...otherwise he'd be down here as well. Even if they have caught him, I'm almost positive he is likewise not dead—they need Ethan more than they need Storm. So again, this is good. Ethan has explained the situation to my parents, so even if they are worried, they at least know *why* I've been abducted. And if Ethan hasn't been caught, he had to have told them where I am and that I am unharmed. Again...good. I'm sure my parents are enjoying *some* relief about that. The situation may not be ideal...but to get through the rest of this, I have to believe that we will come out alive.

Sometime during my abstracted reasoning, I hear a shuffling sound from across the room. Upon opening my eyes, I see Storm scooting over to me. Looking at him with wide eyes, I silently ask him what the heck he is doing sliding across the floor on his butt.

His eyes narrow, and I believe he is telling me to shut up.

I raise one sarcastic eyebrow in response.

His head shakes a couple times, and with his own raised eyebrows, I'm sure he's saying, "*I told you to shut up.*"

I mumble a "humph" beneath the duct tape and turn my head up and to the right, replying with my own, "*You cannot talk to me like that.*"

Storm manages to make it over to me using only his glutes—*which is very impressive to watch, I'll have you know.* He slides next to me and nudges me with his upper elbow.

I'm hoping my scowl tells him I'm still upset, but when I look at him he's trying to tell me something. Mumbling arrested words, he motions towards his upper leg.

"*What?!*" I exclaim, but it comes out as a high-pitched hum. *What the heck is he asking of me? I'm not that kind of girl.*

A smirk sneaks out from behind the duct taped mouth while his dimple dances in amusement. I catch a sparkle in his eye, but just as quickly, it's gone. He motions with his elbow this time towards his front pocket.

Oh. *Oh.*

He taps his elbow a couple more times on his front pocket while he mumbles some frustrated request.

There must be something in his pocket I need to get. I look up at him with questioning eyes. No matter what is in his pocket, it's still going to be awkward reaching for it.

He rolls those intense violet eyes and shakes his head. Then a sigh vibrates from his throat, and he tilts his head in agitation.

I look at him with questioning eyes, but I soon do as requested. With tumultuous hands, I skim the edge of his jeans pocket. My face burns so hot, I'm sure I'm giving myself a sunburn. Storm lifts his right hip off the floor, loosening the material so the pocket won't be so tight. My eyes instinctively close, but I quick open them. *God forbid I find something I'm not supposed to.* Pressing my fingers deeper into his pocket (which is difficult, since my wrists are tied together), I still don't feel anything. Storm groans a deep, guttural groan and shifts his legs. Both of us have become extremely uncomfortable, but when I look up at him, he nods as if I should continue. I inhale through my nose and don't let it out, digging deeper into his pocket as I hold my breath.

Finally, I feel something.

I manuever the hard metal instrument up the inside of his pocket and curl it under my fingers. I pull it out, uncurl my hand and hold it out to him. It's one of those Swiss army knife things. Looking up at him for answers, I find his eyes closed and his face flush. My heart does one of those flippy things and I get all tingly inside. I let out the breath I forgot I was holding.

When his eyes open, he juts out his chin and holds up his wrists. *I'm supposed to cut the rope. Okay. I can do this.* Again, my hand shakes, but I flip up the knife and start cutting through the rope. Luckily it's not that thick and it doesn't take me too long to break through it.

Storm wriggles his wrists around a few times then gently takes the duct tape off my mouth. His duct tape comes off next, and he proceeds to undo the ropes around my wrists and ankles and then his own.

He takes in a deep breath and drapes his arm around my shoulder. "Thanks," he barely breathes out.

Turning to look at him, I notice his face is still red and his eyes are that deep plum I saw the other day. I lean my head against his shoulder and let out my own sigh of relief.

A few silent moments go by before I hear, "Don't get too comfortable, sweetie. We got work to do."

"Work?"

"You wanna stay down here forever?"

"We're gonna break out?" I ask in amazement.

With that amused grin on his face, he replies, "As much as I'd love to stay down here with ya, princess, I'd like to be with you on my own terms."

We let that statement hang in the air while we regard each other silently. Unable to tear my gaze from his, I stand there entranced by the soul behind those eyes. It calls out to me. I want to reach inside him...envelop myself within him. With my breathing growing more rapidly, I try to force myself to look away.

Fortunately, he breaks the trance first. Walking away from me, Storm says, "C'mon, let's see if this knife'll work on the door."

I follow him up the stairs and sit on the top step while he saws on one of the hinges. And I consider intently my feelings for Storm...and for Ethan.

**

An hour later and Storm is frustrated. The small knife is not cutting through the old rusted hinge. Giving up and sitting down next to me, Storm looks at me with tight lips and a heavy breath. I know better than to open my mouth right now. Storm's anger is brewing, and I am not about to let it boil over. We have enough things to worry about.

I lay my hand on top of his leg and try to erase some of that anger.

"You don't have to do that, angel. I won't bite," he says without smiling.

"I know," I whisper.

"I'm sorry I messed things up," he confesses. "I really thought I was doing the right thing." He looks down at his lap and shakes his head. "I wanted to do something right for a change."

A tear strolls down Storm's dimpled cheek. I wipe it away with my thumb, smiling while I do so.

"He should have never come looking for you," Storm says softly.

"But I'm glad he did," I respond, not really sure why I'm glad...whether it's because I've met Ethan...or Storm.

Storm tilts his head. "Yeah. I'm sure you are." Another tear drops from his eye and I know *he* thinks I'm talking about being happy to have met Ethan. I don't correct him.

A set of footsteps screams above us. I look to Storm for instruction. He drops his head in defeat and pulls me close in his arms. "I'm sorry," he cries.

Storm has given up...for both of us.

Chapter Thirty

Cringing as the door thuds open, I brace myself for something akin to a lashing.

"Thank God," Ethan chimes.

Storm hurriedly releases me from his embrace and stands eye to eye with Ethan. "I see you know how to take care of your girl." Storm laughs. "Good thing I was there to do it." He taunts Ethan, and I have to laugh. *This is not the Storm I'd just spent time with.*

"Shut the hell up, Storm, and let's get her outta here." Ethan grabs me around the waist and carries me like he had earlier.

"Please put me down, Ethan," I manage to say with as much dignity as I can. "We'll be faster if you're not carrying me."

Storm snorts as if he's enjoying this, but I see no humor in his eyes.

Adhering fixedly to his idea of playing knight in shining armor, Ethan continues to carry me across the overgrown weeds over to the old Monroe school building.

Whispering into his ear, I beg, "Please, Ethan. Put me down. This is embarrassing."

He scrunches his forehead and looks from me to Storm and back to me again. Realization hits him. Ethan frowns and puts me down. "C'mon. I think I found something," he says quietly, leading us into the building through the wooden shutters he must have previously unhinged. "You first, Honor," he instructs, clasping his hands together to make a footstool for me to step up on to, making it easier for me to reach the window.

Storm jumps through the window, then Ethan, who is holding onto the gray wooden shutter. He puts the board back into place and jams a piece of cardboard under it to keep it in place.

"I had to throw them off course." Ethan talks, but I can hear the hurt in his voice. I can feel it in my heart. I guess it's hard to hide feelings from an empath. I couldn't hide mine from Ethan. He can't hide his from me.

The sun creeping through the cracks in the shutters shines directly on the floor where Ethan is standing. It casts a shadow on a slight groove in the floorboard. Ethan bends down to lift up the piece of wood, evidently familiar with what he is doing. "I took the Dover train into the city, got out, made sure I wasn't followed and hopped on another train heading back," Ethan continues saying, as he lifts the board, sets it aside and removes another. Hopping down into the hole, he signals for Storm to join him.

Uncharacteristically quiet, Storm follows Ethan into the hole. "Hmmm," he remarks.

"I know, right. He had to kill a lot of empaths to get this much." I hear Ethan say, but all I see is the top of their heads.

"What's going on?" I ask, stretching out on the floor to take a peek.

Both of them lift their heads. They're actually kneeling on the floor beneath me, but it's a small cubby that they're cramped inside of. Unable to see what they're looking at, I strain my neck to get a closer look. Hidden in the corner of the cubby are two large glass jugs of dark red liquid—gallons and gallons worth.

"Is that blood?" I ask, disgusted.

"Looks like it," Ethan says. "We have to get this out of here unseen, but I don't know how."

"Just dump it. It's evil anyway, and then this whole thing can be done with."

Both of them look at me like I've committed murder or something. "What?"

"Honor, we can't dump it. We'll have nothing to negotiate with," Storm explains.

"I agree with *him*." Ethan says reluctantly. "We'd have to show them something, but...I guess Honor's right. It is evil...being made from all that evil blood. Maybe we should just hide it for now. If this gets into the wrong hands, it can be dangerous. This wouldn't be enough elixir, either. They'd figure out the ingredients and try to copy it. The only way to do that would be to start killing more empaths...just for their own immortality. That can't be good...not with the Gaffer in charge."

"Then let's just dump it," I say louder than I should. "I just want to be done with this."

Storm and Ethan look at each other.

Ethan speaks first. "We'll figure something out, Honor."

"Let's get out of here," Storm demands in his normal commanding voice now, hopping up out of the hole and helping Ethan close it up. "Even though you led them away, I'm sure someone followed you. By the way, what happened to the guy who was supposed to be standing look-out? How'd you get past him?"

Ethan ignores the question and continues covering their tracks. He helps Honor out of the building and leads them through the woods to the back of the school.

"Where we going?" I ask, wondering why we're not headed out toward the road. Where civilization is.

"We can't risk it." Ethan sighs.

"Where's the guard, Ethan?" Storm asks again.

I catch an eye roll and a slight shake of Ethan's head as he tries to get Storm to drop it.

"Ethan, what'd you do?" I ask him myself.

Sighing, he says, "I had no choice, Honor. He would have stopped me from rescuing you."

"You killed him!?"

Storm chuckles. "Welcome to the club, little brother."

Ethan turns an angry eye at his big half-brother. "I did it out of necessity, Storm." He says enraged. "Not because I wanted to."

With a shrug and a smirk, Storm laughs it off. "We all end up in the same place, little bro...but hey, look at it this way...if he was an empath, then you'll be immortal, it'll take longer to get there. Someone'll just *have* to kill you." Storm pats his little brother on the shoulder. "Oh, but don't worry about that...I'll keep you safe."

I hear the sarcasm in Storm's voice, but I feel the pain in his heart. He's just mocking Ethan to cover up a bigger hurt.

Ethan shrugs off Storm's wisecrack and takes my hand. "C'mon. This way."

"Where *are* we?" I ask, tightening my grip on Ethan's hands. It's getting dark and I'm getting scared.

Ethan doesn't answer.

"Ethan. Where *are* we? Where are we going?"

"The boy has no idea, Honor. Can't you tell?"

"Shut the hell up," Ethan says to Storm.

"Guys. Stop this. Please. Ethan, I want to know where we're going."

"We're getting away. Okay?"

"You don't know. Do you?" I ask.

"No."

Crap.

"I knew I shouldn't have followed you." Annoyed, Storm stops in his tracks. "Before we go any further, we have to have a plan."

"A plan?" Ethan mocks. "Your plan got you locked up in the icehouse with *my* girlfriend."

"And wouldn't *you* have liked to have been a fly on the wall?"

"Storm," I cut in. "Stop."

Storm's smirk disappears and he mouths the words, "I'm sorry," to me.

"Okay. Storm *is* right though, Eeth. We need a plan. Do you think they'll find the elixir and leave us alone?"

"No." Both guys say together.

"Plus, they couldn't have followed me into the school. I was careful." Ethan explains.

"Yeah," Storm chimes in. "But obviously they know it's near. They wouldn't have hid us so close. You think that was just coincidence? They know more than you think. For all we know. They're probably scheming a way to get the blood out of there too."

"The blood?" I ask.

"The elixir."

"Oh."

**

It's now so dark that Ethan turns on the flashlight app on his phone. Since Storm's and my phones went missing during our abduction, we have to rely solely on Ethan's phone.

"Hey. Can't we just call 911 and tell them we're lost?" I ask.

"No. We are not getting the cops involved." Ethan says.

"Uh...this should have occurred to us before, but don't you have a GPS on that phone? Or can you download one?" Storm presents.

Though it's dark, I know Ethan's face is turning red from embarrassment. I guess we all should have thought of that already. He quickly finds the app for GPS and attempts to download it.

"No service." He sighs.

"Damn," I think we all say.

"We're just gonna have to find our way out," Storm says.

Ethan squeezes my hand, and we let Storm lead the way.

"Can I ask you guys something?"

Storm meets my question with silence, but Ethan answers quietly. "What's that?"

"Can we please just dump the elixir? I'm really getting bad vibes from it."

"I guess…" Ethan tries to answer, but Storm interrupts.

"No. We need to hold onto it."

"But why?" I whine.

"Okay." Storm stops walking and turns around. "Suppose we do dump it. What happens when one of *his* men catch up to us and ask us for it? When we tell 'em we dumped it, do you really think they'll be all *'oh, okay, we just thought we'd ask for it. You don't have it anymore? No problem. Thanks anyway.'* No. They'll kill you just 'cause they can. And 'cause they're angry."

"But I don't like the idea of them having it. Who knows what they'll do with it. There's so much. It'll just get out of hand. It'll ruin mankind. I just know it."

While Ethan is still holding my hand, I feel another hand wrap lightly around my other arm. "I don't care what happens to mankind," Storm whispers mere inches from my face. "I only care what happens to you. We *don't* dump it."

His hot breath so near to my mouth makes me think about our kiss earlier and how much I enjoyed it. But the warm tingle where Ethan's hand is attached to mine, reminds me that Storm's kiss should not be on my mind. Digressing from my own thoughts, I turn my thoughts back to the immediate issue at hand—we're stranded in the dark woods without cell service.

"Leave 'er alone, Storm," Ethan shouts.

Storm steps back and says, "Yeah, well at least I'm looking out for her. That's more than I can say for you." He turns and begins walking the way we were headed before we had this elixir discussion.

"I look out for her fine. You're such an ass." After Ethan addresses Storm, he turns to me. "I take care of you, don't I?"

"Of course you do, Eeth. He's just trying to annoy you. I wish the moon were bright tonight. At least we'd be able to see where we're going." *Walking through the woods in complete blackness is making me even more scared than being held prisoner in the icehouse.*

Storm stumbles in front of us, causing me to jump. "Storm," I cry. "Are you okay?"

"I'm fine, Princess, just a branch...I think."

Chapter Thirty-One

A rustle behind us catches our attention, but when we turn, no one is there.

"It's probably an animal." Ethan reassures us, though I don't believe him.

"I wish we could just find our way out of here," I whisper. "I just wanna go home." Unable to help myself, I start to cry.

Ethan unclasps his hand from mine and drapes his arm over my shoulder. Pulling me close to him, he whispers, "We'll be okay, Honor. I promise."

Storm just snorts.

Ethan and I ignore him.

A loud thud against the ground announces that we are not alone...and it is not an animal. A large tree limb has dropped in front of us.

"Maybe the branch just fell loose from the tree," I hope in a whisper.

Ethan blocks my way, while Storm takes the phone from him. Shining Ethan's flashlight on the tree above us, Storm whispers, "Get 'er outta here. Now."

Ethan and I are frozen.

"Ethan, I said now."

But it's too late. Two large ski-masked men drop from the tree, guns in hand. "Hold it right there," one of them commands.

Storm jumps in front of Ethan and me. "It's me you want. Let them go."

The other one laughs. "Yeah. You." He continues chuckling to himself. "You know it's the girl we want." The men come closer, and one of them grabs my arm and pulls.

Storm and Ethan yank me back, but the other guy grabs Ethan, leaving Storm hanging on to me.

"Storm, can we call the cops *now?*" I plead through my sobs.

"No cops," one of the bad guys answers. "Besides...no service out here in the woods."

"Bring us to the elixir," the other man asks of me.

"No, Honor," Ethan yells.

Storm snaps his head around in Ethan's direction. "What're you crazy? They'll kill her."

"Listen to the boy," Masked Man number one says. "Now go," he says, directing us to lead him to the elixir.

Ethan wrestles himself away from the man holding him and puts him in a headlock, grabbing the gun from his hand. Now Ethan is pointing it at him.

Quickly, Storm surmises what's going on and grabs hold of the other guy, yanking him from the grasp he has on me. I scream, "No!" as I see the man cock his gun, ready to shoot Storm in the foot. Storm turns, but I jump at the man to knock him over, giving him more leverage and a better target at both of us. *Damn, that did not go as I intended.* Realizing the man is going to shoot at one of us, Storm knocks me to the ground, covering me with his entire body. A loud crack resonates through the air, and I feel the full weight of Storm fall on me.

I hear another crack soon after, and I see the man who shot Storm fall to the ground. Another crack, another thud and man number two is on the ground. I can't stop to think, but I feel my body go numb. I want time to rewind, because going forward is going to alert my senses to the grim realization that Storm is lying dead on top of me.

"Honor. Sweetheart. Honor!" Ethan exclaims as he runs over and drops next to me on the ground. "Honor. Are you..."

"Ethan," I squeal, unable to use my full voice because of the crushing weight on top of me. *Then it occurs to me. I'm an empath. I can heal. Maybe I can...*

"Oh thank God, Honor." Ethan begins hefting Storm off of me, but I can't let him.

"No. Stop."

"What? We can't just leave him on top of you, Honor. He's bleeding all over you."

"Is he dead?" I ask, hoping that he's not.

Ethan struggles to find Storm's pulse on his wrist. "I...I think he is...I'm sorry."

My heart crushes inside of me.

He's gone.

Never...have I felt such unbearable pain.

His body wriggles above me. "Ethan. No. I said don't move him." I try to yell as loud as I can, but not much sound escapes me.

"I'm not..." Ethan says slowly, but doesn't finish.

"What?" Something's going on. "What is it?" I whisper, scared as hell.

"Um..."

"What?"

"Um..."

The wriggling continues and I smell something smoke-like. *Okay, change of plans. I'm getting scared.* "Ethan, get him off of me."

Ethan moves forward and pushes Storm off of me, creating a soft thud on the ground next to me. I sit and scoot backwards on my rear, aghast at the vision in front of me. *Storm is covered in blood. His limp form, prostrate on the ground. From his back, a dark fog rises above him. His soul? I don't know...but the fog spirals slowly upward. Another murky cloud rises from him...then another. I reach out to touch...something calls me to it.*

"No. Don't." Ethan pulls me from my trance. "Get back. We have no idea what that is."

Looking up at Ethan, I wordlessly tell him that I *need* to touch. I lean forward, extending my hand through the fog. My hand disappears inside it. Quickly pulling it out, I inspect to make sure my hand is intact, then slowly reach back in. The fog lifts high, leaving my hand visible. I lay my hand on Storm's wound while watching the fog.

Momentarily I close my eyes, absorbing the brunt of pain that Storm had recently felt from the bullet. My breathing picks up, my heart races...my body burns. While I soak in Storm's death, I force my eyes open to watch the fog. Lightning crackles in the sky, though not a cloud is to be seen. The fog drops and dissipates. Standing behind it are three people—a young girl and a man and woman.

The flaxen-haired woman, dressed in a long white dress, steps forward, her hand extending towards me.

"Don't touch her," Ethan demands.

While keeping my right hand on Storm's wound, I raise my left hand toward the familiar woman. "Mom?"

The woman's smile lights up the dark. "Oh, Honor. You remember." Her voice, as soft as an angel, comforts me like no other. I move to stand, but she stops me. "*No.* You can save him...go ahead."

"But he murdered you all. You want her to save a murderer?" Ethan walks toward the young blond girl who is also dressed in white. "Summer?"

"Yes, Ethan. It's me...your sister."

I hear a sob escape from Ethan's throat. His sister hugs him...though she's quite translucent. Ethan almost looks as if he's hugging air. "I can't believe you were trapped inside that monster for so long."

Summer shakes her head. "He's not a monster," she says softly.

My head becomes light, and I feel like I'm fading, but I keep my hand on Storm and try to focus on bringing him back to life. The man, who I'm guessing is my birth father, dressed in a handsome white linen pants suit, kneels next to me. His hand on my shoulder reinforces his love for me. Between my sobs and the reeling sensation that I'm going to faint, I'm unable to speak. But his hand reassures me. "He's a good man, Honor. Concentrate."

"A good man? Y'all are crazy...he's killed all three of you." Ethan is appalled at what I am doing—at what they are asking me to do.

I am trying my best to concentrate, but with my birth mother so close, I can't help but focus my energy on her. She presses her hand to Ethan's cheek. "We died at Storm's hand, yes...but not because he was trying to *kill* us. He was trying to *save* us...and he was just a very young boy. He'd run away. We hadn't gone too far to die, but we had found ourselves a small cabin somewhere. I guess Storm was looking for shelter and came across our cabin. When he saw the state we were in, he tried to help us. He didn't know he could kill. Even after, I think he just thought he did it wrong...he's not a murderer...and he's not immortal, because it was an inadvertent kill. That's why he still ages. And he's a good soul."

Ethan looks as confused as I feel.

"How can I put this so you'll understand," she wonders. "There's a *glitch* in his DNA. He can feel like an empath...all the pain and suffering that we feel, he feels. But when he touches you...instead of *healing* you and taking the pain away...he...well, he takes the life out of you." My beautiful birth mother turns to me, "Like he did that day to you in his car."

"You were there?" I ask in amazement.

"Yes, we have no choice but to go where Storm goes...until now that is." She looks to her husband and to Summer. "I think we need to leave, so that Honor can save Storm's life. Us being here may be the reason it's not working."

"But he's dead," I say. "I can't bring him back to life. I can only heal people who are alive."

"No, Honor. You're special." My mom kneels and presses her hand to my face now. "You *can* bring him back to life. We saw you do it with your mother. Empaths can't usually do that, but you can." My mom tells me with a sincerity of a heavenly being.

"No. At whose expense?" Ethan says. "She'll die young."

My mom smiles her angelic smile. "God put us here for a reason, Ethan. To help others. Yes, our lives are cut short, but we are doing God's work."

"No," he insists. "It is not God's work to die saving others. It is *His* work to save them if they should be saved. Otherwise, it is their turn to die. *To every thing there is a season...* remember?"

She still smiles, undeterred by Ethan's rant. "*To every thing there is a purpose,*" she reminds him. "We are heroes," her sweet voice resonates deep in my heart.

Mom looks at me. "You are a hero, Honor," she kisses my forehead. Dad follows and then they walk towards Summer.

Summer gives Ethan a hug and says, "Remember who you are, Ethan." She kisses him on the cheek and grabs both my parents' hands.

In one white moment, they float to the heavens where they belong...leaving us to live as we should.

Mom's words invigorate me.

I lay my left hand next to my right. With all my might, I concentrate on Storm—absorb his pain, his blood, his soul.

Closing my eyes, I allow Storm in. My arms heat up again. I convulse as my lungs fill with pain. Screaming because I'm on fire inside, it takes all my energy not to pull away. I hear a swishing sound blow past my face. In the faint background I hear Ethan yell, "The bullet." Storm's wound burns under my hands, but the hole gets smaller. Though my eyes are still closed, I know his skin is joining beneath my touch. His hot skin turns warm...then cooler. My hands rise...and fall. Rise and fall. I feel his heart beating through his back. And at the sound of his breath catching in his throat, I collapse on the ground.

Chapter Thirty-Two

I wake lying in my bed in my very own bedroom surrounded by flowers, balloons, and...boys. Well, Ethan and Storm to be exact. Ethan is sitting at my desk in one corner of my room; Storm is on my mended beanbag chair in the other corner. I blink my eyes a couple times to adjust myself to the light, then I push myself up on my elbows and lay my head against the headboard.

"Storm," I say first, glad to see him smiling and upright. "You're all right?"

When he stands, I can't help but notice how beautiful he is. The bed dips next to my hip where he sits. "Thanks to you...I couldn't *be* any better." Storm bends to kiss my forehead, but right before he does, I notice that spark in his eye. The same one I see every time he looks at me. And I can't help but think that he sees the same spark in my eyes when I look at him. But, because I wanted to be part of a couple for once, I am Ethan's girlfriend...and I could never hurt him by allowing him to see my feelings for Storm. Though I can't help keep him from *feeling* what I'm feeling for Storm. But I'm sure Ethan will ignore those feelings...just like he has been.

Storm's kiss is warm and tender on my forehead, while the butterflies in my stomach assault me much like stinging wasps rather than the sweet, beautiful, winged things. "I owe you my life, Honor." Storm smiles. "Thank you so, so much. Anything...*anything*...you ever need or want, I will give to you. That is my promise." He rises from my bed, tips his proverbial hat towards Ethan and leaves my room, closing the door behind him.

Ethan sits on the other side of the bed and takes my hand. "How are you? You feeling okay?" he asks.

"Yeah. A little groggy...and weak, but...for the most part, I'm good."

Moving in closer, Ethan kisses my lips, leaving them there for a few wonderful moments. Of course, I kiss him back. When he pulls away, he gazes into my eyes. "Honor," he pauses, unsure of himself. "Um...about your...um...birth parents. Do you remember seeing them?"

A smile spreads across my face as tranquility washes over me. "Yes. I remember." But I don't dwell on the subject. I'd like the memory to remain untouched. "Tell me, Ethan. What happened afterwards...with the elixir, the Gaffer...are we still in danger?"

He shakes his head. "Not for the time being. Hunter and Uncle Tom helped us lug the elixir out of the school. We know we weren't followed. We also buried the dead bodies in the woods and covered the graves with some brush. Hopefully, no one will go digging around. No one has bothered us yet and it's been almost two weeks."

"Two weeks?" I interrupt. "I've been out that long?"

A soft smile plays across Ethan's lips. "Pretty much. You'd come awake a bit, and then you'd fall right back to sleep. Your parents wanted us to call a doctor, but then we'd have to explain the events leading up to what happened. We kinda wanted to keep that to ourselves....Storm was good at convincing them you'd be okay.

"So no one is after us anymore? I find that hard to believe."

"Well...I think taking out two of their men halted them for a while. We're not out of the dark forever, but...I think we're safe for now...Anyway, let's not talk about that. C'mere."

I fall drowsily into Ethan's arms as he slides next to me on the bed. His heart is racing way too fast and I sense his anxiety, so I thank him for loving me. *That's really the best I can do.*

"Always, Honor." He pulls me close and kisses my head. Closing my eyes, I drift back to sleep, this time on Ethan's shoulder, and the last thing I remember thinking was... *how happy I felt knowing Storm was still alive.*

The End of Part One

PART TWO

STORM

Chapter One

I don't normally resort to begging. But since meeting Honor, I'm doing a lot of things I don't normally do.

"I'm gonna ask you one last time, Honor. Where's the elixir?"

"And I'm gonna tell you one last time, Storm. I'm not telling."

The girl is really testing my patience these days. "Why not?"

"I told you already. That elixir is evil. Literally."

"Stop."

"No. I won't. It was made from the blood of murderers…empaths who killed other empaths just so they could live forever. Until Ethan finds a place to dump it, it's staying hidden."

"Well that's just great." Letting out a huge sigh, I jump down from my perch on the picnic table and walk away from the girl who stole my heart…and gave hers to my brother.

"Storm, please, you have to understand." Her sweet voice sings behind me, but I don't turn around to look at her. Instead, I grab the thick limb of the Stevens' newly budding old Maple tree and yank myself up. Climbing up one more sturdy branch, I sit my ass down and lean against the trunk.

"Storm. C'mon, get down. You know why I can't give it to you."

Yeah. She's told me a hundred times. *If I drink the elixir, I'll possess within my own soul, the souls of many self-*

serving, murderous empaths. If I imbibe in the blood-based elixir, I'd not only be able to feel people's pain and heal them...I'd be immortal.

But at what cost? Honor always asks me.

At the cost of my own honorable soul, she always answers.

"Storm. Please," she pleads.

Resisting Honor's requests is like driving the speed limit on the freeway—it cannot be done...not by me, anyway. I look at her sparkling violet eyes staring up at me, and I turn weak. Honor's slightly turned-up nose flares just a bit when the corners of her mouth form into a smile.

"Please come down and talk to me. You know it's only 'cause I care about you...and stop ignoring me," she adds, knowing damn well it is impossible to ignore her.

"You come up *here*," I challenge.

"What?!" You want me to climb that tree?"

"You can do it."

I hear a soft groan escape her throat before I see her pale hands grab the branch below me. Being tall and lean, Honor finds no difficulty in pulling herself up to the strong limb I'm sitting on. Straddling the branch with her long legs, Honor unintentionally causes a stir deep down inside me. *How embarrassing.*

"Now that I'm up here," the beautiful princess says to this violet-eyed frog, "will you let me explain why we don't want you drinking the elixir?"

"We? Please. Ethan doesn't give a crap what I do."

"Yes he does," she lies. "But it doesn't matter. *I* care. You know, if you drink it, you won't be the same. There are evil souls in that stuff. You don't want to turn...like them."

I look at her soft, smiling expression, and I want to agree. I do.

But I can't.

"Do you know what it's like to not be able to hold someone for more than like a minute, because you'd kill them if you did?" What I really want to say is, *"Do you know what it's like to not be able to hold you?"* But I refrain. Her compassion would just make her feel bad that she's in love with my oh-so-great half-brother Ethan instead of me.

"I understand, Storm, I do. Heck, I even *feel* your frustration. But do you really want more souls living inside you? You just got rid of three of them when you...y'know."

"I died, Honor. You can say it, you know. When I died. Go 'head, say it."

"No," she whispers.

"Look. You saved my life. Hell...you brought me *back* to life. That was awesome. I'm so grateful. And yes...I'm glad your mom, dad, and Summer are in Heaven now. Holding them inside me was a drag. I'd feel *their* emotions besides my own...it wasn't fun."

Honor just stares at me with her empathetic eyes and a crooked sympathetic smile.

"But Honor...it's not fun knowing I can never hold anyone...never...for God's sake, Honor, I'm 22 years old and still a..." She can figure it out on her own. I will not say that word out loud. I've never even admitted it to anyone else before.

"You're still a what?" she asks.

After staring at her for several long seconds, her eyes grow wide and her face turns red. By golly, she's figured it out. For such an innocent girl, I'm surprised it didn't take her longer.

"That's right. So you see why I want the elixir. If I take it, I'll be able to heal people...and well, not that I care too much about that, but it'd mean I can actually *touch* a girl without killing her. I could finally hold you," I whisper finally.

Her face turns a pretty shade of pink while her eyes become a gentle lavender. Though she insists she's Ethan's, it doesn't take an empath to know she holds some type of affection for me. I felt it in her kiss two months ago when we were held captive by the Gaffer's men inside the icehouse. Her lips may have only contacted mine briefly, but I felt her desire. I just wish *she* would have recognized it.

"Storm, I'm sorry. That must be terrible, but..." She inhales softly then lets out her breath in five extremely slow seconds. "I'd hate to think what you'd change into. I mean...you're so sweet now."

I can't help but laugh out loud. "Yeah. Tell *that* to my little brother. He thinks I'm the most rotten corrupt person out there."

"Don't worry about Ethan. He's still trying to get over his childhood anger towards you. I mean, now that he knows you didn't intentionally kill Summer, he's *trying* to change his opinion about you. Give him time."

"Oh good, 'cause I couldn't sleep knowing he hates me." I scoff. "Really, Honor, you think I care what that loser thinks of me?"

"You're the loser, Storm," I hear Ethan say from the ground.

"Leave us alone," I order, but know full well that he won't. Honor is his, not mine...unfortunately.

"Storm," Honor scolds before descending the tree. "Hey, Eeth," she says, then gives him a big hug. Which really irks me.

"What's *he* doing here?" Ethan asks Honor.

"He just came to talk," Honor answers defensively.

"Yeah well, I don't like it."

"Get over it, loser. She's my friend too, so get used to it." I need to react to his insensitivity toward Honor's and my friendship.

"Well she's *my* girlfriend, so *you* better get used to *that*," he rebuts.

"Will you two stop," Honor reprimands. "You're brothers, for goodness sake. You shouldn't treat each other the way you do."

I hop down out of the tree, kiss Honor on the top of her head, and tell her not to forget what I asked her. Then I leave.

"What'd he ask you?" I hear Ethan question her.

"He wants the elixir," Honor answers.

"He ain't getting the elixir, Honor." Ethan yells.

I scoff walking out her driveway. *He's such a loser.*

Chapter Two

My morning classes are boring, especially because I'd already attended and graduated high school five years ago when I talked an older roommate of mine into registering me at the local school. Not that it's public knowledge or anything. The only reason I'm redoing this lame school thing is to get closer to Honor. Well, my original intent when getting one of my empath associates to forge documents and make me a fake id was to keep an eye on my loser brother's total lack of judgment in following the legendary Honor Robinson. A big mistake in my opinion, because he totally disrespected the wishes of her birth parents to keep her from danger. In any event, we're here now and I cannot deny that I am more than happy to have met the pale-haired maiden. Which is why my morning classes are so dull—Honor is not in any of them.

Lunchtime cannot come fast enough for me, even though my irritating younger brother will be there sharing a lunch table with us. It is getting a bit tiresome seeing him everywhere Honor is. But she likes the kid, God help her.

Rushing out of class when the fifth period bell rings, I skip going to my locker in the hopes of seeing Honor at lunch before Ethan gets there. Not only do I *want* to see her just because, I also *need* to see her to ask if she's changed her mind about telling me where the elixir is. I wish they'd never moved it from her basement.

After Honor brought me back to life, her birth mother had informed her of my little empath DNA glitch—when I feel someone's pain and try to heal them, I kill them instead. *Who knew?* I mean yeah, it was clear that whoever I tried to help, I hurt, but I never knew why. Now I do. So drinking that elixir would sure help my dilemma. Instead of killing people, I could heal them.

Yeah. Like that's really the reason.

I just want to touch Honor for more than a few seconds without having her gasping for air and struggling for her life.

I just want to hold her, run my fingers through her ass-length blond hair, and kiss her.

I want to kiss her.

And not kill her in the process.

So, yeah. Having that elixir could certainly benefit me. But damn that Ethan for not trusting me. First, he gets Honor. Then, he takes charge of the elixir. It's not even his. It's Honor's. Her gramps left it for her, and who the hell does Ethan think he is telling her not to give it to me?

Honor tucks her long bangs behind her hair while she waits for her lunch buddies to join her at the table. Taking an apprehensive step toward her, I take advantage of this chance to get her alone.

"Hey, princess," I say, sitting my ass down across the table from her.

"Oh hey, Storm." Her smile is big and bright and radiant.

"Did you change your mind yet?" I ask her, hoping she has, though knowing she hasn't.

"Storm." I try to ignore the patronizing tone in her voice. "You know we've talked about this. It's too danger..."

"Dangerous. Yes. You've said that already."

"Then why do you keep asking?"

The way her lips wrap around her straw when she takes a sip of her iced tea, causes me to forget completely what we were talking about. All I can think of is pulling those soft pink lips between my teeth and nipping on them.

"Well?" she asks.

"Well what?"

"Why do you keep asking for the elixir if you know it's dangerous?"

"Oh...well." I shake my thoughts back to the conversation. "*You* said it was dangerous. *I* never did."

"Storm. You *know* it is."

"And you don't think *killing* someone I'm trying to help is dangerous?"

"Who are you trying to help? Who is in pain? Maybe *I* can help them," Honor offers.

I scoff at that. Like I'd let her put more strain on that heart of hers. She's already saved too many people from their pain and suffering...and death. Her big heart won't last much longer if she keeps that up. Besides, I'm not *really* feeling anyone's pain right now. Come to think of it, I haven't felt anything in awhile.

"Storm. Who is it? I'll help them."

"What?"

"What's wrong with you today? You keep zoning out."

"Oh. Sorry. It's noth..." I stop talking. Ethan is walking toward us. "Well look what the cat dragged in." Feeling pretty proud of myself for no reason at all, I reach across to take Honor's drink, and bring it to my lips, sucking it slowly just to get under Ethan's skin. And of course to put my lips on the very straw Honor just had her lips on. Which is also why Ethan doesn't appreciate the act at all.

"What are you doing here, Storm?" My little brother asks. "You know Honor doesn't want you sitting here either."

"Ethan," Honor whispers. "That's not true."

I raise a cocky eyebrow at Ethan and take another sip of Honor's drink.

"Get your own friends," Ethan growls.

"But I don't know how, little brother. Will you teach me how to make friends?" I quip. The mock pout on my face irks the hell out of Ethan, but it gets a stifled chuckle out of Honor. Win!

"Hey, guys." Tamlin climbs over the bench and sits next to me.

"Hey, Tam." Honor is the only one who acknowledges Tamlin's arrival. Ethan is too busy brooding, and I'm content tapping my fingers on the table and pissing off Ethan.

Some other kids sit down at our table, but I couldn't tell you their names...then Hunter shows up. Great. Another little brother. At least this one doesn't irk me the way Ethan does.

"So, Honor," Tamlin begins. "You're really gonna stay after school with hunky Mr. Moore? You're so luck..."

"What?" Ethan and I both exclaim at the same time.

While Honor dips her eyebrows toward that cute little nose of hers, Tamlin smirks. "What's with you guys?" Tamlin asks. "You got something against Mr. Moore?"

Ignoring Tamlin, I turn to tell Honor what I think of Moore, but Ethan opens his mouth first.

"Honor," he says. "I don't know about this. There's something about Moore I don't like. I...I can't put my finger on it, but...he gives me the creeps."

"The creeps?" Honor laughs.

"Yeah. You don't feel anything from him?" Ethan whispers to her.

That's when I realize that my own feelings about Moore are not physical feelings but gut instinct. Why am I not feeling anything? Still. Mr. Moore rubs me the wrong way.

"Honor," I say to her softly. "Don't go to Moore alone."

"Why?" she asks.

"What?!" Tamlin exclaims. "You guys are crazy. He's *so* nice. Not to mention *hot*." Tamlin chuckles. "You're just jealous," she says to Ethan and me. Then she turns to Honor. "Too bad I couldn't bring *him* to the prom."

Honor chuckles now, Ethan rolls his eyes, and I can't believe I'm sitting at a high school lunch table at twenty-two years old. If I could just figure out who's after this elixir, and Honor, I could leave this stinkin' place.

But then I'd never see her.

High school it is.

Besides, I need to get closer to Moore. The more I think about it, the more sure I am that there's something about him I need to know.

"Ethan," Honor says. "I'll be fine after school with Mr. Moore. I'm sure there will be other kids getting help from him. Besides, it's school. What's he gonna do? There are so many teachers still here after three."

"Yeah. I guess you're right." Ethan kisses Honor's cheek and she blushes, turning a pretty peach color as she does. "I'll go to my apartment and check in with Uncle Tom. I'll do some laundry then meet you at your house for dinner."

"Good."

"You sure your parents still don't mind my staying in their guest room?" Ethan asks, causing my blood to raise several jealous degrees.

"Of course not," she says, though I note ambivalence in her tone. "They're happy you're there." Honor scans the room then leans in closer to Ethan. "This whole elixir-Gaffer thing has them worried. So, it's okay. Don't worry." She smiles, but when she catches my eye, her smile fades.

When the first bus bell rings for the other side of town to board their ride home, I take the opportunity to visit my favorite chemistry teacher. Mr. Moore is dismissing his students when I knock on his door.

"Mr. Sutherland, please...come in. I'll be with you momentarily," he says, before turning back to his class and reminding them to read their assigned chapter for homework.

After the class disperses, Mr. Moore pushes a few papers aside and sits on the corner of his desk. With a smug smile, he folds his arms in front of his chest and crosses his long legs at the ankles. "So, Mr. Sutherland, what can I do for you?"

"I'm having trouble with the lab assignment on empirical formulas," I lie, trying to come up with something, anything, to stay in his room. "The one with the iron and..."

"Sulfur, yes. But I'm surprised, Storm," Mr. Moore says with a weary eyebrow. "You're a straight-A student. I don't see you having trouble with *any* assignments." Mr. Moore shoots me a silent stare.

"Can you humor me, Mr. Moore and explain it again?"

"Hi."

Moore and I turn to see my sweet princess smiling in the doorway.

"Miss Stevens, I've been waiting for you. Come in."

While Honor places her backpack on one of the front desks and removes her binder, I watch the way Moore takes her in. There's a huge void in my chest where I should be feeling something. My usual empathic abilities are missing. Now I am sure of that.

In Moore's eyes, I see some type of contradiction, which had something not been amiss with my own empathy capabilities, I'd be able to pick up. But my gut tells me he is out for Honor. And I don't know why.

"Storm, can we do this later, I have a session with another student at the moment." Moore addresses me.

"Oh. No problem," I say, while sitting down at the desk behind Honor. "I'll just wait."

"I'd rather you not, Mr. Sutherland." Moore says with clenched teeth.

"Well, Mr. Moore, I'm Honor's ride home, and I'm sure she won't mind my sitting here waiting for her."

Honor takes a quick look in my direction and asks, *"What's up?"* with her eyes.

With *my* eyes, I tell her to just go along with me.

"It's fine, Mr. Moore," she says. "I really don't mind Storm sitting in with us."

Boy, I'm relishing in the fact that Honor and I can communicate with no words. Just like we did when we were locked up in the icehouse.

Moore grunts inwardly and sits at the desk next to Honor, moving it closer with his ass, to block my view.

***

After Honor and I walk out of Moore's class, she taps my arm with a fake punch. "What was that about?" she asks.

"I told you. I don't trust him."

"So you had to babysit me?"

I drape my arm around her shoulder. "No, princess. I was protecting you."

She chuckles, "From what?"

"From Moore," I answer, confused as to why she doesn't get that. "What do you *feel* when you're around him, Honor. You *must* feel something."

She shrugs her shoulders, and I tighten my arm around her. "I don't know. Sometimes I get those bad shivers up my spine when I'm around him. But mostly," she brightens her face with a smile, "I feel...happy. Comforted in some way. I really don't feel threatened at all. I don't understand why you and Ethan feel differently."

"I don't know," I say quietly.

"Like, shouldn't we all be feeling the same thing?"

"You'd think," I say cryptically, getting increasingly worried about why I am feeling nothing but my own emotions.

Chapter Three

"Thanks for the ride home, Storm." Honor turns up the corner of her mouth in an unintentionally seductive smile. "And...thanks for staying after with me. It's nice to know you're looking out for me."

"That's what I'm here for," I joke, not letting on that I really am in Jefferson, New Jersey to look out for her and my brother. Not that they know it, nor do they think they need looking after, but I know these guys that work for the Gaffer. They will *kill* to get what they're after. And not that I knew this before moving here, but I would *kill* to save Honor.

Even though she *isn't* mine to save.

"Well, I appreciate it. Even though I think you're crazy worrying about Moore."

"Yeah, well, I'm just plain crazy.".

Honor laughs. "I'd have to agree." She offers a full smile now, and my heart expands with my increasing adoration for her.

I shake my head and pinch her cheek. "Who you callin' crazy?"

She chuckles. "I'm just teasin'."

"I know," I say, hoping she doesn't hear the change in my tone from playful to serious. Her playfulness emphasizes the fact that dating my idiot brother, instead of me. Because I don't feel it's my place to play back, I digress and tell her I'll see her tomorrow.

After a quick nod, Honor gets out and walks away.

Leaving me almost breathless.

Because I want her so much.

***

Not even home for five minutes, I'm confronted with a hard rap on the door. "Open up, Sutherland. I know you're in there. Your obnoxious car is parked out front," demands the voice on the other side of the door.

"Jeremy Mills," I sneer, after opening the door to *not* one of my favorite empaths—one of Gaffer's men. "What do *you* want?"

"The old man's got another assignment for you. Ya gonna let me in, or do I have to stand here all night?"

With a grunt and a reluctant wave of my hand, I lead him in to my one-bedroom basement apartment.

"Nice place you got here, Sutherland. Tiny, no?"

"It does what it needs to do. Now what's this about?" I ask, afraid to know.

"Like you don't know." He pauses. "The elixir."

"What about it?"

"Where is it? You were supposed to have found it already. Unless of course you really aren't working for the man. In which case, he's gonna be pissed. And you know what he does when someone pisses him off." Mills cracks himself up, holding his stomach as he bends over laughing. "Yeah...that's right. You already did piss him off trying to save your precious Honor instead of getting what we needed from her."

"It was part of my plan," I lie through my teeth. "I was trying to get her to trust me."

"Yeah right. But that's why he's giving you one more chance. Just in case you really were trying to get the elixir from her."

"I was. Besides, she doesn't even know where it is," I lie again, desperate to get him off Honor's case.

"Yeah well, we don't believe that. We searched that school. It's not there. And we found Toby and Michael buried in the woods. You guys think you're sly throwing some old branches over the shallow grave you dug, don't you? You're just lucky we were the ones who found them...and not the cops."

Staring him down buys me some time to think of a response, since falling for Honor has me losing my edge.

"Why'd you kill them? Part of your plan, Sutherland?"

"They weren't playing games. What was I gonna do?" No need to tell them that *they* killed *me*, and Honor brought me back to life. Then they'd forget the elixir and go right for Honor. The ability to bring life back from death has got to be as appealing as an immortal elixir.

"This time get it right, Sutherland. Otherwise, we take it into our own hands. And we're not gonna be gentle with your precious Honor either."

"I'll get it. Are we done here?"

"Yeah. We're done. For now."

After Mills leaves, I grab a soda and plop down on the couch to fret about the mess I got us into. I came here to try to help, but ended up making things worse. Like I always do. Now, not only do I need the elixir to be able to hold Honor...I need it to save her life.

The thoughts going through my mind cause my chest to constrict and my temper to rise. Each thought brings me to one main target of my anger. Ethan. It was his stupidity that brought us all here. Until Ethan had learned of Honor's whereabouts, she was tucked-in safe and sound in her adoptive parents' home. Now she's their target, and I'm at a loss for how to save her. I could kidnap her and run, but they'd eventually find her. A life on the run would be no life for an innocent like Honor.

Slamming my can of soda on the end table and spilling some in the process, I decide to give my little brother a visit. Maybe I'll know what to say to him when I get there.

Ethan is already pulling out of his lot when I tear in behind him, honking my horn to alert him to stay where he is.

"What the hell, Storm?" he shouts, swinging his door open and treading hastily toward me.

"Tell me where it is. I want it now."

"You're outta your mind, you know that?"

"It's not your elixir to hide and do with as you please, loser. It's Honor's."

"And Honor doesn't want you to have it. She's made that clear on more than one occasion."

My little brother is pissing me off. I'm ready to strangle it out of him. In an effort to calm murderous thoughts, I take several deep breaths while maintaining eye contact with the loser.

"Ethan, I'm going to ask this one more time," I say calmly, pressing my palms firmly on his shoulders to let him know I'm serious. "This doesn't just affect me. If I don't get that elixir," I enunciate each word, "Honor will be hurt."

Ethan throws up his hands and walks back to his car. "Oh. So now you're threatening Honor. That's just great. You know she thinks you're her friend. Go to hell, Storm."

"It's not me who's threatening her. It's him." No need to say who *him* is. By the nauseated look on Ethan's face, I'd say he's figured it out.

He drops his arms to his sides. He looks like he's about to faint. "I dumped it," he whispers so low I actually read his lips rather than hear his words.

"You what?!"

"I dumped it," he says louder. "I fucking dumped it."

"How could you dump it? I *told* you we'd need it to negotiate or hand it over. You don't know what this man is capable of. His men nearly killed us, Ethan. Did you think he'd be deterred because we killed two of his guys? He's got more...lots more. What the..."

"I'm sorry. But you were bullying Honor about giving it to you, and it pissed me off., So I dumped it." He wipes the sweat from his brow. "I really thought you wanted it for yourself, and well, Honor kept talking about how dangerous it would be," Ethan drops his head, "if we gave it away."

I shake my head. He's so pathetic. Looking him in the eye now, I tell him that seeking the elixir for my personal benefit was my original intent...until a visitor decided to come knock on my door this afternoon. *And since when did he start listening to a girl's rationalization about things?.*

"Where'd you dump it?" I ask, not that it matters much.

"Mahlon Dickerson."

"You dumped it onto county property? What are you? Stupid? If someone finds all that blood, they'll be looking for a body. Oh my god, never mind that, they'll take DNA samples and figure out it belongs to someone *two hundred years old*," I yell. "*Several* people two hundred years old."

"No, no. I dumped it in the stream there," Ethan admits.

"Oh great. Even better. It'll flow into the water system; then we'll have a ton of immortal empaths."

"Don't be so dramatic, Storm. By the time it gets there, it'll be diluted."Ethan runs both his hands through his hair, undoubtedly more worried than he's letting on.

"Ethan," I try again to keep my composure, "where are the glass jugs that stored it?"

"There's an attic in my apartment. I put them up there."

"Okay. Maybe I can get something out of them. Maybe it'll be enough to satisfy them."

"Right. Well...I rinsed them out."

"Oh you stupid son of a..."

"Shut the hell up I wasn't thinking. Damn it, Storm, if you just could have been straight with me from the beginning, we wouldn't be in this mess."

"Oh, so now you're blaming me?"

"Well if you'd have just told me..."

"I told you that night in the woods."

"I had other things on my mind that night."

"Just," I hold up my hands, "stop, all right. I'll figure something else out. Just...don't tell Honor. I don't want her to worry."

"At least we agree on one thing then."

I leave without another word, taking off in my Challenger and letting the loud music drown out my thoughts.

Chapter Four

Tamlin barrels through the double lunchroom doors, terror washing over her face. Instantly my thoughts turn to Honor. Something's wrong. Unstraddling the bench, I leap for Tamlin, who is heading our way.

"What is it?" I ask, placing my hands on her shoulders.

"It's Honor," Tamlin cries.

"I know it is..."

"She's in the girls' bathroom. She fainted."

"I'll see to her," Ethan says behind me.

Tamlin takes my hand. "Come on, Storm. You too."

Tam and I follow Ethan to the girls' room, but my throat constricts in an attempt to hold in my emotions. Ethan belongs with her. Not me. My steps slow with this realization.

"What is it?" Tamlin asks. "Why you slowing down?"

Coming to a complete stop, I ask, "What happened? Why'd she faint?"

Tamlin shakes her crimson-haired head. "I don't know. When I walked into the girls' room, she was holding on to some freshman. When the girl turned to leave, Honor went down."

"Damn," I whisper under my breath.

Ethan is already hovering over Honor on the bathroom floor when Tamlin and I walk in.

"Please, there is no room in here. We need to keep the space open for the paramedics. You can stand out in the hall," the nurse commands.

"But..." Tamlin starts, but the nurse cuts her off.

"Thank you, Tamlin. Why don't you stand outside and wait for the paramedics."

Leaving Honor inside the bathroom leaves me feeling helpless. She doesn't need me in there, I know that. She has Ethan. But *I* need to be there. *I* need to know she'll be all right. Her never-ending need to help others is slowly killing her. I cannot let that happen.

Out in the hall, Tamlin squeezes my arm. "She'll be okay, won't she, Storm?"

Tamlin is looking to me for an answer that I wish someone would answer for me. My sarcastic nature nearly impels me to say, *"Does she* look *okay?"* But I hold my impulsive tongue, knowing that Tamlin is Honor's best friend, and she, too, needs to believe that Honor will stop giving in to her empathy to save her own life.

With an apprehensive hand, I rub Tamlin's arm. "Yes. She'll be okay," I say quietly, needing to believe it myself.

***

Tamlin talks me into following the ambulance to the hospital. Though I know Ethan is headed there too, we do not offer each other a ride.

"I'm really nervous, Storm, "Tamlin says, breaking the welcomed silence; welcomed by me, apparently not by her. "What if she bumped her head so hard she doesn't wake up?"

Well that thought hadn't occurred to me until *just now*. In no mood to encourage conversation with her, I stay silent, focusing on the road in front of me.

"What if she keeps doing her healing thing and like, she dies?"

I want to ignore this question. I really do. But it's the same question that is going through my mind right now. "She won't," I whisper.

"But how do you know?" she asks, and I wish she would just shut up. "Ethan has been *begging* her to stop, but she just says, *'If God didn't want me to heal people, then He wouldn't have made me capable of doing so.'*" Tamlin does a good impression of Honor, and she's right. I have heard her say that.

"Yeah, well, Ethan's a loser. I'll get her to stop."

"And how are you going to do that if her own boyfriend can't?"

Without taking my eyes off the road, I say, "You know...you ask way too many questions."

"Uggh. Ethan's right. You *are* an obnoxious ass."

In my peripheral vision, I see Tamlin brush her finger under her eye. When girls cry, it is so irritating. "You're crying?" I mock.

"Go to hell, Storm."

Yeah. I'm already there.

The ER admissions clerk allows us through to see Honor in room seventeen. Behind the curtain, Honor is propped up on the bed. Looking whiter than she usually does, she strains to greet us.

"Hey, princess. You needing attention again?" I tease. There is no way I'm showing how scared she has me.

Honor smiles, but Ethan tosses me a dirty look. "She doesn't do this for attention, jerk. She..."

I cut him off by ignoring him and focusing on Honor. "Hey, babe," I say before kissing her on the forehead. Whispering in her ear, I tell her she has to learn to say no sometimes.

Pretty princess shrugs her shoulders and softly says, "I know."

"They allowed you in here?" Ethan asks. Again, I ignore him.

Fortunately, Tamlin comes to my defense. "Of course they allowed him in, we're her friends." Tamlin squeezes in behind me and takes my place at Honor's side.

"Hey there, Hon. What's going on? You gotta stop doing this to yourself." Tamlin takes Honor's hand and brings it to her lips.

Honor sighs, closing her tired eyes and keeping them shut.

"Oh, sweetie," Tamlin chokes. "You're killing yourself."

"Literally," Ethan says.

I agree...only silently. Standing helpless near the curtain, my attention falls to my chest, where a staggering pain crushes my heart like crumbling stone. Honor is slowly dying. I can't save her, nor am I allowed to love her. My colliding thoughts are warring inside me—fight for her love and safety, or flee. I've always flown. Loving someone is usually never worth the pain.

But knowing Honor has changed me. She's shown me love. The caring kind. The saving kind. Honor brought me back to life, and I owe it to her to stay. If only to be her friend.

"Yo, Storm," Tamlin says, waving her hand in front of my face. "C'mon, let's go get some food. The nurse needs to take her for tests soon, and Mr. and Mrs. Stevens should be alone with her."

"Oh," I respond, not realizing that Honor's parents had even entered the room.

Releasing myself from the raging war of thoughts in my head, I turn to Ethan. "You coming with us?" I ask, biting my tongue to keep from saying some wise-ass remark that might upset Honor.

He looks at Honor sleeping on the bed. "Yeah." He shrugs. "I'll go."

"Thanks, kids," Mr. Stevens says to our backs.

In the hospital cafeteria, Tamlin plops down on a seat and cries. My inner devil rolls my eyes, but I refrain from actually doing it. I'm upset too, so I understand her need to shed tears.

"It'll be okay," I say, my attempt at a "there-there" and a pat on the shoulder.

Her teary eyes look into my callous ones. "How do you know?" she says.

"I don't. I was just trying to be nice."

"You're an ass," she says.

"What'd I say wrong?"

"What did he do now?" Ethan asks, setting a cup of tea in front of Tamlin and a cola and fries in front of where he sits down.

"Nothing for me?" I joke, humorlessly.

"Get it yourself," Ethan says.

Opting instead to spend time alone, I disappear into the hospital halls. What I did to piss Tamlin off, I've no idea, but I don't need to be bothered with high school bull right now. There are better things to be done. Like figure out how to hand over a non-existent elixir.

"See you losers later. Brother, make sure you see that Tamlin gets a ride home." I walk out and don't look back.

Chapter Five

It's two a.m., and I can't sleep. Besides thinking about Honor needing to stay the night in the hospital, my brain slips into overdrive wondering how I'm going to come up with an ancient elixir made from the blood of murderous empaths. The old man is not someone I ought to screw with. However, since Honor became the target, I can't seem to stop myself. I'm just going to have to come up with something before the Gaffer's men come knocking on my door again.

Since sleep isn't going to find me anytime soon, I go for a ride. Allowing my Challenger to lead the way, I shift into auto-pilot so I can empty my mind. Hoping to spark an idea or two. I cannot let them come after Honor. Somehow, someway, I need to send them away...for good.

My mind is racing a mile a minute. Clearing my mind doesn't work, and though many thoughts are battling for my attention, not one is successful in helping me solve this elixir dilemma.

Having not been focused on the road, I find myself pulling into the hospital parking lot. The corner of my mouth betrays my horrid mood when it tugs toward my cheek. I don't *want* to smile, but the fact that I subconsciously drive myself to where Honor lies sleeping, makes me smile anyway. In that moment, I realize that Honor is all that matters. Her health. Her happiness. Her life. Whether she wants me in it or not, she's all that I care about. Whether I *remain* in her life or not, she is *still* all that matters. To me, Honor is everything. Not only did she save me from death, she brought my heart back to life, literally and figuratively. She made me a better man just by being near her. I love her so much, and whether she will ever know it or not does not make a difference. I will fight to keep her safe. If I have to kill to do so, I will.

I back my car into a spot under what I think is her window and turn off the engine, letting the hum of the street lamps lull me to sleep. Images of Honor's pretty face dance beneath my eyelids as I drift away—my heart heavy and wanting.

**

A warm sensation falls over me, gently waking me up. When I open my eyes, however, I'm blinded by the early morning sun glaring in through the windshield. After adjusting to the bright light, I turn on the engine to check the time. It's too early for visiting hours, but I shut the car off and see if I can get into the hospital for a cup of coffee.

The main entrance is locked, so I head over to the emergency room entrance. Fortunately, there's a coffee kiosk at the end of the hall.

I take my double espresso and walk through the halls with the intention of reaching Honor's room without being noticed. As I pass each room, my eye catches one closet-sized area in particular. The stacked bags of donated blood stand at attention on the cart in the center of the room. Suddenly, I have an idea.

With a renewed vigor, I hurry to Honor's room to see my princess and to sit and organize my thoughts. I now have a plan brewing in my head, but I need to work it through before putting it into action.

Chapter Six

Honor's skin is so pale that I swear I can see the violet from her eyes breaking through beneath her fragile eyelids. Her breath is shallow, and her sleep appears restless. If I were a normal empath, I'd touch her and make it all better. But since I'm a defective one, I'd end up killing her, which makes me wonder why Ethan doesn't just heal her. He's certainly capable. Now my blood is boiling. Honor can be cured with a single touch by her boyfriend, yet she's here in the hospital, suffering from pain and exhaustion. My breathing picks up its pace, and I feel the need to break something. Preferably Ethan's head. But since he's not here at the moment, I stand up to leave and go outside before I find something to break. I never reach the door. Something rustles behind me.

"Storm?"

When I hear her call my name, I can't help but close my eyes and smile. Turning around, I see her soft pink lips turned up at the corners.

"Princess," I whisper, choking out the words. It hurts so much to see her like this and know I can't help.

"It's early," she says, implying I probably shouldn't be here.

"Yeah."

I pull the chair up next to her bed, sit, and take her hand for just a second.

"Shouldn't you be like sleeping or something?" she asks, reaching out to touch my hand again after I'd pulled it away. But I set them on my lap.

She frowns...but only briefly.

"Nah," I respond. "I don't need sleep. Sleep's for wusses."

Honor tries to laugh, but I can tell it takes more energy than she has.

"Honor, sweetheart, why do you do this to yourself? Look what helping somebody else does to you."

She sighs, but says nothing.

"You gotta learn to let their pain go. Please, angel. It kills me to see you like this."

After a slow blink, she opens her mouth. "She was hurting. She was depressed and...I think she was having thoughts of suicide."

"Who? The girl in the bathroom?"

"Yeah," she whispers.

"Wait. You could tell what she was thinking?"

"Well, not exactly, but I kind of *felt* what she was thinking."

"And you thought you could take away her sadness?"

Honor nods.

"But you fainted. I don't get it."

"Me neither. I got, like, so sad that my heart really hurt. I actually wanted...to die."

My heart stops a beat. "What?"

"After I touched her...I wanted to die." Honor leans her head into her shoulder.

There was nothing either one of us could think of to say after that. We sit there in silence until Honor whispers my name again.

"What is it, princess?"

"It must be terrible to feel so helpless that you want to die."

"Yeah, it is."

Honor doesn't say anything, but I'm sure she's *feeling* what I'm thinking. *I've been there before. After I killed Summer.*

While Honor slips back to sleep, I gently toss my feet on the edge of her bed and relish in the sweet sound of her steady breathing. Then I close my own eyes, slink back into the chair, and concentrate on figuring out how to put my new plan into action.

***

Sleep must have found me as well, because the sound of Ethan's voice startles me awake.

"I asked you a question," he says in a loud whisper.

"Excuse me? You can't be talking to me."

"Um, yeah...I am."

Remaining in my reclined position, so as to piss him off a little more, I stare him down.

"Why are you here, Storm?"

I shrug my shoulders. "Same reason you are, I guess." I try keeping my voice low.

"She's not your girlfriend, she's mine."

"I never claimed she was. You just must be really threatened by me to keep repeating that."

"Go to hell," Ethan commands.

"Yeah, yeah." I put my feet on the floor and sit up. "You *really* have to come up with a new line. *Go to hell* is gettin' a bit old." Still keeping my voice down, I look to the bed and see that Honor is still sleeping. My heart is screaming *"Stay with her, don't leave,"* but my head knows better. Ethan deserves some time alone with her, if only for Honor's sake.

I inconspicuously blow my sleeping angel a kiss with my fingertips and walk out. Ethan doesn't need a good-bye from me.

In the lobby downstairs, Tamlin is on line at another coffee kiosk. "Hey," I say, for lack of an insulting comment.

"Hey," she smiles. "You going to see Honor?"

"Just did." I get in line behind her.

"What's your poison? My treat."

"Double espresso. I thought I was an ass?"

"You are, but I'm not," she says to me, then turns to the cashier. "A double espresso and a medium mocha latte, please."

After paying the lady, we move to the side to wait for our coffee.

"So what's with the blond hair?" I ask, just making small talk.

"I was sick of all the fancy colors, so I bleached it last night." She shrugs.

"Not in the mood for flair right now?"

She shakes her head. "Not really. It feels...I don't know...disrespectful, I guess."

"To Honor?"

Tamlin nods.

The coffee lady hands us our drinks, and we walk to a couple of chairs in the lobby.

"I'm really scared, Storm. Ethan said last night that if she keeps trying to heal people, she's gonna die soon. He said she's done so much already that he's worried she doesn't even have much longer."

Hearing these words hurt. Bile rises from my stomach, my heart tightens, and when I see Tamlin's eyes pool with tears, my own eyes start to burn. Dammit. I *don't* cry. If I open my mouth to respond, I know my voice will shake, and the tears will actually fall, because there's a lump in my throat that's telling me so. Instead, turn to stare out the window.

"Storm, did you hear me?"

I can't look at her.

"Storm."

"Not now," I choke out.

Tamlin puts her hand over mine. "I knew there was a soft side to you." She leans in to hug me, but I pull away.

"I'm sorry. I..." She trails off, probably embarrassed, but if I hug her back, I'd hurt her.

"Tam, I'm sure Honor's told you about me," I manage to say over the golf ball in my throat.

Her eyes get all squinty, and she shakes her head.

"I can't touch people. *Unlike* Honor, the stroke of my hand can kill."

Tamlin smiles and takes my hand again. "I'm not scared." She looks me in the eyes and wraps her other arm around me, finally pulling me into a full embrace. "If it gets too much, I'll pull away."

Closing my eyes, I let her hold me. Besides Tamlin needing the comfort as well, my body aches for the touch of a female. My instincts tell me not to do it, but my arms have a will of their own. I reciprocate her hug by wrapping my arms around her and pulling her to my chest. Tamlin's not Honor, but she feels good against my beating heart. My breathing picks up, but I try to slow it down. I close my eyes and take slow deep breaths.

That's when I realize it.

Tamlin's not gasping for air.

In fact, she's breathing a nice, comfortable, steady pace, and her crying has stopped.

"Storm?" she asks, still pressed against my chest.

"Yes?" I whisper.

"You're not hurting me at all."

I nudge her back to look at her face. "Nothing?"

"No."

She's staring at me now, and I'm getting this strange feeling. By the way she's looking from my lips to my eyes, I believe she wants to kiss me. My conflicting emotions are confusing me, so I turn off my brain and lean in, setting my lips to hers. Her lips are soft and sweet, but there's no spark. No electricity. She parts her lips and runs her tongue across my lips. Needing so badly to touch and be touched, I open my mouth to allow her in. She hugs me tighter, and I run my hand through her newly bleached hair.

Just then, I break our embrace and pull away.

"I don't understand," I say, breathless.

"What?" she asks, confused as to why I stop our kiss so abruptly.

"You should be dead. Or at least gasping for your life."

Tamlin chuckles.

"I'm serious, Tam. I've never been able to keep contact with someone for so long without sucking the life out of them."

She laughs again. "Your attitude pretty much does that," she jokes.

"Be serious for a minute. Something's wrong."

"Why?"

"First, I can't feel things like I used to. Now I can *touch* people?" I'm so astounded by this, I pull her back against me and kiss the heck out of her—just to be sure.

After several minutes of making out with Tamlin, I am convinced that I am no longer a danger, at least not to Tamlin. Not only that, I sense no emotions from her at all. If I am surmising correctly, I am no longer empathic. Though the thought brings a smile to my face, it puts a damper on my plans to fix this whole elixir debacle.

Chapter Seven

Tamlin breaks the kiss first. "Wow," she utters beneath her breath.

Though I don't feel the *wow* factor myself, the kiss certainly was intense. And I wouldn't be opposed to doing it again. But now's not the time. Not here in the hospital where Honor is suffering only a few floors above us.

"Tam," I whisper, smiling at her. "I should go."

"Yeah. I'm sorry. I don't know what came over me. I shouldn't have-"

"Hey. It's fine. I enjoyed it."

She smiles and hooks her thumb over her shoulder. "Yeah, well, I should get upstairs. I wanted to give Ethan a few minutes alone with her. He's probably wondering now where I am."

"You came with him?"

"Yup."

"Oh, well, I'll see you later?" *Shit. I hadn't meant to sound so eager.*

"Sure," she said, smiling, then giving me an impulsive peck on the cheek.

What have I done? I'm in love with my brother's girlfriend, and I go and kiss her best friend. Shameless. I may not have hurt Tamlin physically, but I'm sure I'm going to hurt her emotionally. Just another reason to keep my distance from people.

In the car, I blast Jack's Mannequin's *Dark Blue*, substantiating my quest for isolation. As soon as I get Honor out of danger, I *will* return to my solitary life. It'll be better than what I'm doing now.

Reaching my apartment in record time, I grab a soda and pull out my laptop. Since my plan to get the old man and his men off Honor's case involves materials, I pull up a search engine and type in medical supplies. Hoping beyond hope that a non-medical person can actually order the supplies I'm going to need.

After searching for nearly an hour, I give up. Not having a medical license is seriously going to hinder my plan. I take a shower, get dressed, and head back over to the hospital to see Honor. When I get to her room, Tamlin and Ethan are still there.

Tamlin's face lights up at the sight of me, causing my stomach to burn. I know I should not have kissed her this morning.

"Hey, Storm," she says, grinning before reaching up to kiss me. Though she's aiming for my lips, I subtly turn so she lands on my cheek. I'm too aware that Honor is in the room. Ethan's eyes are all squinty, because he's obviously skeptical of my intentions. Which makes me feel even more guilty for kissing Tamlin.

Turning my attention instead toward Honor, I notice her smile is pensive. "Hey, princess," I say, barely opening my mouth. Barely hearing my own words.

"Hey," she answers.

"How ya feeling this afternoon?"

"Better."

"Yeah," Tamlin interrupts, "she was even laughing with us."

"Yeah?" I ask, looking at Honor while my heart burns beneath my chest.

She nods. "Yeah. I feel *much* better. They're running more pointless tests on me later, and I should be able to go home tomorrow."

Ethan tries to hide his scowl with a smile that ends up looking like a lopsided grin. "So Tamlin tells us you and she are a thing."

"Ethan, I did not say that," Tamlin snaps. She looks at me. "I did not say that. I just told them...well..."

"That's okay," I reassure her. Truth is, it felt good to be in Tamlin's arms. Plus...she's quirky. *Sometimes* quirky's cool.

"So now maybe you'll stay away from *my* girlfriend?"

"Ethan," Honor snaps at her boyfriend.

Tamlin looks from me to Honor.

"He can't help himself, princess, he's an ass," I quip.

"You do call her princess an awful lot," Tamlin says, laughing.

"Just habit," I say. "No big deal."

Honor starts speaking softly to Tamlin, so I take the opportunity to call Ethan aside. "Can I talk to you a minute?"

"What?" he says quite caustically.

Leaning in close to my dear half-brother, I whisper in his ear, "Had you not dumped the elixir, I wouldn't need to be coming up with a plan to save *your* girlfriend."

Ethan's tightened jaw loosens, replacing his cocksure attitude with a defeated one.

"Honor," he addresses her, "I'll be right back."

She nods and continues her discussion with Tamlin.

"I have a plan, but I need your help," I tell him once we're out in the hall. "I'll need your uncle and Hunter too."

"Yeah, okay, but what do we need to do?"

"I'll need you to get Elijah and any other brothers you got floating around," I immediately feel bad for saying that, because I know Brad was just killed.

Ethan shakes his head. "What? Care to explain before I volunteer my family?"

"Here's the thing. I need your blood."

He just stands there bug-eyed.

"I want to try to fill one of those jugs you got hidden. Fill it with blood."

"What? You mean..."

"Yeah, I mean we pass it off as the elixir. I've been thinking and if we use the blood of different empaths, it may work."

"Correct me if I'm wrong, but aren't elixirs made from more than just blood?" he says sarcastically.

"Yes. But I think Moore might have some of the stuff we need in his lab."

"You're going to trust Moore?"

"No. I'm going to use his lab."

"You mean the school lab?"

"Yeah."

"How do you suggest we do that?"

"We break in," I say, shocked that he doesn't get that.

"Break into the school? We'll never get away with it." Ethan shuffles his feet, obviously nervous.

"Well, little brother, we're gonna have to do something. Once I find out what's needed, I'll know more. Maybe it's something I can do from home. Either way, we're still going to have to play burglar."

"Huh?" My little brother's turning green.

"We're gonna have to break into a blood bank to get the supplies I need to take your blood."

"You're crazy." He throws his hands up and turns to walk away.

"No," I say quietly. "Crazy is tossing the friggin' ancient elixir."

Ethan turns around, looks at me, tilts his head, and closes his eyes.

"Now do I have your help?"

He sighs. "Yeah."

"The rest of you too. You're gonna have to convince them to help. I doubt your uncle will refuse, but what about your brothers? You think you can find Elijah?"

Ethan nods, but his scrunched up face confirms his uncertainty.

"Ya gotta talk 'em into it," I demand quickly. "This is no joke. If we don't come up with an elixir, they'll be going after Honor. Especially if they find out..."

"Find out what?"

"Nothing. Just do it. Get your family to agree, and meet me tonight at my house at nine...and wear something black." I walk away.

"Wait. Tonight? For what?" Ethan says to my departing back.

"Just be there," I yell, not looking back.

Chapter Eight

One drawback of being a loner is there aren't many friends to call upon for help. The people I *have* associated with in the past were never considered friends, and I certainly could not trust them for this. Hopefully, Ethan and his family love Honor enough to keep our plans to themselves.

As I bend down to plug my dying laptop in, my cell rings. Beads of sweat collect on my forehead when the caller id announces a blocked number. This could be *him*. Or one of his men. Stretching out the neck of my t-shirt to alleviate the choking sensation I have, I touch the answer button on my phone.

"Hello," I answer, hoping the higher pitch of my voice doesn't give my anxiety away.

"Storm?" an apprehensive female asks.

The choking feeling disappears—since I know the male-chauvinist Gaffer doesn't employ women.

"Yes?" I ask, my voice back normal.

"It's Tam."

Tam. I hadn't even recognized her voice. Taking a deep breath, I rub the back of my neck. "Yeah. Hey. What's up?"

"Um. Can I, like, come over?"

Damn. "Um. Sure?" *Sure? I said sure?*

"Great. Ethan's driving me home right now, I'll just have him bring me to your house. You can bring me home later, right?"

"Uh, yeah."

"Good," she says. I can actually hear her smiling over the phone. "See you soon."

I toss my phone across the table, pissed that I couldn't tell her not to come. I'm going soft, and I don't like it.

Truth is...I think I want her to come here.

The guilt I feel thinking I'd be letting Honor down is irrational. She's with Ethan. I'm probably not even a second thought in Honor's mind.

Twenty minutes later, Tamlin's at the door. Those tiny spidery things that crawl in my stomach every time I'm with Honor are conspicuously absent. But I'm still kind of happy to see Tam.

"Hey, Storm."

"Hey. Come in."

Pointing to the couch for her to sit, I ask her if she wants a drink.

"K," she says.

"Like what?" I open my fridge and continue talking. "I got cola, water, and yeah, that's it."

Tamlin laughs. "Water's good."

I grab two waters and sit next to her on the couch.

"How's Honor?" The second I say the words, I know I shouldn't have.

"Hey, just a thought, but," she shakes her head, "do you *like* her?"

Inwardly rolling my eyes, I respond, "You just came from seeing her in the hospital, I thought I'd ask."

"Right. But that didn't answer my question. *Do* you like Honor?"

"She's cool," I answer, trying hard to keep my composure and not let on that I'm madly in love with her.

Tamlin's lips twist, like she's biting the inside of her mouth. Then she shrugs. "Yeah. She's doing good. Better."

"Good. Did you eat?" I am so bad at making small talk. "I have chips or something."

"No. I'm good."

Her hand grazes my knee. She bites her bottom lip and runs that hand up my thigh.

Leaning my head back on the couch, I wrap my arm around her and draw her close. She meets my lips with a soft peck, but I part my lips and press more firmly, enjoying the sweet taste of Tamlin's mouth.

As her fingers run through my hair, my mind races with thoughts of taking this further. Her lips leave mine and find a sensitive spot on my neck. My breathing increases and the little hairs on my arms begin to tingle. Fingers aching with the need to touch her. There's a fluttering in my heart that makes it feel like it's popping out of my chest. Her hair smells like shampoo when I breathe in her scent, and that's when I open my eyes and force myself back to reality. I'm with Tamlin. I *want* to be with Honor. Though I may never have that chance, taking advantage of her best friend is just wrong. I am craving to be loved, but if I'm only going to hurt her in the process, I need to stop this now. Before we go any further.

Tamlin's lips slip lower on my neck when I lay my palms on her shoulder and put space between us.

"Tam," I murmur.

"Hmm?" Her eyes are still half-closed, and she moves to kiss me again.

"Tam," I say again, this time more forcefully.

This grabs her attention, because she opens her eyes wide now and sits back, looking embarrassed.

"I just think we should..." I put my hand on her knee, but I can't think of what I wanted to say.

"It's Honor isn't it? I *knew* you liked her."

"No," I lie. "It's not Honor. I just...I'm not sure I feel that way about you yet, and we should probably," I take a deep breath, wanting so badly to continue where we were, "wait."

"You're right. I mean, this was such a random thing anyway. I mean, that kiss this morning was weird, and I don't even know where that came from anyway. I should go," she says. Standing from the couch, she shoves her hands in her pockets and curls her shoulders forward.

"No, Tamlin." I get up to put my hands on her arms. Sliding my hands down her arms, I reach into her pockets and hold her hands. "I like you," I say, trying to get her to look me in the eyes. "I'm trying to be honorable here, I know I don't have much practice," I joke.

Pulling her hands out of her pockets, she moves away from me.

"Can we start over?" I ask. "Be friends, maybe?"

Now fiddling with the hem of her sparkly shirt, she shrugs, all the while keeping her eyes cast downward.

"Listen, Tam," I say, sitting back down on the couch, "I think I've filled my daily quota of playing nice. You want to curse me, go 'head. Ya wanna be my friend, great." Standing back up, because this really is new ground for me, and I'm totally uncomfortable now, I ask, "So, friends? Or you want me to take you home?"

From the corner of her eyes she looks at me. "You're an ass, you know that?" The grin on her face betrays her meek attempt at being angry.

"Yes, actually, I've been told that before."

"Yeah, well...I'm hungry now. Where are those chips?"

Though I know Tamlin's probably not hungry at all, I don't let on. "I can do better than that. How 'bout I take you to the diner to get some real food?"

"Okay," she responds. "I guess you're not *that* much of an ass."

I take her hand, grab my keys, and head to the Jefferson Diner.

Chapter Nine

Tamlin is a good sport and fun to be with. Laughing with her feels good, and though the Honor undertones are absolutely present, we enjoy ourselves at the diner. But anxious fluttering rolls through my stomach when I drop her home. *Will she want to kiss me good-bye? Does she expect me to call her? Will she be hurt when I don't?*

"Ok, well, see you around," she pronounces, before shutting the door and heading up her walk.

"See ya around," I respond to an empty car, relieved that she is so cool.

Ethan, Hunter, and Tom are standing at my door when I pull in my drive. All dressed in either brown or black, they're ready to start phase one of Coming Up With a New Elixir.

"So what's this about?" Ethan scowls, obviously irritated to be in my presence. *The feeling is mutual.*

"It's *about* saving your girlfriend's life, loser."

"Storm," Tom intervenes, "Let's go inside and you can fill us in on what you need us to do."

"Hunter," I address, after unlocking my door.

"Storm."

Like a spring wound too tight, Ethan is about to snap. The enmity between us is rising rapidly, causing the tension in the room to reach the others. If Hunter's foot tapping is any indication, he's worried the impending conversation will escalate to a boxing match between Ethan and me.

To ease the stretching tension, I hand a can of cola to each of them, nodding with what I hope comes across as a smile to Ethan.

"Look, we all agree on one thing," I begin. "We want the Gaffer and his men off Honor's back, right?"

They nod.

"I've come up with a plan." I rub the back of my neck, concerned that hearing my plan out loud may not sound as practical as it does in my head. "We need to replicate the original elixir." I strain not to glance at Ethan. I blame him. He knows that. But looking directly at him right now will cause a shitstorm, and I'm not about to lose focus on what is our priority tonight.

"Ethan has the original jugs in his attic," I continue. "I'd like to fill them with our blood." Pausing for a reaction from them, I'm met with raised eyebrows. "Well, more like all of *your* blood. It's recently come to my attention that I am no longer an empath."

This announcement causes a stir.

"What?" All three respond at once.

"You don't just suddenly become normal," Ethan quips.

"Well, yeah, I did." My tone remains flat.

"Care to explain?" Uncle Tom asks.

"Well, remember when Honor brought me back to life?"

Now met with narrowed eyes, I press on. "I *think* she may have healed the empath right out of me."

Ethan's twisted mouth and wrinkled brow tell me he doesn't believe me. That, and the fact that he says, "I don't believe you. You just don't want to hand over *your* blood."

"Are you high?" I ask him, because truly he must be to think that I wouldn't give my *life* for his girlfriend. "That's not the way I do things, but maybe you think I wouldn't give my blood to save Honor, 'cause that's the way *you* do things."

Ethan meets me chest to chest. "You're a jackass," he leers.

"No. You are. You let Honor lie in that hospital bed, suffering, when you could have saved her. You could have healed her *each* and *every* time, but you chose not to. *That* is why you'll never be more than a loser in my eyes."

Ethan clears his throat and pulls at his collar. "You think I care what *you* think of me?"

"You know what? I don't give a damn. What I care about is Honor, and if it were in my power to heal even a fucking headache that she has, I would. And I can't, for the life of me, understand why you won't."

With the palms of his hands, he shoves me in the chest, but I don't budge. "I knew you had a thing for my girl-friend. You're such an-"

"Then *act* like she's your girlfriend," I interrupt, yelling at him, "and try healing her once in awhile."

"Okay, guys," Uncle Tom intervenes. "Let's talk about the task at hand."

"Right," I say, glaring at Ethan.

"Why *don't* you heal Honor?" Hunter asks.

All heads turn to hear Ethan's response.

His body shifts and his words come out all garbled. "Well...she'd just try to heal me back." Ethan looks down at his shuffling feet. "We'd just keep going around in circles."

"Lame," Hunter quips.

"Forget it, guys," Uncle Tom scolds. "Storm, please finish."

"Yeah." I turn away from the loser and focus on Tom and Hunter. "In order to fill the jugs with our blood, we need equipment. That's where the black clothes come in. There's a blood bank in Parsippany. We need to break in and get some needles and bags and anything else they have so we can take blood."

"Why can't we just steal blood? Why does it have to be ours?" Hunter asks.

"'Cause it needs to be empath blood."

"Why? It's not like they can tell."

"I wouldn't be so sure. This guy's ancient. Plus, remember, he was working with Honor's grandfather. He may not have been a scientist like him, but he must have picked up a thing or two."

"Hmm." Hunter's brain is working overtime thinking about this—he's scratching his head.

"Besides, I'm not quite sure how it works, but if they try out the blood, they may know if it has healing powers or not."

"So..w..wait," Ethan stutters, reluctant to speak. "All someone needs to do to become an empath is inject an empath's blood into them? That seems highly unlikely," he scoffs.

"That's not what I'm saying," my words come out clipped and angry.

"Then what *are* you saying?"

"I'm saying. We don't. Know." I refrain from screaming at him. "But I'm not going to take a chance by handing over just anybody's blood. They'll test it. I'm sure of that."

Uncle Tom nods his head. "Okay then. Let's get a move on. I'll give Elijah a call tomorrow and see if we can't get him to come up and give us some of his blood…also, I have some friends in Pennsylvania who'll help too if we need it."

"Great. Let's go." I command, grabbing my car keys.

"Storm," Tom says. "Let's take Ethan's car."

"What?"

"It's less conspicuous." Tom says.

"Yeah. Sure." Ethan sighs.

The blood bank is surrounded by huge, empty, well-lit parking lots, but fortunately for us, the area behind the blood bank is dark. We turn off the car, and I grab the tool kit I brought to break the locks. In it are some wire cutters to clip the alarm system, if there is one.

"Okay, we need to be quick. If there's an alarm, I can cut the wires, but I'm not sure if it'll alert the cops before I do. So look for anything you think we'll need and get the hell back in the car. Quickly."

Handing everyone a pair of gloves and a big black garbage bag, I nod my head and turn to attempt picking the lock. After about two full minutes, I break through a lock and two deadbolts, putting to use some techniques the Gaffer's men had taught me before I headed to Jersey. To my surprise, no alarm sounds.

Then I think, and say, "There may be a silent alarm that goes right to the police, so just take everything you can."

Scrambling through every drawer and cabinet there is, we sweep everything into our bags and are in and out in sixty seconds flat. Following the directions I found earlier online, Ethan tears down a back road that leads behind the bank opposite the way we came. Luckily there's a path within the trees that outline the road, because in the near distance, we hear sirens. The alarm must have alerted the cops.

"Shut down the lights," I instruct Ethan. "Go slow and follow the path. It'll lead us outta here, I saw it on the satellite map. Just move slowly."

As the sirens fade in the background, we find the road we need. Once we're on Route 10, I relax, fairly certain we've made it undetected.

"Now, get us home and forget this night ever happened," Uncle Tom directs. "Don't utter a word to anyone, and no one will be the wiser."

An hour and a half later, after Ethan and his family drop me off, and all the blood supplies have been sorted, I'm confident we have what we need to make this work. My head throbs. The stress has definitely wreaked havoc on my mind. But for Honor, it's all good.

The thought of keeping her safe is the last thing that enters my mind before nodding off on the couch.

Chapter Ten

Though Ethan and Tamlin return to school after missing the last two days to be with Honor, I take another day off. It's Friday anyway, and it's not like I haven't graduated high school already. Plus, I really need to see Honor without my loser brother busting in.

A gleam of burnished gold shines over her pale blond hair, causing an ethereal image that sends bursts of heat throughout my chest and limbs. She is beautiful.

When I finally get strength back in my knees and air back in my lungs, I tap on her hospital room door frame. "Hey, princess."

She looks up, and her face is flush from the warm morning sun. "Storm," she marvels, as if my visiting her is unheard of. "What are you doing here?"

I sit at the edge of the bed, facing Honor. "I wanted to catch you before you went home."

Her smile lights up my heart. "You could visit me at home you know."

"Yeah, but then I'd have to contend with my precious little brother." I smirk.

Honor shrugs, but her smile disappears.

"I'm sorry," I say, shifting on the bed, because suddenly I'm uncomfortable. "I guess you don't like my berating him all the time. Understandable."

She tilts her chin into her shoulder. "It's okay. I know he's not your favorite person."

"No. Not at all. But I shouldn't bring you into our problems."

Honor straightens her back and sits forward on her chair. "So...Tamlin said you kissed her?"

I knock the side of my fist to my mouth while I compose my thoughts. "Uh, I did." *So not what I wanted to say.*

"You like her?" she asks, sounding disappointed.

"Well she's nice and all..." What am I going to say? Tamlin's her best friend. I can't be cruel and say "no, but I'm a guy, and I need the touch of a girl, now that I can finally get close to one without her dying."

"Why'd you kiss her?" Honor's frowning, and I'm thinking I know why. I'm *hoping* I know why.

"You're jealous." I smirk, trying to hide my grin but failing big-time. Honor's jealous.

"What?" Honor asks, sitting back into her chair and shaking her head. "Jealous?" She crosses her arms in front of her chest. "I am *not* jealous," she insists, turning her head away from me.

"Mmm," I mutter, enjoying immensely, watching her squirm.

"I'm not," she asserts again, but the corners of her mouth quiver. She's trying not to blush.

"I believe you," I lie, unable though to remove the smile from my face.

Honor sighs.

"Hey, princess."

She looks up at me.

"There's nothing to be jealous of."

I watch the corner of her mouth curl.

"Can I ask you something?" she asks quietly. "How? I mean, I thought you can't, like, touch anybody for too long."

Crossing and uncrossing my legs, I settle on standing and leaning against the wall, my arms shoved deep in my pockets. "That's just it. I'm not sure, but I think when you brought me back to life, you healed me."

Honor opens her mouth to speak, but instead, she says nothing and leaves her pretty mouth dropped in awe.

"I also think you cured me of being an empath. I feel nothing anymore, and for that," I bow to Her Highness, "I thank you."

"Really?" she smiles.

"Really."

"Like," she tugs on her bottom lip with her teeth, "is it just with Tamlin or like...everybody?"

"Um, you volunteering to test it out?" I raise my eyebrows, really hoping that is exactly what she's suggesting.

She denies it with the click of her tongue and the shake of her head.

I take a step toward her.

"I'm not volunteering...uh...is your hair darker?"

Another step closer, and my eyes are only focused on her mouth as she curls her bottom lip inside it. "Probably...'cause I'm not an empath anymore, there's nothing to drain me of my color." Taking another step forward, I think, *wow, that explains my sudden tan.* "Hey, you're changing the subject."

Honor rolls her violet eyes. I'm now close enough to touch her.

I do.

Picking her hands up off her lap, I lift her from her seat. Her soft hands inside mine tease me. While she unknowingly seduces me with the tender touch of her hands, I move to slide my right hand up her arm.

"Am I hurting you?" I ask, staring directly into her eyes.

She takes a swallow and moves her head back and forth.

My eyes linger on hers for a few very intense moments before both my hands are cupped just behind her ears.

"Anything?" I purr, unable to speak in my normal voice, due to my breathlessness.

Her breathing picks up and she shakes her head, almost imperceptibly.

I move my gaze to her parted lips, tempted to taste her. When her tongue darts out to skim the edges of her two front teeth, I lose all restraint. With a gentle tug of her head, and a trepid hand, I crash my lips to hers. Tiny tremors race through my veins when our tongues meet. Her hands wrap snugly around my waist, and I tangle her silken hair in my hands. A guttural groan escapes me, and I want to pull her inside of me. I want her to become part of me. I want to become part of her.

Her tongue, still dancing with mine, assures me I am not hurting her. Not draining her of life. I know now with complete certainty that I am not the murdering empath I once was. Honor has cured me of that. For the first time in my life, I can love someone physically...and possibly be loved in return.

Is it too much to ask that it be Honor?

Chapter Eleven

In a mutual burst of verity, Honor and I separate.

"Oh my god," she breathes, plopping back down in her chair.

"I didn't hurt you did I?" I ask, wondering, even though I know it was the reality of kissing her boyfriend's brother that has her flustered.

She drops her face into her hands. "No. You didn't hurt me," she says, her words muffled by her hand-covered mouth.

Sitting on the edge of her bed, I touch my hand to her arm. "I'm sorry. I shouldn't have done that."

Honor doesn't move.

I stand from the bed and glide my hand down the length of her golden hair. "I won't do that again. You have my word." I kiss the back of her bowed head and walk away, sensing she needs to be alone.

In the empty elevator down the hall, I bang the back of my head against the wall and curse myself. Now I've risked her friendship. For what? A minute in her arms? Sixty seconds kissing the sweetest girl in the whole world? Though it was the best sixty seconds of my twenty-two years, it was not worth ruining our friendship and possibly never speaking to her again.

Though the elevator door opens on the lobby level, I press the button back up to Honor's floor. Walking away now, I fear, will only sever the friendship further. It must be resolved before this gets worse. My breath hitches and my stomach clenches, but plodding forward anyway, I reach Honor's room in slow motion.

Her back is to me when I get there. She's staring out the window. The way the blond hair floats down her back and reaches her ass causes a falter in my step. Grabbing the door jamb helps me compose myself before walking in.

"Honor," I start, clearing my throat before continuing.

She takes hold of the chair's back when she stumbles turning around. "St...Storm," my name gets caught in her throat. Her cheeks are wet.

Each step I take feels like ten pound weights are bound to my ankles. "I...I'm sorry. I had to come back."

Instinctively, my hand reaches for hers, but I drop my arm awkwardly, avoiding the touch of her skin. Tears slip into her mouth when she smiles, and her tongue darts out to lick them.

"I *am* sorry I kissed you, princess. I shouldn't have put you in that position. Please. Please still be my friend. Please." I shake my head and catch my breath. "You're the reason I get up in the morning. The reason I stay here in Jefferson. I know you love my brother. I swear, I will not let my feelings get in the way of our friendship. I just. I can't. I cannot. I need you. To be my friend. Please."

"Really?" she asks, licking her lips again and wiping her cheek with her sleeve.

"Really what?" I wonder. *She doesn't think we can be friends now?*

"You really feel...that way?" she questions quietly.

"That I want you to be my friend? Of course I do."

While she bites her lip, her hand cups her stomach. "No. I mean...about...you staying here...in Jefferson."

As if my heart weren't strained enough, just thinking about repeating my declaration makes it feel as if it were going to explode. "Um," I nod. "Yes. You. Are. The reason. I'm here." Though a smile creeps up my face, there's no happiness behind it, only irony—declaring my love to someone unable to accept it.

Honor's hand moves from her stomach to her mouth, where she slowly starts tugging on her bottom lip with her fingers. "I had no idea." Her words come out so slowly and so softly that I have to ask her to repeat it.

"I had no...idea...that you felt that way," she says, still just above a whisper.

"Yeah. Well. I do." My neck cracks when I stretch it sideways and backwards. "But please. Don't worry. I won't kiss you again." I smile despite the breaking of my heart. I silently curse myself for having fallen in love in the first place.

Honor uses her sleeve again to wipe her tears. "I'm sorry. It's all just so...complicated."

"I know that." Taking a breath before each thought helps to drive away my own imminent tears. "That's why I'm sorry." Inhaling her scent, while trying to calm myself, exacerbates the pain in my chest. "I should have known better."

She smiles. "Me too." Reaching for my hand, she's surprised when I stick it in my pocket. "Storm," she says, tilting her head. "Forget about this. Let's move past it."

My brain is saying, *"Sure, let's move on,"* but I can't form the words, so I nod.

Honor glances down at the floor then out the window, and it seems she's uncomfortable, so I switch the subject.

"So what's with your boyfriend? Why doesn't he just heal you so you won't have this heart problem anymore?" Probably not the best subject to divert the tension, but it's been on my mind.

Her big violet eyes grow bigger. "Storm. Stop. I don't want him to heal me. Why should he?" She sits back on her chair and bites the inside of her mouth.

I move back onto her hospital bed and adjust the settings, propping myself against her pillow. Clasping my hands behind my head, I cross my legs at the ankles—looking cooler than I feel.

"I just think if he loves you the way he says, he'd wanna take your pain away." My smirk is smug, but my heart is heavy, wishing I could be the one to take away her pain.

"He loves me," she snaps. "I just...I told him I don't want him to heal me. I'd just heal him back, and then we'd just...never stop. It's crazy."

I drop my hands from behind my head and sit forward. "It's *crazy* that he doesn't try. What if he could heal the empath right out of you? Then you could be done with this bullshit for good."

She returns her gaze to the window, avoiding looking at me and facing the truth about her loser ass boyfriend.

"You know I'm right, princess. He should be at least trying."

"No."

Watching her shake her head in denial is more frustrating than I thought. No longer can I remain nonchalant on the bed. I hop off and pull her up out of her chair. "He has to try, Honor. You're dying. Your heart can't take much more. He has to," I demand, feeling like a crazed lunatic, my voice is so loud.

"No. He doesn't. He...he doesn't like to do that. He...he's learned to shut out...others. You know...because of his parents dying so young."

"His parents? That's bullshit."

"Storm. Really. He's healed the little things...like when I'm sad and stuff. He just..."

"He what? Oh c'mon, Honor. He makes you not sad anymore?" I mock, disgusted by my little brother's behavior.

"He's just scared about being vulnerable. I...he's closed his heart, his feelings...to people."

"Then why you with him?"

"What? He loves me. "

"Yeah. How can he love you if he's closed his heart? You're not making any sense, Honor." My teeth are clenched, and my body is tense. It is maddening to hear her talk about him like this. She doesn't see how selfish he is.

"Look, Storm. I don't *want* Ethan to heal me. He *knows* that. And as for healing the empath right out of me, I'm staying the way I am. Even if I have to die young." Her voice catches when she says this, so I know she doesn't really mean it.

"Checkmate? Fine."

Honor only nods, and I see her eyes grow wide. She's trying to prevent tears from escaping.

"You got a ride home?" I ask.

"Yeah."

I blow her a kiss. "See ya around, princess." With a heavy heart weighing me down, I walk out of her room...barely aware of who I am anymore. Once collected and cocksure, at least on the outside, I can no longer hide my emotions. I cannot even fool myself anymore.

"Storm?"

Her voice halts my steps. I turn and see her standing in her hospital room doorway.

"I don't love your brother." Her fingertips fly to her lips. "Before, you said, 'I know you love my brother.' I don't." She nods and quickly disappears into her room.

I leave the hospital a much more satisfied man.

Chapter Twelve

At home in my apartment, I practice taking blood from myself using the paraphernalia we swiped from the blood bank. Aside from making a bloody mess on my kitchen table, by the seventh or eighth time, I finally find success. Cleaning up everything takes some time, but I put the stuff in a box and set it aside for later.

My intention now is to research how to at least *fake* a base for this friggin' elixir. It's ridiculous how many sites offer recipes for immortal potions. If they really worked, wouldn't they be selling the stuff for a mint instead of posting to the world the entire ingredient list? Plus, not one recipe I find has the same list. I jot down a few ingredients that look easy enough to pick up locally and then set out to find them.

An organic whole food market in Butler may have most of the raw ingredients, but I may have to find a Chinese store for the others. Hopefully the guy in Butler will know where to send me.

My cell rings on the way down to the store.

"Yeah?" I don't recognize the number.

"Storm. It's Tom."

"Hey. What's up?"

"I'm not sure if you spoke with Ethan today, but Elijah's taking the red-eye up from Florida tonight."

He pauses, probably waiting for my reaction. "Oh. Good."

"So what's the plan?" Tom asks.

"I need their blood as soon as possible. I have no idea when someone's gonna pay me a visit again, so I want to have something to give them."

"Right. Did we get everything you need to take the blood? Do you even know how?"

"I've been practicing on myself, but yeah, I should be able to do it. I just wish there were more empaths around."

"Why can't you use just anyone's blood along with it? How will they know?"

I hope Tom isn't as stupid as his nephews are. "Tom, they're smart. I'm sure they'll test it. That's why I'm even going so far as to add some organic herbs as a base. This way, maybe they won't figure it out for years...when they realize those they gave it to are not actually immortal."

Tom laughs. "I hope it works."

"Yeah. Me too. I figure they're not really gonna know for sure if it'll make them immortal for at least twenty years or so...I hope. I don't know, Tom." I sigh. "I'm grasping at straws here."

"Well, it's better than nothing, kid."

"Yeah."

"We'll all be over in the morning. You stay calm, 'kay?"

"Mmm. Catch ya later."

The dude at the health food store knows his shit, I'll tell ya that. He has the wild reishi I need, the chaga mushroom, and the Chinese coriander. The only items I need to get are the *ho shou wu*, the deer antler tincture, and the turkey tail, which he said I could get at the Chinese produce market down the highway.

By the time I'm finished picking up the rest of the items and get home, Tamlin's sitting on my front step.

"Hey, Tam. What's up? Everything okay?" I ask, getting the bags out of my car.

"Yeah." She jumps up to help with the bags and follows me upstairs.

"Then what's going on?" The grumbling in my stomach hits as soon as my brain registers why she's here.

"Ethan went straight to Honor's, so I thought I'd come here."

Crap. "Oh."

"So whatchya got there?" Tamlin watches me place my funky purchases on the table.

"Um..." I know I don't want Honor finding out that Gaffer's after us still, but it's doubtful that Tamlin will tell her. She loves her as much as I do. "It's stuff."

"Stuff."

Pulling out a seat for her to sit, I do the same for myself. "Listen, Tam. You cannot say a word to Honor about this."

She makes an *X* across her heart and holds up the two fingers on her right hand.

"There are men after her grandfather's elixir."

"That's old news, isn't it?"

"Yeah, but they're looking for it. They want me to hand it over."

"When?"

"I have no idea...but soon. If they don't get it, they're going after Honor herself."

"Then hand it over," she says, looking at me like I'm crazy for not thinking of that myself.

"I can't. Ethan dumped it."

"*He what!?*" Tamlin's dropped jaw and raised brows mimic my feelings about the whole thing.

"Stupid. Right?" Leaning back on my chair, I open the refrigerator and grab a can of soda. I slide it across the table to Tamlin and reach back to get myself one.

"What was he thinking?" She pops the lid and takes a sip.

"I really don't know. I think he was trying to do what Honor wanted."

"Honor wanted to dump it?" Tamlin shakes her head.

"Yeah." I sigh. "She didn't want it to get into the wrong hands." I ponder this a moment. *Was* he just trying to do right by Honor? "Anyway, it's gone, and I'm trying to concoct a new elixir."

Tamlin's hand flies to her chest. "You know how to make an immortal elixir?"

"I think all that dye and bleach on your head has seeped into your brain. No. I do not know how to make an immortal elixir. I'm faking it...to fool them."

It's cute how her head jerks back in laughter. "Oh," she continues cracking up, "I was gonna say..."

"Anyway...I need to make it at least *seem* real. I'm sure they'll test it." Squeezing the bridge of my nose, I realize how tense I am. The thought that I may not pull this off leaves me on edge. There's not much time to do this, yet for me, time moves backwards—like in a dream when you're trying to run but you can't get your legs to move.

"Storm." Tamlin nudges my elbow, and I drop my hand to the table. "You look worried. You think it's not gonna work?"

We stare into each other's eyes, and she reads the truth—no, I do not think this will work. But Honor's life depends on it, so I *need* to make it work.

Tamlin pushes away from the table and slowly approaches me. Standing behind me, her hands feel cool on my neck. Her firm touch begins to ease the tightness there. In slow circular movements, her thumbs press the knots I wasn't aware I had. I take a breath and inhale. It feels so good. As she continues massaging my neck and shoulders, I drop my head forward, encouraging her to continue. A guttural groan escapes my throat, and I realize I'm enjoying Tamlin's touch. Again.

Her hands slip underneath the front collar of my shirt, and her fingertips play with the hair on my chest. I caress the back of her hand and stand up. Still touching her hand, I turn to face her and lift my other hand to her face. Her lips taste like cherries, and at the same time she kisses me, her hands fall to the hem of my shirt. She lifts it over my head then continues running her hands over my chest.

She tastes so good, I don't want to stop. As her hands slide to my back, warm tingles flutter over my skin. Though I'm afraid to lead her on, I press my body closer to hers. Her hips grind into mine, and I'm unsure if she's sending out signals to do what I think she wants to do. Her shirt slides off easily. After tossing it on the floor, I wrap my arms around her back and push her gently toward the couch, not breaking lip contact as I do so.

Tamlin falls to the couch and scooches herself against the arm. She lifts her legs, wraps them around my waist and pulls me down on top of her. My hips dance on top of hers, but when I move my lips to kiss her neck, I get a glimpse of the joy I see on her face. Despite the fact that her eyes are closed, ecstasy shows in her cheeks. With an abrupt stop, I get up and sit on the other end of the couch. She opens her eyes and licks her lips.

"What is it?" she asks, understandably confused.

"We're going too fast. I think we need to slow it down a bit," I lie.

"Storm." She sits up and moves next to me, placing her hand on my knee. "You're twenty-two years old. Surely you've done this before."

I snap my head towards her. "Of course I have," I lie again. "I just don't think it's a good idea. With us. Not yet."

I see disappointment sweep across her face.

"I'm not saying *ever*." I do like Tamlin. I'm just not sure how much. "Just...right now. Let me sort all this stuff out first, then maybe?"

"You mean...get over Honor? Then I'll have a chance?"

A huge sigh escapes from my throat this time. "Something like that."

She nudges me with her elbow. "Okay, but just don't take too long. I won't wait forever."

I look at her, smile, and drape my arm around her, pulling her into me. "Why are you so cool? There aren't many girls like you around." And I mean it this time. Tamlin is cool. Maybe if I could get over Honor, she and I *would* have a chance.

Chapter Thirteen

After a restless night's sleep, I drag myself to the kitchen to put on a pot of coffee. Even the lazy energy of a Saturday morning is lost on me. I can't enjoy it, knowing what's ahead today. Concocting some freakin' elixir. *With Ethan's blood*. It just doesn't sit well in my gut. I want nothing to do with the guy, yet I *need* him. I need him to help *his* girlfriend, whom *I* love. Sometimes I want to throw up my hands to this whole thing, grab Honor, and take off. But she would never go for that. She'd never leave her parents. And even though she told me she doesn't love Ethan, she'd probably never leave him either.

As I sip my coffee, I contemplate running over to Honor's and declaring my love for her. Of course, my flippin' brother lives with her now. Like he *needs* to be there. He thinks he's protecting her? No. Sleeping in Honor's guest room is not protecting. Coming up with a solution to this messed up elixir issue is protecting her. She wouldn't even need protecting if he didn't *dump* the original.

Coffee splatters everywhere when I slam it down on the table. Sitting here feeling sorry for myself is getting me nowhere. After wiping the coffee mess off the table, I gather the stuff I bought yesterday and lay it all out in front of me.

The pot I use for boiling my ramen noodles is the biggest pot I own, so I pour the spring water I got from the running stream on Berkshire Valley into it. One by one, I add all the ingredients, leaving the deer antler tincture and turkey tail for last, like the website instructed. The elixir base smells horrid, but I can only imagine the stench once I add the blood. Yuck.

At that thought, the doorbell rings. It's Hunter and his Uncle Tom and a face I haven't seen in years. Though Elijah is looking more and more like the fifteen-year-old man he's become, his face still resembles the five-year-old boy I remember. That...and he's the spitting image of my father.

"Storm," Tom starts, "this is Eli. I'm not sure if you remember him."

Without taking my eyes from his face, I nod. "Yes. I do," I say softly. I'm embarrassed by the way my father's face haunts me. He loved these boys. *Left me for them.* The blood is pooling in my wrists. It must be, because my hands are clenching so tightly that I'm sure no blood is reaching them. My teeth start to ache from grinding them. Elijah had nothing to do with my father's betrayal, yet the anger inside me races through my veins faster than a tornado races through flat land.

Forcing myself to close my eyes and get my father's image out of my head, I turn away and walk back to the kitchen.

A huge hand rests on my shoulder. "What was that?" Tom asks.

"Nothing."

"*That* was nothing?" He squeezes my shoulder and pulls out two chairs. "Sit," he demands. "He's a ringer for your dad, isn't he?"

With a reluctant nod, I sit but say nothing.

"Don't blame the kid, he barely remembers your father."

Unfortunately...I do. But I still don't say a word.

"Your dad loved you, y'know. He just...he didn't love your mom anymore. That's all."

"That's messed up," I finally respond. "He left me for *her*..." I toss my head in the direction of the living room. "And *them*."

"No. He left your mother for their mother. You *chose* to see it the other way."

Tom covers my forearm with his hand. It's funny, but I can actually feel him taking the hurt away. It's a strange sensation. Aside from Honor bringing me back from the dead, no one's ever done that for me before. No one's ever been able to *touch* me.

"Don't take your hate out on your brothers. They *are* your brothers, whether you think of them that way or not."

He gets up and pours himself a cup of coffee. "And this thing with Ethan...drop it...he may have Honor now, but I see the way she looks at you. Step back. Give it some time. I'm pretty sure you're the one she wants."

Tom sits back down, sips his coffee, and peers at me from over his mug. When he slaps the near empty mug down on the table, he has a lopsided grin pasted on his face. "Give the boy a break though. Don't tell him. Let him figure it out himself."

I go get my own coffee, and with my back to Tom, I can't help but smile. I hope to God he's right.

**

Sticking needles in my brothers' arms is satisfying, to say the least. Though sticking Ethan's arm would feel even better...if he were here.

"Where's Ethan?" I ask, his name tasting like vinegar on my tongue.

The boys shrug.

"He knew he was supposed to be here at noon," Uncle Tom says.

Yeah. If I got to wake up in the next room from Honor every day, I wouldn't be able to leave either. It pisses me off.

"Well, the loser better get here soon," I demand...to nobody. "I need to get started on combining all this."

"We can't start without him?" Eli asks.

"I guess. I just...I really need strong empath blood, and well, the loser's is unfortunately the strongest," I say reluctantly, "we have right now."

"Why? What makes *him* so strong?" Eli asks, quite defensively.

After an involuntary snort, I respond. "Your loser brother actually killed two people recently."

"What?"

Uncle Tom jumps in. "Two of Gaffer's men were after them. One of 'em killed Storm. Ethan shot them both."

Eli's eyebrows are now about an inch higher on his forehead. "Ah, now I see why you call him loser—you're jealous. Gotcha."

The knife on the table is the closest thing to me, so I grab it. Instinctively raising it to my shoulder, I point it at Eli and plunge it right into the table. I walk out of the kitchen and straight out my door, leaving the knife standing upright on the table.

"Great," I mutter to myself, throwing up my hands in a huff. Ethan's here...with the empty elixir jugs. Not interested in talking to him right now, I duck out through the side of the house. If I let my temper get the best of me, I'd be failing Honor. I lean against the side of the house and slide down until I'm sitting on my ass, my knees at my chest.

How did I get here? My curiosity about the legendary Honor Robinson and my distaste and distrust for the son of the bastard who broke up my family got the best of me. I should have never stepped foot in Jefferson Township. And now I can't leave. Not until I see this thing through—save Honor, then get the hell out.

Hopefully taking Honor with me.

Chapter Fourteen

Fifteen minutes later, back in my apartment, my *family*, for lack of a better word, is making themselves at home. Hunter's eating my leftover pizza, Eli's downing one of my cans of soda, and even Tom is flicking channels from my leather recliner. The only one looking uneasy is Ethan. And somehow this softens my heart toward him. I *hate* myself for it.

When I see Ethan looking at me, I direct him, with my eyes only, to follow me to the kitchen. I'm still not ready to talk to anyone. Since all the blood bags and needles are on the table, Ethan doesn't need an explanation. He sits and holds out his arm. I sit across from him and bring the needle to his vein. So I don't have to look at him, I watch his blood ooze through the tube. Slow and thick. My stomach tenses, hating the fact that *his* blood is what will save Honor's life. *His* blood will allow the elixir to pass for the real thing.

When I've got the pint from him, I pull out the needle, press a cotton ball to the inside of his elbow, and signal that we're done. The rest I can do by myself. Tom and the boys are clearly confused when I stand at the open front door.

"I guess we're done?" Tom asks.

I nod.

After they leave, I grab a cola and begin combining their still warm blood with the base I made earlier. My stomach isn't as strong as I suspected, because cutting open the bags of blood and pouring them into the pot is making me nauseous. I carry the pot back to the stove and figure the ingredients will combine better if I cook them—the thought making me dry heave. Turning the flame on low and standing an arm's length away, I stir the blood. And gag. As it warms over the fire, my eyes tear, the stench is so bad. Honor. I'm doing this for Honor. She is the only reason I'm playing with my half-brothers' blood. The only reason I'm brewing up an elixir-like pot of dark red, foul-smelling human blood.

I run to the toilet and vomit. Heaving over the bowl, my thoughts are still on Honor. They have to be. The Gaffer's men are dangerous. I've no idea what they'll do, but if they aren't given the elixir soon, I don't think it'll be me they'll go after. Honor will be their target. I cannot let that happen.

Since it seems my stomach has nothing left to come up, I wash up, brush my teeth, and get back to my brew. I turn off the stove and leave the apartment, needing fresh air.

The next step is to funnel the blood into the containers. Surprisingly, Ethan didn't really wash the jugs like I'd thought. When he said he'd rinsed them, it looks like he merely ran a little water through them. A thick coating of fog and dust still remain on the outside, keeping the vintage look I'll need to pass this off.

Hopefully, the Gaffer is not as scientifically gifted as Honor's great-grandfather. Lord, help us if he figures this out.

Chapter Fifteen

She's here. In the cafeteria. I don't know how I missed her in the halls this morning, but when I walk into the cafeteria for lunch, she's sitting at her table. She couldn't even give herself time off to recuperate?

My stomach flips a little when I approach her. "Honor?"

She turns around. "Oh. Hi." Her eyes drop down, avoiding mine.

"What are you doing here?" I straddle the seat beside her. "Aren't you supposed to be resting?"

Honor turns back to the table and fiddles with her food. "I guess," she mumbles.

My hand instinctively goes to her thigh. "Honor. Your heart is weak. You should be home in bed."

This stirs a chuckle from her, causing her to finally look at me. "I'm seventeen, Storm, not some old decrepit lady."

The corners of my mouth tug, even though I'm serious about her resting. My heart swells at the sight of her, but I keep from smiling. Moving my hand to her forearm, I tell her, "I know you're young, princess, but your heart is not. It has to have aged quite a bit after saving your mother and me. And then Shelby and the girl in the bathroom and whoever else you've been trying to help."

A tiny grunt escapes her throat. "Stop. I'm fine." She turns her head and looks away, but doesn't pull her arm from my light grasp.

"I just worry about you," I whisper, averting her eyes as well. There's a makeshift Band-Aid on the inside of her elbow. I see a bruise forming around it. "What's this?"

Honor looks at her arm and shrugs. "Oh, Mr. Moore had us testing blood-types today."

"From your elbow? That's illegal. He's not a nurse or something. What the..." I stop myself from swearing, though it's hard. "He can't do that, Honor. He did this to everyone?"

"Well, no. We all pricked our own fingers, but he wasn't getting a reading on mine. He said we probably needed to take it from another spot."

"So he pricked your arm?"

"Well, no, not exactly," she says, pulling her arm away now. When I look up, I see why. Ethan is walking toward the table. He just nods, and so do I.

Turning my attention back toward Honor, I ask, "Not exactly...meaning what?"

"He used one of those needle things with the vial thingy."

My chest starts to burn. My temper is rising. "Vial thingy, Honor? You're smarter than that. A teacher is not *allowed* to do that."

"What's going on, Honor?" Ethan asks.

She shakes her head. "Nothing. Just...we took blood-type samples in chemistry today."

Ethan looks to me for explanation.

"Moore took Honor's with a needle and vial, not just a finger prick like everyone else got."

"What!?" Ethan's floored.

"He couldn't get a reading on mine," Honor explains. "He said he probably needed to get a little more."

"A little more?" I say again, extremely angered this time. "Honor, come on. Did you bump your head in that bathroom, because it certainly seems like you must have."

"Hey. That was uncalled for," Ethan scowls.

Honor sits up straight. "Oh thank God," she says to Tamlin, who sits next to Ethan, across from us. "Tell them we were just doing blood types in chem—nothing sinister." Honor forces a giggle.

"Did Moore take a vial of blood from you, Tam?" I ask.

She shakes her head. "No. I did find that odd though. Why would he need three vials just to get her blood type?"

"Three!?" Ethan and I both gasp. We look at each other, suspicion as evident in his eyes as it is in mine.

The lunch trays bounce when I slam my hands on the table and stand, racing out the door to find Moore.

Chapter Sixteen

"Who the hell *are* you?"

My question is met with wide eyes and a dropped jaw, but quickly he presses his lips tight, narrows his gaze, and stands from his desk.

"Mr. Sutherland. Now what?" Moore composes himself and crosses his arms in front of his chest.

Restraining from decking him before he explains, I stand rigid about a foot from him. "I want to know who you are and why you need three vials of Honor's blood."

He loosens his stance and sits back down in his chair, picking up a pen and turning from me. "Mr. Sutherland, we're done. Please leave."

His hand starts moving along his paper, but it's shaking as he writes. I've hit a nerve.

Moving to stand in front of him, I place my hands, palms flat, on his desk, lowering myself to look him in the eye.

"Who *are* you? And what do you need with Honor's blood? What do you know? What do you want?"

He places his pen down and meets me eye to eye. "Mr. Sutherland, do yourself a favor and get your own girlfriend. Honor belongs to your brother...no?"

This distracts me momentarily. I shake it off. "What does that have to do with my question?"

"Jealousy. Resentment. It'll eat away at you. Make you do things you wouldn't normally do." He peers deep into my eyes. "Leave it alone now, Storm. Before it's too late."

He picks up his pen and goes back to his work. "We're done," he says, keeping his focus on his work.

Pounding my fist on his desk, I attempt intimidation. He merely raises his eyes at me, not his head. "What are you talking about?" I ask, suddenly mentally exhausted.

"Brothers, Storm. I'm talking about brothers. Back away from your brother's girl before it turns you into a monster who only wants revenge."

I shake my head. "You're crazy, you know that? You think I'm worried about Ethan? If you haven't noticed, we're pretty much indifferent toward each other." I lie.

"We're done, Mr. Sutherland."

Pushing his desk right into him gets his attention. He stands. "That's enough. Leave or I'll call the principal and get you suspended."

"Go 'head. I don't care if I get suspended. Besides, I'll just tell them you took three vials of one of your student's blood."

His face shows little sign of being affected by my threat. "That's right. Of course you don't care if you're suspended. You've already done this high school scene." He shakes his head. "So let me ask *you*. Why are *you* here, and what do *you* want with Honor...besides that sexy body of hers?" He smirks, making the hairs on the back of my neck stand up. "That's right, Mr. Sutherland. We *both* have secrets, don't we? If you don't want the school finding out who and what you are, and what your precious Honor is...you'll back away from me. You come to class, keep your mouth shut, you leave class. Got it?"

I feel my shoulders drop but hope he doesn't notice. He knows. He knows we're empaths. And that's why he wants Honor's blood. Who *is* he?

My eyes stay on his, and I want so much to shake information out of him. But I won't. Who knows how serious he is about outing us? Until I have something substantial to hold against him, I need to keep my mouth shut.

Dropping my gaze first, I turn and walk out. But I'm not done with him. I *will* find out who he is. And I *will* find out why he's here.

Chapter Seventeen

The doorbell rings, and my hands are covered in blood. Pouring blood into a two-inch wide mouth, even with a funnel, is messy. The blood plops. It doesn't pour. And since it's thick, it doesn't flow consistently, overfilling the funnel and spilling over my hands every time.

When the doorbell rings a second time, my soapy hands are under the hot water. Mentally, I wish the person to go away, but since my car is parked out front, they probably realize I'm home. I'm just about done scrubbing all the blood off when it rings again.

Damn it. "I'm coming," I yell, not too pleasantly, silently hoping it's not someone looking for the elixir.

"What!?" I say abruptly, opening the door and stilling. My chest tightens. My breath hitches.

"Hi, Storm."

Standing outside my door, Honor's smile is as bright as the sun shining behind her. "Hey. Uh. Yeah. What's up?" Her presence at my home has me stumbling over my words.

"I just..." She averts her eyes again, looking as nervous as I am.

"Sorry, Honor. Come in."

"Is my bike okay here?" She points to her boardwalk-style bike leaning against my house.

"Uh, yeah. It should be, but what are you doing riding a bike? Honor, I keep telling you...you need to rest."

She smiles again, and my heart does another flip. "It's only like a mile. No biggie."

"Yeah. No biggie." I sigh. "Come." Holding the door for her to walk in, I close the door behind me—nervous as all hell that I have her alone in my apartment.

"Soda or water?" I ask, pointing to the couch for her to sit.

"Oh, water's good. Thanks."

When I go in for her water, I slip the jugs under the sink and quickly wipe the counter to get rid of the spilled blood.

Gulping the rest of my cola, I attempt to gather my composure—something I'm not used to losing.

"So, princess," I swallow, walking toward the sweet-smelling angel sitting on my couch. "What brings you here today?" Trying hard to hide my sudden uneasiness with being alone with Honor, I hand her the water, sit, throw my elbow onto the top of the couch, and turn my body to face her.

"I, uh," she hesitates.

"Oh. I wanted to ask you," I interrupt, kicking myself afterward. "Uh, no, never mind. I'm sorry. You first."

"No. No, that's okay. What?"

"About this afternoon. First, I'm sorry I took off like that, but Moore really pissed me off."

"Yeah, why?" She crumples her face, obviously not seeing in Moore what I see. Which is odd. Honor's an empath. She should be able to read him well.

"Honor. He's..." I stop. My intent has always been to keep her from worrying. I can't now tell her what I think I know about Moore. "Why did you let him take your blood like that?"

She tilts her head and shrugs. "I don't know. I didn't see anything wrong with it."

"Really?" I'm amazed. Honor is intelligent. She's earnest and resolute. To take in Moore like the rest of the flighty girls in this town is so unlike her.

"Really. He's a good guy. I don't understand what you and Ethan have against him."

"You don't *feel* anything from him? What are his emotions, Honor? Do you sense something good about him? I'm curious."

As she is now facing me, sitting in mirror position to me, she leans her elbow on her thigh and tucks her curled hand under her chin. "I don't know. I guess I feel curiosity coming from him. I sense *something*, but I'm not sure what. No pain or anything like that. No sadness. Just. I don't know. I trust him."

I nod and gnaw at my inner cheek. "You trust him?" Shaking my head, I let out a "hmmm," then utter, "I don't get it, but...be careful, princess. I *don't* trust him. I know I don't have my powers," I use my fingers to make air quotes around the word power, "anymore, but I still have my intuition. Don't get too close to him, 'kay?"

"'kay." She smiles. "By the way, are you, like, going to a tanning salon or something? You're, like, so tan. And your hair...it's the color of honey. You were, like, bleach blond. Did you dye it?"

"Nope, and nope. I think it's 'cause I'm not an empath anymore."

"What?" She chuckles.

"Yeah. Feeling everyone else's emotions is draining. Maybe it drains all your color too. Who knows? I mean, look at how pale you are. You're almost ghost white." I laugh, making sure she knows I'm just teasing her, despite the fact that she really is void of any color.

"Ha, ha," she retorts, but laughs along with me.

"So, why'd you ride your bike all the way here? I'm sure it wasn't just for a pleasant visit. Ethan wouldn't allow that."

"Well, Ethan doesn't know." She darts her eyes to the floor. "He went straight to his apartment after school."

I raise my eyebrows, wondering conspicuously why she's here. "Oh?"

The lower part of me stirs when her breath hitches and she turns to me with half-lidded eyes. I inhale—taking in the sight and smell of her. Quickly she shakes her head back to reality.

"Um." With the tip of her tongue, she darts it over her bottom lip—an act I realize is unintentional on her part. "Some man gave this to me to give to you." She holds out a small envelope with "Storm" written in block letters across the front.

"Some man?" I take the envelope from her. "Why didn't he just give it to me?"

"That's what I asked him. He said he needed the letter to come from me. That you'd understand."

The blood must be draining from my face, because I'm suddenly lightheaded. With a trembling hand, I slide my thumb under the sealed flap. For a moment, staring at the open envelope is all I can do.

"Storm," Honor nudges. "You're white as a ghost now. What is it?"

Still unable to pull the letter from the envelope, I keep my gaze on it while I whisper, "What did the man look like?"

"Older. But nice looking. He had like light greyish hair, but nice. Almost blond. He was all dressed in a suit and, like, he had a driver and everything. I don't know. He *was* kinda creepy too. I remember that. Not just 'cause he was intimidating, but what I felt when he handed me the letter." She shakes her head and crunches her face in disgust.

"What did you feel, Honor?" I ask, finally taking my eyes off the envelope and focusing on Honor.

"Odd. A mixture of fright and revenge."

"They're two completely different emotions."

"I know. But...maybe I was confusing my emotions with his. I don't know."

Gulping down some courage, I close my eyes and pull the letter from the envelope. My hands are clammy and shaky. When I unfold the letter, small black block letters spread across the page. The words cause a shiver down my spine.

Ah. So you got my letter. Sweet girl, that Honor. I'm going to love having her all to myself soon—having her blood all to myself. I hear she's quite powerful. Yes. I'll be having some fun with that. Unless of course you have that elixir of mine. You know, the elixir that was stolen from me.

So you hand that over and precious Honor will be saved...maybe. I just may need them both. Hmm. Something

to think about, don't you think? One thing is for sure—I don't
get that elixir, you won't see Honor anymore.

And obviously...I know where to find her.

Tootles,

G.

Gaffer. The man himself. Holy shit, what am I going to do? He's seen Honor. He's following her. She'll never be safe. Handing over the elixir is not going to be enough. If I don't think of something, Honor will never be safe.

Chapter Eighteen

"Storm. Storm." The sound of Honor's voice pulls me from my state of shock. "What, what is it?" Her question is wavering. She doesn't really want to know. My heart pounds in anticipation. Not sure what to say, I say nothing.

"Storm, c'mon, what is it? I'm scared. I wanna throw up, so I know it's something bad," she insists.

How am I going to hide this? "Honor, it's nothing." Not the best explanation, but all I can think of.

"You're lying. I know it's bad." She nudges my knee. "Tell me," she nearly cries. "I'm feeling you. What is it? Please, you have to tell me."

Bringing my head down, I'm ashamed. How do I keep her from worrying when she can feel every emotion? I wrap my hand around the inside of her knee. "Honor." I pause a long while. "You're just gonna have to trust me. Yes, I'm scared, but it's nothing I can't handle. So please, don't worry. Everything'll be fine."

She pushes my leg harder. "This is about that man who wants the elixir, isn't it?"

I shake my head. She shouldn't know this. Ethan must have told her. "What are you talking about?"

Honor pushes my leg one last time and stands. "You and Ethan are lying to me. I know it. I feel his anxiety every day. He's scared. And I just know it has to be that man. He came back. Or he sent his men, didn't he? Who was that guy who left me the note?" She's standing with her hands on her narrow hips.

"I'm not sure."

"He was one of them though?"

I nod. "Yes."

My body grows warm when she sits back down, this time right next to me so that our thighs are touching. Her hand grazes my leg when she asks, "Why are you hiding this from me? Do you think I can't handle it?"

Crossing my arm over hers to place my hand on her thigh, I take a breath. "I know you can handle it. I just don't want you worrying. Your heart doesn't need the extra stress."

"Stop." She raises her voice. "You treat me like I'm going to break. I'm not made of glass, Storm. I'm stronger than that." I watch her eyes roll. She's annoyed. I get it.

"I'm sorry...I just...it's bad." My voice drops at the end of my sentence. Disheartened and out of control, I cannot bring myself to tell her that her life may be in jeopardy.

"How bad?"

"Very."

"Is there anything we can do?"

Her scent is so sweet, it's overwhelming, and I cannot help but bring my hand up to her face to touch her. Since she doesn't back away, I let my fingers caress her ear and her neck. She's beautiful. And so soft. "I'm trying."

When her head leans into my hand, I pull her close and wrap my arm around her. With her head on my shoulder, I hear her whisper, "What are you trying?"

"I've concocted another elixir."

Her head pops up. "What?"

"Yeah, well, since you wanted Ethan to get rid of the original...*and he actually listened to you*," I shake my head in disbelief, "I had to come up with a new one."

"How do you make an empath immortal elixir?"

"I have no idea. But I used the blood of empaths," I say, silently asking her to believe the unbelievable.

"Whose?"

"Ethan's. Tom's. Hunter. Eli."

"Oh...well...that's all you need to make one?"

Shaking my head and pulling her back to me, simply because I want to be holding her again, I tell her about all the organic ingredients I had to buy.

"Turkey tail?" she asks. "What the heck is that?"

"What it sounds like."

"Yuck."

I laugh. "Yeah, tell me about it. The whole process was yuck."

Popping her head back up, realization sets in. "*You* had to mix all that blood with all that stuff?" Her eyes narrow, trying to comprehend what I'm telling her.

"Yup. And cook it too."

"Eww. Gross."

"Yeah," I answer, trying hard not to remember the stench.

"So now what? You have to give it to them?"

"Yes."

"When?"

"Whenever they show up. It's ready though." I get up and walk to the kitchen, signaling for her to follow me.

"This is it," I say, lifting the jugs and placing them on the table.

Her fingers reach out to touch the old glass. "You think it's gonna work? Will it really make someone an immortal empath?"

"No, princess. It won't. I'm just hoping to trick them for fifty years or so." I say it as a joke, but we both know it's not.

"Aren't they going to be able to tell?" Honor pulls a chair from under the table and sits.

Sliding out another chair, I sit too. "Maybe," I say, wishing I could know definitely. All this worrying has exhausted me. So, when I rest my cheek in my palm, Honor asks me if I'm okay.

"Don't worry your pretty little head, sweetheart. We'll be fine." But the words come out monotone and she frowns.

"Don't talk to me like that."

My head jerks up. "Like what?"

"Condescendingly."

"Where in the hell did that come from?"

"I don't know." She sighs. "Like calling me *pretty-little*. I'm nearly as tall as you, so obviously you meant it in a way that you think you're superior to me."

"Oh my god, Honor. Really? How 'bout I say my pretty large sweetheart? Oh, but wait, then I'd be calling you fat." Making sure I smile so she doesn't get offended, I bat my eyes at her.

It works. She laughs.

Relief washes over me when she finally breaks into a smile. Then tingles stream up my arm when she reaches for my hand.

"I'm sorry, Storm. I'm just touchy because of all this. Your emotions and Ethan's emotions—they're scaring me. And until you just told me, I didn't know why. You always try to protect me and..." She shrugs. "It makes me feel stupid."

I drop my shoulders in realization. "Oh, Honor, that is not my intent. At. All. I just don't want to see you hurt. I know you can take care of yourself."

"Then stop treating me like I can't, and tell me things. I can handle it."

Turning my hand to grasp hers, I squeeze it. "Okay. You want the truth?" I ask with as much warning as I can, just to give her a chance to change her mind.

Her teeth graze her bottom lip. "Yes," she says resolutely.

Taking both my hands in hers now, I scoot closer and look her dead in the eyes. "If this man doesn't get the elixir," I pause, hoping for courage to continue, "he will come after you. He knows your blood is powerful. I don't know how, but he knows you're different. Maybe because your grandfather was, I'm not sure. What I do know is, if he takes you, that'll be it. He'll use your blood for *his* good only." I wait for her reaction. It's just a swallow. "There's even a chance that when he gets the elixir...he'll still take you."

This time her hand shoots to her mouth, and I hear a soft gasp.

"I will do my best to keep him from doing that," I promise, now taking her one hand in both of mine. "Even if I have to find him and kill him myself."

Chapter Nineteen

Her bulging violet eyes scream at me in terror, arresting my heart and suspending my speech. My own chin trembles in fear along with her. My deep love and concern for her causes empathy I've never felt before—even when I actually could feel the pain of others.

My throat closes and my lungs are tight. Honor's eyes, still unblinking, glisten with tears as she sits there zombie-like at my kitchen table. I need to find my voice. I need to suppress my own fear in order to provide her comfort.

Though my chest is tight, I force myself to inhale big and slow, exhaling even more slowly before I speak. "Honor," I whisper, pushing out my chair to stand and pulling her up with me as I do. "It'll be okay. I promise. We'll figure it out."

Still holding onto her hands, I lead her onto the couch. She sips the water waiting for her on the end table.

"We just have to come up with a plan," I tell her and hope to begin alleviating some of her anticipation.

Honor still holds her glass—staring into it as if it has the answers.

"First of all," I proceed cautiously, speaking to the side of Honor's head, since her gaze hasn't left the glass. "I know you are capable of taking care of yourself," and I think, obviously in this situation, she feels incapable. "But in this case, you *will* need protection. *Every minute*," I emphasize.

She finally turns toward me but says nothing.

"What's this with Ethan going to his apartment after school? Why doesn't he just stay with you?"

She just shakes her head slightly.

"Honor. We need to talk about this."

Sitting back against the couch, she places her glass down and puts the bottom of her palms against her temples.

"I know it's hard to hear. You're only seventeen and someone's after you, but now that it's out there, we have to discuss it."

She leans her head back against the couch and moves her palms to her forehead before dropping them on her lap.

I scoot over.

"Storm," she says quietly. "I'm afraid. What will my parents do without me?"

"Your parents? That's what you're worried about—what your parents will do? Aren't you afraid for yourself?"

She shrugs and looks at me with big eyes. "Sort of. I mean, yeah, definitely. But...I'm all my parents have. They'd be worried sick if someone else took me. They barely made it through the last time."

I can't help but laugh. A good, hearty laugh. Not that what Honor says is funny, but it cracks me up nonetheless.

Draping my arm around her, I pull her close. Her head feels nice on my shoulder. I kiss the top of her head and leave my lips there for a few seconds. "Honor, does Ethan always just drop you off and go to his house after school?"

"No, just a couple times a week to get more clothes or do his laundry. He feels funny doing it at my house."

"Well then on those days, please let me know and I'll come over. Your parents are usually working then, right?"

"Yeah."

"Will you be honest with me? Let me know when you're gonna be alone?"

"Yeah. I'll be honest."

I sigh. "I'm sorry it has to be this way."

Honor says nothing, but I hear her moan beneath her breath.

"There's another matter we need to talk about."

She raises her head from my shoulder but stays in my arms. "What?"

"Moore."

"*Mr.* Moore?"

I nod.

"Why?"

"I'm almost positive he has something to do with this."

Her eyes grow wide, and she raises her eyebrows. "What?"

"I'm pretty sure he's an empath. And I'm pretty sure he's up to no good."

Chapter Twenty

"But his eyes aren't violet," Honor exclaims.

"Maybe he's wearing contacts. I don't know. All I know is...there's something not right where he's concerned. I have to figure out what it is."

"How you gonna do that?"

I unwrap my arm from hers and lean back into the couch. "I don't know yet."

"Can I help? He likes me, maybe I can find things out."

I lean forward, turning to her. "You *cannot* be alone with him. I don't trust him."

"Well," I see in her eyes she's searching for an idea. "What if I go for help again after school, and you can stand outside in the hall? I'll put your phone on speed dial, and if I call, you run right in."

"Hmm," I think out loud. "That may work...let me think about it—what we can ask and stuff."

She nods.

We stare at each other now. Since some of our fears have been appeased, other emotions take over. She has that look in her eyes. The one that makes me want to kiss her. But we've been here before. I do not want to go there again...not right now.

"I think I should get you home," I whisper, still gazing into her eyes.

"Um, okay," she says, holding my stare with the want she shows in her eyes.

I know she wants me. I think. Maybe she's absorbing my desires and bouncing them back to me unintentionally.

But who knows. Whatever it is, right now we want to kiss each other. Her eyelids drop just a hair, but I know the look. She's inviting me. My heart races. My breathing picks up. While still looking into her intense violet eyes, I catch her chest rising and falling quite rapidly. When she leans in, it takes all I've got to break the connection and stand up. I want her, yes, but not until she can give herself fully to me.

Not until she is done with Ethan.

"Well, princess." I resort back to my cool, distant self—a protective tactic I've grown very good at. "Let's get you home." Grabbing my keys off the table by the front door, I say, "We'll put your bike in my trunk so you don't have to leave it here."

Reluctantly, and pleasing to me to know she likes it here, Honor rises from the couch and follows me out.

"Cute bike, princess. Love the basket," I add. "But you shouldn't leave your purse where anyone can take it."

"Oh my god," she cries. "I forgot I had it in there."

When we pull into her driveway, Ethan's sitting on her front step. He sees us and storms toward the car.

"Where were you, Honor? I've been worried sick. Why didn't you answer your phone...or call me back?"

"Oh, Ethan," she says, barely out of the car, "I left my purse with my bike and forgot about it. I'm so sorry."

Ethan gives me a stern look of the eye before responding to Honor. "You had me worried, sweetheart," he says more calmly.

"I'm sorry, Eeth," she says, giving him a quick peck on the lips. And don't think I missed the fact that she darted her eyes at me right after.

Ethan eyes me up and down but talks to Honor when he asks, "What were you doing with him?"

I wheel her bike up to the garage door, and I hear him ask, "And why does he have your bike?"

"He didn't want me driving it home." Her voice is quiet, as if she's unsure of what to tell him.

So I interject. "Ethan," I snap. "We need to talk."

His eyes shoot from me to Honor, and I can't help but chuckle at what he must be thinking. "Calm down, little brother, I'm not talking about Honor and me." Though I wish I were. "It's *him*, he's made contact with Honor."

"What?" he exclaims, livid as hell.

"Let's do this inside. I don't trust it out here," I suggest. "Are your parents home, Honor?"

"Not yet."

"Good. Though we'll need to tell them soon."

Honor's eyes close for a second, her shoulders drop, and she sighs.

We walk into Honor's house with me lagging behind. I take a quick look around, swearing I feel something dark around us. I close the door.

Chapter Twenty-One

"Your girlfriend's in trouble, Ethan." I get right to the point when we get inside. There's no way I'm pussyfooting around this. Honor's too important. "And I think Moore might have something to do with it."

"What? Where'd *that* come from?" he asks with a tone in his voice that tells me he thinks I'm crazy.

"You said it yourself, you don't trust him."

"Yeah, but I wasn't thinking anything like that." His eyebrows are crunched, and he's still not getting it.

"You're an empath, Ethan, you should be feeling this. Moore is hiding something and looking for something. I think that something is in Honor's blood."

Ethan's shoulders drop, and he rubs his jaw. "What makes you think that? What's in Honor's blood?"

"Are you blind, man? She brought me back from the dead. That's crazy shit. I bet *you* can't do that."

"Well, no, I guess not. Hanna did say Honor was special."

"Hanna? She's dead, what are you talking about?" It's my turn to look at him like he's crazy.

"Oh that's right," Honor says softly. "You didn't see her."

I shake my head, waiting for her to go on.

Honor walks up to me and sits me down on the couch like I'm a child. "When you died," she pauses, worry inching across her forehead. "Um, there was like this white puff of smoke lifting from your body."

She must have paused for my reaction, because she doesn't say anything. "And?" I ask, quite agitated.

"And...after the smoke disappeared, your sister and my parents were standing over you...all of them dressed in white."

I chuckle and turn to Ethan. "Is this a joke?"

He shakes his head.

"Storm," Honor continues. "You had been holding onto their souls."

"Yes," I interject. "I'm aware of that."

"No, but you don't understand. They went to Heaven now. They were released from your body." Honor smiles and rubs my thigh.

"Yes, I know, you already told me that, but..." I stand, feeling like I'm going to lose it, and pace the floor. I remember Honor explaining to me that her mother spoke with her, I guess it didn't register that she saw her too. "You *saw* them? Like they were real?"

"Yes," Ethan says calmly, "It's true. I saw them too."

"You saw Summer?" I hear myself whisper.

Ethan smiles. "Yeah, I did. She was beautiful."

"Oh my god." Feeling nauseous, I sit back down. My sister. The one who died at my hands. I want to throw up.

"It's okay, Storm," Honor says, returning her hand to my leg. "She's good. She knows it was an accident. They all do."

All the memories come flooding back. Especially the day I killed Summer.

**

"Hey, kid," I force a smile when I see her on the bed. She's so pale and drawn, her little body shivering under the covers. "How ya doin'? Feeling any better yet?"

Summer's smile is bright despite her sallow, speckled skin. "Yeah, my mom says my fever's down. I should be all better by my birthday." She beams.

"That's right. Your birthday is in two days. How old now? Five?"

Summer laughs. "Oh stop, Storm, you know I'm gonna be nine."

"Nah, you're not that old yet. You can't be catching up to me."

"Well I am, so ha, ha." She brings her hand to her face and starts scratching.

"You itch?"

"Yeah, I got chicken pox. That's why."

"Mmhmm, I know." I sigh. Why hasn't anyone healed her? "Hey, hasn't like anybody tried to take your sickness away, kid? I mean we live with a bunch of people who can do that."

"Mommy says they try to save their powers for the big stuff. She says it's good to get chicken pox. Then I'll be amused."

"Amused? Are you amused you have the chicken pox?"

"You know, like when you can't get it again."

"Oh," I laugh. "Immune."

She giggles.

"Well guess what?"

"What?"

"How 'bout I try to take the itch away at least?"

"Really?"

"Really." Her smile is spread from cheek to tiny cheek, and I can't help but smile just as wide. She's the best. "Here goes, kid."

I place my hand over her arms and concentrate really hard, like I always see my mother do, at taking away those stupid pockmarks she doesn't need. When I open my eyes, she's gasping for air.

"What is it, Sum? Are you choking?"

Her eyes grow wide, and she shakes her head.

"Summer." I move my hands to her face now. Her eyes roll behind her head. "Summer. Summer." Her eyes close, and she starts turning a funny color.

"Summer," I yell, then quickly put my hands over her heart. "Summer, please, I didn't mean it. Wake up." Oh my god, I think. I killed her. Oh my god.

"What's going on in here?" my step-mother asks, then she runs to Summer and picks her up. "What did you do?" she yells to me. "What did you do?"

My step-mother is crying. And shaking. And shaking Summer. "Summer, Summer, baby, wake up. Please," she cries. "Go get your father...now," she demands in a voice I never heard before.

But I don't get my father. I'm scared. So I run.

**

I feel the tears on my face. There is no way they will see me like this. Finding a steady foot, I flee from the house and catch my breath out by my car. With my hands on the roof of the car and my head against the window, my breathing slows down. The memory of Summer is too much for me to bear. I need to let it go, but I can't. I killed my little sister. The only sibling I have ever loved, and I killed her. With my bare hands.

"Storm?" I hear my angel's voice. I don't deserve her...even as a friend. I need to get rid of the people after her and leave her for good. "Storm?" Her voice is closer. "Are you all right?" Her hand is on my back. "Were you thinking about her?" she whispers.

"Honor," I whisper back, my eyes closed.

Now her other hand is on my arm. "Hey...it's okay," she speaks softly into my ear. "Summer knows you didn't mean it." I know Honor's an empath, but it still floors me that she knows exactly what I'm thinking. Well, feeling rather, but I guess the two go hand in hand. "She even said so to us. Storm. It's okay. My birth parents even told us...they know you were trying to save them. They know, honey. You're a good person. Please don't think you're not." She leans her head on my shoulder. "Please, Storm. You gotta stop hurting like this. You're always hurting," she whispers. Her touch becomes more intense.

"Don't," I insist and pull away. But I do look at her. She's beautiful. Her violet eyes are glassy and her cheeks are pink. "I'm sorry. I didn't mean to yell. I just...you can't do that. You can't try to take it away. *I* own my pain, Honor. *I* hurt the people I care about and only *I* deserve to hurt. So don't."

Her bottom lip quivers, but she smiles anyway. "I'm sorry."

My arms instinctively go around her, pulling her to my chest. "Don't be, I'm sorry I yelled. Thank you, though. For your words. I appreciate them."

When she sighs into my shoulder, her breath warms me, rousing my desire for her. Damn that Ethan. I play with the long strands of her hair and inhale her scent. I want so badly to kiss her. To have her. To love her...like no one has before.

"Okay, that's enough," Ethan yells from the doorway, and we unlock our embrace. "What the hell's going on, Honor? Every time I see the two of you, you're in each other's arms. Do you like him?"

"Ethan, um, I was just comforting him. The whole Summer thing. It's hard on him. I just—"

"Then he shouldn't've killed her."

"Ethan," Honor scolds. "That was cruel."

I'm choosing to remain quiet. I'd like to see what Honor will say. Of course, I'll come to her rescue if she needs me to.

"No, him holding you all the time is cruel. He's in love with you, Honor. I know that. But tell me right now. Do you feel the same way about him?"

Her shoulders tighten. "Ethan, stop. That's unfair. I was only—"

"Do you?" he interrupts.

"Ethan," she cries.

"I want an answer, Honor. Do you love him back?"

I see her struggling. She shouldn't have to do this now. "Leave her alone, Ethan. She was just trying to take away my pain. I wouldn't let her. Just leave her alone." Honor is looking at the ground, I know she's embarrassed. "You have to stop being so suspicious. We're good friends. She saved my life. You gotta accept that we've formed a bond because of that. Nothing else."

Ethan eyes Honor, but her eyes are cast down.

"Listen, drop it, Ethan. We have more important things to worry about. I'll let Honor fill you in for now." I open my car door and put a foot inside. "I'm not up for it right now. I'm going home to figure out something."

I get in, shut the door, and peel out of her driveway. Needing to think. Needing to figure out how to save Honor, and then get the hell out of Jefferson.

Chapter Twenty-Two

Icy prickles nip at my spine on the ride home. Someone is following me. Though no one appears in my rearview mirror, someone is after me. At this very moment. I may not have my empath powers, but years of recognizing the inner feelings of everyone besides myself have left me with super intuition. And right now, I'm intuiting something bad.

The floor beneath the gas pedal prevents me from pressing any further, but as fast as my Challenger will take me, I gun it on Berkshire Valley Road, heading for home as quickly as possible. I want this over with. Hopefully, once the elixir is in his hands, Honor will get a reprieve from any harassment before it even begins.

I'm not in my driveway thirty seconds when my car hops forward.

Cursing out loud, I throw open my door and walk straight for the black Navigator jammed up against my car. "Was that freaking necessary?" I yell to the closed black window.

The back door slowly opens and out steps a black wing-tipped shoe. *Wingtips?* I was not expecting that.

The suit that follows matches the shoes, and the gray-streaked blond man that wears it matches the description that Honor gave me when he paid her a visit earlier. Only she didn't mention he was this fancy. Or this intimidating—for a little man. Though, I guess I knew damn well he was.

"Mr. Sutherland," he greets me with a crooked smile.

"Mr...Gaffer," I respond with no knowledge of his real name.

"I believe you have something that belongs to me."

"I do." I just stand there, uncharacteristically frozen where I stand. I need to shake this fast. "*Sarcasm. Use it, Storm,*" I say to myself. "I'm flattered you dressed in your Sunday best for me. Really. You didn't have to." Hopefully that came out as cool as I intended it, because inside I'm quivering like a little girl.

The passenger side door opens up and out steps the biggest person I've ever seen in real life. He's huge. Like seven-feet-tall huge.

Then his twin slides out the back passenger side door.

"Hey, G., you need assistance here?" Thing Two says.

"No, Jimmy. We're good," Gaffer says to his bodyguard before turning to me. "So, Mr. Sutherland. My elixir?"

"Yeah. I'll go get it. Be right back," I say quickly and turn to go inside.

"No so fast. Jimmy and me will be going with you," Gaffer commands.

I close my eyes to take in a huge breath. "Sure."

In the kitchen, I fumble with the jugs underneath the sink while silently praying that this works. When I plop the jugs on the table, Jimmy's in the doorway. "You want 'em?" I say, pointing to the jugs. "They're yours."

Jimmy lifts them like they're loaves of bread. I follow him out to the living room where Gaffer is having a look around my apartment. I don't like him snooping.

"Jimmy's got your jugs. You can go now," I tell them, hoping it'll be that easy.

He silently instructs Jimmy to put the dirty jugs on my end table. *No. It won't be that easy.* G. inspects the jugs, pulls the cork out of one of them, and sticks his finger in the concoction. Retrieving his bloody finger from the jug, he sticks it in his mouth and sucks on it. *Puke. That's what I want to do right now.* G. looks at me as he slips his finger out of his mouth. "Tasty," he says with that crooked smile.

"You got what you want. Now, can you leave?"

"Not so fast there, Mr. Sutherland."

I fight to hide my disappointment. "We're not done here, you know. Just 'cause I got these jugs in front of me, doesn't mean I'm satisfied with what I'm getting. I *will* be testing this."

Like I knew he would. "I wouldn't expect anything less," I say, hoping to convince him of my confidence in this handover.

"I know every move your precious Honor makes, so make no mistake, if this isn't the elixir her grandfather made, I will come after her faster than you can blink, Mr. Sutherland."

Of course he will. I nod, too afraid to speak.

G. instructs Jimmy to take the jugs, and in an instant, they're gone.

I remain frozen where I stand. How long will it take him to find out that he doesn't have the original elixir? Will I even be made aware if he finds out? Will he go right for Honor without forewarning?

I manage to pull my cell out of my pocket and slide onto the couch. Though my fingers are trembling, I dial Ethan. He doesn't answer.

Instead, I grab my keys and head straight to Honor's house.

And sit out in my car across the street.

Telling her what the Gaffer said would destroy her. She'll start worrying that he'll find out the elixir is a fake. I just need to alert Ethan to not let her out of his sight. I try his phone again, but it goes straight for voicemail. Instead of leaving a message, I text him—alerting him to stay near Honor at all times. I even ask him to please stay in her room at night, afraid Gaffer will just take her in the middle of the night.

When my phone alerts me I have a text, it's Ethan.

"*She broke up with me*," the text says. "*I left right after you did*."

Oh.

I'm not sure what to think of this just yet, but there is no time to think. Honor is alone. I don't know if her parents' cars are in the garage or if they're just not home, so I do the first thing I can think of.

Ring her doorbell.

Chapter Twenty-Three

The tears that fill her violet eyes make my whole body hurt—and not because I'm an empath, which I am no longer. I hurt because I am so deeply in love with this girl that I can't stand to see her hurting.

She just looks at me and starts sobbing.

"C'mere, princess," I say so softly that I barely open my mouth. Pulling her into my arms, I try with all my might to take away her pain the only way I now know how—by loving her. And showing her through my hug.

Without breaking our embrace, I walk forward through the doorway and shut the door. Her sobs slow down to a hiccup-cry combination. Leaving one arm wrapped around her back, I move the other beneath her knees and carry her to the sofa—where I sit and keep her on my lap. My intuition tells me she doesn't want to hear any words of wisdom, so I lean against the couch and bring her head to my chest. The silent tears she cries hurt me just as much as her hysterical sobs...more so, if that's possible.

As I let her cry against me, I close my eyes, kiss her head, and leave my lips there. Right now I wish I had my empathic abilities, because it's killing me to see her so sad. After some time, I'm not sure how much time has actually passed, her breathing returns to normal.

"Can I get you anything, princess?" I ask, breaking the sad silence.

Her head moves back and forth against my chest, and I cup my hand over her damp cheek.

When she looks up at me, she attempts to smile. "I had to do it. It wasn't fair to Ethan."

I nod. Because really, what was I going to say? I realize she may have feelings for me, but I also know how much she adored Ethan. This can't be easy for her.

"Why'd you come back?" she asks, suddenly realizing my presence wasn't expected.

What was I gonna say?

The truth.

I had promised her I wouldn't keep her in the dark about this elixir nonsense. So I won't. "Well, I had a visitor today."

She looks at me wide-eyed and hops off my lap. Sitting down on the coffee table, she now faces me. "Was it the same man? The one who gave me the letter?"

I nod.

She leans in forward, very interested. "Did you give him the elixir? Is it over now?" Her smile is hesitant. My thoughts are seeping into my emotions and she's reading them. It doesn't take her long to frown. I don't even have to say a word.

"It's not over, is it?" She sits back and drops her shoulders. "What did he say?"

"Well, that's why I'm here, princess." I take a deep breath. "We can't leave you alone. I tried to call Ethan to tell him not to leave your side, but when I didn't get an answer, I swung over here to tell him in person. It hadn't sunk in that his car wasn't parked in your driveway, so I texted him to not leave you alone." I paused. Her eyes were too sad. I give her credit though, she hasn't shed any more tears yet. "That's when he texted me that you broke up with him." This time I just stop talking. Maybe she had questions.

She didn't.

"I didn't know if your parents were home from work yet, so that's when I rang your bell."

She shakes her head. "What does that tell me, Storm? Nothing." She's agitated now.

"You can't be left alone."

"Yeah, you told me that. Why?"

"Because he's going to test the elixir. If it's not the original, he's coming straight for you."

Her eyes fill again, and her head drops. When she slides her hands down her lap, she crosses them—almost in prayer position.

"Honor." I lean forward so my knees touch hers, and I lift her chin with my fingers. "I won't let anything happen to you. I promise."

"You can't promise something like that. You don't know. He knows where I live. He'll just come here and get me."

Bringing my hands to her thighs, I try to calm her. "Princess, I'm not leaving your side. At all. Until this whole thing is over, I'll be right next to you."

She pulls away from me and stands up. "What are ya gonna do? Move in? What are my parents gonna say? I have one boy move out and another one moves in?" She shakes her head, gets up, and paces the room. Knowing she needs to think this through, I sit back into the couch, and wait for her to come to a decision about what she wants to do about this.

When a car pulls into the driveway, Honor runs to window and cries. "Oh my god, it's my mother." Turning to me, she asks, "Do we have to tell her?"

I nod. "Yes. Even if I take you away from here, your parents will still be in danger. I'm sure of it."

"Take me out. Right now," she says nervously, grabbing her purse off the front table.

"What?"

"I can't face her right now. She'll know something's the matter. Just take me out to the diner or something, just let's go now," she says in one breath, simultaneously opening the front door just as her mom walks in.

"Hi, Mom," Honor chirps. "Storm's taking me to get a bite. We'll be back soon."

"Oh. Okay. Sure. You need money, sweetheart?" Mrs. S. asks.

"No, ma'am, I got it," I say, trying hard to paste a smile on my face when I talk to her.

"Okay. Have fun. Not too late, Honor. You have school in the morning."

"I know, Mom. Be home soon. Love you."

When her mother closes the door, Honor sighs, and the mood she was in previously returns. Silently, we walk to my car, and I open her door for her. Once we're on the road, Honor's gaze is out the passenger window, so I don't try to make small talk. Instead, we drive in silence. But I don't take her to the diner. That'll be way too crowded, and something tells me Honor is not all that hungry anyway.

But maybe she can go for a hot drink. I know I can go for a cup of coffee at the moment.

When I pull into a small coffee shop parking lot up a few miles from Jefferson, she finally turns toward me. "This isn't the diner."

"No. Was your heart really set on the diner?"

"No," she says quietly.

"C'mon, I'll buy you a drink."

I open her door and take her hand, feeling way too guilty that I'm happy her hand is free for the taking now. When I get to the counter, Honor whispers that she wants a vanilla chai tea. After we get our drinks, I lead her to a secluded corner in the old shop.

"In the mood to talk?" I ask.

She only shrugs.

"Mind if I do the talking then?"

She shakes her head.

"Let's forget about Gaffer for a minute. I wanna talk about you and Ethan."

She lets out a cynical laugh. "I almost forgot about that." Then she puts her head in her hands.

I continue talking to the top of her head. "I hope he wasn't mad at you because I was hugging you before. I hope it wasn't a fight that led to your decision to break up with him. Because...because that would just be wrong."

"Uh...," she says, raising her head.

Holding up my hand, I stop her from talking just yet. "I know we have feelings for each other, but what you have with Ethan, well, that's a relationship, and sometimes they need a little work...instead of just walking away." That was so hard for me to say, but I needed to say it. If she was going to be available for me, I'd want her to be truly available. Having her by default would be so unsatisfying.

"We did have a fight about it, but that's not really why I broke up with him."

My heartbeat quickens, and I try to steady my breathing.

"I do like you, Storm...a lot." She takes a couple sips of her tea before she continues. "But I like him too, and I don't want to hurt him."

Another sip of tea takes precedent to finishing her sentence and I feel like I'm going to scream. I want to tell her I'm so in love with her, but that would be unfair. She needs to decide her feelings without bias.

"I'm just so confused. Ethan is such a nice guy. He is only ever wonderful to me. He really is. But...when he kisses me...it's nothing like what I feel," her face turns the prettiest shade of pink, "when you kiss me." She nips at her bottom lip and looks down at the table.

I'm at a loss for words. All I really want to do is take that lip and bite it myself. My smile has a sigh along with it. I rest my chin on my hands. "My whole world shatters when I kiss you," I whisper.

Her sigh is guttural. "That doesn't make this easier."

"What, darlin'? It doesn't make what easier?"

"I was afraid that when you heard that Ethan and I broke up, you'd think I'd, you know, want to go out with you, but I do, but...I don't either," she says, and I hear the regret in her voice.

"Princess, it's fine. I wasn't expecting anything," I lie. "Really, I'm just concerned that you may have broken up with him for the wrong reasons. That's all."

Her pretty violet eyes narrow. "You don't even like Ethan. Why are you so concerned about that?"

"I like *you*. I worry about *you*. That's all."

The way her mouth is moving back and forth, I can tell she's mulling it over.

"Listen, let's drop it for now. Can we talk about the other matter we need to discuss? Or is that off limits still?"

Immediately, I regret asking her. Fear cloaks her pretty face like a black cloud covers the sun. It's so damn hard to see her afraid. She's normally so strong.

My heart breaks for her.

My heart breaks for me.

I wish I could just offer myself as a sacrifice to this man, but he won't have it. I'm of no use to him. It's Honor he wants. And I damn well better find a way of keeping her from him.

I damn well better come up with another plan.

Chapter Twenty-Four

"Do you need to take me away, Storm?" she asks, fussing with her fingers and skewing her lips.

"I should. But I'm afraid for your parents. You know we have to tell them," I state firmly. I want her to make no mistake that they need to be on guard as well.

"Tell me what we have to do. I don't even know where to begin."

I take her hands in mine and caress her long fingers. "We begin by telling your parents tonight. We'll stop by my place to get a few things before we go to your house. I *have* to stay with you, Honor. We have no choice, really. I hope your parents are okay with it."

She nods. "Well, they were okay with Ethan staying, so I'm sure—"

"I can't stay in the guest room, Honor. I need to stay in your room."

"What? Why?" She worries her lip again. "I don't think they'll allow that," she says quietly.

"Honor, this man, he'll stop at nothing. I wouldn't put it past him to enter through your bedroom window in the middle of the night."

Honor closes her pale eyelids. "Oh my god," she whispers under her breath and covers her face with her hands again.

"Sweetheart," I say, pulling her wrists from her face. "I am not going to let anything happen to you. That's why I'm staying in your room...And I have a gun," I offer as an afterthought.

Honor gasps. "How'd you get one?"

"I stole it," I say as a matter of fact. "Back when I was roaming the country on my own. No biggie." Honor's eyes are wide in surprise. "Just don't tell anyone, princess, especially your parents."

"Why hadn't you used it when we were in the woods with those guys?"

"I didn't have it on me."

"Why not?"

"Boy you have a lot of questions. I don't know. I don't think I really thought I'd need it then. I'm not sure. I...I don't have an answer for that. But I do know this...I'm not putting you in a vulnerable position this time. I'm ready this time."

She smiles.

"What's the smile for?" My heart always skips a beat when she smiles at me.

This time her eyes smile along with her mouth. "There are just...so many things about you." She blushes.

"Things?"

"Like...layers. Like when I first met you, I was almost scared of you. I don't know, I remember thinking you were like evil, but..." She turns red again. "That was probably Ethan's feelings I was feeling. And then you had this soft side. And then you have a tough side."

I can't help but laugh. "Isn't that the same as being evil?" I joke.

She curls her lips into her mouth, still smiling. "Not at all. Your tough side is your protective side. You're loyal too. And even though I know you can't stand Ethan, I know you love him. You're sweet, Storm, and even though you hate for people to know that, *I* know it." She bites the corner of her mouth and casts her eyes down in embarrassment. "I'm sorry. I shouldn't have said that."

All I can do is stare at her. As much as I do hate for *anyone* to know I'm soft, something about Honor thinking I'm sweet makes me feel special—like someone is actually taking the time to see through me.

"Cat got you by the tongue?" she quips.

"No cat," I say, looking Honor straight in the eyes. *She's* got me...by the heart.

She's reading my thoughts because her face is turning pink again. When she blushes, my chest feels warm. It's hard to hide what I'm feeling with her. She may as well be a mind reader.

"What's so funny?" she asks, still pink. Still smiling. Still stopping my heart.

"Nothing." I smile back at her then take the last sip of my coffee. "You wanna get going?"

Honor's smile fades. "Yeah," she says with a soft groan.

"It'll be okay, princess. I'll help you tell your parents. If you want, you can just stand there while I do the talking."

She nods then takes the hand I'm holding out for her. With our hands clasped together, we walk to the car. Ready to face the music.

Chapter Twenty-Five

"Please just take care of her, Storm," Mr. S. asks of me after Honor and I tell them the whole Gaffer story. "We can't let anything happen to my daughter."

"I promise. Her life means more to me than my own. Whatever it takes, I'll keep her safe."

"I still wish we could go to the police. I'd feel so much better."

"I really don't think they could do anything for us right now," I tell him. "Maybe if they do approach us here, then we can. I just hope they'll keep our empath thing quiet."

"Hopefully," Mr. S. says quietly.

There's an awkward silence. Five minutes ago, Honor took her mom into the kitchen to also explain what happened between her and Ethan. She began telling her in the living room, but her face dropped when she caught my eye. I guess she wasn't comfortable telling her parents about her feelings for me just yet. That's okay. I can be patient.

After Honor's dad helps me move the guest room twin bed into Honor's room, he gives us some privacy. Though he makes us leave the bedroom door open, I'm perfectly okay with that. If it were closed, I'm afraid I wouldn't trust myself in the room alone with her. Yes, I'm trying to be someone Honor can trust, but I'm also a guy...a guy who has never been able to touch a girl until recently. So yeah, it'd be hard. The door open is fine by me right now. If Honor ever chooses me though, that's another story.

Now that we've put on the sheets and blankets, Honor and I stand face to face on either side of my bed. Her face is that pretty shade of pink I'm getting used to seeing.

"Ya nervous, kiddo?"

She shrugs and says, "No." Honor drops to her bed and sits on her hands. "This is gonna be weird...you sleeping right next to me."

"Well, I'm not *right* next to you, the *bed* is next to your bed. There's a difference." I wink, wishing like hell I *were* sleeping right next to her.

"Listen," I change the subject, "we need to talk about Moore. I think we need to try your plan tomorrow."

"You mean me going to him after school while you're in the hallway?"

"Yup. We need to go over some questions or things you can say to get the answers from him."

"Okay."

Sitting back against my headboard, I try to get comfortable and forget the fact that I'm in the same bedroom as Honor.

She sits cross-legged and attempts to relax as well.

"I wouldn't even know what I'd say," she tells me.

"Truthfully, I'm not sure either, but we'll come up with something." I lean my head against the headboard and close my eyes.

I open them when I have a thought. "Honor, why don't you go for help on an assignment, then you can maybe cry about Ethan or something."

"What? What would that do?"

"I don't know, break him down a little. Men aren't equipped to deal with female tears," I say honestly. "Maybe he'll get all flustered and tell you things he shouldn't. I don't know. I'm at a loss here myself. You can't very well just come out and ask him what he has to do with the elixir. He'll get suspicious and shut down."

"Wait. Maybe not. Maybe he will just come out and tell me. Maybe he's not a bad guy."

I roll my eyes. She can be so naïve. There's evil in everyone. Everyone besides Honor, that is. "Honor, we can't trust him. I told you that. Why don't you cry over Ethan and mumble something about how you broke up with him because he took something that was in your family for hundreds of years."

She looks at me like I'm crazy. "Wh...what?"

"We'll see if he goes after Ethan. Of course, if he's working for Gaffer, he may already know we've handed the elixir over, so who knows. We'll play it by ear, okay?"

Honor's hand comes up to cover a yawn. "Okay, I'll try," she says in the middle of her yawn.

"Let's talk about this tomorrow. It's late. You're tired. We have school in the morning."

"Yeah," she starts, "I'm going to brush my teeth, unless you want to first."

"Nah. You go. I'll just get changed here while you're gone."

When she closes the door behind her, I yank my jeans off and pull on a pair of sweats. I usually sleep in my boxers, but I'm thinking that's not a good idea tonight. I head for the bathroom to brush my teeth after Honor comes back, but as I open her door to come back in, she's in a small tank top and boxer pjs, and she's bending over to let down her bed. Her legs go on forever.

Realizing I'm now back in the room, Honor turns and stares at me. "Hey," she says, as if she didn't expect me to be in her room. She looks down at her legs and blushes. "I was...uh...trying to get under the covers...before you came back."

"Don't worry," I assure her, "I'm not looking." *Yeah, right.* I pull my t-shirt over my head and get under my own covers, but only cover my legs. I stay sitting up against the headboard. I have to chuckle, because when I look over at Honor, her wide-eyes are staring directly at my chest. "Like what you see?"

"Huh." She shakes her head and looks at my face. "Uh, uh...yeah. G'night, Storm." Turning off her light, she also turns on her pillow and faces the wall.

"Good night, princess." Lying in the dark in the bed next to Honor is difficult to the say the least. What I wouldn't give to crawl underneath her covers and hold her all night. To feel her soft body cuddled up next to me would be Heaven here on Earth. To smell her scent directly underneath my nose for the night's entirety would leave me breathless and intoxicated. Having her sleeping in my arms...well my life would be complete.

A clanking at my window startles Honor and she jumps into bed with me. I turn quickly to her then to the window. Though my wish to have her next to me in bed has suddenly presented itself, I can't take the time to appreciate it. Someone's at her window. I grab the gun I hid underneath the pillow and leap for the window at the same time the predator lifts it open.

"Come any further and I'll shoot," I threaten before hearing my brother's voice.

"Storm?" he asks, confused.

The light between our beds is turned on and I'm face to face with Ethan. But he's not looking at me. He's looking at Honor sitting up in the bed that's closest to the window. The one that Ethan must know is not hers.

"Honor?" He looks at her then at me. "You move quick, don't you, Sutherland? You couldn't even give us a full afternoon before you made your move. You suck." He spits at me.

"Ethan," Honor scolds him for the second time today. "That was uncalled for. Apologize."

"Apologize? Seriously? Is this why you broke up with me? And you're already in his bed. I thought you weren't ready for that yet, Honor. Or were you waiting on Storm to be your first fuck?"

That's all I need to hear. When my fist hits the side of Ethan's face, the crack is low and fleshy. It feels disgusting under my knuckles but satisfying to see him fall flat against the wall. As he slides down the floor with his palm to his face, I start to feel bad.

All I hear is Honor's cry. "Ethan, oh my god. Storm, what'd you do?" She kneels down, but at the same time, Ethan jumps back up and pounds me right in the gut. With his other hand, he pelts me in the face. With all my might, I pound him again right in the eye. For the second time, at my hand, he goes down.

Honor, in shock and still on the floor, reaches for Ethan and pulls his hand off his face, replacing it with her own hand. Without taking her eyes off of Ethan, she orders me to go get ice from the freezer downstairs.

I feel bad that I hit him like that in front of Honor, but he pissed me off talking shit about her. He can't do that and expect me to stand there and do nothing. Besides, he hit me back, so why is she upset with me?

Chapter Twenty-Six

Honor is still kneeling on the floor fussing with Ethan when I come back with the ice and a rag for the blood. Her expression when she looks at me is filled with disgust. I've shown her my dark side and I guess she doesn't like it. But like I said, there's no way I was going to let him get away with talking like that to her.

"Here you go." Handing Honor the supplies, I notice she doesn't even look me in the eyes. She doesn't even say thank you. I've pissed her off.

In an effort to appease her, I say, "I'm sorry, Ethan, " but my voice is strained because it's not easy for me to apologize, especially to him.

He tries to lunge toward me from his sitting position, but Honor pushes him back.

I continue. "When you said that about Honor. It made me furious." I'm still battling with my innate nature to offend versus the call to be humble, but my love for Honor and her opinion of me means more than my desire to be spiteful. So, I try my best. "I...I really shouldn't have punched you over it, and...I'm sorry."

This time they both look at me. I barely get a nod.

I help him up and onto my bed. He's holding the ice to his eye, and Honor's finishes wiping up his bloody face.

"I'm sorry, Honor," Ethan says. "I shouldn't have said that, but seeing you in his bed—"

"*His* bed? Ethan, I jumped in it because we heard something at the window. I was scared. This Gaffer guy...he's threatening to take me. I thought you were him."

Ethan closes his eyes in regret then looks to me. "It's that bad?"

"Yeah. It is."

"Oh, Honor," he continues. "I'm sorry. I should have come as soon as I got the text from Storm, but, well, I was feeling sorry for myself. That's why I had come now though. To make sure you were okay."

Honor gives him one of her smiles, and I'm filled with jealousy. I need to let it go.

"Storm thought it best that he stay here...in my room. Dad thought so too."

Ethan nods. "Yeah. I guess it's best." Though his words sound forgiving, the scorn on his face shows his disdain. I'm sure I wouldn't forgive him for punching *me* in the face. Nor would I forgive him if I had caught Honor in *his* bed. Though she'd have had every right to be in it.

"Listen," I say to change the subject. "We were discussing Moore. We need to figure out how to get information from him," I tell my brother.

"Okay," Ethan says straight-faced. "Tell me what you want me to do."

I know that asking me to tell him what to do must have been hard for him, because it would have been hard for me, so I try my best to smile at him, but it feels false. I don't smile. I quickly wipe it away and begin telling Ethan the sort-of-plan that Honor and I came up with.

"So, do you want me to stand out in the hall too? Or should I stay away?" he deadpans, which tells me he's trying hard to swallow his pride.

"Whatever you think is best. I'm not sure what to think of Moore yet, so we may need the two of us. I mean, I don't think he'll hurt Honor, but it would be good if you're close by." I look at Honor now. "Maybe you can call one of our phones *before* you go in to see Moore, and you can leave it on speaker. Like under your book or something. This way, Ethan and I will be able to listen to the whole conversation."

Honor wiggles her mouth a little while she thinks. "Okay."

Now that we've settled the Moore plan, we approach a painful silence. Ethan needs to say good-bye, and I don't think he really wants to. Though I feel bad for the guy right now, I will not relinquish my bed to him. I've moved in. There is no way I'm going back to my basement apartment. Not now anyway. When it comes to Honor, it's only me I trust to keep her safe. Ethan may *want* to, but I'm not quite sure he'd give up his life for Honor.

I *know* I would.

"Okay, well," Ethan chokes out, "I, uh, guess I'll get going. See ya tomorrow," he says to only Honor.

"Yeah," she says. "I hope your eye feels better, Eeth," she whispers wistfully. *Maybe she's having second thoughts about getting back with him.*

She and I go back to our respective beds and fall quietly asleep. Well *she* does. I lie still wishing things would have gone differently, so that Honor wouldn't be upset with me right now..

Chapter Twenty-Seven

As I hit the snooze on my phone for the last time, Honor walks in the room fully dressed and ready for school. "Holy shit, what time is it?"

"Seven fifteen," she answers quietly.

"Damn, we're gonna be late." I quickly jump out of bed, and grab the clothes from my bag.

"Ethan's picking me up." Honor is speaking to me, but not looking at me. Instead she's putting some books into her backpack.

"Oh. All right. Were you at least going to wake me up?"

Her back still faces me and she shrugs.

"Fine." I continue to gather my things and walk past her to go into the bathroom. "See ya at school," I say, not turning to look at her.

She's mad. Or regretting giving up Ethan. Either way, if we didn't have plans to question Moore after school, I'd ditch today and go for a ride. Instead, I get ready for school and go, taking the cup of coffee that Mrs. S. offers me on the way out the door.

The veins in my temples must have ruptured inside my head because my brain is screaming to jump ship. My headache came on shortly after period one began and it is now ten minutes until lunch and I want a boulder to fall on my head—it'd certainly be less painful. While I wait for the period to end, I lay my head on my arms on the desk and ignore the teacher's plea to wake my ass up.

"Storm," she says, "tomorrow morning I expect you to come to class wide awake." She tsks and sends me on my way.

Skipping my locker to get to lunch, I'm able to grab Honor before she reaches the lunch room. "Honor," I say, foregoing the impulse to call her princess. "I need to talk to you for a minute. Please," I add, after seeing her solemn face.

"Okay," she answers, but doesn't smile.

I walk, shoulders slumped, into the alcove by the front of the school. Honor walks alongside me. "Listen, Honor," I start, reaching for her hand, which fortunately, she doesn't pull away. "I'm sorry I hit Ethan. I realize that's why you're mad, but really...it was an impulse. I saw red when he talked about you like that."

She sighs. "That's just it. Your impulses are violent. And he's your brother. You don't do that to your own brother. When are you going to finally accept that he's your own flesh and blood? It hurts me, you know?"

"I'm sorry, but why does it hurt you?"

"You're kidding, right? I *feel* everything. Aside from feeling the punch to Ethan's face in my own face, I feel the pain he feels every time you put him down...And I feel yours also. It pains you to be mean to him, I know it does."

"Honor, he was talking shit about you. That didn't make you angry? Because it sure as hell made *me* angry."

"Well, yeah, I mean it wasn't nice, but they were just words. *You* made him bleed, *and* he has a huge swollen black eye."

"Well, I'm sorry. And I'll apologize to him again. I get defensive when it comes to you, I can't help it."

The way her mouth tugs toward her right cheek, I know she's suppressing a smile.

I take her other hand and pull her closer. "I can't stand to see someone hurt you, Honor, physically or emotionally. You have to understand that. Although I may not be empathic any more, when it comes to you, my senses are heightened. I lo...like...you when you're feeling happy. When you're hurting, I'm hurting. But I promise, I'll refrain from using my fists again on Ethan. All right?"

"All right," she whispers. "Thank you."

I let go of her hands, but we just stare at each other. I want to kiss her. Hell, I almost just told her I loved her. Averting my eyes from her eyes is impossible for me. If she doesn't break the stare first, I'm going to grab her right here in the hallway.

"Um." She bites the corner of her bottom lip and retains her gaze. "We...uh...better..."

"Get to lunch," I finish.

"Yeah," she says. "Um, listen, I'm sorry I didn't wake you up this morning."

I close my eyes to break the stare. When I open them, I say, "It's fine, princess. No worries. Let's get going."

Ethan and Tamlin are already at our table with Hunter and Eli.

"What's Eli doing here?" I ask Honor.

"Uncle Tom enrolled him."

"Great. Another Sutherland at Jefferson," I mock before sitting down next to Elijah on the bench across from Ethan. This way I won't have to *look* at my father's clone.

Honor sits safely in between Tamlin and Hunter, purposely choosing to not sit near Ethan or me.

Hunter leans across Honor to get my attention. "Ethan says you all are seeing Moore after school," he whispers. "You really think he has something to do with the evil empath world?"

"Yeah. I do." I look at Honor. "I'm going to get a soda. You want anything?"

"Nah. I'll just share Tam's lunch." Tam slides half her sandwich to Honor.

I get up to get my soda, and when I turn around, Honor is leaning behind Tamlin and talking to Ethan. She's smiling at him and gently touching his bruised eye.

Me and my damn temper. I single-handedly sent Honor running right back into Ethan's arms.

Chapter Twenty-Eight

After the last bell rings, Honor, Ethan, and I meet outside Moore's class. Honor calls my phone, and we both put them on speaker. She tucks it securely inside her binder, then walks into the classroom.

"Miss Stevens," we hear a muffled Mr. Moore greet Honor. "To what do I owe this pleasure?" he asks much too sickeningly sweet.

"Hi, Mr. Moore, I was just wondering if you could help me with today's assignment," Honor says and then I believe I hear her sniff.

"Sure, Honor. Have a seat." The desks shuffling on the floor comes through as a screech on the phone. "Is everything okay?" Moore asks.

"Yes," she sniffles. "I'm having trouble with what you taught today, that's all."

"And you're crying because of chemistry? Honor, you're a good student, sweetheart..." Moore pauses. "What's going on? I can't believe you're only crying because of chemistry."

Ethan and I look at each other—anticipation apparent on our faces.

Honor sniffs again. "It's just...I broke up with Ethan...and I'm upset about it."

My stomach clenches, and I feel queasy hearing Honor say that. Because from what I saw today, maybe she really is upset about them breaking up.

"Why'd you break up with him?" Moore sounds genuinely concerned—no ulterior motive. But I don't believe the act.

"He was trying to steal something that's been in our family for a really long time."

"*Ethan* was?" Moore sounds surprised.

"Yeah, and I just, I don't think I can trust him anymore."

"Hmm," Moore mutters. "You can't trust Ethan." He sounds like he's making a mental note of it.

"No, and then there's Storm. He and Ethan are fighting all the time. And it's starting to really affect me."

Why the hell is she opening up to him about us? That was not part of our plan.

"Brothers will do that. Especially when there is something, or someone, that they both want." Moore explains.

"You think Storm wants our family...heirloom too?" she asks, surprised.

"Maybe. But more so I think he wants you. And Ethan has you."

Ethan and I glance at each other again, but only momentarily. We are much too uncomfortable sharing this space between us right now.

"Not if I can't trust him," she reminds Moore, getting back to the whole reason she is sitting in his classroom.

"So, did he actually *take* the heirloom, or do you still have it?"

"Um..." she's faltering. Honor backed herself into a corner.

I'm trying my hardest to tell her through telepathy that I took it and hid it. This way, Moore will come after me and not her. I know she can't read minds, but she can certainly read my emotions, so I try really hard to force my thoughts into my emotions.

"Um...no," she says. "I...uh...I gave it to Storm to hide."

"Oh, so Storm has it." Again, it sounds like he's making a mental note.

If Moore doesn't know that I've already handed over the elixir, then maybe he isn't working with Gaffer. *Then who the hell is he?*

"Yeah, look, I'm sorry, Mr. Moore. I shouldn't have brought my problems to you. Really. I just came for you to explain today's lesson, but—"

"That's all right, Honor. Sometimes teachers play the role of therapist too. Please don't apologize." Moore does sound like the sweet guy Honor makes him out to be.

But I'm still not buying the act.

It takes Moore about ten minutes to explain the lesson to Honor when she tells him it finally sinks in. "Thank you so much, Mr. Moore. I appreciate your help."

"Anytime, Honor."

Honor slips out the door and begins walking down the hall right away. We run to catch up to her.

"Now does that sound like a man who has something evil to hide?" she scolds us both. "And all I felt from him were good intentions. I even felt his *relief* when I told him you had it," she says to me.

Ethan and I remain quiet.

"And by the way, Storm, were you, like, *sending* me your thoughts?"

I smile. "I knew you would get them. Just like when we were trapped in the ice house and talked to each other silently," I boasted.

"Yeah, well...thank you." She smiles at me, and I'm hoping all is not lost between the two of us.

"Why don't we all drive over to Honor's house. This way we can talk and keep her protected at the same time. I'll meet you guys over there." I want to be the bigger guy—to prove to Honor I can be—so I let them ride over together. Maybe they still have things they need to talk about.

Honor pours us all some iced tea and we sit at the breakfast bar that separates her kitchen and living room.

"So what did you guys make of it? You still think he's up to something?" Honor asks.

"Yes," we both answer.

"Really?" she doesn't believe us.

"I do," I say first. "I'm just not sure anymore that he's working for Gaffer. If he were, he wouldn't have seemed so surprised that I was hiding the elixir...or the *heirloom* rather." I chuckle. "Nice word you came up with."

"I had to think of something."

"Honor," Ethan addresses. "What did you feel from him? Anything significant?"

"I felt what I always feel—someone who cares. He was scared for *me*. I think he is a genuinely nice guy. Whether you guys think so or not."

"Okay...I'll give you that," I tell her. "But he knows we're empaths. He knows I've already graduated from high school and I'm here to protect you. So the questions are...why does he know? Who the hell is he? And why is he here?"

"You're sure he knows we're empaths?" Honor asks.

"I am. He told me one day that he would spill our secret if I spilled his."

"What secret? He told you a secret?" Ethan asks, annoyed I hadn't told him.

"No, he told me nothing, but I was threatening to tell the principal that he took three vials of Honor's blood. That's when he said he knew what we are. He especially said he'd tell what Honor is. So, I need to know what he wants from her."

"If he wants something from me, then he's hiding it well."

"Maybe all three of us should go to him," Ethan suggests.

"I think he'll see it as an attack if we all show up."

"Honor's right," I respond. "He'll get defensive."

"Do you think what he wants is relative to the elixir anyway? Maybe it's just a coincidence."

"No, Honor, I don't think it's a coincidence," I tell her.

Taking a sip of my tea, I am at a loss for words. I have no idea what to make of Moore and if I should even proceed in my investigation against him. Maybe it is irrelevant. I wish I knew for sure—to guarantee Honor's safety.

"I have homework to do." Honor goes for her backpack. "If you guys want to join me, fine, otherwise...I need to get working on it. I've got a headache, and I'd like to get my mind off of all this empath stuff."

"Who's staying with her?" I whisper to Ethan when Honor goes up to her bedroom.

"You are. I discussed it with Honor on the ride over. We both agree that you'll be the best one to protect her. You're more..." he trails off.

"Violent?" I finish his thoughts.

He snorts. "Yes, but I was going to say that you're more experienced in this kind of stuff. I've never been involved in things like this. You're just the better choice. Besides," Ethan sounds sad, "Honor and I need a break. I don't open up enough with her...I've been alone too long."

"You? I've been alone much longer. What are you talking about?"

"I closed my heart a long time ago. I hadn't even considered opening it until I met Honor. But it's still hard. You said it yourself—I don't even try to heal her when she's sick. I've taught myself so well to tune every feeling out, that I've even been able to tune her out also." Ethan runs his hand through his hair and shakes his head. "I don't know how you do it. You've been away from family nearly your entire life, yet you're able to feel Honor's pain and sadness and hopelessness...how do you do it? Out of everyone, I thought you'd have been the most callous." Ethan's eyes seem to gloss over, but I know he's too proud to have me see him cry.

"I've wanted for so long to be wanted—by my dad, by my mom, by *your* mom. I was jealous my whole life. I *am* callous. And sarcastic. And nasty. But I was never able to close my heart and not care. It's all on the outside. What I let you all see. Inside, I'm a crumbling mess." I swallow my pride and let him in. "Honor was the first to actually see through the walls I built. Right away she saw that I was good—or at least part of me was. No matter how nasty I would be, she knew it was an act. I've lived with empaths before—*none* of them ever felt what I felt, besides maybe Summer, but then again she was just a kid. She trusted everyone." My heart was aching from being so honest, but relief was pouring from my shoulders like warm maple syrup. I always wanted a brother to talk to.

"You're not even empathic any more, yet you know what Honor needs. You know it right away. How?"

"Because I love her. I love her so much, Ethan, that it hurts. My heart feels everything she feels, because it is totally one hundred percent in love with her. I fell in love with her the first time I ever heard her speak. And I'm sorry about that. I'm sorry I fell in love with your girlfriend. That was never my intention."

"Yeah, I was wondering... what *were* your intentions anyway? Why did you follow me to Jefferson?"

"When I was on the run, I ran into people...Gaffer's people. They were after Hanna and Daniel's daughter. I remember that Hanna and your mom were best friends, so I kind of stayed interested in what they were doing. I also remember respecting Hanna and Daniel for giving up their daughter to regular humans. I thought, *'wow, finally, someone is being set free from this life.'* But then their daughter showed up on the news. Word spread that you followed her to Jefferson, New Jersey, and I knew that couldn't be good. Gaffer's men would find you and Honor in no time. I didn't know you anymore, and I couldn't trust that you would protect her." I started pacing Honor's living room. "Ethan, you didn't even know anyone else was after her, so I knew you wouldn't be able to handle it. I had to follow you...her...I know Hanna and Daniel were like family to our family. I also knew I owed them for...killing them. And well, when you're harboring their souls...sometimes they also like to tell you what to do." Mirthlessly, I chuckle. "Anyway, that's why I followed you both here."

Ethan nods. "Yeah, well...thanks. You're right. I have no clue what I'm doing. Without you..." Ethan struggles to say something. "Without you, I think Honor would be dead already." He nods nervously several times. Then he sits on the couch and drops his head in his hands. "I messed up. I love her too. But I messed it up. I'm not good enough for her."

I sit down next to him and place my hand on his back. "I don't think you messed up, bro. I think Honor just needs time, y'know, to figure things out. She's confused." This is hard for me to say, but my heart is opening for Ethan and I don't know how to slam it shut. "We can both take good care of her. I believe that. When this whole elixir-Gaffer thing is over, and Honor makes her decision...and it's you...I'll back off. I'll leave town and won't look back. I promise, Ethan. She'll be all yours." I feel my throat closing, so I stop talking.

With his head still in his hands, Ethan shakes his head. "No. I'm not going to wait for her to choose. My heart's been closed for so long, I don't think I'm capable of loving her enough."

"You can't leave, Ethan. She needs you here. We have to see this thing through."

"No, I mean, I'll stay until I know she's safe, but afterwards, I'm going back to live on my own." He lifts his head and looks at me. "I trust you to keep her happy."

I pat him on the back and stand up. "Let's drop this, we're getting too maudlin. Go do your homework with Honor. I'm going to sit out back in the tree."

Ethan laughs. "No homework for you?"

"Nah. What for? I already have my damn diploma. Now go." I fill my glass with more iced tea, grab a bag of cheesy garlic bread potato chips and head outside to climb the old tree.

Chapter Twenty-Nine

An angel's voice wakes me from my nap in the tree.

"Honor. Hey." She is sitting on the branch across from me.

"Storm, you were sleeping. Do you know how dangerous that is? You could have rolled off."

I crumple the empty bag of chips and stuff it into my empty glass—which I'm surprised is still sitting in my hand. "I couldn't have been sleeping too hard, princess," I say, widening my eyes to force myself awake. "I was still holding onto my glass."

"You're crazy. If you're tired, you should have just taken a nap."

"I did."

"On the bed," she scolds. "Not in the tree."

"Don't fret about it, darling. I'm fine. Did you finish your homework?"

She nods. "Yeah. Ethan's gone too. What did you say to him? He told me you were a good guy and I shouldn't let you go. Did you threaten him or something?" Honor's face is all serious.

"Thanks. You think highly of me, don't you?"

Honor shrugs, but then she blushes.

"I guess I haven't given you any reason to believe I'd be nice to Ethan, so I understand. But no, I did not threaten him. We just had a long overdue brother to brother talk."

"Really?" she says with a smile so big she blinds me. Well, not really, but it was a huge smile.

"Really. We needed to come to terms with a few things and I...I think we accomplished that. I hope so anyway."

Placing my glass securely between my legs, I reach my arms overhead and grab the branch above me. Being in one position for so long, I was in dire need of a good stretch.

"So what is our plan next?" Honor asks, her smile disappearing immediately.

I run both my hands through my hair and sigh. "I don't know, sweetheart. I really was hoping I'd get some answers today from Moore. I'm not accustomed to just waiting for something to happen. I like to make things happen. But I'm really at a loss right now. I'm sorry. I hate letting you down."

Honor forces her smile now. "You're not letting me down. I know you're doing everything you can. I just wish I could come up with something. Anything."

"We'll come up with something." I say softly. "When are your parents due home?"

"Shortly. They usually walk in about six. Why?"

"Wanna fix dinner for them? Is there anything here to make?"

This time Honor smiles *and* laughs. "What? Storm Sutherland is gonna cook?"

"Uh, yeah. How do you think I managed to survive on my own all this time? I had to eat more than just fast food." I tap her on the knee. "C'mon. Let's get dinner going."

She hops down the tree first, and I'm disappointed. I wanted her to fall into my arms on the way down.

In the kitchen, Honor's reaching for the pasta in one of the higher cabinets, and I can't help but notice her shirt riding up—showing the very edge of her bra. If she only knew what that was doing to me, she'd refrain from reaching so high. It's getting harder and harder for me to keep my hands to myself. When she turns around, I'm caught staring at her. Her blushing face puts a huge smile in my heart and I show it on my face.

"The pots are in the cabinet under the toaster," she informs me. "Get the big one and fill it with water."

"Okay, boss, but I thought I was the one that was going to do the cooking."

She looks at me with an expression that says, "Yeah, what's your point?"

I say, "That means I do the bossing around."

Honor gives me a pretty little smirk and says, "Be my guest, I'll go watch TV."

My hand wraps around her elbow. "You know I'm teasing, don't you?"

She allows me to keep my hand on her while she moves in just a bit closer. "Yes, I know you're teasing." When her eyes find my mouth, I'm tempted to kiss her, but I'm afraid of rejection. What if her feelings for Ethan get in the way? What if she's not ready for me yet? I'm still not sure I'm sticking around Jefferson after this is all over. Maybe she'll run back to Ethan; I won't be able to go through that pain. Loving her hurts already. If she turns me down for good, I don't know if I could stick around.

Laughing to myself, I think, *living on my own, answering to no one, is a much easier life to endure. Love is for people with courage. The more I get to know myself, the more of a coward I realize I am.*

In the midst of my pity-party, it doesn't register that Honor is still looking at me. And I at her. My mouth does an involuntary quirk to the side, which causes her to make a little tittering sound. Her lower lip disappears inside her mouth while her top teeth graze them. Without thinking, I lick my own bottom lip and inch forward, moving my hand from her elbow to her upper arm. My other hand slides around her waist, and before I can change my mind, I lower my mouth to hers. When her hands wrap around my neck, I pull her so tight I am afraid I am going to break her. She parts her lips, and I slip my tongue inside. When our tongues meet, I taste peppermint—like maybe she'd just brushed her teeth.

While one of her hands runs through the hair above my neck, her other hand caresses my face. Hoping I am not making a huge mistake, I clasp my hands beneath her ass and lift her up. Her legs naturally wrap around my waist as I start walking toward her bedroom. I know Mr. and Mrs. S. don't want her bedroom door shut, but I use the back of my foot and close it anyway.

Lowering Honor to the bed, she parts her legs and I move in between them, never taking my mouth off of hers. I slide my hand around her waist and under her shirt, slowly advancing toward her bra. Her breath hitches, so I stop and look at her. "You want me to stop?" My question comes out hoarse and raspy, barely audible.

"No," she breathes.

I continue edging toward her bra, running my thumb underneath the band. Her skin is soft and warm, and I can't help but reach around back and unclasp her bra. When she doesn't flinch, I bring my left arm around and cup her in my hand. My god, I need more. I can't stop. For so long, I have needed to touch a girl. For so long I have *wanted* to touch Honor. Recklessly, I lift off her shirt and bra and bring my mouth to her breast. She gasps, her hands pulling on my hair. Looking into her eyes, I silently ask her again if I should stop.

She shakes her head. "I...I've never done this before," she whispers so low I can barely hear her.

I lean on my elbows and touch her nose to nose. "We don't have to," I say breathlessly into her mouth.

"No, it's okay. I've..." I kiss her lips before she finishes.

"We can stop," I say when I pull back again.

She grabs my t-shirt and pulls me back down. Into my ear, she breathes, "I've never *wanted* to before...but...I do right now." She nips my earlobe and I feel my body quiver above her.

She pulls up on my shirt and whispers, "I want to feel your chest against mine."

I tear my shirt off, and pressing my chest to hers, I lift her and turn her simultaneously, sitting her on my lap—her legs around my waist.

"Oh, Honor...I love you so much." And as soon as I say it, I'm totally embarrassed. I had not wanted to say that yet.

"Oh," she says, as if realizing this for the first time—which probably she is. I'm not sure she had realized just how much I was into her. "Oh," she breathes out again.

Tucking a strand of her hair behind her ear, I say, "Honor, I...uh...didn't mean that. It...it just came out. I'm sorry. Don't—"

"Shh." She puts her fingers to my lips. "No. Don't be sorry. I just, I don't know if I...you know..." she's turning red, "if I feel the same...'cause Ethan...and all. I'm...I'm sorry." Honor stays on my lap and doesn't pull away.

I kiss her again on her luscious mouth, kissing her softly...without tongue. "Don't be sorry," I ask of her. "Please don't be sorry for being honest."

I run my fingers down her back and embrace her soft skin beneath my fingertips. "Why don't we stop right here? Your parents will be home soon anyway."

Honor kisses me hard on the lips. "Thank you," she says after pulling back.

"For what?"

"It was the first time anyone's ever touched me like that. Thank you for making my first time so special."

Now it's my turn to blush. And then it registers. "You and Ethan never...?"

Shaking her head, she says, "I wasn't ready yet."

My heart is smiling again. *With me, she was ready*. And that thought is the best news I had heard all day. Maybe I stand a chance after all.

Chapter Thirty

The next day in lunch, Honor is not at our table. I know she's in school today, because she drove in with me.

"Tam, do you know where Honor is?"

She tilts her head and looks at me from across the table. "No. I thought she was coming to lunch. She said she'd meet me here, she was just going to run to her locker."

"Oh." That's not so bad. I go buy a burger and cola and sit back down across from Tam. Eli and Hunter are now at the table.

A few seconds later, Ethan puts his tray down. "Where's Honor?" he asks me.

Shrugging, I tell him I have no idea.

While everyone else makes small talk, I can only think about Honor and what she's doing. She isn't one to stray from her normal schedule, so it worries me.

"Storm." Tam gets right in my face to get my attention. "What's going on in that head of yours? Why you so worried?"

"It's just not like her to be late, that's all."

"What're you worried about?" Ethan asks.

"For all the time you've known her, have you ever known her to not be where she says she's supposed to be?"

He laughs. "No. But she's a big girl. I'm sure she's fine."

"Unless she went and *healed* someone again and is passed out in the girls' room." I say it sarcastically but realize that she could have really done that.

I run out of the lunch room in search of her.

After checking all the girls' rooms nearby, I go the nurse's office, but Mrs. Wentink hasn't seen Honor today. Plodding down all the hallways now in search of every girls' room, I pass Moore's class. Always suspicious of the man, I look through the tiny window in his door. He doesn't have a class this period, but he is talking to a student.

Honor.

I push open the door frantically. "What the hell?" I scowl at Moore.

Honor runs over to me. "Storm, it's not what you think." She grasps my arm and turns toward Moore.

He nods his head. "Shut the door, Mr. Sutherland."

"Yeah?" I ask, my pulse elevated, wondering what the fuck Moore wants from Honor now.

"It's okay, Storm. I came to see *him*. He's not against us." Honor tries to calm my temper.

What the hell kind of lies has he been feeding her? "Talk. Now," I urge him.

A cocky Moore leans against his desk, half sitting on it with his hands on either side of his hips. "I don't work for Gaffer. Never have. Never will."

Whoa. What the...? I turn to look at Honor. "What did you tell him?" I ask her, my teeth clenched, I am so angry right now.

She gasps.

"Whoa, Sutherland. Don't be angry with her. She did nothing wrong."

"Don't tell me what to do," I demand. "I don't know what kind of bullshit you're feeding to Honor, but I don't like it."

"I don't think he's lying," she says quietly.

"I'm not." Moore attempts to assure me. "I know Asa...but in no way am I working for him. I don't even *like* the man."

"Asa?" My temper is not subsiding. My ears are pounding with the pressure from holding in my anger at Moore right now.

"Gaffer. His real name is Asa. And he's no friend of mine. But I assure you, I am solely on my own here."

"Okay." I sit on the edge of a classroom desk across from Moore. Folding my arms, I ask him, "I'm listening. What is your part in this? What do you know and what do you want?"

Moore looks up at the intercom. "Let's not talk about it here. Meet me at four at Mahlon Dickerson...by Saffin Pond. Bring your little empath troop with you. But say nothing to anyone else," he implores.

"Mahlon at four," I reiterate, trying to read his face. "I still don't trust you, but we'll be there."

"I don't like this," I say to Honor out in the hall.

"I don't know why," she says. "I feel nothing but honesty coming from him. I trust him."

"Then why did he need your blood? He was sneaky about it. Right there tells me we can't trust him."

"But I'm usually so good at reading people. I mean, I do realize now that taking my blood was kind of suspicious and all, but...I don't know. I didn't really wanna say anything, because it's crazy and all, but I get the feeling that he, you know, cares for me...like a lot."

I freeze. "He's in love with you?" The question comes out from deep in my gut.

"Shhh...Storm." She squeezes my forearm. "Shut up. No. Not in love with me. Not like that. Just...I don't know. I can't explain it. Sometimes it's there, and sometimes it's not. Just...don't make a big deal of it."

"Don't make a big deal that your chemistry teacher is in love with my girl...with you? That's a *huge* deal, Honor."

We've reached the lunch room.

"I'll drop it for now. Maybe the guys can feel something from him when we're at the reservation later," I say.

"Where the heck have you guys been?" Tamlin makes a show of her question, wagging her arms around.

"Calm down, Tam," I tell her.

Honor just laughs at her silliness, which borders on the ridiculous, then squeezes in next to her. I sit back down in my spot across from Tam.

Turning toward Ethan, I tell him about the meeting today at Mahlon.

"What do you make of it?" he asks.

"I don't know." I sigh. "Honor seems to trust him. I don't."

"He wants us all there?" Eli asks.

"That's what he said—'bring your empath troop.' But you have to keep it quiet."

"Like we don't already know that," Hunter remarks, shaking his head.

"What about me? Can't I go too?" Tamlin asks. "It's not like you guys keep your secrets from me."

I nod. "Yeah, Tam. I think it'd be okay."

Chapter Thirty-One

Honor rides with me to Mahlon Dickerson. Hunter, Elijah, and Tamlin follow us in Ethan's car. After parking in the gravel lot, we walk the trail towards Saffin Pond.

"I sure hope this isn't a set up," Elijah says from behind me, Tamlin close at his side.

"Oh, you sound like Storm," Honor quips before I have a chance to answer.

"I'm hoping the same thing." I say, looking him in the eye for the first time since that day in my apartment. Since opening up to Ethan, my heart has gone soft. Forgiving my father will never happen, but his sons' aren't to blame for his betrayal, and I'm trying to get over my hatred towards them. I guess what they say about love and hate being a fine line is true, because underneath all this hate I'd carried towards my half-brothers these past years is a layer of love for them I didn't know existed.

Becoming soft is another result of falling for Honor. Her openness and honesty, combined with my unconditional love for her, is wreaking havoc on my bad boy persona—*not sure I like this side of me.*

Reaching the beach at Saffin Pond, everyone but Honor takes a seat on one of the several wooden benches scattered about the sand. I stand back up and follow Honor to the dock she's headed for. "Hey, wait up," I call out to her.

When Honor turns, I see a frown appear on her face.

"Do you not want me with you?" I ask, catching up to her and taking the space alongside her.

Stepping onto the dock, she shakes her head. "No. It's not that. I'm nervous, I guess."

"Ah. So you don't completely trust him."

"No. I do. I just feel like something's gonna go wrong."

I take her hand, and we sit on the dock, taking off our shoes to dip our feet in the water. "What do you think is going to go wrong?"

Honor leans her head on my shoulder. "I wish I knew, but something bad. I keep getting these vibes from him."

"From Moore?"

"Yeah. I can't explain it. I trust him, but something's gonna happen."

"Today?"

She lifts her head from my shoulder and looks at me. "I don't know," she answers, then puts her head back on my shoulder.

Draping my arm around her, I tuck her in close and kiss the top of her head.

We sit there for a while before Moore walks up the trail and leans against the back of one of the benches. I help Honor up and head for Moore.

All eyes are on him. We're here for answers, and I see it in all my brothers' eyes. They, too, don't know what to make of the man.

"Moore." I'm the first to greet him.

"Sutherland," he mocks.

"Hi, Mr. Moore," Tamlin says with a giggle, and Eli nudges her in her side.

"Hey, Honor," Moore addresses her, and that's when I see it. He does like my girl. It's in his eyes.

I'm so pissed at this, I clench my fists. "Cut to the chase, Moore. Who are you?"

He smiles one of those sly crooked smiles. "I'm Jared Moore. I've never lied about my name."

"Keep going," I order.

"I'm Asa Moore's younger brother." He pauses, waiting for our reaction.

But since Honor and I are the only two who know that Asa is the Gaffer, he doesn't get the reaction he's looking for.

"Okay. So you're ancient," I wisecrack. "But you said you had nothing to do with the guy."

"I don't."

"Wait, back up here a minute," Ethan says. "Who the hell is Asa?"

Honor is biting her lower lip, and I can tell she's nervous about the impending doom she expects to happen. Reaching over, I take her hand and gently squeeze it.

"Asa is the Gaffer," I explain. "The one causing all this trouble."

"So what do you want if you have nothing to do with him?" Ethan asks.

"I want revenge." He pauses for effect again.

"Okay, I'll bite," I quip. "Why do you want revenge?"

"He took something that was mine. Or should I say someone."

Ethan and I look at each other. Then it clicks. Didn't Moore tell me to leave Ethan's girl alone once? "So this is about a girl?" I'm disgusted with him. He is freaking out Honor all because of a girl.

Moore smirks. "No." He looks from me to Ethan, then keeps his gaze on Honor—which pisses me off. "Though I can see where you'd think that." He flashes that crooked smile, and I wonder—*what is it that Honor trusts in him. He's slimy.*

"Cut the bullshit, Moore. You may be their teacher, but really, you're no one to me."

"I beg to differ, Sutherland. I think you may need me now more than ever."

"Yeah? Why?"

It seems while everyone else is processing what's being said, I'm the only one carrying on the conversation with Moore.

"Because I can get Asa to come to me."

"And why would I want that? I need to get him *away* from here. *Away* from Honor."

He shifts a little against the seatback of the bench. "Because once we have him," he holds out his arms as if he wants us running into them, "we can kill him."

"Whoa, whoa," Ethan chimes in.

Honor squeezes my hand so hard, I know she's holding back tears.

"Who said anything about killing anyone?" Ethan asks. "I ain't killing anyone else. Two is my limit."

Okay, that was funny.

"Explain it to me, Moore." Pulling Honor under my one arm, so it's draped around her shoulder, I'm able to rub her arm. "Why do you want your brother dead?"

He folds his arms across his chest. "Because he deserves to die. He has it coming to him."

"That's no explanation," I say, lowering Honor to the bench next to us. When I look at her face, she is whiter than white, so I sit down next to her and hold her. "Why does he deserve it? What has he done to you? Who did he steal from you?"

Moore swallows hard and looks directly at Honor. "He stole my partner. Honor's great-great-great granddad was my business partner. We worked on that elixir together."

All of us, including me, gasp at this statement. I was not expecting that.

Moore continues. "He put me in a coma. Of course he thought he'd killed me and left me for dead, but I came to. It took a while. I'm not even sure how long I was out. All I know is when I woke up, blood had dried all over me. But my heart was still beating. He drove a stake through my chest." He laughs. "Maybe back then he thought one killed empaths like they killed vampires. I have no idea. Guns had been invented for goodness sake. I mean we've been killing for years." He ponders that for a moment. "I made my first kill when I was thirty-three.

"Anyway, it took a while to find him. Evidently, he fled the state. I found him in Pennsylvania a couple months later. He had convinced Seth, Honor's granddad, that I was working against him—using his elixir against him. When I caught Seth alone, he'd said he'd had it with both of us and he was taking his elixir and leaving it someplace safe."

Honor is shaking under my arm. I shift her atop my lap and try to comfort her with my embrace.

Moore continues his spiel. "I was pissed. I had worked so hard on that elixir, but Seth had kept the ultimate ingredient a secret. We had everything else."

I didn't like where this was going. From the way my lap was shaking because of Honor's tremors, I'd guess that she felt the same way.

"What was the ingredient, Moore?" I ask with clenched teeth.

He looks at Honor, then at the ground.

"Tell us," I demand.

With his eyes still cast down, he whispers, "Seth's own blood."

I close my eyes, leaning my forehead against Honor's.

"So that's why you need Honor's blood," Ethan declares, since I was stunned into silence.

My biggest fear has come true—Honor is not *safe.*

Moore nods, than inches toward Honor.

Instead of sticking around to see what he's going to do, I pick up Honor. With my arm tucked under her knees and my other arm around her back, I make a run for it.

There is no way I'm taking a chance at having him come after her. Who knows if he has a gun? He's not going to care about witnesses. He'd kill us all.

Well, all I care about is what he will do to Honor, so we flee.

Chapter Thirty-Two

The fading voices behind us are demanding that we return, but I won't. It may seem cowardly to them, but I'm too afraid for Honor.

Not uttering a word since bolting from Moore, Honor keeps her face buried in the crook of my neck.

"I need to put you down, princess. I'm sorry, but we need to run faster. I'm not sure if he's coming after us."

I put her down, grab her hand, and continue running at full speed. There are two trails up ahead. Following my gut, I lead her up the trail that goes directly into the woods. Once we've reached an area where the gravel ends and the dirt path begins, I take her up behind some large trees and overgrown bushes. We hide behind some seven-foot broken tree trunk that at first glance looks like a huge black bear.

Sitting her down on a rock behind the tree, I settle next to her. "Are you okay, princess?"

She nods. "You thought he was going to kill me right there, didn't you?"

"I'm not sure, baby. I just knew we couldn't take the chance."

Honor nods again.

"Did *you* think he was going to kill you right there?" I ask.

Shrugging, her eyes fill up, and she says, "I don't know. I felt at first that he was okay, but then, I'm not sure if I felt your fear or mine. I do know I was scared."

"I'm sorry," I apologize quietly.

"I wish I were able to distinguish, y'know, between my fear and yours. But he really was scaring me."

"Me too." My head aches from thinking about this.

"What do we do now? Do we stay here? You know they're going to look for us. What if he killed Ethan and Tam and them just so they wouldn't tell? Oh my god."

I pull Honor back on my lap. "Princess, shh. We're okay. I just, I wish I'd grabbed my gun before school. I should have had it on me."

"Your gun?"

"Yeah. That's why I brought it to your house in the first place. To protect you. But what good does it friggin' do me in your dresser? I just didn't think I'd need it at school. Fuck." Realizing, too late, that I said the F-word in front of Honor, I say, "I'm sorry, I didn't mean to say that."

"It's okay. It doesn't bother me."

I run my thumb along her bottom lip. "Yeah, but you make me want to be a better person. I'm trying not to curse in front of you."

My thumb moves along her lip as a smile forms on her face.

"Thank you," she whispers.

We stare at each other a long time, but before I move in to kiss her, my cell phone dings.

"It's a text from Ethan," I inform Honor and continue reading it out loud. "He says that Moore's gone. They walked out with him and watched him drive away. Moore doesn't want to kill you. Yes, he wanted your blood, but just to be sure you were Seth's granddaughter." I look at Honor who is looking at the phone with me. "Ethan says Moore insists you are safe with him, but not with Asa. We need to talk with Moore some more."

"What if he killed them and took Ethan's phone?" she whispers.

God bless her, she's thinking like me. "How 'bout I give Ethan a shout?"

A tentative smile forms on her face.

"Storm," Ethan answers his phone.

"Just making sure it was you who texted."

He laughs. "What'd you think Moore killed us and took it?"

I say nothing.

"Lighten up, dude. Why the hell did you take off like that?"

"I wasn't taking a chance with Honor's life. I'm not an empath anymore. I can't actually *feel* what's going on. Sue me."

"Hey," he says. "I'm joking. It...it makes me feel good that you protect Honor like that. Now get her ass back home before her parents worry. We'll talk about Moore later."

"Yeah. Okay. Thanks."

Honor watches me slide my phone back in my pocket. "Did you hear?" I ask her.

"Yeah. I'm sorry."

"For what?" I ask, running my thumb down her cheek.

"For making you scared or whatever. You're usually so, I don't know, unaffected. I'm sorry."

"It's not your fault, Honor."

This time, instead of waiting and chancing another interruption, I kiss her mouth. At first it's a tender kiss—I lightly touch my lips to hers, taking her bottom lip in between both of mine. But as my heart pounds, my kiss gets stronger—as if I would die right now if her lips were not fully engulfed by mine. When she parts her lips, I slip my tongue inside and let my passion take over. I lift her so she straddles my lap and vigorously pull her down on top of me. Our kiss deepens while I thrust my hips up and down. Her body rhythmically moves with mine, and I want to take her right there.

When I pull back, she looks at me as if I've rejected her. "Don't stop," she pleads.

"Princess, if I don't stop, it's not going to be pretty. And I'm sure you don't want me tearing your clothes off out here in the woods."

She lets out a loud disappointed sigh. "Oh, don't test me. But, I guess you're right. Not yet," she finishes her sentences softly.

"Not yet," I repeat. Wrapping my arms around her, I let her lay her head on my shoulder. With her arms and legs wrapped around me, it feels so natural. This is where she belongs—in my arms forever.

Chapter Thirty-Three

First through fourth periods suck. Not knowing if Honor is safe scares the shit out of me. She texts me at the beginning of each period to let me know she made it to class, but still, it drives me crazy. Third period she has Chemistry. And really, can I honestly trust Jared Moore? No. I cannot.

Therefore, sitting in third period class is for the birds. Raising my hand, I get the teacher's attention.

"What is it, Storm?"

"I need to see the nurse. I'm not feeling well."

She writes me out a pass and sends me on my way.

Obviously, I don't go to the nurse. Instead, I stand outside Moore's classroom. Through the long narrow window on the door, I see Honor diligently sloping over her books, speed-writing whatever it is Moore is yammering about today. Moore's crooked grin appears as soon as his eyes make contact with mine. Shit. He shakes his head and turns back to teach his class, uttering something I can't hear. Then Honor's head pops up. Next thing, she's getting out of her chair and heading towards the door. I roll my eyes at Moore's big mouth and step aside so Honor can open the door.

"Is everything all right, Storm?" she asks innocently.

I close my eyes and let out the breath I hadn't realized I'd been holding. "Yes, princess. I was just worried about you. That's all."

She gives me a resigned sigh. "Storm." She places her hand on my forearm. "I'm fine. As a matter of fact, without your fear interfering with my own emotions, I'm not afraid of Moore."

I roll my eyes like some ineffectual wimp. "Just be careful," I tell her. "I'm not trusting *anyone* until this is all over."

Her genuine smile brightens up her beautiful face before she reaches up and kisses me on the lips. "I'll be fine, Storm. See you at lunch."

I nod and let her close the door, but I lean against the wall, arms folded in front of my chest, and wait for third period to end.

After the bell rings, Honor walks back out and shakes her head at my still being there. At least she's smiling.

"I just wanted to walk you to your next class," I explain. "Save you from a text."

She laughs.

"Don't laugh at me," I joke.

"But you're funny."

"Yeah, well, just forget it, princess. You're not going to change the fact that your life means more to me than anything. I'm not apologizing for that." I grab her hand and walk with her to her next class, hoping to just shut her up about my being whipped over her.

"Okay, *now* I'll see you at lunch," she says when we've reached her classroom. "Unless you're going to be standing outside the doorway when I get out."

"I just may be." I watch her walk to her desk, and then I head for my own class—missing her as I do.

In the hallway on my way to lunch, I spot Elijah caging in Tamlin against her locker. This makes me smile. Tamlin's a great girl. She deserves someone who'll give her his full attention. Hopefully Eli will do that, even though he *is* two years younger than she is. I'll have to talk with him about that later .

Honor is already sitting at the table alone. Rushing to sit down next to her, I straddle the bench and kiss her on the cheek. "Hey, princess."

"Hi, Storm."

"You mad at me?" I'm afraid my overprotectiveness freaks her out.

Her sweet smile relieves my fear. "Why would I be mad at you for caring about me?" She leans in and kisses me.

A kiss like that is such a simple act, but it sends a warm flow through my body that I can't help but close my eyes and embrace it. Placing my hands on her thighs, I whisper, "Thank you."

"Are you eating?" she asks, changing the subject.

"I guess. Can I get you anything?"

"Nah. I have the sandwich Mom made me."

"Just like a princess to have her mom make her lunch," I joke.

She nudges me in the stomach. "Stop. She always asks if she could make you one. You always say no."

"Yeah, peanut butter and jelly's not my thing."

"Don't knock it. It's good, especially with white bread."

Chuckling, I get up, kiss her on top of her head, and get on line for lunch.

When I get back, Ethan and Hunter are sitting at the table.

"Hey." I greet both of them with a nod. "So tell me about Moore." I put my lunch down and sit next to Honor.

"First of all, he laughed that you went running off like a baby," Hunter says, laughing the whole time.

"Yeah, yeah. Get on with it."

Honor gives my thigh a squeeze.

"By the way, where's Eli?" Ethan wonders.

"Sucking face with Tam." I take a bite of my sandwich after supplying him with that information.

Honor laughs.

"You knew about this?" I ask her.

"She mentioned they liked each other."

"Ah. Anyway, tell me about Moore." I look at Hunter. "Without the jokes."

"He's not after Honor's blood. Not the way you think," Ethan makes clear.

I look at Honor to make sure she's okay. It must be hard knowing all this is about her. But she's cool today.

"He admitted to taking those vials of blood for his own use, but only to make sure she was, in fact, Seth's granddaughter, like he said." Ethan takes a bite of his burger before continuing. With his mouth full, he continues. "But Gaffer...Asa...will not stop with the elixir you gave him. Moore's an empath too."

"But his eyes," Honor interjects.

"Contacts," Ethan informs. "Anyway, Moore realizes you made a fake elixir."

"How?"

"He's been an empath for a long time. Not only can he *feel* emotions, he can read what you're thinking based on those emotions."

"So now what?" I ask.

"He said his brother's not an idiot. It won't take him long to figure out that he's not dealing with the real elixir." Ethan pauses and looks at Honor, a frown deepening on his face. "He said once his brother realizes it, he won't only come after you for trying to pull shit over on him, he's going to come after the missing ingredient."

Honor gasps and covers her mouth with her hand.

Taking Honor's hand, I mutter, "Honor?"

Ethan slowly nods. He looks at Honor and apologizes to her in a whisper.

Eli and Tamlin finally grace us with their presence. "Hey guys, what's up?" Tamlin says with her happy grin, which quickly fades when she sees Honor frowning. "What is it, Hon?"

Ethan, Hunter, and I all utter a loud sigh.

"Oh. Mr. Moore's brother?" she asks, finally realizing. "It's gonna be all right, Hon. Moore said he has a plan."

"A plan?" I look at Ethan. "What plan?"

"I was about to fill you in before *she* interrupted."

"Sorry," Tamlin says.

"The plan," I remind Ethan.

Holding onto Honor's hand and rubbing her forearm with my other hand, I listen to Ethan tell me how Moore wants to lure his brother into the woods near the reservation by telling him he has Seth's granddaughter's blood and he doesn't need Storm's bloody elixir.

"Wait a minute," I interrupt. "What if Moore is lying to us? What if that was the whole reason he took Honor's blood in the first place? We can't trust him."

"What else we got, man? We're gonna have to trust him. Besides, the three vials is not enough for the elixir. He'd need pints of it."

"And what if that's why they want Honor back in the woods? The whole reason I took off in the first place."

"It didn't sound like that, man," Hunter chimes in.

Sighing, I relent. "Okay. When does this *luring* take place? And are we supposed to be there with him?"

"Moore said he could use our help," Ethan starts, "He said Asa never shows up anywhere alone. He said we'll disperse throughout the woods. Maybe get there way ahead of schedule to beat his brother there."

I nod.

"It'll be risky, I'm not gonna lie. We're going to have to have some kind of ammunition."

Honor glances at me quickly. She's referring to the gun, but I don't want anyone else, besides her and Ethan, knowing I have it. "We'll think of something."

"We better," Tamlin says.

"You shouldn't be there, babe," Elijah tells her.

"Oh, Eli, stop worrying about me. You can't *pay* me to stay away."

"Moore said he'll get in touch with you when he schedules the meeting with his brother."

"Me?" I ask.

"Yeah, he says though you were a wimp the other day, you're the only one he trusts to see this through."

I shake my head. I sure hope I'm strong enough to see it through. Loving Honor has turned me into a pussy. "Yeah, I'll see this through. And I'll make sure we have some means of protecting ourselves." I look at Ethan. "Can you take care of Honor today? I need to do some things."

"What?" Honor asks.

"Things. I don't want you with me." I turn back to Ethan. "Will you?"

"Definitely," he says.

"Don't leave her alone...At. All. I'll be back before it gets dark."

I kiss Honor on the mouth and let it linger. "I'll see you tonight, princess."

"You're leaving right now?"

Bringing my finger to my lips, I whisper, "Shhh." Then I walk out of the lunch room and out the school doors. I'm cutting the rest of the day.

Chapter Thirty-Four

Mahlon Dickerson is right up the road from school, so in five minutes, I'm there. Today, I'm going to scope the place out. If we're going to do this right, I need to know this place backwards and forwards. Passing the beach where we convened the other day, I decide to forego looking into that area. Anything sinister that's going to happen will not happen out in the open. Instead, I head up the trail towards the new bridge. Though it's fairly open, there's room underneath the bridge to plant one or two of us. I take some pictures with my phone and head up another trail. This trail, different from the trail Honor and I took the other day, is much more secluded. Taking several pictures of most of the area, I continue up the hill. There are so many overgrown trees and bushes, that we could certainly hide. But then, so can Asa and his men. Storing that information in the back of my mind, I make a mental note to tell Moore to give his brother no advance notice as to where he'll meet.

After combing the area for several hours, I now search for some large branches I can whittle into something akin to a stake. I'll have my gun on me, but no one else will be armed. They're going to need some type of protection, and I can't get my hands on another gun.

In the midst of carving my third stake with the Swiss Army knife I carry with me at all times, my cell phone rings.

"Honor. What's up, princess?"

"Just wondering if you're okay. I was worried."

She was worried about me. Sweet. "I'm fine, sweetheart. I'll be heading home soon. Ethan stayed with you, right?"

"Yes. Even though my parents are now home, he insisted on staying."

"Good. Can I talk with him?"

"Yeah."

"Yeah, Storm. Whatchya find?" Ethan asks.

"Nothing. I wasn't looking for anything in particular. I came to scope the place out. Y'know, to get the upper hand when Moore meets his brother."

"Ah. Makes sense."

"Yeah. Listen. Do me a favor. Try to contact Moore. Did he give you his number?"

"No. Did he give it to you?"

"No. I don't know. Find a way to contact him. The sooner the better. I need you to alert him *not* to give his brother the location of where we're going to meet. Just the day and time."

"What? Why?"

"'Cause he's smarter than me. What makes you think he won't come up here and set traps or something. I don't want to take the chance. Just tell him. Maybe email him through the school page and tell him to call you. Just leave your number. For goodness sake, *do not* put anything private in the email."

"I'm not an idiot, Storm. Fine. I'll get in touch with him."

"Good. Let me talk to Honor."

"Hi," she says, and her soft voice turns me to mush.

"Hey, sweetheart. I'll be home soon, 'kay?"

"Yeah."

"Don't worry about anything. We're gonna kick this guy's ass."

She chuckles, but I know it's not heart deep.

"See you soon."

"Bye, Storm."

I slide the phone back into my pocket and finish the stake I'm working on. Since it's just about dusk, I figure I'll come here tomorrow with more supplies and make some other ammo.

Before leaving the reservation, I hide the stakes where no one will find them and take pictures of where I hid them.

Then I head home to the love of my life...and maybe make her my girlfriend for real.

Chapter Thirty-Five

The Stevens are sitting at the dining room table eating a late dinner, Ethan included. They're all laughing and enjoying each other. A spasm of jealousy shoots through me. I don't like it.

"Hey," I say with a smile as I approach the table.

"Storm," Mrs. S. greets me. "We set a place for you. Sit and eat."

"Thank you, Mrs. Stevens." I sit down next to Ethan, across from Honor. I blow her a soft kiss with my lips, trying hard to keep it inconspicuous.

She smiles, but I'm still jealous; I guess I expected her to blow a kiss back. Part of me didn't want to leave Ethan in charge of her, knowing damn well she still had feelings for him. But I can't trust Hunter or Elijah to protect her like Ethan would. Trying not to let my doubt show on my face, I paste on a smile and tell Mrs. S. how delicious her meal is.

"Thank you, Storm. Honor and Ethan helped."

"Mmm. Nice." Well, if that didn't just kill me. I wonder if their cooking led to the same thing it led to when Honor and I tried to prepare dinner. "If you'll excuse me," I say before finishing dinner, "I'm really tired. Would you all mind if I excused myself?"

"Not at all, honey," Mrs. S. says. "Go ahead. Get some rest."

Not even looking at Honor, I take my dish to the sink and head for my bed. I don't change into shorts or anything. I just plop down on top of the covers fully clothed and kick off my shoes. I lay my head against the pillow and close my eyes, my intentions of asking Honor to be my girl-friend flying out the window the minute I caught the guilty look on her face at the dinner table.

A light knock on the door startles me from my nap.

"Yeah?" I call out.

"Can I come in?" Honor asks.

I sit up against the headboard. "It's your room, princess. You don't need to ask permission."

She leaves the door open, like her mom requires, and sits on the side edge of her bed facing me. "Why did you leave the table? You don't get tired. What's wrong?"

"I don't wanna talk about it."

"Storm. Stop. This is about Ethan isn't it?"

I sit up and face her, knees to knees. "Is that your guilt talking or are you *feeling* what I'm thinking?"

Her lower lip tremors and it makes me feel bad for being sarcastic.

"That's not fair." Her voice is quiet, but she continues looking me in the eyes.

"What are we doing here, Honor? Is there something between us or not?"

Her knee bounces up and down, causing mine to do the same. "I thought so," she says, her voice still barely above a whisper.

"I thought so too." I can't seem to hide my aggravation.

"Then, I don't understand. Why are you mad?"

"Is there something between you and Ethan still?" I ask her, needing to know the answer as if my next breath depends on it.

She shrugs. "I...I don't know...it's just..."

"It just sucks is what it is, Honor. I can't be holding you in my arms one day then watch you swoon over my brother the next. I may be a wiseass son of a bitch, but when it comes to you, my heart just can't take it."

"Swoon?" she says, her voice clipped. "Who's swooning? I'm certainly not. Give me a break. You're being totally unfair and irrational."

"Oh. Really? I don't think so at all. I saw your face at the dinner table. You had guilt written all over it."

"Maybe if you thought to ask me instead of storming off, you'd have found out why I had guilt written all over my face," she mocks.

"I don't think asking you at the dinner table would have been appropriate, do you?"

"Well, no, but you didn't have to excuse yourself from the table in a huff."

"I didn't think it was in a huff. I thought I remained quite calm," I admit. "You're the one getting all defensive right now."

"Uggh," she groans. She shakes her head and goes to her dresser.

"Honor."

She turns around. "What?"

"I'm sorry." I stand up and move toward her.

She closes in on me, so I take her in my arms. Over her head, I ask her in the calmest voice I can why she had that look on her face at dinner.

My chest feels warm as she sighs into it. "I was feeling guilty *for* Ethan...not *because* of him."

I pull her away to bring her at arm's length and look at her face. "Why? That doesn't make sense."

"Sure it does," she says. She takes a few breaths and looks like she's composing her thoughts. "Before we started helping Mom with dinner, we, uh, had a long talk." Honor clears her throat, obviously stalling for time. "He, uh, told me he wanted to give us...another try."

"Who? You and Ethan?"

She only nods.

"What the fu...hell? He knows how I feel...never mind. What did *you* say?"

"I told him I didn't think that was a good idea right now."

"Right now?" I jump in.

"Well, I couldn't just, like, tell him no right out. I felt bad for him."

"Okay. Did you say anything about me?"

She shakes her head this time.

"But he knows about us, Honor. He sees me holding you all the time. The fact that you didn't mention your feelings towards me, gives him reason to try again." I'm pissed again. And I hate being pissed. Especially since I've been so happy with Honor recently.

Her back is facing me now as she walks toward her window.

"I don't know what else to do, Storm." She turns around to face me. "Having a boyfriend is new to me. I've never dealt with all this before."

"That's just it. Tonight, I had wanted to ask you officially to be my girlfriend. Then I come home to this. You say having a boyfriend is new to you. Who do you mean? Who is your boyfriend?"

Plopping back down on her bed, she looks like she's about to cry.

Her inevitable tears do me in. I sit next to her on her bed and drape my arm around her. "Listen, Honor. You're obviously not ready to...be my girl, so I'll just have to accept that. But I need to know one thing...did he kiss you today?"

When her eyes meet her lap, I regret asking her that question. "Did you kiss him back?" I ask, knowing damn well I do not want to know the answer to that.

Her eyes remain on her lap while she fidgets with her fingers.

Shit.

I remove my arm from around her and go to the bathroom to get ready for bed. There is no way I can deal with this right now. When the heart breaks, the mind either shuts down or goes crazy. And I'm about to go freaking crazy, so I need to shut down. Now. Sleeping is the only way I know to do that.

After spending some time in the bathroom, Honor is still sitting on the bed where I left her. From the look of her heaving shoulders, she's crying. I'll go crazy if I look at her, so I keep my gaze down, take off my shirt, let down my bed and climb in—making sure to face the window as I do.

That lasts about thirty seconds, because I hear her hitched breathing and I melt. Sitting up in my bed, I look at her and wave two fingers in my direction. "C'mere, princess."

I pull her between my legs so we're sitting with her back against my chest. She rests the back of her head against my shoulder, and I think, *this is where she belongs...whether she knows it or not.* "I'm sorry I walked away," I say into her ear. "It's best though, when I'm angry, to walk away."

"I'm sorry I made you angry," she says, her voice sounding so weak.

"No, princess. You have nothing to apologize for. You haven't even broken up with Ethan that long ago. I should have never even considered being with you until you had healed from it. I'm really sorry."

"Thanks," she whispers. "I do like you, Storm. Sometimes, I think I lo..." She pauses and takes a breath. "I love you."

I kiss her cheek. "You don't have to say that."

"But I want to, and I do...love you, that is. But when I'm with Ethan, I get confused. I wish I weren't an empath, because then I wouldn't have my feelings fighting with everyone else's. It gets difficult to decipher. You know what I mean?" Honor's huge violet eyes look up at me.

"I think I do, darling. But to be sure, after this is all over, you know, the whole Asa-Mr. Moore thing,maybe you and I should take a break too. This way you'll know for sure if you actually love me, or if you are just feeling my love for you and confusing the two."

She looks up at me with watery eyes. "But I'll miss you."

"And I'll miss you too. But it's the only way. I don't want to keep you in a relationship that you're not even sure about."

"Yeah. I guess not. Maybe I'll go away with my parents or something. They probably need a vacation after all this too."

"I'm sure they do." I kiss my princess on her cheek and hold her for as long as I can. Honor has become my every thought lately. Living without her, even for a short time, is going to kill me.

Chapter Thirty-Six

When Honor's alarm clock rings, we wake in each other's arms. Sometime during the night we must have slunk down under the covers and continued holding each other. My arms are wrapped around her so that both my hands are clasped together, and she is huddled tight inside my arms, her head still firmly against my chest.

Unclasping my hands, I reach over to the end table and shut off the blaring alarm.

"Morning, angel," I whisper over her head.

"Morning," she breathes into my chest.

Neither one of us wants to make the first move.

"Princess, I don't have a problem cutting school in order to stay in bed with you all day, but something tells me your parents won't exactly approve."

Her giggling against my bare chest makes all the little hairs around my pecs tingle, sending the most fabulous sensation right down to the hairline on my stomach. I kiss the top of her head.

"C'mon, princess. We need to get up," I say, my words betraying my actions, because I am still holding on to her as tight as I can.

Lifting her head, she kisses my chest then looks at my face. "I like the way I feel when I'm with you, Storm." Her eyes get more intense as she looks deep into mine. "I hope they're my own feelings, because I don't want to let this go."

I sigh with a smile. "I hope so too, angel. I really do. But a little time apart, and we'll know for sure." I continue to smile though my heart is trembling with fear that she'll have realized a different truth while she's away.

My high from waking up with Honor plummets when I see Ethan getting out of his car. Needing to protect Honor, I keep her by my side as we walk into school, but I want to kick his ass for hitting on her.

"Hey," Ethan says innocently.

"Hey," Honor replies.

I keep quiet for fear if I open my mouth, I'll let loose on his skinny ass.

Honor keeps her head down the whole while walking to her first period class. Ethan's presence unnerves me. He insists on walking with us. When I finally blow a kiss goodbye to Honor, Ethan is still by my side.

"What?" I ask, agitated by his refusal to leave.

"I talked to Moore this morning."

"And?"

"Today. We're meeting today." Ethan's words don't come out calm. He's a nervous wreck.

"Today? When did you talk to Moore? We just walked in."

"I emailed him like you said and left my number. He called me as I was driving in."

I run a quivering hand through my hair and start pacing. "I'm not ready. Why today?"

Ethan shakes his head. "I don't know, man. Mr. Moore didn't explain anything.

"Shit. Fine. I'll go talk to him, and we'll talk it out at lunch."

"Yeah. Okay." Ethan starts to walk away.

"Oh, and little brother?"

He turns to face me.

"Don't you fucking make a move on her again. She's mine." I turn and walk away.

"Fuck you," he says, and I swear...he laughs.

Pushing past the pesky teenagers sauntering to their second period class, I race to Moore's class before the bell rings.

"Moore," I say with a ragged voice.

"Sutherland." He looks at his swelling classroom. "Not now."

"But—"

"Not. Now."

My heart slumps along with my shoulders, and I cover my fist with my other palm. Nervous energy is taking me over. I am so not ready for this to go down—especially without talking to Moore first.

"Your lunch hour," I hear behind me as I'm walking out his door. Turning around to make sure he is talking to me, I see that he is. "If you need help with the assignment," he continues, "come during your lunch hour. I have a free period then."

My tension settles a little, and I crack a half smile. "Thanks."

As usual, Honor is the first at our lunch table, so I sit next to her and kiss her on the cheek.

"Hey, Storm," she smiles. "I was just thinking about you."

"You were?" My heart wants to warm to this fact, but the empty pit in the bottom of my stomach is overriding any good sensations I'm feeling.

"Yeah. I was just thinking about waking up with you this morning." Her cheeks turn that rosy shade of pink I love so much.

"That was nice, wasn't it?" I say, hardly feeling the sentiment. My palms sweat so much I need to wipe them on my jeans. "Listen, Honor. I just came to tell you that I'll be in with Moore this period."

She looks at me with big questioning eyes.

"It, uh, appears he's meeting with his brother this afternoon. I need Ethan with me, and Tom and the boys too, so I'm going to ask Tamlin to go straight home with you—"

"Hell no, Storm." She cuts me off. "There's no way you're leaving me out of this. No freaking way."

"Honor," I say with as much sternness as I can to get this across to her. "There is no way I am putting you right in the line of fire. No flippin' way. Now, you'll go home with Tamlin like I said, and you'll lock the door behind you and stay put."

I shake my head and don't give her a chance to respond. Turning and walking away, I head for Moore's room.

"Sutherland, sit down." Moore puts his pen down and leans back in his chair.

"No. Why today?"

His shoulders drop in exasperation. "My brother gave me no choice. He said if I have the girl's blood, he wants it immediately." He looks down momentarily, and I get that sick to my stomach feeling that there's more to it. "But he already warned me that a pint or so will not suffice. He wants all of it."

"All of it? Honor's blood? No fucking way. You're crazy, Moore."

"Sutherland, calm down. I have no intention of draining her dry. I like Honor. I wouldn't do that. But she should be there with us."

"No way. I'm not putting her in danger. No."

"I promised him." Moore informs me. "If I don't have all her blood in bags, then he wants her alive so he can drain her himself. She needs to be there so it looks like I'm doing what he wants."

"Sorry, but no. I'm not putting her in danger like that. I don't even trust you yet. For all I know, this was your plan with your brother all along. No. She stays put." I make a mental note to tell Tamlin to take Honor to Tamlin's house, not Honor's house. She'd be too easy to find at home. "You'll have to come up with something else."

"Fine. We still have to meet today. He agreed with the reservation though."

"Fine. Right after school?"

"Yeah. I told my students that I wouldn't be here for afterschool help today. So meet me there then."

"Yeah. I'll make a few calls then I'm going over now."

"Now?"

"You don't think I'm going with no plan do you? I need to set up. So, if you can cover for us Sutherland boys for skipping classes this afternoon, I'd appreciate it."

"Yeah. Sure. Death in the family or something like that," he quips while handing me several blue passes that will excuse us for the afternoon.

"Somethin' like that." My feet aren't even out the door when I send a group text to my brothers to meet me at Ethan's car in five minutes, I quick call Uncle Tom, then I send a short text to Tamlin about taking care of Honor this afternoon.

After stopping at my car to retrieve the gun and bullets I fortunately put in my glove box this morning, I meet the guys by Ethan's car.

"What's going on? We're meeting today?" Eli asks.

"Yeah. And I don't want my car there. Asa knows it, it wouldn't look good."

"And you don't think he knows mine?" Ethan asks.

"Well, at least it's less conspicuous." I say, making sure to keep my gun hidden while Eli and Hunter take the back seat. Then I have a thought. "Ethan, park by the old ski area."

"Why?"

"It's a longer trek, but no one will see us walk through the woods to the reservation. I'll text Tom to meet us there too. Then, I think one or two of you should ride to Saffin Pond with Tom and enter that way. Just try to stay out of sight."

Ethan tsks. "What makes you sure they won't be looking for all of us?"

"I'm not sure. You got a better plan?"

"No."

"Park here," I tell him when we get there. There's a private parking area set off to the back of the lot. "I'm going to head in by myself, you guys wait for Tom, then Ethan, you follow my path." Before heading up through the woods, I remind them to keep in close contact via our phones. "And set them to vibrate. We don't need anyone hearing us."

On my way up the trail, I say a silent prayer that Honor remains safe through all this. Then I say a selfish prayer asking that if I come out of here alive today, she'll choose me after our break. I make the sign of the cross then pat my pockets. My gun and extra bullets are all safe and secure.

Chapter Thirty-Seven

Adrenaline flows rapidly through my body, causing my heart to feel like it's going to flee from my chest at any moment. Honor's life depends on this mission, and I'm doubting myself—*not* a good sign. Where there's doubt, there's room for error.

There is *no room for error.*

Closing my eyes, I try to breathe out all of my fears and instead welcome the sounds of nature. If I can tune into the rustling of the leaves and the calls of the animals, I will be able to decipher the noises that don't belong. When my stomach calms, I open my eyes and take out my phone. In order to let Tom and my brothers know where I've hidden my wooden stakes, I send them all the pictures I took yesterday. I inform them of what I hid where and press send. Then, to make sure Honor is not mad at me for walking out on her during lunch, I send her an apology text and ask her to please stay safe and stay at Tamlin's. Without waiting for a response, I slide the phone back into my back pocket and take hold of my gun.

With a slow and cautious gait, I make my way towards the bridge. Under the rocks, on the outskirts of the brook, I reach for my stake and place it upright, point pierced into the ground and ready to grab hold if needed. I text Moore and tell him we're here.

Hunkering down beneath the bridge, I hide for the time being. If there's a chance Asa and his men will see me now, it may ruin everything. So I wait, rapid heartbeat and tense muscles not lacking, for Moore to alert me what to do next.

Tom's group text alerts us that Moore is here. Asa too. Though Moore hasn't seen him yet—only his car. Great. That means he's here somewhere in the woods. Confused, I ask Tom if he's talked to Moore himself. He assures me he has and that we should head toward the swim team's side of the pond. In an attempt to stay hidden, instead of taking the trail, I walk through the overgrown brush that parallels the trees. That's when I see Ethan walking the trail in plain sight. Stupid boy.

Staying within the brush, I keep my eye on Ethan, just in case he needs my assistance. Fortunately, he'd grabbed a stake on his way down. When Ethan meets Moore, I see Hunter and Elijah with him. They're stiffly turning their heads, either searching for me or for Asa. Or Tom, wherever he is. With a few waves of his hands, he instructs my family to disperse. Each one takes a different direction and finds a tree to hide behind.

Just then a text comes in. Moore.—**stay hidden. He's here. I feel him. I'm sure he feels y'all too. When I told your brothers to head towards the pond, the assholes didn't think of staying out of sight. Fuck.**

Moore puts his phone to his ear. I don't need to read lips to know he just let out an exclamatory "fuck" when he runs his hand through his hair and starts pacing. His brow furrows and he rubs it with his phone-free hand.

Something's happened.

Something bad.

As Moore paces the beach area, I get a sickening knot in my stomach. Approaching Moore is out of the question, so I text him. When he looks at his phone, I'm surprised when he doesn't acknowledge my text. Shit. What's happened?

Staying cautious, alert, and out of sight, I head to where I watched Ethan hide. I stay low behind a bush, but Ethan catches glimpse of me.

"What's up?" he whispers, not turning to look at me.

"No idea. But I need you to go back out there. If Asa's here, he's already seen you. I'm sure he knows exactly where you're hidden." I keep my voice as soft as I can, barely whispering the words so that only Ethan can hear me.

With a nod of his head, Ethan's gone, and I get a better look so I can witness whatever's being said.

And within sixty seconds, my greatest fear is realized.

My pulse races, and my knees go weak, as I watch as Ethan collapse on the bench, his hand splayed across his heart. Suddenly, I'm dizzy and hyperventilating. But I know why he's down. He felt her. He fucking felt her. Forcing my feet to move, despite my legs' unwillingness to follow, I bolt down to the beach and grab Moore by the collar. "Where the fuck is she? How'd he get her?"

Moore looks at me with bated breath and bulging eyes. "You said...she wasn't coming?"

"She wasn't!" I yell, shaking the hell out of him. "Tell me where she is!"

He shakes his head.

"Get the fuck out here!" I yell to whomever will listen. "Get out here now."

I guess I'm signaling for my brothers, but I want Asa to hear me. "Asa, you old fuck. Get out here now. Make this a fair fight. You hear me, you fucking old man."

Tom puts his hand on my shoulder, but I brush it off.

"What direction did you see him come?" I ask Moore, still frantically exclaiming my words.

"I didn't. I only...I only saw his car...and got his call."

If I'd only brought her with me, she'd be safe by my side.

Tamlin. I phone her.

It goes to voicemail.

"*Feel* your way to her," I tell them all. "You guys are empaths, right? Well use your fucking superpowers and find Honor. *Now.*"

Closing my eyes, I reach deep inside my gut to listen to what it says. I head back towards the bridge and hope to God that my instincts are right.

My gun clutched in my right hand, I worry that my trembling hand will cause me to miss my shot. Though my empathic abilities are gone, my bond with Honor is so strong, that I know she is near. And in danger.

Taking a hidden path all the way back to the bridge, I must show myself in order to reach the part of the bridge I left my stake. Ducking as I maneuver my way down the rock decline, I see Tamlin rushing down an unused trail.

Huffing, she drops her hand to her thighs, bending over to catch her breath. "Storm, help," she says between breaths. "He has her...he took her...and..."

"Where?" I beg.

She points into the trees. "He...he's lost...he doesn't know his way...around. That's..."

"What, Tam? Hurry, I need to go after her."

"Go that way." She points again. "I got away because he was trying to get his GPS to work."

Taking her by the arm and hiding her beneath the bridge, I tell her, "Stay here. Don't move. Call Eli, tell him where you are and take this." I hand her the stake I had hidden.

Not looking back, I race back up the trail Tamlin just came from. When I come to a fork, I need to rely on gut instinct to tell me which path to take. I choose the one on the right and say a quick prayer that I'm headed in the right direction. Following the path up another steep incline, I hit a dead end, and though my instincts are to scream for Honor, I don't. Instead, I text the guys and tell them what's up.

Rather than return back down the trail, I cut through the woods hoping…praying…I'm on the right track. The adrenaline takes over my body, and I can't help but run. Though running will get me there faster, my reasoning will be impeded. I want to break down and cry. This evil man has Honor, and I feel so helpless.

That's when it occurs to me what Tamlin had said. Asa is lost. He can't find his way out. I know that there are only two ways out of Mahlon Dickerson. The way Ethan and I came in and the way Tom and the others entered. I am nowhere near either. I text Moore and tell him to guard the front entrance, then I run for the path that leads to where we parked. When I reach the lot, Ethan's car is there. And Tamlin's is parked next to it. I remind myself to kick her ass later for bringing Honor here.

Taking the trail back this time, I don't stray from the path. I do, however, take it slow, scaling every inch of the woods around me for any movement. Not even an animal scurries through. A new text comes in and it's Eli. He's with Tamlin and they're staying put. He lets me know that Ethan is on his way up the trail heading out to the lot, while Hunter and Tom are headed up the trail that circles behind the lake. With all four pathways surrounded, the dread inside my chest lifts a little.

Gripping my gun, my eyes are peeled on everything around me. When I've combed every inch of woods on the outskirts of the trail, my hope diminishes, and I wonder if I need to travel inside of the woods as well as the paths. Acre upon acre of rock, brush, and trees lie before me and I think, *it'll be dark before I've even searched a tenth of the place.*

Fatigue takes over. My desperation heightens, and no longer do I feel the hope I had in finding Honor before she's harmed. Not one for giving up, I trudge forward, vowing to die before giving up on finding her.

As the bridge where Tam and Eli are enters my line of sight, I hear a shuffle in the woods beside me. Shaking off my weariness, I stride up to where I hear the noise.

And there she is.

Her back against the chest of a lithe Asa.

A gun to her head.

"Storm," she cries.

"Honor," I cry back.

Holding my gun in his direction, I hesitate to shoot, fearing I'll clip Honor instead.

"Drop the gun," he commands, while still holding his gun to Honor's head.

"You won't shoot her," I reply, hoping he won't. "You won't be able to drain her blood if you shoot her." I try to stall. "It won't hold her powers if she's dead." The chill in my voice betrays the heart that's pounding at my chest, searching for a way out.

I can't know what he's feeling, but I can certainly read the resignation on his face. He won't shoot her. My gun remains in my hand. If only I could trust my shaking hand to shoot him in the head while sparing Honor.

His smirk lets me know that he's read my thoughts. "I'll just shoot *you*. Now that I got what I need, who the hell needs you, Sutherland."

"Go 'head. I'll trade my life for Honor's any time. Just know though, there are others here who will fight you just as hard to save her."

With Honor still firmly in his grasp, Asa walks forward, his gun now pointed at me.

I don't back down.

"I'll be long gone," Asa says.

"You've got that right," Moore says from the brook behind me. "Because I finally get to kill you."

From my peripheral vision, I see Ethan running down the trail, and I say a quick prayer that he gets here in time to grab Honor before Asa sees him. But Moore fires his gun, and in that tenth of a second, I think he's going to tag Honor at the same time. But when Asa goes down, falling forward on his knees, I realize Moore purposely hit his brother in the back of his calf to spare Honor.

It works. She's freed.

But she runs straight toward me, and knocks the gun out of my hand as she catapults into my arms. As I bend to pick up my gun, keeping my arm securely around Honor's waist, I hear another gunshot. I look up just as Moore goes down from a bullet to his chest.

Honor yells, "Noooo," when she catches what happened.

"Who's next?" Asa mocks, standing as if he hadn't just been shot in the leg, though the pool of blood surrounding his foot is proof that he was. Just as Asa aims his gun at me, Ethan makes it down the hill just in time and impales him with one of the stakes I'd made.

At the same time, Honor peels herself from my grasp and runs toward Moore.

"No!" I yell. "Don't." As I run for her, Ethan lets go of the stake, and runs for her as well. "Honor, no. You can't," Ethan demands.

But before we grab her, smoke rises from both dead men, halting Honor from touching Moore.

Making my move, I wrap both my arms around Honor. "You can't save him. You don't have the energy left. You'll kill yourself."

"I won't," she cries. "He helped us. How can we just let him die?"

Tamlin and Eli head up from the bridge.

"Honor," Tamlin cries, still holding the stake that I gave her.

"Stay back," I tell her. "She's trying to save Moore."

Hunter and Tom, their makeshift stakes in hand, make it down from their trail, running and out of breath.

Behind me, footsteps plod down the hill. I turn to look but keep my hold on Honor. Two armed men approach us and I recognize them as Thing One and Thing Two. But when they see what appears through the smoke, they halt.

My attention returns to Honor, who is still struggling to release herself from me. "He's a good guy," she cries again, and the tears pour from her eyes.

Ethan runs to my side and holds her with me. "Honor. Look. They're killers. Look at all those souls leaving their bodies." *Hundreds of them.*

"Why would you want to save a mass murderer?" Hunter asks.

Still pushing to break free from my grasp, Honor cries, "Noooo. Noooo. He can't die like this. He helped us."

While she cries on about saving Moore, the rest of us are stunned into silence by what appears before us.

One soul manifests itself from Moore's body. Honor gasps, and halts her efforts to release from my hold, but I keep my arms wrapped snugly around her. When the image has transformed into a solid figure, he smiles.

At Honor.

"Do you know him?" I whisper in Honor's ear.

She shakes her head, and then totally starts nodding. "I think." Her words come out in tiny breaths.

The man glides forward, rustling nothing beneath his feet, and when he opens his mouth, he says, "Sweetheart."

Honor falls listlessly in my arms.

When I sit her down, he man steps forward and kneels down in front of her, placing his ghostly hand on her knee. "It's me, Honor," he says softly. "Gramps."

Every single one of us gasps this time, excluding Honor.

"Gramps?" she whispers.

"Yes, baby. Oh how I've missed you."

As I watch Honor's frown turn into a huge bright smile, she leaves my embrace and hugs her grandfather—which is odd to watch, because though he looks solid, he really isn't. Honor ends up falling forward. I catch her before she falls flat on her face, and her grandfather apologizes.

"How?" she asks.

Her grandfather raises his eyebrows. "He killed me."

"Mr. Moore?" she asks incredulously.

Nodding his head, he says, "But he's not all bad. He listened to me these past few months."

"I...I don't understand," she says.

"Some souls are persistent. They refuse to die within their host body. They wait it out until it's time to finally flee...when their host is finally put to rest."

I look around, and I'm amazed that everyone, including the two armed strange men, are speechless and intent on listening to this dead man speak.

"So," Seth, I believe Moore said was his name, continues. "I refused to rest. I knew that eventually you'd be in danger and I wouldn't allow it. I willed my thoughts and feelings onto that man and insisted he help save you."

"Hmm," I utter, despite trying to remain silent.

Seth looks at me. "The doubting Thomas."

I point to myself.

"Yeah, you. You insisted Honor was crazy for trusting Moore. But she knew. Her powers never lie. She felt me inside that man. Yes, Moore was evil...but I wouldn't let him act on anything that would harm my granddaughter. Never."

"Okay, I need to ask...why did he kill you?"

Seth smiles. "Sibling rivalry."

Instead of responding to that, I look at Ethan and then back at Seth.

"When we were in our thirties, the three of us—Jared, Asa, and I—worked tirelessly on the elixir. I finally got the formula right when we realized that I had all this power that they did not. We had worked on every ingredient together, until one night when I decided to add a couple pints of my own blood. I was about to tell them what it was—they were my best friends for goodness sake. I thought I could trust them. Until the two of them turned on each other, claiming one or the other had the idea first and that they each earned the rights to it over the other. No. I earned the rights to it. I created it."

Seth stands from his kneeling position, holding on to Honor's hand. I help her up but don't loosen my hold on her.

"I decided to run off without giving them access to the elixir. I ran clear across the country from out west to New Jersey. I had hid the elixir in my house, but I figured they'd find it eventually if they ever caught hold of me. Instead, I found the old schoolhouse in Hardyston and figured I could hide it away there. Class was not in session since it was summer, so I thought I could hide it without consequence. The basement was so deep underground that even if they knocked the building down, the elixir would probably remain."

He runs a hand through his phantasmal thick head of blond hair and smirks. "It stayed hidden for many years. I was always on the run, flitting from one place to the next—even after I married and had children. My poor kids barely saw me. Then one of my great-grandaughters gave birth to her own daughter and I met my Honor. I'm not sure what it was, but Honor made me want to be a better person."

"I know the feeling," I interject.

Seth laughs. "That's when I decided to leave a clue for her...just in case she ever needed it. I told her mother to keep the photo. Told her it may not look important, but it meant more than my life."

Seth starts fading away.

"Gramps," Honor cries.

"I think it's time, sweetheart."

He hugs her this time, and it hurts me to see the tears spill from her eyes.

"I love you, baby. Always will."

"I love you too, Grandpa."

When he fades, Honor turns into my chest and cries.

Seth rises up in a puff of smoke and the two men lying on the ground are nothing but dead men in possession of no more innocent souls.

Chapter Thirty-Eight

After the shock of watching hundreds of dead souls vanish into thin air, not to mention one of them stopping to chat, I realize we are still standing in front of two very armed large men. Turning to face them, and positioning Honor behind me, I look them in the eye and hold my gun back out.

They laugh.

"Put that thing away," the larger one of the two says. "We're not going to hurt you."

"Then why are you here?"

"To get Honor."

Without taking my eyes off of the men, I motion with my hands for my brothers to build a wall around Honor. "You're not getting her."

"We don't need her now," they laugh. "Asa's not around to pay us to hand her over."

"So, you *don't* want her?" Ethan asks.

"No. We wouldn't even know what to do with her. We just worked for the guy...got him what he wanted. We're not empaths or anything like that. Asa just paid us a ton of money to do his dirty work. As you just saw, he's not the largest of men."

"So—"

"So," the larger man interrupts, "if you'd like help disposing of the bodies, we can help. We'll take them to where Asa had us dump all his bodies."

"Where's that?"

"Now, we won't be giving that away, will we? No. Then you can implicate us. Though, we can implicate you, too, for murdering Asa. But we never liked the guy, so just help us drag them out."

The other large man speaks up. "I'll go get the bags, but we'll have to watch. We're lucky no one was around today. We should probably stick around 'til dark before carrying them out."

Yeah, we are lucky. All the time thinking about saving Honor, I forgot that it was daylight. "Okay, let's drag them into some bushes until we can get them out," I offer.

"How 'bout all this blood?" Tamlin asks out of the blue.

"He'll get stuff for that with the bags," the larger man says.

"Um...Tam," I say slowly, forgetting who brought Honor here in the first place. "Why the hell didn't you take Honor to your house like I'd asked?"

"Storm." Honor puts her hand on my arm. "I forced her to take me. There was no way I could stay away. I wasn't going to sit back and drink lemonade while you all were fighting to keep me safe."

"And you listened to her?" I'm still talking to Tamlin.

"Uh, well,..."

"Stop, Storm," Honor reprimands. "She could have taken me to her house, but I just would've jogged home and got my car. Stop protecting me like that. I mean, I appreciate it, and I certainly couldn't fight my way out of the Gaffer's hold, but..." she trails off, unsure of what to say.

"But what, Honor? If you'd listened to me in the first place, you wouldn't have had to fight your way out of his hold, would you?"

Honor sighs, and I inwardly chastise myself for getting angry.

"Okay, can we just stop this now?" Elijah says, not really asking us to stop, but demanding that we do.

"Fine. It's dropped," I say. Softening my resolve, I hug Honor. "Now that you're safe, why don't you and Tam go home? We don't need you to help clean up. Go put some normalcy back in your life, and be glad it's done."

Honor and Tamlin look at each other and shrug.

"What do you think, Honor?" Tamlin asks. "You want to get going? I need to have me a big piece of chocolate cake."

Honor chuckles. "You have cake?"

"Of course. Then, you can help me dye my hair. I'm thinking of trying green this time."

"Green?" Honor and Elijah cry in horror.

"Yeah, like a mint green," Tamlin says.

"Why don't you two go," I suggest again.

"C'mon, Hon," Tamlin grabs her by the arm.

"Yeah," Honor says. "Thank you," she looks at me, "for getting me away from that man...and killing him."

Hugging her again, I kiss her on top of the head. "That was my only goal, princess—to save you from that man. Now you're safe. It's over."

She rests her head on my shoulder, and she tightens her arms around my waist.

"It's over," she whispers, and I know exactly what she's thinking. *Now that it's over, we need to take that break.*

"I'll still stay with you tonight. We'll talk about it later."

I give her a soft kiss goodbye, Elijah and Tamlin break their embrace, and the girls walk away. The man with the bags and the clean-up material comes walking back around the lake, a backpack on his back.

After gruelingly stuffing the dead bodies into the bags while Hunter stands guard, we drag them up the hill and behind some torn down huge tree trunk. Then, we proceed to clean up the blood on the dirt with some bleach and some brushes Asa's men had packed away.

All the while cleaning up our fatal mess, I think about how tonight would be my last night with Honor for a while. And if she realizes that her feelings for me are only rebounded feelings of mine, then it'd be my last night with her forever.

I silently pray that I could handle it if that were the case, but I doubt it. A life on the run would be my fate again...if Honor doesn't choose me.

Chapter Thirty-Nine

"Hey, princess, I'm home." I greet Honor in her bedroom about nine at night.

It seems that though Mahlon Dickerson by Saffin pond is not a popular place to be during after school hours, it certainly is a hopping place for the after work crowd. It is necessary to wait until all the walkers and runners leave the reservation before carrying the dead guys out.

"Hey, Storm," Honor says with sleepy eyes.

"Were you sleeping already?"

She holds up the book in her hands. "No, reading, but I may have dozed off a little." Putting her book aside and sitting up against her headboard, she pats the bed for me to sit. "How'd it go?"

"It went. There were just all these after work exercisers getting their miles in that we had to wait until they left."

"Oh my god, did they see you?"

"Well, we didn't hide. We just...acted like we were supposed to be there. Eli and Hunter went walking up some trails while Tom and the big guys hung out talking near where we hid Asa and Moore."

"What about you? Where were you?"

"I just sat on a rock nearby."

"You weren't up for talking with anyone?"

I settle myself more comfortably on Honor's bed by sitting next to her and holding her in my arms. "Nah. Wasn't in the mood." All I had been able to think about was what would happen to Honor and me if she decided she wasn't in love with me.

"Oh," she says with a sigh. "Storm," she says after a long pause. "Do we have to take that break?"

"I think we do, princess. I wouldn't be comfortable not knowing whether you really are into me or if you're just into me because I'm into you. Does that make any sense at all?"

She shrugs beneath my shoulders. "I guess."

"Besides, you still have feelings for Ethan. I want to know for sure that you're done with him before you and I make any commitments to each other."

"Yeah." She sighs and rests her head against my chest.

I kick off my shoes and grab the pillow beneath us. Placing it behind my head, I settle back and enjoy holding Honor for what may be our last night together.

"I'll still see you at school, right? And at lunch?" Her voice breaks.

"Well, I've been thinking of withdrawing from school."

She whips her head up to look at me. "You can't. Please don't leave school."

"Baby, I finished high school like five years ago. They just have my fake school records which say I'm eighteen anyway. I can just sign myself out."

She leans her head back against my chest. "But I like having you there."

"Sweetheart, in June I'd be graduating anyway. There is no way I'm sticking around for that. Besides, I was only here to watch over you. That job is done."

"No," she cries. And after a few seconds her tears seep through my shirt and onto my chest.

Gliding my hands through her long hair, I whisper, "Don't worry, princess, I'm not leaving Jefferson...not until I know what *you* want."

The sweet scent of Honor right beneath my nose lulls me to sleep. I'm not sure who falls asleep first, but when I wake up, the sun is rising and Honor is still in my arms.

"Morning." Honor surprises me by being awake. She was lying so still in my arms.

"Morning, princess."

"Um, Storm? I was thinking. What is everyone going to think about Mr. Moore not showing up at school?"

"Hmm, I hadn't thought of that. I don't know." Now that it's on my mind, I'm worried about it. Plus, withdrawing from school will probably not be the best thing for me, especially since everyone knows how much Moore annoyed me. Not that jumping to the thought that I'd killed him because of my dislike for him would be the natural conclusion, but I can't take that chance. "You know...I think I'm going to stay in school until graduation."

"Why? What changed your mind?" She looks up at me with wide violet eyes.

"I guess I'd like to see how this whole Moore thing plays out."

"Oh," she says. "That's a good idea...I still feel bad. He was a nice guy."

"I don't know about that, but at least he tried to help us."

"Yeah, and I'm glad I got to see my grandpa."

I squeeze her hard. "Yeah. That was pretty cool."

While Honor gets ready for school, I pack up all my things and run it to my car, feeling sad about moving out already. When I return, Honor is sitting at the counter with her mom.

"Storm, coffee?" her mother offers.

"Sure. Thanks, Mrs. Stevens," I say, taking the already poured mug from her hand.

"Honor filled me in last night about yesterday."

"Oh. Well, I'm happy to say, she's safe now. No one will be out looking for her blood or that elixir anymore."

Mrs. S. smiles, but a frown follows. "She also told me about the three of you all needing a break from each other."

I just nod.

"She said it was your idea," Mrs. S. continues.

"Yup," I say with a frown.

"I think that was very admirable, young man. It takes a real grown up to face the truth like that." She smiles again and whispers in my ear, "I'm pulling for you."

I chuckle.

"I told Mom about my vacation idea. She said she'll talk to Dad, but she likes the idea too. She said maybe an island or something," Honor says with half a smile.

"Sweet." I find it hard to be happy that she's going away. What if she finds her feelings for me have totally disappeared? I guess I'd just have to deal with it.

"Anyway," Honor says. "We should get to school."

"Yeah, uh...just let me brush my teeth. Be right back."

"Mom really likes you," Honor says in the car on the way to school.

"Yeah? Well, that's good." My heart is just too sad to get excited about it.

"I'm nervous about going to school. How are we going to hide what we know about Mr. Moore?" When I take a side glance at Honor, she's biting her lip.

"Princess," I say while rubbing her thigh. "Just act natural. It's only suspicious to us. No one else would have any idea what to think, so c'mon, just act like normal."

"I'm not feeling well all of a sudden."

"You know what, babe. I'm gonna drive you home. I think you need the day off."

"But..."

"No buts. You and your mom can plan that vacation, and you won't have to deal with this today."

"Okay," she says, and I can see the relief pass her face.

We turn around, I take her home, and I kiss her goodbye at the front door.

"So...I'll see you soon, I guess," I say, giving her a long hug after the kiss.

"Oh. Oh. Does our break...start...now?" she asks, her hands still around my waist.

"I think it does."

I kiss her forehead and look into her violet eyes. "Call me when you've made your decision."

She nods.

"I'll be here waiting." My voice comes out hoarse, because I'm trying hard to hold back tears. Tears that I don't usually shed.

But when I see Honor start to cry, I can't help myself.

I don't cry.

I hate crying.

But here I am...crying.

Giving Honor one last strong hug, I turn and walk away.

Not even bothering to wipe away her tears.

Chapter Forty

Walking through the school halls without Honor is like walking through life without a purpose. Honor's week-long vacation in Berry Islands is almost over and I'm dying to know where I stand.

The only reason I attend classes is so I don't go crazy sitting at home. That, and the fact that gossip has run rampant about Moore's disappearance. Every high school teacher has been questioned about any personal issues they may have known about their peer. Teachers are worried and students are intrigued. Evidently, Moore had no family members. Faculty was concerned about his disappearance, so they were the ones to inform the officials. Now there's a case, and my brothers and I can't wait until it's closed. Trusting that the two large men, who Tom says are named Jimmy and Jack, hold true to their word, Moore won't be found and his case will close—unsolved.

At lunch time, instead of going to the cafeteria and socializing, I go out to the track and take a run. Trying to outrun the pain in my chest is futile, but it beats staying still and feeling the pain. When the end of lunch bell rings, I continue running right up the hill and into school, stopping when my cell goes off.

Not recognizing the out of state number, I let it go to voicemail and head to my next class.

"Storm," Tamlin says as I pass her in the hall. "What are you doing after school?"

"Not much. Why?" I ask, not enthused at all.

"Eli, Hunter and I are going to the diner. We want you to come. You've been so sulky all week." She takes my hand and squeezes it. "You need to get out. We're not even asking Ethan to go, since that'd probably make you sulk more."

I crack a smile.

"Is that a yes?" she says with a big grin.

"I guess."

"C'mere." Tamlin gives me a big bear hug. "She's going to choose you, you know. There's no doubt in my mind. I think Ethan even knows it. So come on already, smile. She'll be back in like what two days?"

"Yeah, she's flying in from Berry Islands today and then they're staying in Nassau for two nights," I explain as I unlock myself from Tamlin's death grip.

"See, that's two nights. You can go two more nights, can't you?"

"Yeah." I sigh.

"Good." She punches me in the arm and laughs. "Meet us in the lot, I'll drive."

"Oh great." I roll my eyes. "I would like to stay alive two more nights."

"Jack-ass," she calls, walking away and holding her middle finger up in the air.

Though weary from a mind that hasn't shut down, even with sixteen hours of sleep a day, the trip to the diner is a welcome diversion. Tamlin still manages to make me laugh, and I'm envious of her relationship with Eli. They fit well—as well as I thought Honor and I had. But to watch them brings a small smile to my face. There's no one cooler than Tam, and she deserves to be happy.

"So, Storm," Hunter says, a forkful of pancakes entering his mouth as he speaks. "We're going to the drive-in tomorrow night. Wanna come?"

"Uh, I don't know. We'll see."

"Ah, c'mon, you got anything better going on?"

"Hunter," Tamlin reprimands him from across the booth.

"It's fine," I tell her. Turning back to Hunter, I say, "No nothing better going on, but I'll let you know if I'm up for it."

"Okay. But it's Friday night. Don't sit home and sulk."

As firmly as I can, I repeat, "I'll let you know."

"'Kay, have it your way," Hunter replies.

Tamlin gives me one of those pity smiles, but I don't take it to heart. I finish my burger then order another milkshake. Not eating this past week has made me surprisingly hungry. It's still hard to feel happy though and I have a bad feeling. Even if she doesn't choose Ethan, something tells me she may not be choosing me either. And I won't know how to live with that.

When Tam drops me back at my car, I thank her for inviting me. If anything, it lifted my mood for a couple hours. Revving my engine, I peel out of the lot and head for home—where I'll go right to bed so I won't have to think too much. My nightmares will keep me from forgetting altogether, but at least I'll get some sort of reprieve from grief.

What a wuss I've turned into. Once so callous and cocksure, I don't even recognize myself anymore. Reclining on my bed, I grab my second pillow and hold it to my chest—the pillow filling the void where Honor should be. Attempting to recapture her scent is the last thing I remember before falling off into a restless slumber.

**

Clutching the sheets, I wake up drenched in sweat, my heart weighted in fear. Honor never comes back. She never returns from her trip. I sit up and clutch my chest. The pain is so intense, the nightmare so real, I can taste the foreboding rising up in my esophagus. Rubbing my sweaty palms on my blanket, I replay the nightmare in my mind.

Honor. Saving. Healing. Dying.

That's all I can recall. Why can't I remember my dream? It doesn't make sense. In my dream, I watch her die. I watch her fall. Her hands, I remember her hands. Dammit, why can't I remember everything?

Dragging myself out of bed, afraid to make a movement but afraid to stay still, I pad clumsily to the bathroom, clutching my stomach. My knees betraying me, they buckle and I fall against the sink. *Think, Sutherland. Think. What is my dream telling me? It has to have some meaning. I feel it in my chest. Know it in my mind.*

It's when I'm splashing water on my face that I remember the long-distance phone call I never picked up. Running to the chair I threw my jeans on last night, I pull my phone out of the pocket and retrieve the voicemail.

It's Honor's dad. He's calling from the Princess Margaret Hospital in Nassau. Oh my god, his voice is shaking. He's muttering something, but all I hear is that something has happened to Honor. His voice goes on and on, but his words don't register.

When the message ends, I take a huge breath and will myself to calm down so that I can hear his voicemail over my pounding heartbeat. I press replay and hold my breath.

Storm. It's Jack Stevens. There's no cell service here, so I'm calling from the Princess Margaret Hospital in Nassau. There's been a terrible accident and Honor is ...oh my god, Storm.

Mr. Stevens pauses to swallow some tears. He's choking up.

I'm sorry. I'll try to stay calm so I can get this out. The plane went down. Right on the island. A lot of people were hurt. Honor and her mom included. But...Honor wasn't hurt too badly. She would have...

Jack's voice cracks and he hesitates again.

She would have gotten away with just some bruises, but...she couldn't help herself. Oh, Storm.

Jack cries again, making me wait even longer for his explanation.

She had to go saving as many people as she could. Wound after wound, she wouldn't stop. Until finally...she collapsed...fell unconscious. It...It was horrible. She was turning all sorts of colors...wounds started appearing on her skin where before there weren't any. It...oh my god, it was awful.

Jack catches his breath again, while I listen to his sobs over the phone.

And oh, Storm...

His crying is scaring the hell out of me.

She...she...

BeepBeepBeep. Three fast beeps end the call.

She what goddammit? Oh my god...she what?

I drop to my knees with the phone clutched to my chest. He never told me. He never said...

He never said if she was still alive.

Forcing myself to grab hold of my emotions, I get up off the floor and pull open my laptop. The first thing I do is book a one-way ticket for the first available trip to Nassau, Bahamas. This gives me hope before going on to the second thing I do –dial the long-distance number that displays in my recent calls.

After listening to the recording, I press the option to reach the receptionist. When she finally answers the phone, I ask to reach Honor Stevens' room. When she tells me to please hold, I wait impatiently listening to some cheesy Chicago song called *Wishing You Were Here*—which pisses me off big time, because it's sad...and I'm already sad.

When the woman comes back, she tells me, "I'm sorry, sir, but I cannot connect you at this time."

"Can you tell me if she's at least there? Is she alive?" I beg. I plead.

"I'm sorry sir, but I'm unable to offer you information. You can come in and speak to that department face to face, but we cannot give out that information over the phone."

"I'm in fucking America. I can't just take a bus over there. Please. I'm begging you."

"I'm really sorry, sir, but I can't."

Before I plead one last time, the line goes dead.

And so does my heart.

Chapter Forty-One

The incessant replaying in my mind of yesterday's phone call is all I remember about the flight to Nassau, Bahamas. The melting ice in my glass and the three empty miniature bottles of Jack Daniels tells me I was articulate enough to request a drink and coherent enough to show the correct form of id—considering I have two different ones. But don't ask me what my attendant looks like or whether or not she's male or female. All I know is, though my body is numb, my heart and mind have a permanent vise clamping down on them. The pain is unbearable.

"In five minutes, we will be landing in beautiful Nassau, Bahamas," the pilot announces. But all I care about is getting to Princess Margaret Hospital and finding out if Honor's alive.

God I hope she's alive.

Since I spent no time packing, there is nothing to stop and retrieve. So when I get off the plane, I hail the closest taxi and somehow communicate to the driver where I need to go. I don't even hear the words come out of my mouth. It's as if someone else is operating my body. I'm floating above myself in a way, because everything that is happening to me since the moment I got the phone call is hallucinatory.

The eight stairs leading up to the front door may have been the seventy-two stone steps leading up to the Philadelphia Museum of Art. It took me that long to make it into the building. And even longer to make it to the receptionist. Yes, I was in a hurry to see Honor. No, I was not in a hurry to hear terrible news. So I let time stand still by hovering in the lobby a few minutes before asking for information about her.

"You can go up to the Intensive Care Wing on the second floor. There's a reception area where you can sign in," the woman behind the circular desk says.

My heart struggles to pick up its pace with the vise constricting it, but God bless it, it tries. "Are you...are you saying...she's alive?" I ask between labored breaths.

"Yes, sir, I am, but she *is* in ICU, so you'll need to cover up. The nurses will give you a gown upstairs."

She is alive. Like one of those religious people who drop to their knees and sing "Praise be the Lord," I feel my own body screaming in celebration. "She's alive," I whisper only to myself. "Praise be the Lord."

Upstairs, the lady in blue makes me put on a yellow gown and a mask and gloves. When I walk into her room, I'm greeted by two grim faces and a body hooked up to all types of tubes.

"Storm," Mr. and Mrs. Stevens say together.

Taking slow steps toward the bed, I feel that vise clamping down again. She's not breathing on her own—she's breathing through an oxygen mask. My eyes stay drawn to a sleeping Honor, but I manage to speak softly. "What's going to happen to her?" I ask her parents.

"Well, it's a waiting game," Mr. Stevens tries to say as a matter of fact, but his voice cracks, and I know he's trying his best to stay strong.

"What are we waiting for?" My voice is still quiet, my eyes, still on Honor.

Mrs. Stevens' breath hitches and her hand covers her mouth.

"We're waiting to see...if she'll make it." Though he tries not to, Honor's dad cries.

This is where I drop to my knees. Right next to her bed. And cry. I don't just let the tears slip from my eyes. No. I let them rain down. And I don't stop crying until sometime later in the evening when Honor's mother brings me a cup of coffee.

"It was nice of you to come," she tells me.

My struggle to stand is met with two lower limbs filled with pins and needles. I turn anyway and hug the shit out of Mrs. Stevens.

"I'm so sorry. I'm just so so sorry."

"It's not your fault, Storm. Stop," she cries.

"The break. If I hadn't...oh my god, if I hadn't asked to take a break, she wouldn't be here right now." I'm still squeezing Mrs. Stevens so hard, I finally realize I could be hurting her.

She lets me pull away and then looks me in the eyes. "Storm. We might have taken this trip anyway. You don't know that we wouldn't have. Lord knows we needed it." She laughs through her tears, leaving me to wonder where she finds her strength.

"I don't know what to do," I cry in exasperation.

"We fly back home. They'll be flying Honor to Morris-town Hospital on Tuesday. We'll meet her there. That's all we can do."

Nodding my head, I say, "Okay. Okay."

I sit down in the chair next to the bed, manage to swallow a few sips of the hot coffee, and cry. Again. Going through my mind this time, though, is making a deal with God.

God, if You allow Honor to live, I will no longer be the asshole I've been. No longer will I make Honor choose between Ethan and me. If You allow Honor to live, Ethan can have her. I will not stress her out over it. I will make things easy on her and just be her friend. Her very best friend. If You allow Honor to live, I will be only good. Good to everyone. Especially Ethan. Please God. Please.

After my meltdown, I think - this affects him as much as it does me. He should know. It's only fair that he knows.

And in a matter of minutes, I'm in the hallway calling Ethan. Giving him what has to be the worst call in his life. And it breaks my heart, because I know he loves her as much as I do.

PART THREE

ETHAN

439

Chapter One

I will never forget the moment my heart opened for the first time. It may have been the thought of losing her for good. Or it may have been the thought of losing her to Storm. Whatever the reason, healing Honor had become my priority.

**

Honor is finally going home. Living in that hospital room for the past month, everyone involved is happy to see her leaving, especially Honor. Not that I'm patting myself on the back, but if I hadn't done what I did, Honor would still be there dying of wounds she could have easily avoided. But unlike when Honor had saved her mother from a heart attack, the doctors and nurses are suspicious of *why* she made such a miraculous recovery. They also have their eye on the fact that Honor saved a plane load of people from dying in that plane crash.

How many times have I told her to shut them out? *The pain of everyone else is not worth killing her own heart.* I know I told her that a hundred times.

But she was never willing to listen to me, and now her heart is so weak, she needs another. At least she's able to come home and wait for the heart. The doctors say as long as she's resting, she doesn't need to wait it out in the hospital.

"Thanks again, Ethan," Honor says from her couch about an hour after her parents bring her home from the hospital. "Are you feeling all right? I mean, how come you're not like weak? You saved my life. Why are you not drained of all your energy like I always am?"

Storm, standing over Honor like a gargoyle on a cathedral, says "Thank you so much, Ethan," for the thousandth time. It's kind of getting sickening.

"I guess," I say in answer to Honor's question, "because I don't go saving every suffering person I see." I don't want to offend her, but I have to let her know. "You can't save everyone who needs saving, Honor. It just doesn't work that way."

"Maybe because you're immortal," Storm says, "you're not prone to the weaknesses that Honor is. You think?" There are no resentful undertones. No anger. No signs of Storm's usual hostility. And that irks me.

Irritated, I respond with, "Yes, of course I'm not prone to the same weaknesses that Honor is, but I also think, Honor," I turn to her, because I don't want it to seem like we're talking about her as if she's not right here in the room, "you wouldn't go down for the count every time you tried to make someone feel better if you would just avoid it most of the time." I wink, making sure she and her self-appointed guardian Storm know I have only her best interests at heart.

"I know, Eeth." Honor sighs. "But I can't help it. Their pain is just so real to me." Storm starts sliding his hand down the back of her head. "It's like, if I don't do something, I feel like I'm gonna die. Like the teenage girl whose skin was burned off. She was in so much pain, and her mother was screaming because her daughter was dying? How could I not have saved her? How could I let her die...and in so much pain? Ethan, I felt those burns all over my body. She was dying from the pain, and it made me feel like I was dying too. Literally."

"Well, *literally*, you will." I love her, but she needs to know the truth.

And why the hell isn't Storm on her case about this? Ever since the accident, he's been so cautious with what he says around her. I'm not sure why it's pissing me off, but it's like he's a different person since Honor nearly died.

"I'll be fine."

I look to Storm for some type of reaction, but he just continues stroking her hair.

"Dammit, Honor, you won't be fine. You need a god-damn new heart. Storm, back me up here. You know I'm right. Her actions are killing her."

"What do you want me to say, Ethan?" he asks from his perch on the arm of the couch. "She's heard this all before. I'm not going to upset her anymore. Her heart can't take the stress, so—"

"So," I interrupt, "when she gets a new heart and she does this again, then what?"

"Ethan, please," Honor says quietly. "I'm sorry."

Her apology breaks my heart. Moving my hand from her forearm to her hand, I clasp it in mine. "No, I'm sorry, Honor. I don't mean to be stressing you out, I just don't wanna see you like this. You're young. You should be healthy."

"I feel fine, Eeth. Really. Thanks to you. I mean, that was so cool. Thanks."

"Yeah, but I couldn't save your heart!" Why I was able to heal all of the wounds and bruises on her body but not her heart makes no sense. Uncle Tom thinks it's because her heart has just taken on so much in such a short amount of time that it may be incapable of healing completely.

But that's not good enough.

What if they can't find a heart in time?

What if her heart gives out before someone gives her one?

Chapter Two

Mrs. Stevens makes us leave. She says Honor needs to rest. So, after dinner, Storm and I say goodbye to the one girl we are both in love with, and then we walk out together.

"I'm sorry I didn't back you up in there, Ethan. I should have, but I'm just so scared to lose her, and I can't risk putting even more strain on her heart," Storm says with clenched teeth then balls his hand into a fist and plugs the side of his car, leaving a softball size dent in the space behind his window.

"Yeah. I get it," I say dryly. I'm in no mood to be his friend right now. Not when he won't even be honest about Honor's welfare, and not when he's still fighting to win her heart. But then, I chuckle. One of those hard ironic laughs that aren't even funny at all.

"What's so funny?"

"We're both trying to win her heart, right?" I shake my head. "Yet, when she gets a new one, she may not love either one of us."

The truth hits us right in our guts. Storm's pained expression mimics my feelings of having the breath knocked out of me.

"That's true, isn't it?" Storm finally says when he's able to catch his breath.

"Yup," I say so disappointed at the truth of it. The feelings of love come from the heart. Without her own heart, will she even love us anymore? 'Cause right now, I know she loves us both. Figuring out which one of us she's *in love* with will probably be a moot point soon.

"Well then," Storm blurts, "I think we should start being brothers for a change." He holds out his hand for me to shake, but I cock an eyebrow at him and he drops it. "But I'm not racing you for her. I made up my mind in Nassau that I would let you have her if that's what she wanted. I love her too much to cause her all this strain. Besides, like you said, when she gets that new heart...well, we're just going to have to be happy to be her friend."

"And you believe that?" I ask callously, still suspicious of this other side of Storm.

"Believe what? That she'll be our friend? Why wouldn't she be? She's not having a brain transplant. It's not like she won't remember we were in her life."

"No asshole, I mean, you actually believe that we're just gonna stop fighting over her? Because I'm sorry, I won't."

Storm drops his shoulders and sighs. "I said I was done. You do what you have to, but I'm not going to fight over her. Especially, if it means killing her before she gets the transplant. Besides, it's up to Honor anyway, and I don't even think she's thinking about either one of us in that way now. Her only concern is surviving." He opens the door to get in his car.

"Oh. So, now you're the good guy? What's up with you anyway? When did you become such a pussy?"

"Forget it, Ethan. You wouldn't understand." He goes to shut his door, but I won't let him.

"No. This is your way to win isn't it? You go all soft in the hopes Honor falls for that. Well, I'm not buying it."

"Then don't. I'm too exhausted for this, little brother." He starts his car while still looking up at me. "This whole thing has knocked the fight out of me. The only thing I want. No, the only thing I *need* is for Honor to come out of this whole. With or without me at her side. You want her, take her, but you better only have good intentions toward her and you better never hurt her. Or I'll rip your throat right out of your mouth with my bare hand." He shuts the door and peels out of her driveway. Leaving me to feel like the lowlife I've become.

**

At home, in my now empty apartment since Uncle Tom took Hunter and Eli and bought a house on White Rock Boulevard, I sit on the couch and stare at the blank TV screen. *The only thing I want. No. The only thing I* need *is for Honor to come out of this whole. With or without me.* I mock Storm to myself. As if *I* don't need the same thing. Just because I'm angry that Honor uses her power to save every living thing that's hurting, doesn't mean I don't love her just as much as *he* does. Didn't I prove just that by placing my hands down every inch of her bruised body so that she could heal? I don't *heal* anyone. Haven't since my parents made us orphans when we were young. I vowed to myself then that no one, ever, could make me do what my parents had done. They were selfish when it came to their boys. Sure, they were heroes to everyone else—saving children from bicycle accidents, curing cancer from young mothers, rescuing the mentally ill from a lonely life—but what about their sons? What about us?

From the moment I took that vow, I had shut down my heart to the world. Storm may have been the one who lived a solitary life—the lone teenage runaway—but I had been the one that ran away from my own heart. It may have taken up residence in my body, but my brain had no connection to it. Its only purpose was to pump blood to my veins.

Until I met Honor.

And slowly, the walls to my heart began to crumble, until one day, I found them completely gone.

It was when I'd gotten the call from Storm that Honor was being transported via helicopter to Morristown Memorial Hospital, in the state of congestive heart failure and unable to breathe on her own, that I had realized there was nothing left surrounding my heart to protect it. It hurt worse than any pain I had ever endured. Even at the distance from Nassau, Bahamas to Jefferson, New Jersey, Honor's pain had entered my body at the speed and force of a freight train.

At that moment, I had known what I needed to do, and so I did. For the first time in my life, I had used my powers to really heal. But it wasn't good enough. I could not heal Honor's heart, and so she was told she'd need a new one.

Because Honor's parents do not want her taking on everyone else's emotions anymore, Honor is being home-schooled again. Honor isn't happy about it, but she knows it's necessary. And though she's upset that she'll be missing prom and graduation, her parents insist, saying that emotions will be at their highest during those events, and they will not allow her to take the risk of straining her heart even more.

Prom is this coming Thursday night, and I have a plan. If only Storm would leave her side for more than a minute, I can make it happen. As it is, he gets to be with her all fucking day long, since he thinks it's no longer important to show his face at school now that the whole Mr. Moore fodder has settled down—which leaves me with seeing Honor half that time, and working double-time to win her heart. A heart that won't even be hers much longer.

Chapter Three

Honor emerges from inside her confined walls into the setting sun that shines on her front porch. Her lavender sundress makes her eyes a brighter violet. She is beautiful. The long braid that drapes over her shoulder teases me the way it covers her left breast, accentuating her cleavage. I take a deep breath and focus on her flawless face.

"Ethan." Her smile is huge and captivating. "How was school?"

"The same. Boring without you." I wink and give her a chaste kiss on the top of her head.

Then Storm walks out. "Ethan, hey."

"Storm." I keep my tone formal, but then I feel bad. We had made such strides becoming friends, and then I let my jealousy set us back at square one. Not wanting to cause undue stress on Honor's heart, I decide to swallow some pride. "Storm," I say much more amicably. "Sorry about yesterday. You just caught me in a bad mood."

"It's fine, brother." He holds out his hand, and this time I shake it.

"It's been an emotional few weeks," I add.

"You ain't kiddin."

Storm takes the seat next to Honor, and I sit on the porch railing across from her. It's okay, though, because a few seconds later, Honor straightens out her legs to stretch and I grab one. I rub my hands gently around her ankle, and she visibly relaxes. Storm actually does too. That's when I realize that he really is more concerned with her health and well-being then winning her over. He loves her unconditionally—whether she loves him or not—and I'm not sure I can compete with that. My love for her seems purely selfish when I think of it, and I vow that I will take a good hard look into my feelings before attempting to play a game of tug of war with Storm. And I'm pretty convinced he'd let me win anyway.

Inwardly I laugh. *It's up to Honor anyway, and I don't even think she's thinking about either one of us in that way now. Her only concern is surviving.*

"You got a game we can play, Honor?" I ask. "Scrabble, maybe?"

"Yeessss," she drags out the word. "You know I have Scrabble. You wanna play?"

Storm shakes his head, though a smile plays on his face.

"Yeah, I do," I say. "I'll go get it."

"No, Ethan," Storm says. "I'll get it. You just got here. Spend some time with Honor."

After Storm closes the door, I look at Honor and question her with my eyes.

"He knows you probably want to spend time alone with me. He asked me if I'd like that too and I, well, I said I did miss hanging with you, so..." she shrugs her right shoulder, "he said he'd leave us alone after school every day if we, uh, wanted."

"Wow. But he's going to get the Scrabble game? Is he leaving?"

"Only if we want him to."

"Do you want him to, Honor?"

She shrugs her shoulder again. "I like when we all just hang out. It, it takes my mind off of being home-schooled again. I hate being home-schooled."

"Yeah, I would too. Hey, I got an idea. Why don't I text Eli? Maybe he and Tam will come over too."

"Okay." She looks down at her phone and starts texting away.

"Who ya texting?"

"Tamlin."

"Oh." Okay. "Do I still text Eli?"

"Yeah, silly. They may not automatically be together."

"Oh, I think they are." I laugh.

She laughs too.

When her cell dings, Honor says, "They'll be right over. They're at the store getting snacks, so they'll just bring them here."

"'Kay."

Storm comes out with the game and places it on the dining table on the side of the porch.

"Tam and Eli are coming," Honor tells him.

"Great. Then...I should stay?" he asks Honor.

"Yeah," I answer instead. "You should stay."

He nods, but it's much more than a nod. It's an understanding—no more fighting to win Honor's heart. We fight to keep it for as long as she needs it until someone is ready to offer her their heart.

When Tamlin pulls up in her silver Civic, she parks the car cockeyed in the driveway and hightails it up the steps to give Honor a huge bear hug. I watch Eli shaking his head in disbelief.

"Tam, give me your keys," I say. "I'm going to park the car the right way." Because Eli isn't sixteen until next week, I figure it would be better if I move it.

"I can do it," he says.

"Nah, you might hit a mailbox or something."

"Funny. I turn sixteen next week you know."

"Yeah. And you're dating a girl almost two years older than you."

"Lucky me."

I sigh. He *is* lucky. Not 'cause his girl is older than him, but the girl he likes actually likes him back. But then I think—there is so much more going on than just trying to hook up with my ex-girlfriend. My girl is dying. So yeah, he's lucky.

"Why the long face?" Eli asks when I walk back up on the porch after parking Tamlin's car.

Out of my peripheral vision, I see Honor looking in my direction. Following Storm's lead, I avoid causing her extra stress by saying, "No long face, I'm just waiting on those snacks you brought. Unpack 'em already." I laugh and notice that Honor does too.

She wants things back to normal. I don't blame her.

Chapter Four

Prom night is tonight.

I had talked to Mrs. Stevens earlier in the week to tell her my plans and ask her to have a dress ready for Honor.

Now I call Storm.

I hear his longing for Honor in his voice behind the words, but he is quite the gentleman when he says, "You know what? I think she'll *love* that. I'm glad you thought of it."

He says nothing after that, so I just say, "Okay. I just wanted you to know," and then I hang up, not sure why I had wanted him to know in the first place. Is it because I don't want him there when I ring her doorbell? Probably. Is it because I think I have to check with him first before planning anything with Honor? Pretty much. But I have no idea why. She doesn't belong to him. Nor has she ever. She did belong to me once. So, why am I feeling like I'm horning in on Storm's girl? It doesn't make any sense.

After picking up my tux at the mall, I stop at the florist and get the corsage I'd ordered two days ago. My nervous stomach reminds me of how it felt the first time I asked Honor to go out with me—in the library's vestibule. I think I fell in love with her that day. And if I hadn't known for sure that day, my feelings were definitely sealed the night I watched her save her mother. Seeing Honor so raw that day exposed emotions in me that I'd never felt. And now, after all we've been through together, my own heart is raw—open, vulnerable, broken. Just like hers.

**

Because I arrive unannounced, when I first get to Honor's house, she is dressed in a pair of dark blue sweats and a white t-shirt, her blond hair falling over her shoulders in two long braids. Her mother winks at me knowingly and walks out of the room. The look on Honor's face when I show up in my tux is a look of disappointment—the frown on her pretty little lips is unmistakable. "Oh. You're going to the prom tonight?" She says quietly. Sadly.

When I shake my head and smile, her frown picks up. Then I look over her shoulder at her mother holding up the peach dress she must have bought for this occasion. The tag is still hanging from the strap.

Honor looks at me, and then back at her mom. "But...but I can't go. There'll be too many people you said," she says to her mother.

"Ethan has other plans for the evening."

When Honor looks back at me with expectant eyes, I tell her, "I'm taking you to our own prom tonight."

Her huge violet eyes smile. Her mouth follows. "Really?"

"Yes, now go put on that pretty dress your mom bought you."

When she floats through the room in her pale peach gown, held up by only the thinnest straps on her shoulders, she resembles a goddess. Missing are her braids, and in their place are soft waves that tumble down her back and a small gold clip clasped above her forehead. Her eyelids sparkle and her long black lashes accentuate her eyes, making them look almost purple. The soft glimmer of peach on her lips makes me want to kiss the gloss right off them, they look so delicious.

Her smile is shy and sweet when I slide the corsage on her left wrist. I try to hide my tremulous hand, but Honor catches it and blushes. I slip my hand in hers and tell her mom we won't be back too late.

After helping her into the car and getting in myself, Honor asks where we're going.

"Somewhere where we'll be alone."

Her pale peach cheeks blush again. Hopefully, that's a sign that she wants to be alone with me too.

We don't talk the whole ride, but I chalk that up to nerves. I'm sure she's as nervous as I am; it's been awhile since we've actually been alone together. I miss how easy it used to be with her. Riding around Lake Hopatcong for a while, I finally pull into the parking lot of The Jefferson House, where my stomach has reached maximum anxiety.

"I've never been here before," Honor says softly.

"No?" I ask, turning off the ignition. "Well, good. I like being the one to introduce you to some firsts." I'm hoping my smile comes across as sweet and not creepy.

"No...but...is it a good idea to, you know, be in a crowded restaurant?"

I look around the near empty parking lot. "It's Thursday night, Honor, it's not that busy. Besides, I reserved a private area for us."

A shallow dimple peeks when she gives me an adorable lopsided smile.

After closing her car door, I take her hand and lead her inside.

When the waitress brings us to the deck overlooking the lake, Honor's hand flies to her mouth. "Oh my God, it's so beautiful out here. And look, a table for two."

"That's what I asked for. A place just for us," I say, pulling out a chair for her to sit.

"Thank you," she whispers when I push in her chair.

"You look beautiful tonight, Honor."

Her peach cheeks blush a rosy pink again, and her dimple deepens. "Thank you." She looks down at her hands and bites her lip. "Ethan," she says slowly. "Thank you so much for this. It was really sweet of you."

"Well, you deserve a night out. It's not fair for you to sit home while everyone else is at prom. Out of everyone, you deserve it the most."

Honor's blushing smile is interrupted by the waiter who takes our drink orders. But as soon as he leaves the table, I ask Honor to dance.

"But there's no music."

"Ah, but that's where you're wrong."

I pull my mini Bluetooth speaker and iPhone out of my tux pocket. Taking Honor's hand, I walk her to the open deck area and place the speaker on a small table next to the railing. I choose the playlist I put together for tonight and press play. Laying the phone on the table, I take Honor in my arms and begin dancing with her to "Patient Love" by Passenger, a deliberate choice on my part. With my arms around her waist and hers around my neck, my stomach screams in anticipation when she lays her head on my shoulder. I press my cheek against her temple and silently wish for this night to continue forever.

When the song ends, Honor lifts her head and peers into my eyes. "Thank you," was all she said. The next song on my list is "Your Song" by Ellie Goulding. Again, a deliberate choice on my part to put this song on the playlist for tonight. Not only because the words make sense to me, but because I know it's one of Honor's favorite songs. She gives me one of those huge endearing smiles, and her dimple sets me off. I can't help myself—I kiss her. Her lips are soft and sweet, but as I open my mouth to let her in, she pulls back. "I'm sorry, Ethan." She breaks our embrace, says, "I'm sorry again," and steps back against the railing.

Meeting her at the railing, I put my hand on her shoulder and apologize. "I crossed a line. I shouldn't have done that. It won't happen again."

"It's, uh, just..." Honor struggles with what to say, so I hold up my hand to stop her.

"No explanation needed. Let's just enjoy the night. I promise, it'll be like it never happened." I open my arms and she walks into them. Her head falls back on my shoulder. She's not ready for kissing me. I understand. It could be me. It could be Storm. It could be the fact that she's dying. So, I won't take it personally. She just needs to enjoy this night, and I won't complicate it by putting my feelings into it.

When Ellie Goulding's soft voice finishes telling us how wonderful life is, Honor and I walk hand in hand back to the table, where our drinks are already waiting for us.

Desperately needing her to forget that I just kissed her, I say, "So, Honor, talk to me. You must have thousands of thoughts running through your head these days. I'm sure you want to scream."

She lets her lips linger on her straw when she's done taking a sip of her soda. "Yeah. I do."

"You do what? Want to scream or have a thousand thoughts going on?"

"Both." One little peach strap lifts when she shrugs her shoulder. "But mostly, I want to cry."

"I'm sorry."

"What are you sorry about? Not saying I told you so?"

"I would never do that." I take her hand in both of mine. "Honor, yes, I wish you would have thought twice before saving all those people, but part of what makes you you is your ability to feel and empathize." I laugh at myself, because what I just said is so lame. "I mean, it's your nature, but you also are just a truly genuine person. You trust your heart." And again, I'm sad for her. "I just wish your heart was trustworthy."

Honor lets out an ironic laugh. "Yeah. It did kind of fail me, didn't it?"

"In a way." I take a roll from the basket and butter it. Then I hand it to Honor and butter another one. "But don't think about it. What's done is done. I know they'll find you a new heart. I just know they will. I feel it."

A smile is on her face, but it doesn't reach her mouth. "Do you *empath* feel it, or is it wishful thinking?"

With a sad sigh, I tell her the truth. "I guess it's wishful thinking."

A frown replaces her shallow smile.

"But hey, wishful thinking is a good thing. It means we're thinking positively, and good things come from positive thinking." *Lame, lame, lame.*

"Thanks," she says.

When the waiter comes to take our order, Honor apologizes because we haven't looked at the menus. My chest grows warm when she promises to look at it right now.

"Honor, you're too nice," I say, opening my menu to follow through on her promise.

"It's just courtesy." She blushes.

"I know. Something not taught in public schools." I sip my soda while focusing on my menu.

"Oh, that's not true. I think we're just not paying attention," she retorts from behind her menu.

"And by *we*, you're talking about in general, because certainly *you* always pay attention."

When her finger brushes her hair behind her ear, I want to be the one to do that. "Are you calling me a nerd, Eeth?"

I smile and tease her. "If the name fits."

She slaps my hand teasingly, but I don't let her take her hand away. I grip it in mine. "You know I'm teasing, right?" I ask.

I'm the recipient of another wholesome beautiful smile. "Of course."

We hit a lull in the conversation, leaving time to actually look at our menus, so when the waiter comes back, we've made our decisions.

"I'll have the vegetarian enchilada," Honor tells him.

"And I'll have the house sirloin. Can you bring us an order of onion rings and sweet potato fries,too, please?"

"Sure." He takes our menus and leaves us alone again.

"Let's go." I take Honor's hand and lead us back to our dance floor on the lake.

I press the play button on my phone and let Ingrid Michaelson's version of "Can't Help Falling in Love with You" lead us into dance. Of course I pick this song, because I hear Honor playing it on her piano all the time. I know it's this version too, because she has her iPad sitting atop the piano while the song plays and she accompanies it. In my heart, I pretend she's playing the song for me, but I can't get past the idea that it could be Storm that her heart feels when she hears the song.

"I love this song," she says so passionately while hanging on to me.

"I know you do," is my simple reply.

"This whole night has been so sweet, Ethan. I can't believe you did this."

"Only for you, angel."

My whole body turns warm when Honor's cheek inadvertently touches mine mid-dance. The smell of coconut that rises from her neck reminds me of the sweet summer sun, and I smile to myself. Honor *is* the human equivalent to the sweet summer sun. Honor is *my* sun. She makes my world go 'round. I just wish I could be the reason her world goes around.

Chapter Five

During dinner, conversation is light until Honor brings up Shelby Marcus.

"What did you just say?" I ask, afraid I heard her wrong.

"I said that Shelby's coming over Monday after school." Honor puts a forkful of her enchilada in her mouth.

"Why?" I hold back from telling her that's a bad idea.

Honor's mouth still full, she shrugs and shakes her head. Waiting impatiently for her to swallow her food, I take a bite of my own food before saying something that will ruin this evening even further.

"She called me today to see how I've been. We talked a bit, and she asked if she could come over." Honor, unaffected by my reaction, takes another bite of her dinner.

"Honor, I don't like the idea of her hanging around you." I push my plate away, because suddenly I'm sick to my stomach.

"Why? What's the matter with Shelby? We kind of became friends after the whole incident."

"That's the whole reason, Honor." I tap my fingers on the table, because I'm trying to keep my cool, but it just doesn't happen. "I don't like her," I say honestly. "She's the whole reason you're...you're here in the first place. Had you not saved her from dying of bone cancer, your heart may still be strong enough to beat forever on its own." Because I can't stay still, I stand.

"Where're you going, Ethan? What's the problem?" Honor puts her hand to her chest as if it hurts.

Instead of walking away, I kneel down beside her. "I'm so sorry, Honor. I'm causing stress. Your heart hurts?"

"No, Ethan. Sit down. I'm fine. The food is spicy, that's all. I just felt a little indigestion. But I do feel angry, so I know that's coming from you."

"I'm sorry. I just...I've had a problem with Shelby since the beginning. I hate that she used to bully you, and then you went and saved her life." I stand back up and motion for Honor to follow me. At the farthest railing that overlooks the lake, I say, "If you hadn't pulled her from death, you might not be here like this today."

Honor chuckles. "And saving a plane load of people had nothing to do with it?"

It has everything to do with it, but because I don't understand it, nor do I know those people, of course I need someone to blame. So I blame Shelby Marcus. "Why *did* you do that, Honor? Why did you risk your life for them?"

She nibbles her bottom lip and closes her eyes. When she opens them, tears are threatening to escape. "I told you. It hurt so bad I felt like *I* was dying. It was impossible to ignore them. Impossible. Ethan," she wipes at a stray tear, "if you felt what I felt, I think you would have done the same. It's like...it's like, I hear the screams, you know, of all these people. Some of them kids. And I *feel* the screaming. The torment. The agony. They were all crying in the *worst pain* they had ever imagined. And to stand there, knowing I could take that away from them...well, how could I have chosen to turn away? How could I do that?" Another tear falls, but she ignores it, letting it drip over her lip as she asks. "How could I live with myself if I just ignored them?"

I move in and pull her close. My eyes are tearing now. It's not just her words that get me. It's what my heart is *feeling* that causes my wrecked emotions. Like I had said earlier, my heart is unprotected now. Especially wh

"I'm so sorry, Honor," I say, taking her hand. "I'm sorry I doubted you. I'm sorry I made you tell me the whole fucking story again. I'm just...I'm just so sorry."

At this point, I don't know whether I am comforting her or she is comforting me, but we're both holding on to each other as I we couldn't breathe without the other. I can feel her heartbeat against my chest, it's pounding so hard. Then again, mine is pounding too, so it could be both of our heartbeats competing with each other. Now that I've opened my heart, I feel so selfish for keeping my powers locked up inside me. Though I hate to see Honor suffering the way she is now, I don't blame her for saving the lives she's saved. Because right now, my chest hurts so badly that all I want to do is save Honor from herself. Alas, I can take away her immediate pain, but I can't heal her heart.

The one and only thing she needs to keep her alive.

Holding on to her snugly yet comfortably, I use my hand to press firmly on her back, right behind her heart. I close my eyes and concentrate on releasing her suffering of the memories of that night. Gradually, I feel her heart slow down and her breathing return to normal. Thankfully, because we had been so wrapped up in our emotions, she doesn't realize I am trying to take away her pain.

When both of us have shed our last tear, she looks me in the eyes. "What other songs you got on that playlist of yours?"

Planting a smiling kiss on her forehead, I take her hand and lead her back to the dance floor. The next song on my playlist is Passenger's "Let Her Go" - a song I chose for me. I wrap my arm around her waist as she drapes her arms above my shoulders, clasping her hands behind my neck.

"Thank you for making me feel better," she whispers into my ear.

Not knowing whether she's talking about purposely taking her pain away a minute ago or just in general, I say, "What do you mean?"

She slaps me gently on the shoulder. "I mean, I know what you just did back there. Thank you."

"Oh. You felt that?"

Looking into my eyes, she says, "I feel everything."

"You do, don't you?" And I'm sad when I say this, because it's not fair for such a young girl to have to take on the weight of the entire world.

When the night is over and we've eaten the last of the tiramisu we'd ordered for dessert, I'm sad to see the evening end. It may not have gone how I intended it, but it was nice to be with Honor alone again.

"I appreciate tonight, Ethan. Thank you," Honor says again in the car on the way home.

"You're welcome." I glance at her, still keeping my eyes on the road. "I'm sorry you had to miss the prom though."

"It's okay. I really never thought I'd ever go to one. I mean, my mom always home-schooled me until this year, so it's not like it's something I always dreamed about."

Nothing I say to that would sound appropriate, so I say nothing.

"But tonight, it was really special. I loved it."

"Again, you're welcome. You deserve good things, Honor."

The rest of the ride is silent, but when we get to her house, I walk her to the door and kiss her on the cheek. "I'll see you tomorrow?"

"I'd like that," she says smiling.

I give her another kiss on the cheek and stand there until she goes inside and closes the door. When the light in the window turns dark, I turn, and with my head held low, I walk back to my car.

Chapter Six

Today, I wake up with a smile. All night, I'd dreamed about dancing with Honor, and this morning, I can still smell the coconut scent she was wearing last night. I grab my pillow and hold it across my chest, longing for a day a could hold Honor in my bed. I let my thoughts linger for a while before getting up and showering. Because most of the senior class is headed for the shore this morning, I decide to bring bagels to Honor and hang with her for the day. Maybe we can even go for a drive. I'll let her decide. It may not be the shore, but at least she won't be alone.

When I show up at her front door, Mrs. Stevens tells me she's out back with Storm. I'm not going to lie, I'm disappointed but not surprised. I go around back from the outside instead of going through the house, and find her up in the tree with him. The exact same place I found them when he was begging for the elixir. It almost seems like a lifetime ago. They don't hear me approach, but before I can let them know I'm here, their conversation stops me in their tracks.

"So, he really made a playlist?" Storm asks Honor.

"Yeah. He was sweet."

I feel guilty listening in on them, but I know they are talking about last night, and I'm really curious about what she says.

"Were you happy at least?" There's a tone in Storm's voice that tells me he is genuinely concerned about her happiness.

"Yeah. I was. It was nice to go out like that."

"He's a good kid," Storm says, and I just can't get used to this side of him.

"What's up, Storm?" she asks.

"What do you mean?"

"I mean, why the turnaround all of a sudden? You don't call him loser anymore, and, well, you seem like you, I don't know, like, maybe you...*want* me to be with him."

"Is that so bad, princess?"

"Well, you're not the same. You're, you're not you."

Storm struggles to laugh. "Then who am I?" I can tell he's trying to downplay it.

"Storm, stop, you're not the same. You're too, you're too calm or something."

"Princess, please, I'm fine."

"Are you eavesdropping?" I jump, startled by the voice behind me.

"God, Tam, you scared me."

"You *are* eavesdropping, aren't you?" she whispers.

"No."

"Come 'ere," she whispers again, pulling me back to the front of the house.

"I wasn't eavesdropping. I was just—"

"Cool it. I really don't care," Tamlin interrupts. "I just wanted to ask you what your plans are today."

Sticking my hands in my pockets, I shrug. "I don't know. I just figured I'd hang with Honor today, but I see that someone else already had that idea."

"Storm?" she asks.

"Uh, yeah," I reply, shaking my head.

"Nah, he's just checking up on her. He'd leave you alone if you wanted him to."

"Yeah, what's his deal? Before the accident he would never have let me alone with Honor. Now he's encouraging it? I don't get it."

Tamlin gives me one of those pity smiles, but I think she's feeling sorry for Storm, not me. "He's a mess, Eeth."

"As in?"

"As in he is so afraid of losing Honor that he won't do anything to stress her out. He's popping Xanax like they're candy, just so he'll have no emotions around her. It's crazy."

"I don't understand," I tell her, because I don't.

"He's trying to just zone out. He doesn't want her to feel his fear or sadness or anything at all, because he thinks she'll feel it and stress herself out. I don't like what this is doing to him. He's like a...like a zombie or something." Tamlin clicks her tongue in disappointment.

"So...what? Are we not as good friends to Honor because we're not hiding our feelings?" I say, knowing I'm being defensive.

"No, Ethan. That's not what I'm saying at all. I'm saying Storm's crazy. Honor is worried about him anyway, so it's not doing any good for him to be doing this."

"He sounded fine to me." Maybe not, but I'm not going to act all concerned about him. I'm still trying to figure out his angle.

"Then you weren't eavesdropping long enough." She crosses her arms in front of her chest.

"I wasn't eavesdrop—"

"Yeah, I don't want to hear it. Listen, the reason I asked what you were doing today is because my mom is letting me take the boat out, and I thought we could go for a drive on Lake Hopatcong." She uncrosses her arms and rubs her neck.

"You have a boat license?" I don't believe her.

"Indeed I do, bud. So…you wanna go? Your uncle called Eli and Hunter out sick from school today and Shelby said she'd like to spend some time—"

"Shelby? No fucking way. Talk about upsetting Honor. She's the one who put her in this position in the first place." I rub my hands on my jeans. I'm getting very tense.

Tamlin knocks me on the arm. "Stop. Shelby and Honor are friends. They were awkward at first, but in class and stuff, they were always laughing together. Shelby cares about Honor. She owes Honor her life, and she realizes that."

"Yeah, but why today? Isn't she going down the shore with the rest of the prom crew?"

"Nope. She was at the prom last night, but she went alone. Hung out with Eli and me."

"Eli. Was he the only sophomore at the prom?" I joke.

Tamlin chuckles. "Yeah. He loved it." She yanks my forearm and leads me to the backyard. "C'mon, let's go tell Honor and Storm about the boat."

"Storm?" I stop in place.

"Yes, Ethan, Storm. We're all friends. C'mon. For Honor."

Shaking my head, I head again to the back.

"Yo, tree people," Tamlin yells when we reach the yard.

"Hey," Honor says with a smile and climbs slowly down the tree. But not before I see her give Storm some kind of secret look—maybe a look of apology, maybe a look of regret.

Shaking it off, I approach Honor and give her a hug and a soft kiss on the cheek.

Storm stays up in the tree and leans his head against its trunk.

"Tam has a surprise," I say, taking Honor's hand momentarily.

Honor looks at her best friend. "Oh yeah? Hey, how was the prom?"

"Boring. How was yours?"

Honor smiles at me and blushes. "Wonderful." Looking back at Tamlin, she says, "So what's your surprise?"

"Wanna go on the boat?" Tamlin is beaming.

"Your mom's letting you take it out?"

"Yup. So how 'bout it? You up for a ride on the lake?"

The sun dances off of Honor's huge smile. She seems genuinely excited to go for a boat ride. "I'd love to."

"Great. Go get ready." Tamlin gives her a big huge hug again before Honor skips inside.

"Boy, didn't you just make her happy," I tell Tamlin.

"What are friends for?" Tam answers me, but keeps her gaze on Storm. "So what about you, Storm? You coming too?"

"Storm. She's talking to you," I yell up to him.

"Oh. What?" Storm jumps down from the tree.

"You want to come on my boat today? Mom's lending it to me." She's practically dancing, she's so full of life. So opposite from what Honor has been these days.

"Thanks. But I'll hang back," Storm deadpans.

Because I really have nothing to say about the whole thing, I sit on the picnic table, propping my feet on the bench. But I do watch Storm's actions, which are very sluggish. If he's not popping Xanax, he's sure on something.

"C'mon, Storm. This could be her last—" Tamlin stops herself from finishing that sentence, but Storm tenses. His eyes get big, and his face turns red.

I hop off the table, because I'm afraid he's going to rush Tamlin.

"I...I didn't mean that," Tamlin apologizes, her voice shaky. "Honestly, I just...it's been on my mind, and I'm trying not to act it, and I just, I'm sorry. I wasn't thinking when I said that."

Wrapping my arm around Tamlin's shoulder, I try to console her. "It's okay. It's on all our minds."

When I look at Storm, he's relaxed a bit, but he's staring into space.

"Hey," I say and poke him in the shoulder. "You okay?"

His eyes move to mine, but his body doesn't.

"Storm," Tamlin says. She leaves my side and takes his arm. "Storm, you need to get a grip." Tamlin walks him to the picnic table and pushes him down on the bench. Her pale blond hair flips in the wind. That's when I realize she's down. She may act all chipper, but when she's depressed, she bleaches her hair back to its normal color.

"You know, Storm," I start to say. "She'll be okay. I'm sure they'll find her a heart in time." I do believe that. I do.

Again, he just looks at me, but this time, he closes his eyes. He keeps them closed, even after Tamlin sits on his lap.

With her finger under his chin, she brings her face close to his. "You need to get off that stuff you're taking. You're not supposed to pop Xanax like they're M&Ms."

Storm's eyes are still closed, so Tamlin shakes his arm.

"Stop this," she screams in his face. "You're making Honor hurt even more."

This got his attention. His eyes jerk open and he stares at Tamlin, who's nearly nose to nose with him. There are tears pooling in his eyes.

She stares at him nose to nose. "I'm sorry, Storm, but it's the truth," she says much softer now. "She's worried about you."

Storm's hand slips around Tamlin's waist. I find it odd to see him so fragile and distraught. Though, I'm usually jealous of him, I kind of hope Tamlin's able to get through to him.

"I don't know what else to do," he whispers, and the shakiness in his voice tells me if it weren't for the Xanax, he'd be crying harder than he is.

Tamlin keeps looking at him while she caresses his face. "Just be her friend, Storm. That's all we can do. Pray that someone...well, that she gets a heart soon and—"

"Pray someone dies soon. That's what you're telling me?" Storm quips.

"Well, no, but—"

"You think I care if someone has to die for Honor to live?" His laugh is sardonic. "Think again." His eyes roll up behind his head for a second. It's freaky. "Someone better die, and soon."

"That's the Storm we're all missing." Tamlin gives him a kiss on the forehead. "Now go home and get what you need to go diving off the boat. Ethan and I will pick you up in about thirty minutes."

"I don't know."

"I won't take no for an answer. Now go. I'll tell Honor."

Storm looks at me and I just shrug. *There's no use fighting with a girl on a mission.*

Chapter Seven

With Eli and Hunter in the car, I follow Honor, Storm, and Shelby in Tamlin's car to the marina. Eli's yapping all the way there about being the only sophomore at the senior prom. Hunter teases him about going with a cougar. He takes it all in stride. I'm too busy thinking about Honor and the fact that I had wanted today to be just about her and me. Instead, we're spending it with everyone else. Hopefully, she'll have a good day. That's all that matters anyway.

When we get to the marina and out of the car, it doesn't slip by me that Shelby had ridden shotgun and Honor had ridden in the back seat with Storm. Yes, I'm jealous; I'd love to have sat in the back seat with her, possibly holding her hand or pulling her close in my arms.

"Hey, Eeth," Tamlin calls. "Help us untie the ropes from the cleats."

Like I know what a cleat is. "Sure."

When I walk past Shelby, it's all I can do not to sneer. She's cute, but she rubs me the wrong way.

"Hi to you too, Ethan," Shelby says as I walk right by her, keeping my eyes on the dock ahead of me.

I ignore her. It's hard for me not to blame her for Honor's fate. She started this. There is no way I can ever forgive her.

I watch Elijah and Tamlin untying ropes from these horn looking things on the dock, so I follow their lead and start untying one. From my peripheral vision, I see Honor, Shelby, and Hunter standing together chatting. When I look for Storm, I find him untying the rope behind me, so I finish what I'm doing and go over to him. Putting my hand on his back, I ask him how he is.

"Fine," he says with no emotion at all.

"Really?" I ask, sitting down in front of him. "Because you don't look fine."

He finishes untying his rope and tucks it away before he sits down next to me and answers. "Are you surprised by that?"

Shrugging, a hmph sound escapes from my throat. "I guess not. But what are you doing, Storm? Tamlin says you're taking drugs?" I push at his leg with my hand. "That ain't cool, bro."

He rolls his eyes. "I'm not taking drugs. I'm taking Xanax. There's a difference."

"Not really. Xanax is legal, but you're taking a ton of 'em a day, she said."

While shaking his head, he says, "Tam should mind her own business. She's got a big mouth."

I rub my hands on my jeans. "She's worried about you. What's up? Are you really that scared?"

When he turns his head to look me in the eyes, I see a man in tremendous pain. The only life in his eyes is the suffering he's bearing. "I'm fucking petrified."

Yeah. I'm upset too, but petrified? Not exactly. I feel pretty confident that Honor will find a heart in time. And I trust my feelings over Storm's. I am an empath after all. "I wouldn't be too scared. I know they're going to find a heart for her soon. I *feel* it."

Storm cracks his knuckles and shoots me a smirk. "Since when do you start *feeling* anyway? I mean, wasn't it you who said you would never turn out like your parents? Then you go and save Honor from...I mean, don't get me wrong, I am so grateful you did heal most of her, but why? Why all of a sudden?"

"You're not the only one who's afraid of losing her, Storm." I run a hand through my hair. "Before, I mean, there wasn't this risk, but when I saw her there with all those tubes and unconscious, well, I didn't have to think twice. I had to save her."

"Thank you." Storm says, resigned, but smiling.

"C'mon," Tamlin calls to us. "Y'all ready to ride?"

She's funny at the front of the boat. So confident and cute. And such a good friend to Honor. Even though I had wanted to spend time alone with Honor, I'm glad Tam thought this day up. It's much better for Honor to be among a lot of people. A lot of happy, drama-free, people.

The wind whirls through Honor's hair, carrying her coconut scent through the air, reminding me of how close I held her last night. That probably wouldn't happen today with all these people around, but at least I can admire her while she enjoys being on the lake. Taking the initiative, because she is currently sitting alone—Eli is up front with Tamlin, Hunter is talking with Shelby, and Storm is brooding alone at the back of the boat—I move to sit next to Honor.

"Hey, girl. This seat taken?"

Honor chuckles and pats the white cushion next to her. "Hey, Eeth. I barely got to talk to you since last night, I'm sorry."

"Don't be. This was a nice idea, no?" I'm so nervous, I don't even know what to talk about.

"Yeah," she says with a big smile on her face. "Tamlin's too funny...planning this. But I'm glad. Cookie?" she asks, holding out a bag of Pepperidge Farm Milano cookies.

Sticking my hand in the bag, I say, "Thanks."

When I go to continue the conversation, Tamlin calls Honor to come up front by her.

She looks at me for permission.

"Go. I'm not going anywhere."

"Thanks," she says with a huge grin, patting my leg and tossing the cookies on the cushion next to me when she leaves me for Tamlin.

That's when Shelby comes walking over to me.

"Hi, Ethan," she greets me apprehensively.

"Shelby."

"Can I sit?" she asks quietly.

Without looking at her, I say, "Yeah, go 'head."

She's quiet in the beginning, but then she turns toward me. "Ethan," she says softly. "I know you don't like me, but I wish you'd give me another chance." Her voice is weak, not at all like the voice I remember in the lunchroom a few months ago.

I turn to look at her. "Okay," I say, not meaning it. Why should I give her another chance? Honor may not get another chance at a healthier life.

Her eyes look sad as her teeth nibble on her bottom lip. "I *am* sorry about what I used to do to Honor. I know it was wrong. And I know that's why you don't like me very much." She keeps looking me right in the eyes while she talks, and it makes me feel like a heel. I force myself not to cast my eyes downward. It'll only make me seem guilty of something. *Am I?* I'm guilty of judging her on behavior from her past. She has made amends with Honor. Honor's forgiven her. I'm guilty of holding on to my anger towards her. And I'm guilty of not forgiving her. But I ignore the better side of me and give her a cold look anyway.

My stomach knots up when I look at her fumbling with her hands on her lap. I don't mean to be cruel, but I can't help it. She was nasty, and Honor helped her anyway.

While Shelby sits quietly next to me, I see Honor slowly making her way to Storm.

"Hey, princess." I *hate* when he calls her that. But at least he's backing off of her.

"Hey." Her smile can actually be heard, and I can only see her back. "Mind if I sit?" she asks him.

"Of course not." Though he's still quite emotionless, he perks up when she sits down right next to him—practically on his lap. "You having a good time, angel?"

"I am. You're not." Her hand slides effortlessly over his thigh.

He naturally covers her long, slender hand with his large one. "I'm fine, princess. Please. Stop worrying about me."

"How can I stop worrying about you?" she whispers it to him, but I'm good at reading lips, and so I *hear* her anyway.

"It's easy. Go have some fun with your friends." His words sound forced, almost as if he's holding something back—maybe a good cry or something.

"I want to stay here...with you," she whispers again.

I'm trying not to stare at them, but I'm reading every expression on their faces. Especially Honor's.

"Well, I'd rather you go be with them right now." He says the words, but he doesn't mean it. He's looking down, playing with her hand with both of his.

Honor looks like she's about to cry—her lower lip trembles, and with the hand Storm's not holding, she curls her fingers and brings them to her lips. She's trying to hold back tears.

"Ethan?" Shelby's voice interrupts my eavesdropping.

Pretending to look out at the lake instead of Storm and Honor, I ask her what she wants without looking at her.

"Give them some privacy. They need to talk."

This infuriates the hell out of me, and causes me to finally look her in her eyes willingly. "Who the hell are you to tell me what to do?" My words come out louder than I expected them to come out.

She shakes her head and gets up. "You're a bastard. I should never even have tried to make amends with you."

Now that's the Shelby I know.

But I don't let it go. Instead, I stand up. "Whoa there, chickie," I grab her by the elbow and turn her around.

"What the fuck you doing on this boat? We don't need you as a friend. We've got plenty."

"Whoa, Ethan, man, give her a break," Eli says, coming to her rescue.

Honor seems to have forgotten about her broken heart, because she jumps up and runs to Shelby's side. "You okay?" she asks her.

"I'm fine, Honor." Shelby is sweet and soft-spoken, but when she looks at me, her eyes could slice me in half. "Don't. You. Ever. Lay. Your. Hand. On. Me. Again."

"What's your problem, man?" Eli asks.

"*She's* my problem." I look at Honor. "How can you be friends with her?"

"Ethan. That's so unfair." Honor is disappointed in me. It's written all over her face. "You don't even know her. You don't even give her a chance. I'm just so..." she clenches her fists as well as her jaw, "I'm just so mad at you right now."

I drop my shoulders and turn away, turning right in Storm's direction. He's expressionless. But I walk over to him anyway. "You don't find her infuriating?"

He looks at me a little amused—as amused as Storm can be these days. "She's not bad, Eeth. Try talking to her."

"What? I thought you of all people would hate her as much as I do for doing what she did to Honor." I pound the side of my fist down on the edge of the boat behind me.

"What? She was dying and took it out on Honor. When she was well, she apologized. Don't tell me you don't take your anger out on the wrong people?" He smirks and raises his eyebrows.

"I don't," I say, grabbing the bag of chips that are sitting beside me.

"Bullshit. You're taking your anger about Honor's weak heart out on Shelby. I've been watching you." Storm sticks his hand in the bag of chips and takes a bunch.

"Yeah, well, at least I'm not a pill popper."

"Fuck off." He reaches in for more chips, so I hand him the bag.

"I'm going crazy, Storm."

"Tell me about it. I can't feel my body, but my friggin' chest is killing me. I just want to...I wish I could rip my heart out and give it to her for chrissake. I'm telling you, I'm thinking about it." His eyes are dark, and I can tell by his expression he's serious.

"Storm, you can't do that. Honor could never live with that. She'd rather die than know you killed yourself for her. I don't even like you very much, and *I* couldn't live knowing you'd given me your heart."

"Well lucky for you, I have no intention of giving you my heart, asswipe."

"I'm serious, Storm. Don't do that to Honor. It'd kill her." Even *I* know Honor loves Storm too much for that—as much as I hate to admit it. "Promise me you won't do that."

"Yeah. Whatever," he says flatly, before sticking a handful of chips into his mouth.

Now I wasn't only scared for Honor, I was scared for Storm. He's too unstable these days to make rational decisions. I'm afraid for his life that Honor will get that call.

And it'll be his heart they plant into her chest.

Chapter Eight

Tamlin throws the anchor into the lake. It's time to swim. Watching Honor pull her shirt over her head and her shorts off those long lean legs of hers makes my blood pulse quickly through my body. I feel all sorts of shivers running over my skin. Her milk-white complexion looks beautiful against her mint green bikini, and out of the corner of my eye, I see Storm sit up straighter. He's looking at her too; most likely having the same reaction that I am. A guttural sigh escapes him, and it echoes my own.

When Shelby exposes her little body, I'm taken by surprised when my body reacts to her as well. Those cartwheels and backflips she does as a cheerleader have done remarkable things to her body. She's so tight and toned, and I'm feeling guilty about looking at her the way I am. I mean, I hate the little bully. I turn to look at Storm and notice that he only has eyes for Honor. Her body hasn't left his gaze, and he still has that longing expression on his face.

"You swimming, Storm?" Shelby asks him, intentionally ignoring me.

Bitch.

"Nah." Storm answers..

"C'mon," Hunter calls as he dives into the lake.

Elijah follows him.

Tamlin walks out from the front of the boat still in her shorts. "You're not swimming, Tam?" I ask her.

"Of course," she says, pulling her top over her head. As she shimmies out of her shorts, I notice that her body is amazing too, but I don't have the reaction I had had with Honor and Shelby. Probably because she's my brother's girl. Then again, that doesn't seem to affect Storm and me where Honor is concerned.

"You coming, Storm?" I ask while I take off my own t-shirt.

"Nah. You guys go, I'll just lay down and take a nap."

"Those pills are making you sleepy. Stop taking them." I say, before diving off the edge of the boat myself.

After coming up for air, I look around and notice that everyone is in the lake except for Honor and Storm. Of course, this makes me curious—well, jealous—so I swim closer to the boat to see if I can hear if they are talking to each other.

"Why do you keep pushing me away?" Honor asks him. I hear the hurt in her voice.

"I'm not."

"You are."

"Princess, go have fun with your friends. Don't ruin your day by spending it questioning me." Storm sounds so detached, it doesn't make sense. Is he distancing himself from Honor to spare himself pain if she doesn't make it? Well that's just cowardly.

Something wraps around my ankles and pulls me down. I barely struggle out of its grasp, or rather, someone's grasp, when I see Shelby under the water next to me. She pops up with a big grin on her face.

"What the *hell*?" I say, annoyed, then push my palms through the water to splash her in the face.

"You're an ass, Ethan."

I practically growl at her I'm sneering so hard. "And that's why you're pulling me under?"

"No," she says. "I'm pulling you under to give them some privacy." She lifts her chin in the direction of Honor and Storm on the boat.

"What is it with you and telling me what to do?"

"I'm not telling you what to do. I just think they need to work things out, and you're constantly watching them."

"What are they trying to work out?" Again, I'm annoyed.

"They're hurting right now."

"Hurting?" I'm totally annoyed right now, so I swim away from Shelby and toward the shore.

She follows me.

"What is your deal, Shelby? You don't like me, yet you insist on following me and telling me to mind my own business. A little ironic, no? Since you're not bothering to mind *your* own business." I sit on the beach and dig my feet in the sand.

Sitting her tiny ass next to me, Shelby punches me in the arm. "You deserve that," she says. "Listen, Ethan. Can we call a truce?"

I nod. "Fine."

"I know you're hurting too right now, but I also know that you and Honor seem to have a healthier relationship than she and Storm do."

I close my eyes and massage them with my thumb and middle finger. "What are you talking about?" I ask, keeping my eyes closed.

"Well, you seem to be handling Honor's situation fairly well. From what Tamlin says, you have a good attitude about it. Even Honor is handling it okay when she's with you. We've been talking on the phone, and she says she feels safe when she's with you. But with Storm...she's afraid."

This has my attention. "Does he hurt her?"

Shelby laughs. "Of course not. But he *is* hurting himself. Tamlin says he's not only taking all those pills, but he's been drinking too—after he leaves Honor. And Honor feels it."

"I don't want to talk about Storm anymore. Are you done now?"

"Fine," she says with a frown.

I don't understand why I'm finding her wildly attractive. I can't stand the girl.

"Ethan." She interrupts my thoughts. "Is the only reason you don't like me because I was a bitch to Honor when she first started school?"

"Yes."

"So, even though I've apologized over and over, and even though Honor and I are now friends, you still feel the need to hate me?"

Okay, maybe I am an ass. Maybe I haven't been fair. Recalling Storm's words from earlier, maybe I am taking out my anger about Honor's situation on Shelby. "I'm sorry," I say, looking at her. "I think I needed to be angry at someone, and so I chose you," I admit, resentfully.

"I get that. Boy, do I get that." Again, I think of what Storm said before and realize he has a keen insight on people. I won't admit that to him though. "So, can you stop being an ass now?" she asks, patting my knee.

This time when I look at her, I actually smile. Mockingly patting her on the knee too, I say, "I'll stop being an ass." Then I try to ignore the slight charge I feel when I touch her.

"Let's get back," she says, looking out toward the boat. "It looks like everyone is getting back on."

"Yeah." I get up off the sand and pull her up with me.

"Race ya." She tears out into the water and swims effortlessly out toward the boat.

As I climb the ladder into the boat, I hear a commotion.

"You don't get it, do you?" Storm is yelling at Honor.

Everyone's jaws are dropped while they watch.

"What don't I get, Storm? Tell me. What don't I get?" I've never heard Honor raise her voice before. "You're giving me mixed signals. One minute you're all sweet and protective, the next, you're cold and telling me to leave you alone. Then, I see you all detached and on something. So, tell me what I don't get? Because you're right, I don't get it." Honor stands face- to-face with Storm. They're inches apart and yelling like no one else is around.

I want to step in and stop them, but after my conversation with Shelby, I'm thinking that would be a bad idea. They probably do need to work some things out. Otherwise, Honor wouldn't be this upset.

"You're killing me, Honor." He runs his hands through his hair and shakes his head. "You're *killing* me." Storm is on the verge of tears, and I think he is yelling to cover up that fact. "Why the *fuck* did you have to save all those people? Why couldn't you leave them the fuck alone?" His voice hitches, and it's only moments before the tears follow.

Honor's rigid stance loosens, and her face drops.

So Storm does *feel the same way I do about her saving that plane load of people.*

"You're not the fucking Savior, Honor. And now...now you're dying...and there's nothing I can fucking do about it. *Fuck you* for doing this." Storm grabs onto Honor's shoulders and yanks her against him before wrapping her so tight he looks like he's trying to hurt her. But her arms wrap around his waist and she begins rubbing his back. Her face is buried into his neck, and I can't help but fill with fury over the scene. Just last night she was holding onto me like that.

But she wasn't crying like that when she danced with me.

Tamlin looks at all of us and shrugs her shoulders. "What should we do?" she mouths.

Not that the boat is all that big, but we all jam into the front of the boat, leaving Storm and Honor to work through whatever it is they're feeling. Though all *I* want to do is rip them the fuck apart.

Chapter Nine

"Don't go and think that hug makes everything better. I'm still pissed at you."

Because I never really took my attention off of Honor and Storm, I hear him say this to her. I walk slowly back toward them to eavesdrop again, thinking this *is* becoming a bad habit of mine.

"I love the hell out of you, princess, but I can't take this anymore," Storm says as he backs away from her. "You care about all these other hurting people, but you don't give a fuck about the ones *you're* hurting. The people who *love* and *need you*. It's just not fair to us, the ones you're leaving behind. It's bullshit."

Honor sees me, and a knowing expression crosses her face. *She finally understands what I've been telling her all along—it's a selfish thing she is doing...at least in the eyes of the ones she's leaving behind.* Just like my parents did to my brothers and me.

"I don't know what to do anymore, Honor." Storm continues. "Short of killing myself and giving you *my* heart, I don't know what to do anymore. I can't...I can't be around you knowing you're dying. I can't be around you if you live, because you'll just keep on being you." Storm doesn't hide the fact that he's crying now. He doesn't even wipe his tears away.

But he does wipe away Honor's tears. He cups her face in his hands and wipes at her tears with his thumbs. "Maybe Ethan knows better what he can do for you, but I'm fucking scared to death, and when I'm scared, I run.

You know that about me, and I have never been this fucking frightened in my life."

With his two large hands still cupping her face, he kisses her hard on the lips. They passionately make out right in front of me. Turning my head so I don't have to watch, I'm startled to hear a splash. I look back, and Honor is standing alone. Crying. Storm has jumped overboard.

Honor looks at me and shrugs her bony shoulders. "I'm sorry," she whispers.

Dropping my own shoulders, I walk over and take her in my arms. "It'll be all right," I whisper in her ear.

"I'm doing the same thing your parents did to you. I'm so, so sorry," she sobs.

"Shh. You're just being you. I get it."

"But now I'm hurting all of you. Oh my God, what have I done?" She pulls back to look at my face. "I'm dying, Eeth. Oh my God, I'm dying."

"No," I reply adamantly. "No, you are not dying. They *will* find you a new heart. I promise. They will."

Tamlin comes running over to Honor and hugs her from behind. "Oh sweetie, you're not dying. Please. I know you're going to get a new heart." Honor turns to give Tamlin a hug.

I'm feeling guilty that I even put those thoughts in Honor's head. She was only acting on what comes perfectly natural for her—healing the hurting. Now she is hurting because of the abilities God had given her. A natural empath is born to feel. Now she is being punished for it. I get what Storm is so angry about, but I also finally get what Honor is all about.

Hunter, Eli, and Shelby have all gathered around us.

"Honor," Hunter says softly. "It'll all be all right. You'll see. Storm will come around too. Just give him time. He's never loved *anyone* in his entire life. He doesn't know how to deal with the kind of emotions he's probably feeling right now."

"She's not worried about Storm, Hunter," I chime in. "She's upset because she needs a new heart."

"No, Ethan," Honor rebuts. "I *am* worried about Storm. The only reason I'm worried about dying *is* because of him. I didn't mean to do this." She wipes at her eyes with her knuckle. "What if he never comes back?"

Eli laughs. "It's Lake Hopatcong, Honor, not the ocean. If he doesn't come back to the boat, he'll find his way home, babe." He walks over and rubs her back. "Let's forget about Storm right now. Like Hunter said, he needs to cool off. He's upset enough that he'll probably jog all the way home. Tam," Eli addresses her. "Start the boat. Let's go for a ride again."

Eli rides up front with Tamlin, while Shelby and Hunter sit towards the middle of the boat. I sit at the back with Honor in my arms.

"I'm scared, Ethan," Honor says so no one else can hear. "I want them to find me a heart, but I hate to think someone has to die for me to have it. What if it's a child?"

I really don't know what to say to that. "I'm sure God knows what He's doing. You just have to believe that He has a plan. I really don't know what else to say about that. It doesn't seem fair—to have one person survive at the death of another—but you have to try not to think about that."

She nods on my shoulder.

Honor's pretty silent after that, so I look around the lake, enjoying the scenery. White puffy clouds are scattered generously across the bright blue sky. The cool breeze ripples the water, while the sun paints shadows across the lake. You'd never know it by the appearance of the day that hearts are hurting. People are suffering. It's an irony that causes a lump to form in my throat. When I turn my attention to Shelby, her face mirrors my emotions. Could she be coming to the same realization that I am? The incongruity of this perfect day? Hunter doesn't seem to have the same thoughtful expression on his face. He's too busy playing with his phone.

A small smile appears on Shelby's face when she looks at me. I respond without thinking by smiling back. Something changed today. On the sand, somehow, Shelby had earned my respect. And maybe I had earned hers.

**

At the end of the day, Tamlin invites all of us to her house to play cards. Because no one wants to end the day yet, we all agree—until Honor tells me in the car that she would rather just go home. I can't say I am not disappointed, but I do understand. Her weakened heart causes her to fatigue a lot faster than the normal teenager. Plus, I know she's bummed about Storm taking off. When she found his phone sitting on one of the cushions in the boat, she nearly started crying again.

I take Honor's hand and walk her to the door. "I can stay if you want," I tell her.

"Thanks, but I just want to go to bed." Even in the fading sunlight, Honor looks so drawn and pale.

"Ok. Do you want me to come by tomorrow?" I ask, still holding her hand.

"Please," she says.

I kiss her quick on the lips and say goodnight.

Everyone else had driven with Tamlin, so I contemplate just going home myself. But since being alone is not very appealing to me tonight, I drive over to Tam's house, stopping first to get some chips and dip at the store. When I get there, they're all sitting around a table in her basement.

"Hey, Eeth," Eli calls. "Honor didn't want to come?"

"Nah. She's beat. I'll check on her tomorrow."

Tamlin comes down with the chips and dip I gave her when I walked in. She sets the bowls on the table and hands Eli a deck of cards, pulling out a suitcase full of poker chips.

"Poker?" he asks.

"Strip?" Hunter asks.

For some reason, I immediately look at Shelby, who is looking at me and blushing.

"Keep dreaming, Hunter." Tamlin laughs.

Since I'm not great at poker, I fold one too many times and quit, taking the bowl of chips with me when I sit on the couch.

"*Breakfast Club* is in the DVD player if you want to watch it," Tamlin yells from the table.

"That eighties movie?"

"Yeah. It's really good. You can watch it if you want."

There's nothing better to do, so I turn it on. The red-headed chick on the screen is sitting in the car talking to her father when Shelby sits down next to me. "Mind if I watch?" she asks me.

"Sure." I move over to give her room and hand the bowl of chips to her.

"No thanks."

A strange feeling comes over me while watching the movie. I'm getting turned on. By Shelby. It's one thing making amends and being friends. It's quite another to have intimate feelings for her. The thought disturbs me. Without being too obvious, I shift my body so I'm not so close to her. But the whole time the movie is on, I can't stop thinking that she's sitting on the couch with me. Of course, she has no clue I'm feeling this way—her eyes haven't strayed from the screen. But I am all too aware of these feelings of mine that seem like a betrayal to Honor.

Chapter Ten

Not so subtly, I move over again, this time spreading my legs out diagonally across the couch to avoid any type of physical closeness to her.

Catching her attention by doing this, she looks at me with a weird expression on her face, "Getting comfortable?" she asks.

"Yeah."

Shelby chuckles and says, "Good idea." Her feet swing up onto the couch, and crossing them at the ankles, her top foot dances while she leans against the arm. Turning to watch the movie again, Shelby's dark hair falls over her shoulder, blocking my view of her face. Though I'm facing the television, my thoughts are on my conflicting feelings for Shelby. Early this morning all she made me feel was hate because of what she did to Honor. Feeling sexual desires for her is frustrating. I'm not even sure why I'm reacting this way to her; her glossy dark hair and olive complexion is such a contrast to Honor's pale locks and milk-white skin. Though I love Honor, I can't help but find Shelby attractive. Maybe my perceived feelings of rejection from Honor are to blame. Maybe not. But I am feeling uncomfortable.

Just as I move to get up, I hear Shelby say my name under her breath. "I'd like to explain why I treated Honor the way I did," she says so softly and timidly that it takes me by surprise.

I move to lower the volume of the television, but she touches my hand to stop me from doing so.

"No. I don't want them to hear." She tosses her head back in reference to our friends playing poker.

I put the remote down and nod my head.

"When I was sick, I was told there wasn't anything more they could do. They told me I had at least a year left and that I should just enjoy the time I had. A teenager should never hear those words. No kid should." Shelby looks down on her lap, but only briefly. She brings her head right back up and looks me in the eyes. "Anyway, I was ready to explode. I couldn't handle the news, but I couldn't let anyone see me break like that. My popularity was still important to me, at least on the surface, and I wanted everyone to see me the way they always had. But I needed a friend. A real one. Not the ones I actually hung out with. They didn't give a shit about real life." Shelby scratches the side of her nose, but I think it's to cover up that she's wiping a tear from her eye. "Since I didn't have a friend to release all my emotions, I let them out in the form of anger...against Honor. She was the easiest target." She shakes her head and her lip quirks to the side a bit. "She was the new kid. No one knew her. I hated every moment I was nasty to her, but it was hard to stop myself. There was so much hostility inside me." Shelby pauses to take a deep breath, but she doesn't speak.

"Well," I start to say, but she holds her hand up and I see that she is actually fighting back tears and *can't* speak.

After a few moments of composing herself, she continues. "That's why I need to be there for her now. I know she doesn't need me. She has so many friends that really care about her. Truly care. Like you and Tam and Hunter and

Eli...and Storm. But still, I think I need to be there for her. Maybe it's selfish, but I really want to be her friend, because I know what it's like to be given a life sentence. Honor doesn't deserve that."

I try hard to hold back my tears, but that life sentence line strikes hard. Until now, I've been hopeful that Honor will find a heart, and so I haven't looked at her situation as dire. But what if? It's a huge possibility that there won't be a match in time. Honor can die.

I'm so thrown back by this that I don't realize Shelby is shaking my leg.

"Ethan, are you okay?" I hear her voice in the distance, but it takes a while to register.

"Ethan." She tries again, and this time I return back to reality to answer her.

"Yeah, I'm fine."

"Did I upset you?" Shelby is still hanging on to my ankle.

I position myself upright, removing my leg from her grasp. "I hadn't thought about Honor being served a life sentence. But you're right. If they don't find one in time—"

"Oh boy, I didn't mean it like that. Of course they'll find one in time," she says, putting both her feet on the floor and sitting forward on the couch. "I'm sorry, Ethan."

"It's okay. It just hit me. That's all. I guess...I guess that's why Storm took off today. It's a lot to deal with..." I fade off, not in the mood anymore to talk.

Shelby must sense my mood, because she turns back toward the television. From the somber expression on her face, I don't think she's watching the movie. She's adrift somewhere in her own mind.

Behind us, Tam and the guys are laughing heartily while they play cards. "You cheat, Elijah," Tamlin says while chuckling with a mouth full of chips or something.

"Nah," Eli says. "You're just bad at cards."

They're all laughing and having a good time while Shelby and I are busy mourning the loss of Honor's freedom.

"I'm sorry I upset you," Shelby says again, this time without taking her eyes from the television screen.

Her glistening eyelashes prompt me to move closer. Laying my hand on her knee, I tell her, "*You* didn't upset me, Shelby. The situation did."

"I wish there were something we could do to help her."

"Short of getting her a heart somewhere, I don't think there really is anything we can do."

"I know something we can do," Tamlin shouts from behind, obviously listening in our conversation.

Shelby and I turn back to look at her.

"Throw her a birthday party." Tamlin is beaming. "A real big one."

Shelby looks at me and shrugs.

"I don't know, Tam," I remark, "she can't be around too many people."

"No." Tamlin hops up and stands behind the couch.

"Hey, Tam, we're in the middle of a game here," Hunter scolds.

Ignoring him, Tamlin continues talking to Shelby and me. "Not big as in a lot of people. Big as in—something out of this world. Like the city or—"

"The city," I interrupt, "is filled with too many people."

"I know," Shelby interjects. "A dinner cruise. Maybe we can reserve a whole ship or something."

"A dinner cruise. That's perfect." Tamlin exclaims, bouncing up and down, her fragile blond hair flying in front of her pallid face. It occurs to me now how exhausted she is from worrying about her best friend. I guess you don't really have to be an empath to empathize and take on the hurt of your loved ones. "My dad has tons of money. I bet he'll help us secure a boat for a party. Awesome idea, Shelby."

Tamlin grabs Shelby by the sides of her face and kisses her right on the lips.

"Eww, Tamlin." Shelby wipes off the kiss with the palm of her hand. "A hug would have sufficed."

Tamlin chuckles and then kisses me. "She is gonna love it."

Chapter Eleven

In Honor's backyard, the pool glitters from the rising sun. A zillion tiny sparkles dance across it, getting me excited for the first swim of the summer. Though school hasn't ended yet, Mr. Stevens opens the pool to give Honor and her friends something to do on the weekends.

"Hey, Ethan," Honor deadpans, which is so unlike her. "Daddy said you were out here. Why didn't you just come to the front door?"

"I saw your father skimming the pool, so I thought I'd come through the back. Besides, I thought you wanted to go swimming today." I step towards her, but I'm afraid to get too close. She doesn't look happy to see me.

"Yeah, I did." She sighs and sits on the picnic table. Stepping up on the bench, I sit next to her on the table, making sure to leave a fair amount of space.

"You don't now?" I'm surprised, because she just texted the group of us at like seven o'clock this morning asking us to come swimming. She said her mom would make us waffles and Taylor Ham.

"No, I do. Tamlin and Shelby are on their way right now." The stray pieces of hair sticking out from Honor's disorderly bun fly around like dandelions on her father's overgrown lawn. A pain knocks on my heart. This family is losing hope. First Storm. Now Honor and her father. I can't let her lose hope. Without it, she'll lose her motivation to live, and I cannot let her do that.

"You got your suit on?" I ask her.

"Yeah." She pulls down the shoulder of her long white pullover to reveal a bright yellow strap.

"Good. Pull off your dress."

"What?" she asks with a little more expression.

"You heard me," I say, pulling off my t-shirt and hopping off the table. Tapping her on the knee, I signal for her to come in the pool with me. "Come on. Before anyone gets here. We'll have a race."

"A race? But I'm not really-"

"C'mon, Honor. You don't have to swim well, just move your body across the pool. I'll even let you have a head start."

A moan escapes from her throat, but she still lets down her dress. The bright yellow bikini hugs her hips just below the bone. I have to jump in the pool to cool off, and it's not even hot out yet.

Honor steps in one foot at a time, still no smile on her face.

"C'mon slow-poke, before everyone else gets here."

She rolls her eyes, but sinks under water.

When she's at least half way up the length of the pool, I swim to meet her. And pass her up.

"No fair," she mock whines. "You know I have no strength right now."

Her bun has now unraveled, sending her hair in wet knotty waves down her back. Her beauty is unsurpassed. Even sick, Honor is the most beautiful girl in the entire world.

"Did you want me to let you win?" I joke.

"It doesn't matter." The glint of excitement I had just witnessed is gone.

She is so freaking light when I lift her out of the water to set her at the edge of the pool. I hop up and sit next to her. "Honor," I say seriously. "You gotta get happy, hun. I know this is some serious shit, but damn, it can't be good for you to be so depressed. Has the doctor given you anything for it?"

She nods. "I'm on a whole bunch of stuff. My mother gives all my pills to me when I need them. I have no idea what I'm on."

"You know you'll pull through this, right?"

She nods again. "I'm not even worried about that, Ethan."

"Then what?" I hear my own voice crack. "If you're not worried about your own heart, then why are you so damn depressed?"

Honor just blinks and bites the side of her lip.

"Storm." It's not a question. I am so fucking stupid. Of course she's depressed about Storm taking off. It's always about him, and this pisses me off. "What the hell, Honor? You're so worried about him, but where is he? He leaves without telling anyone where he is going, and then he leaves his phone so you can't even get in touch with him. Instead of worrying about him, be pissed at him. He just left you. You call that a friend?"

I made her cry. Dammit, I didn't want to make her cry.

"Honor," I whisper, squeezing her knee in the meantime. "I'm sorry."

"No, I know you mean well…it's just…I'm worried. It's not like him."

"It damn well is like him," I shout, raising my hand in the air. "He's been running his whole life. It's all he knows. Things get rough, Storm takes off."

I push my wet hair off my face and try to calm down.

"We're here," Tamlin yells from the driveway. "Let the party begin."

Walking in next to Tam, Shelby is shaking her head.

Honor and I put aside our uncomfortable conversation and get up to greet the girls. "Hey, Tam, Shel…thank you for coming," Honor says softly. It pains me to hear her voice so weak. It kills me to know it's because she's missing my arrogant, self-absorbed brother.

"So where are those waffles I heard about?" Tamlin is joking, of course, but at least she is lightening the mood.

Honor actually smiles. "She's making them now. You want to eat inside or out?"

"It doesn't matter, Hon, wherever. It's nice outside. We can stay out here if you want." Tamlin gives Honor a bear hug.

Shelby leans in and gives Honor a hug when Tamlin lets go of her. "You feelin' okay today?"

"Yeah, I'm good." Her smile is forced, but at least she's trying.

Shelby takes her hand and leans in. "Are you scared, Honor?"

Honor looks at me, then back at Shelby. "Yes," she whispers. "I am."

Why couldn't she just tell me that? Why did she have to make it about Storm?

"Hey, kids," Mrs. Stevens addresses, a smile on her face, but not in her eyes. "Waffles are done." Plates of waffles, Taylor Ham, a bottle of syrup, bowls of fruit and chocolate chips, and a can of whipped cream adorn a huge tray that she sets down on the picnic table.

"Wow, Mrs. S., this looks awesome," announces Tamlin. "I'm starved."

When Mr. Stevens comes out with coffee and juice, Honor steps up to take the mugs out of his hands.

"Thanks, hun. I have your favorite mug," he says softly to her.

After she puts the mugs down, she pours some coffee into a mug that has two smiling pieces of toast popping out of a smiling light-blue toaster. Classic Honor. It's such a vintage mug, just like the old-fashioned soul inside the girl herself. Seeing her drink from it makes me wish I was still living here with her. She drank from that mug every morning when I was there. Shaking it off, I return to eating my breakfast.

"Well look what the cat finally dragged in," Tamlin remarks when Hunter and Eli walk into the yard. "Mrs. Stevens gave us all this food, babe," she says to Eli. "Grab a plate and sit." She pats the space on the bench next to her.

"Hey, Honor, how ya feeling?" Hunter asks.

"Okay. Thanks." She's sipping her coffee, but touching none of the food.

"Honor," I pipe up. "Eat."

She looks at me, but ignores my request and takes another sip of her coffee. She's not even a coffee drinker. She drinks tea. What the heck? It's like she doesn't care about anything anymore and this just floors me.

Not able to endure this any longer, I stand up from the bench, taking her by the elbow as I do. "We need to talk. Now."

When she pulls her white cover-up over her head, her drying dreadlocks whack me in the face. "Look at this," I say as I lift up her hair, "your hair's a mess. Yesterday on the boat it was okay, but what happened? You didn't comb it since? You woke up and decided not to comb it?"

"No. I didn't comb it. Why does that bother you?" Her voice is so flat it pains me.

"It bothers me because it's not like you. Every morning and every night you used to brush out your hair. Didn't you tell me once how you love to brush it out?"

"Ethan. It's one day. Why are you making such a big deal out of this?"

"Because. I don't want you giving up hope. It's a sign." I run my hand through her hair, catching my fingers in the knots. "You're giving up one of the things you love to do. What's next? Look at you. If we're gonna survive this, we need to be hopeful."

The veins in her eyelids are so pronounced when she closes them and takes a deep breath. "I'm tired, Eeth. And Storm taking off, well...it just knocked the fight out of me." She sighs and sits on the old swing in her backyard.

"What does Storm leaving have to do with your fighting for your life?" I ball my fists at my side wishing he were here to punch.

"I don't know. I...I really don't know, but it does."

Fuck. She's in love with him. Why else would his leaving bother her to the point of giving up her fight for life?

"Listen, Eeth, I know you mean well, but can we just hang with everyone? I don't really feel like talking about this right now."

When I cup my hands around her face, my heart rumbles. I want to kiss her so badly. "Okay," I say in lieu of a kiss. "I just wanna see you smile."

She does. And it is the first real smile I've seen today. "Thanks."

I take her hand and walk her back to the table. "Please eat something," I whisper before she sits down.

Her thin pale arm reaches for a waffle, and I relax.

**

After we spend most of the day submerged in water, by nightfall, Mr. Stevens lights the outdoor fire pit, and Mrs. Stevens brings out hot dogs and marshmallows. The two of them are trying so hard to make the day special for Honor. I can't even imagine what they must be going through right now.

"Ethan," Shelby shouts above the music playing from Honor's iPod station. "You going to join us?" They're all sitting around the pit. I'm hanging back at the pool and dangling my legs off the diving board.

Because Honor is sandwiched between Tamlin and Hunter, I sit on the ground next to Shelby, who happens to smell amazing. I don't know how after being in the chlorinated pool all day she still manages to smell like pears, but I take a deep inhale and enjoy it nonetheless.

"She's a whole lot happier than she was this morning," Shelby comments about Honor, who is cracking up across the pit at something Hunter or Tamlin must have said. I may not have been able to get her to laugh, but at least she's laughing. As each hour passes, her mood brightens, which is a good thing.

"Yeah."

Shelby reaches behind her and grabs two sticks. "Hot dog or marshmallow?" she asks, holding up the sticks.

"Hot dog."

I watch her tiny hands fumble with a hot dog and drop it.

"Nice." I laugh along with her. "Here." I reach in front of her to pick the dog off the ground, grazing her bare leg in the process. Trying my best to ignore the electricity that immediately courses through my veins, I brush off the dog and slide it on my stick. "I ain't afraid of no germs," I joke.

Shelby's laugh sounds more like a titter, and again, I ignore the prickling sensation I get hearing her nervously chuckle. She slips a marshmallow on her stick and holds it over the fire.

"You love her?"

Did she just ask me if I love her? I assume she's talking about Honor. "Yes...but..." I don't even finish that sentence. I don't know how.

"But...she doesn't love you?" Shelby completes the thought for me.

Looking at her big brown eyes looking back at me, I say, "That is *not* what I was going to say." I laugh, because for some reason I find it funny. "I was going to say, I'm not sure in what capacity."

"Oh. So you love her as a sister?" Shelby jokes. Her laugh is honest, and her smile is sincere.

"Not exactly, no." I nudge her in the shoulder with my shoulder. "But...I don't know really. Loving anyone is so new to me that I don't know what these feelings are inside me." I lick my lips and run my free hand through my hair.

"Ooh, it's burning," she shouts, yanking her flaming marshmallow out of the fire. Taking the stick from her, I blow out her marshmallow at the same time she goes to blow it out—leaving us face to face, mere inches from each other. My eyes freeze on her lips. When her tongue darts out over her full bottom lip, she takes such a deep breath that her shoulders raise a few inches.

I break the stare first, only because I hear Honor talking across the fire. Naturally, my attention turns to her—she is chatting with Tamlin. But the moment with Shelby is lost, because I hear her sigh before she turns back towards the fire.

"Here's your marshmallow," I say, handing it back to her.

Only one side of her mouth tilts up when she says, "Thank you."

This leaves me with a slightly wrenching gut. While I'm contemplating why it bothers me so much to have been pulled from Shelby's trance, Hunter grabs her ear. And instead of joining in on any conversation, I let the fading voices disappear as I stare intently on the burning flame in front of me. While letting the words to Ed Sheeran's "Photograph" sink deep into my psyche while it pipes in the background.

Chapter Twelve

My bed is warm and comfortable, but it's Monday morning and finals week, which means I have to get up. I am so not looking forward to finals. With everything going on in Honor's life, I have not even opened a book, let alone studied.

As I let the warm water rain down on me in the shower, I recall slighting Shelby for Honor. It took all I had to fall asleep last night because of it. *Why does it bother me that Honor's voice stole my attention from Shelby?* Honor is who I love. Until this weekend, I couldn't stand Shelby. So, why has she been constantly on my mind since Saturday night? My heart hurts for Honor, but when I'm with Shelby, all I want to do is smell her and kiss her. *Am I picking up her feelings about me? Is that what this is about?* Now that I have unwillingly tapped back into my empathic abilities, could I be picking up more and more of what other people are feeling? I'd think I could detect which emotions are mine and which are not, but I've been closed up for so long, maybe my signals are getting crossed. In any event, I need to figure out my real feelings. I need to get back to solely loving and protecting Honor.

After a long morning, I finish my first exam and go to lunch, where not only Tamlin, Eli, and Hunter are sitting but Shelby as well. No more cheerleader table? I don't know if I'm happy about this or pissed. Why all of a sudden is she sitting with us? She's Honor's friend. Honor's not here.

"Hey, Eeth," Tamlin calls to me as I walk towards our table.

"Tam."

"Why the long face?" she asks while everyone else just nods their hellos.

"Not in the mood today." I'm not. I don't feel like talking to anyone. My final in first period sucked, and I am not looking forward to this afternoon's.

"Ooh, crabby."

"Shut up, Tam. Not kidding." I slam my lunch on the table and stew in my own despair. When I finally look up, I catch Shelby looking at me. Though not in the mood to smile, one naturally appears on my face.

She remains silent, but she does give me a quick genuine smile before bringing her attention back to the conversation.

"It's just not the same," Tamlin says, "without Honor or Storm. And where the heck is he? Have any of you heard from him?"

"Nope," Eli says, his voice clipped, obviously not giving a shit where the obnoxious ass is.

"No, I haven't," Hunter answers. "But I'm sure he's fine. He's been living on his own since he was twelve. There isn't anyone on earth who could hurt Storm."

"Except for Honor," Tamlin states.

"Well, I meant physically," Hunter rebuts.

"I know. But I still want to know where he is and *why* he ran off. His car hasn't been at his apartment. I keep checking."

"You keep checking?" Elijah sounds angry. "Why do you care where the hell he is?"

"'Cause he's a friend, E. A good friend."

"Yeah, but I know you two were a thing," he shouts so that the whole lunchroom turns in our direction.

"Geez, Eli, get a grip. We shared a couple kisses. Besides, his heart belongs to Honor."

I wish the two of them would shut the fuck up about Storm. I'm beginning to hate the guy again. Abruptly, I yank my uneaten lunch from the table and go throw it in the garbage. Instead, I go sit out on the school's patio until it's time for the next exam.

After another long exam, I decide to drive over to Honor's house to check up on her.

"Hey, kiddo," I say when she answers the door. "Feeling okay today?"

"Yeah, I'm good. Come in." The sun is not reflecting off of her smile today. Even the sun is sad for Honor. Which is so befitting, since the sunshine has finally left what was once the most vibrant of all human beings. My heart finds a way to break just a little bit more.

"Sorry I didn't call yesterday. I stayed in bed all day and watched some movies. Wasn't really up for doing much."

"Join the club," she says, smiling at least. "Sorry about the other day, Ethan. I didn't mean to yell at you. I know how much you care. I'm just being selfish. I'm sorry."

"Honor," I take hold of her shoulders and look into her eyes, "there's no need to apologize. You *should* be selfish right now. Hell, what you're going through is rough. I don't think I could handle knowing I'd need a new heart or I'd die." As soon as the words come out of my mouth I want to take them back. Asshole. "I meant—"

"I know what you meant, Eeth." She laughs. Then she bursts out in hysterics. Honor isn't crying. She's cracking up.

"What the hell is so funny?" I follow her into the kitchen where she pulls out a pitcher of iced tea.

Reaching up to the cupboard to get the glasses, she's still laughing. When she turns and puts the glasses on the counter, she stops. "I don't know what's so funny. That's what's funny. I. Have. No. Idea. Why. I am laughing." She pours the tea and hands me my glass, leading us to her couch. "But it sure feels good."

I smile huge, but I don't have it in me to laugh along with her. "Then laugh every second, darling. It looks good on you."

"You know Shelby is coming over?"

Suddenly I don't feel like smiling anymore. "No. I didn't know." This is going to confuse me even more.

"Yeah, like any minute now." Honor says, squirming to get comfortable on the couch.

"Oh, well, maybe I'll just go. I'll come over tomorrow." I kiss her on the nose and stand from the couch.

Standing as well, Honor comes face to face with me. "No, Ethan, I don't want you to go. I'm glad you came. Unless, of course, you and Shelby still hate each other." Honor's thin nose scrunches beneath her brow.

"No. There's no hate between us." Too bad I don't know *what* it is between us.

At that thought, the doorbell rings.

When Shelby walks in, I'm mesmerized by the smell of pears, but no more spell-bound than I am when in the presence of Honor. Shelby may be cute, but I realize just then that Honor holds my heart.

"Hey, Shel," I greet her after Honor has let her in. "I was just leaving, so—"

"Don't leave on my account, I don't mind if you're here, unless Honor minds." Shelby looks at Honor and waits for her reaction.

"I told him he doesn't have to," she says to Shelby. Looking at me, she asks, "How 'bout you stay for another glass of iced tea at least?"

"Sure." I stick my hands deep in my pockets and follow Honor back into the kitchen.

At the breakfast bar, Honor seems more like herself. It suddenly occurs to me that her hair is free of the knots she had two days ago. It's amazing that the heart can smile as easily as it can break—for that I am grateful. Every smile helps.

"How are your exams going, Honor?" Shelby asks, her finger circling her glass.

"Exams?" I ask. "You have exams?"

Honor chuckles. "Yes, Eeth. I still have to follow a curriculum." Though we're inside, the sunshine returns in her smile. "They're going well, Shel. I have one more tomorrow, and then I'll be done. Mom has me going to school online now, instead of her homeschooling me. They have this whole new program. It's cool though."

"Good," she says. "My grades have gone up this last semester." Shelby hangs her head a moment, and then lifts it back up. "I have you to thank for that, so...thank you."

Honor waves her hand in dismissal. "I'm glad you're healthy again."

"As you will be soon. I really believe that," Shelby says before grabbing Honor's hand across the counter.

"Yeah. I usually don't let things like this bother me," Honor pointedly looks at me, "but when I get sad, it's hard to pull myself out of it."

I decide to join in the conversation. "Do you still feel everyone else's emotions, Honor?"

"Yes. Unfortunately. My parents are really sad. They try to hide it, but I feel it." She lets out a mirthless chuckle. "They want to protect me from everyone else, but *their* emotions hit me the hardest."

I only nod. What can I say? Nothing. There is nothing I can say that would make her feel better, so I just sigh. And nod again.

"You feel guilty too, don't you?" Shelby chimes in.

Her violet eyes grow wide as she exclaims, "Yes, oh my God, yes. I feel so guilty about their sadness. You felt that too?"

Shelby nods. "Yes. I hated to think that I was the one causing their tears. But unlike you, I let it make me angry."

Honor again looks at me and whispers, "Not so unlike me, right Eeth?"

"Honor. Stop. You were barely angry. Just annoyed maybe."

When her pretty lips turn into that beautiful smile, I feel my breaking heart mending just a little.

"Thank you," she mouths to me without any sound.

So I blow her a kiss.

Shelby catches the exchange, and it makes me feel guilty. Why? I love Honor. I don't love Shelby. But I certainly find her attractive and enjoyable. Trouble. That's where this will lead me, and since Honor has already said she still feels everything, I'm sure she'll figure this out too.

So I need to block Shelby from my thoughts.

I can't ruin anything with Honor.

I want her so badly it hurts.

And right now our relationship is on such fragile ground, that I can't let anything cause it to crumble.

Chapter Thirteen

Honor turns her back on us to grab a bag of pretzels out of the cabinet. "Listen," she tells us, her back still facing us, "I'd like to drop this whole subject." She turns back to us and pours the pretzels in a bowl. "I don't want to be depressed today."

"Sure," I say and grab a handful of pretzels.

"Wanna play Just Dance?" Honor suggests.

"Okay," Shelby says with a smile.

"Yeah. That's what I want to do." Of course my response is sarcastic.

Honor comes around the bar and takes me by the arm. "Come on, Eeth. It'll be fun."

Her voice is so light and sunshiny that I can't resist. "Okay...for you." I shake my head and let her hold my arm as we walk into the living room.

The first song on the Wii that Honor puts on is "Moves Like Jagger." Honor and Shelby dancing is highly seductive in an innocent way, but they are definitely two polar opposites. Where Shelby's moves are deliberate and spirited, Honor's are graceful and refined. Where Shelby's short athletic legs are tan and sexy, Honor's long, lean ones are flawlessly classic. I should not be so blatantly enjoying this, but I am.

A slight nudge in the arm interrupts my appreciation for the dancers in front of me. "C'mon, Eeth." Shelby's grinning. "It's fun." Then she quirks her head towards Honor and points to her own smile. I get what she's telling me. *Honor's having a good time. Let's keep her smiling.*

So I get up and join them—feeling like an ass while shaking my ass. I barely spend any time dancing when the song ends. "Oh darn," I tease. "Song's over." I move to sit on the couch.

"Not so fast, buddy." Honor pulls me up by my bicep. "There's plenty more songs where that one came from."

That sun-shining sparkle that I love to see in her eyes is so bright now that I can't refuse to dance in their sunlight. My mending heart is doing its thing as I silently thank God for her smile.

When that deep southern drawl starts crooning "Jailhouse Rock," my body seems to lighten up. I ignore the dance moves suggested on the television and perform a very easy "king of all things rock" impersonation.

Shelby shakes her head and starts laughing, while Honor doubles over in hysterics—cracking up at my uncharacteristic display of cutting loose, which now causes me to laugh, because never in my life have I acted so silly. I believe the pile up of emotions has finally gotten to me. My life has always been one string of solemn events. It feels good to laugh—to really laugh—and when I catch the brief darkening of Honor's eyes, they reflect what I'm thinking. She feels good right now. This has to be great for her heart. Maybe more days like this and her heart just may heal itself. *Hopefully.*

By the end of the night, the three of us had danced, laughed, eaten and joked around. We bonded as a group and before walking out the door, I had an even greater respect for Shelby Marcus. She knew what Honor needed and made sure she received it—laughter. Probably something Shelby hadn't gotten during her own illness. Which makes me wonder. Did she get her laughs by bullying? It so, it doesn't make it right, but I can certainly understand where she had been coming from.

But Shelby is a different person than the one we met in the beginning of the year. Whether it was her cancer or Honor's generosity, Shelby has evolved into a compassionate human being. I'm suddenly thankful that Honor has her as a friend.

Chapter Fourteen

"Can you believe we're graduating this Friday?" Tamlin sings, stuffing a sandwich in her mouth at the lunch table on Tuesday.

"Yup. Three more days," Shelby adds. "I'm glad it's over, that's for sure."

"Yeah?" Tamlin wonders.

"Yeah. I'm so done with high school." Shelby sips her water.

"What are your plans after you graduate?" I ask, curious to peel more layers from this former bully.

"I'm going to CCM for nursing. Then probably William Paterson University to finish my degree."

"That's cool," Tamlin says.

"Yeah. I want to help sick kids. Maybe work at that children's hospital in Morristown." She bites her lip then picks up a carrot and puts it to her lips.

"That's cool," I say, impressed by her choice of profession. "Good for you."

"What about you, Tam?" Shelby asks.

"Law School. I want to have my own practice. Wouldn't that be cool? Maybe in a big city like New York or L.A...or Paris."

"Very cool," Shelby agrees.

"Yeah, well, no moving to L.A. 'til I graduate," Eli commands, very weakly if Tamlin's raised eyebrows are any indication.

"Right." Tamlin laughs. "We'll see about that." Maybe Tam isn't as serious about Eli as Eli is about her. Time will tell.

"What about you, Ethan?" Shelby asks quietly.

I shrug. "I didn't apply to college."

"Why not?"

Again, I shrug. "I don't know. I just never thought about it. My parents left this huge insurance inheritance that I always just thought I'd live off that."

Shelby just says, "Oh," but looks really sad.

Tamlin, however, says, "That is just sad, Ethan Sutherland. What a waste of an intelligent mind. You can do so much. Why waste it living on money you didn't even earn?"

"Oh, I earned that money," I say with so much agitation I slam my fist on the table. "I had to grow up with no parental guidance. No one telling me they love me. No one feeding me a warm dinner. Uncle Tom didn't do that. Don't get me wrong, he was a great guy, but all he gave us was a roof over our heads. So, I went out on my own and took care of myself. So, don't go and tell me I didn't earn the right to use my inheritance."

Shelby is looking down, playing with her food, and Tamlin looks ashamed.

"I'm sorry, Eeth. I wasn't thinking. Forgive me?"

Glaring at her for several long seconds, I decide to forgive her. "Yeah. Forgiven."

"Thanks."

"So let's talk about Honor's birthday party," Shelby suggests, urging us to change the subject.

"Ooh. Good idea." Tamlin taps the table with both hands. "I can't wait to surprise her."

"Surprise her?" *Is Tamlin nuts?* "We are *not* surprising her. That is way too much for her heart."

"Why would surprising her be bad?" Tamlin looks confused.

"The same reason she couldn't go to prom—she feels all the excitement and it overwhelms her."

"Well in case you haven't noticed," Tamlin snaps, "Honor is depressed. That is not good for her either."

Shelby and I glance at one another. Clearly we're both thinking about yesterday's Just Dance extravaganza.

"Tamlin, did you ask your father? Does he have any pull to rent the whole Spirit of New Jersey ship? Maybe we can get a band to play on the ship or something." Shelby shrugs her shoulders, letting us know she is just thinking off the top of her head.

Expressionless, Tamlin stares straight at Shelby for several seconds before shouting, "That is a *great* idea. Awesome. And yes, my dad said he knows the manager of the ship."

A proud smile brightens Shelby's face.

"And hey, I know the lead singer of that local band Two Way Street. Maybe they'll play for us. I can get my dad to pay for the whole thing." Tamlin is so excited she's bouncing up and down on the bench.

"Whoa, Tam," Hunter finally stops eating long enough to say something. "Watch where you're bouncing. You almost landed on my lap."

"Get off his lap, Tam." Eli looks serious, but I'm not sure.

"Go fly a kite," she tells him.

I guess things are not so good in Paradise. That was a short run. Maybe Tamlin is finally realizing that Elijah is just too young for her right now.

"Anyway." It's my turn to change the subject. "Do you think your father can pull this off Tam?"

She pins her hair up into a ponytail while she answers, "Definitely. He's the CEO of the biggest bank in the city, people do anything for him."

"Good," I say, clearing my tray from the table because the bell just rang.

"And I'll take care of Two Way Street."

"Yeah, but I still think we shouldn't surprise her. We'll have to tell her while we're on the way there."

"Whatever, Ethan. See ya later." Tamlin skips off to her next class and I think, *that is* not *someone I would have chosen as a friend, but because she's Honor's best friend, she's my friend.*

After school, the senior class assembles for graduation practice. It seems odd not having Honor here. She would have been right next to me during the ceremony, considering our names are alphabetically in order. Storm would have been on my other side, but we won't mention him. I don't know if I am grateful he ran off or pissed that he left Honor, knowing she would worry about him. Oh well, he's gone, and there have been no tears shed on my end because of it.

My mind is not on this stupid graduation. I'd rather be visiting with Honor, but graduation practice is mandatory if we want to receive our diplomas. Not that it matters if I get one. Like I told them at lunch—I intend to live off my inheritance, so it's not like it will make or break me to not get my high school diploma. But then I begin to think of my life after high school. Will I get bored just hanging around? What if Honor is going away to college? Come to think of it, we never even discussed what her plans were after high school. She's probably just going to one of those online schools.

And again, just like that, I'm sad. *Will Honor's life consist of studying inside her own four walls—never venturing out because of her ability to feel too much? Is there some way that I can protect Honor from that but at the same time allow her to run free—just for a bit?* She lives in a bubble that I wish I could pop, if it would only keep her safe.

Maybe that is what I will commit myself to after graduation—finding a way for Honor to finally enjoy life without the worry of being an empath or being found out about being an empath. I want her to enjoy a worry-free life, and I will make it my duty to see that she does.

Chapter Fifteen

"Don't be sad, Eeth. I'll be fine. I'm getting my diploma in the mail. It's no big deal." Honor is smiling, but I know it's just a front. It's in her eyes—she wants to graduate with her friends. The whole reason she talked her mother into allowing her to go to public school in the first place was to experience her senior year the way it should be experienced. Now, the very events she'd wanted to be a part of are the ones that were taken away from her.

"Well, I *am* sad. But at least we have tonight," I remind her. Tamlin, Shelby and I are skipping Project Graduation and having our own party in Honor's backyard. Her parents had asked us if we'd want to celebrate our graduations this weekend, but Shelby suggested we do it right on graduation night.

"Exactly. I'll be helping Mom set up while you guys are out, so don't worry about me. I'll be plenty busy."

And then, without thinking, I do it again. I pull her into my arms and press my lips to hers. When I attempt to pry open her lips with my tongue, she pulls away. "Ethan—"

"I'm sorry, Honor." I press my fist to my mouth. "My god, I'm sorry. I did it again, I just..." I sigh, again, at a loss for words. "I'm sorry."

"It's okay," she lies.

I hold up my hands and take a step back.

She takes a step toward me, but I back up again. "Ethan, if I'm sending you the wrong signals, I don't mean to."

Again, she steps toward me, and for each step forward she takes, I take one back, until I tumble backwards over the porch rail.

"Oh my God, Ethan." Honor jumps over the edge, landing on her feet next to my sprawled out body. "Oh my God."

Lucky for me, I land on the grass in front of Honor's house and not against the stone wall that stands five feet from her porch.

"Ethan. Are you okay?" She's panicked.

"Yeah. I'm good."

"Were you like afraid of me or something? Why were you backing away from me?"

I sit up and pick at a blade of grass. "So I could take a tumble over your porch?"

"Seriously, Eeth. Why?" Honor starts picking at the grass as well.

"Because." The words are stuck in my throat, but I know I need to be honest with her.

"Because why?" Honor pushes her knees up to her chest, hugging them the way I wish I could hug her.

"Because I want more from you than you can give me," I say in one breath. "Because I love you." I turn to look her directly in the eyes. "The way a boy loves a girl when he's madly in love with her."

"Oh," she says, returning her attention to the blades of grass. I can almost see the thoughts churning in her mind.

"Honor, I didn't mean to make you feel uncomfortable."

"Storm, it's just...I mean Ethan. Oh my God, I'm sorry. I didn't mean—"

"I get it, Honor, you love Storm." The wrenching in my heart hurts more than anything I've ever felt.

"Oh, Ethan, it's just, I just...I can't get him out of my mind. I'm worried about him. As strong as he seems, I'm not quite so sure he's stable." Now she's picking the grass so fast that her front lawn is going to be one huge patch of dirt. "What if he, like, hurt himself or something?"

I doubt he would, but her feelings are real and I don't want to undermine them. "He's strong-headed, Honor, but I don't think he's stupid. I'm sure he hasn't hurt himself. Please don't worry, it's not good for you."

"But, Eeth, what if I'm worrying because my *powers* are causing me to worry?" A tiny tear escapes the corner of her eye.

"Well," I say, taking her hand and saving the lawn, "if that were the case, I think I would be feeling it too. And I'm not."

She allows me to keep holding her hand, so I run my thumb along the space above her wrist. "But...you're so closed off. Maybe you just *can't* feel it."

Patting her hand with my free hand, I reassure her. "Unfortunately, since healing you that day in the hospital, my emotions won't let me block out anything. Hazards of the job, I guess." I laugh, to make sure she knows I don't regret saving her life...well at least saving her from her wounds. It's a shame I couldn't save her heart.

"Really?" she asks, her eyebrows lifting high. "You're *feeling* again, like, everyone's—"

"Yup." I pull her up to stand. "I better get going. I am so late for graduation." I kiss her on the nose and tell her I'll be back soon.

And again, I walk away...feeling like a dog who's lost his best friend.

Chapter Sixteen

Because the graduation ceremony is so boring, I text Tamlin to tell her that Honor called me Storm. Of course, she texts back with an LMAO. After she gets my text telling her to grow up, Tamlin responds with **He's probably just on her mind 'cause he's missing.**

"Yeah, that's what *she* said," I text her back.

The rest of the ceremony drags on until Storm's name is called before I even get to retrieve my diploma. Everyone starts chattering about Storm, and even the principal who's handing me my diploma pays no attention to me. My cell buzzes.

When I get back to my seat, Tamlin's name flashes on my screen—**LMAO. Storm. That was funny, don't you think?"**

Yeah. Funny that Storm steals my spotlight once again.

I get an **LOL** from her.

Once graduation gets back on track, it doesn't take long to finish out the alphabet. Then the principal asks for a moment of silence to think about Honor and pray she gets the heart she needs. It's ironic, because I'm sure many of our classmates barely got to know Honor since she was new this year. Do they even know that the heart she currently has is the most generous and worthy heart anyone can have? Do they even know how special her heart truly is? Probably not. Hopefully, they'll ask God that a new heart come her way anyway.

We sing one last song and toss our caps in the air. My classmates may be in a celebrating mood, but my mind is on Honor.

After grabbing Elijah and Hunter from the stands, I meet Tamlin and Shelby in the parking lot and follow them to Honor's house. An angel in a long pink sundress and silver flip-flops is lighting candles around the backyard. The flames give her straight waist-length hair a celestial glow, while the moon makes her smile more radiant than usual. Honor is breathtaking under the moonlight, and I am a boy who can't stop looking at her.

"Hey, guys," Honor says when she finally sees us walking into the yard. "How was graduation?"

"Good," we all seem to say in unison.

We give Honor a celebratory hug then huddle around the fire pit that her dad set up for us—complete with all the snacks we could ask for. This time, instead of pairing off into separate conversations, we all talk together. Most of it lighthearted and cheerful—an unspoken vow to keep Honor smiling. And she is. I'm so proud of her for putting on a smile in spite of her broken heart.

Elijah, who incidentally was dumped by Tamlin according to Hunter's outburst in the car on the way over, suddenly belts out the first chorus of Queen's "Bohemian Rhapsody." After everyone stops laughing out loud, we all jump in and join him, trying hard to keep our laughter in check. And when Hunter hits the high notes at the end, we crack up so hard that we can't finish the song.

"I didn't know you were a soprano," Shelby asks in between breathless chuckles.

"There are a lot of things you don't know about us Sutherlands, babe." Hunter wiggles his eyebrows at Shelby.

And I can't help but feel a little annoyed. "Shut-up, Hunter, she doesn't need you making a move on her." I say this without thinking and then get an inquisitive eyebrow raise from Shelby. Damn. I hadn't meant to say that out loud.

"Yeah, you don't need those upper classmen, they'll just dump you when they're done with you," Eli shouts, almost drunkenly, though I know we have no alcohol here.

"Shut up, Eli," Tamlin adds.

"C'mon, guys. We were just having fun. Stop the bickering." Everyone stills at Honor's request.

"Sorry, Honor," Tamlin's the first to apologize.

"Yeah, sorry," Eli and I say at the same time.

"Really, I am," I whisper in her ear.

Honor looks at me and then really peers into my eyes. "You like Shelby, Eeth?" she whispers back.

I shake my head.

She nods.

But my earlier declaration of being madly in love with Honor has probably lost any credibility in her eyes now. Though, I still very much am madly in love with her.

The singing continues, this time with that old song the day the music died or something. But rather than join in with the karaoke imitation, I tap Honor on the shoulder and silently ask her to follow me to the diving board.

We sit dangling our bare feet over the edge. "I don't like Shelby, you know."

"It's okay, Ethan. I don't need an explanation, it's not like we're, you know..."

Though I've learned this long ago, it still hurts. "I did think there was something between us though, at one point."

Honor doesn't say anything, so I continue. "I've been nothing but honest with how I feel about you, Honor. Even when I knew you didn't feel the same way. I did not lie about loving you."

"I know," she says, turning away. "Why are you saying this again?"

"Because I don't want you to think I like Shelby. That's why." I take her by the shoulder and make her look at me. "I don't like Shelby," I say shaking my head.

"That's the thing, Eeth." She looks down at her lap, but I once again make her look at me. When I hold her face with my two hands, she says, "It's okay if you do. I'd actually prefer it if you did."

I'm still holding her face, but she closes her eyes so she doesn't have to read the pain in mine. Even though I'm sure she's feeling the pain. *Honor does not love me. She never will.* I drop my hands from her face, and rising from the board, I leave the yard...and go home.

Leaving her in the exact same way Storm had.

Chapter Seventeen

To assure Honor I am still in her life, I attend her dinner cruise birthday celebration three days later. I don't drive in with her. Tamlin and Shelby have that honor. Instead, I meet everyone in Weehawken where the ship is docked. Hopefully, Honor is excited when the girls tell her what they had planned, thanks to Tamlin's father's connections. They should have told Honor on the way to the cruise. All they had mentioned prior was that she had to wear a dress. So, already I know my heart is in for a stomping. I cannot resist Honor in a dress.

I was not, however, expecting to be swept off my feet by the looks of her in a tight, strapless, silver-sequined mini-dress with little poofs of silver roses trimming the bottom of it—the bottom of it only coming just above mid-thigh. I take a swallow. Honor's legs go on for miles and miles before they end at the skimpiest, strappiest silver heels. My hand actually flies to my chest, where I grab hold of my heart. It takes me a moment before I am able to restart my heart and move towards her—the silver goddess. *Oh how I wish she were mine.*

"This is too much, Tam." I overhear Honor say to Tamlin.

"Nah. That's why it's on a Monday. The ship is closed on Mondays, but because Daddy asked, they opened it for us. They didn't mind at all, and neither did Daddy. So enjoy, Hon. You deserve it. We have the whole ship to ourselves." Tamlin hooks her arm around Honor's shoulders.

"Really?" Honor gasps. "Just us?"

"Well, yeah, just us, the waiters and waitresses, the captain, and of course Two-Way Street." Tamlin and Shelby wait for Honor's reaction.

"What?" Honor exclaims. "Two-Way Street is here? Oh my God, you're kidding, right?"

"Nope. They were happy to be here." Tamlin grabs Honor by the arm. "Now c'mon, they're probably up on the ship already."

As Tamlin pulls Honor up the ramp, Honor sees me standing there and waves me to follow. "Thank you for coming, Eeth," she says when I reach them.

"I wouldn't miss it." Which is the truth. To see Honor happy and excited is worth reliving the heartbreak of my unrequited love. Honestly, though, I don't need to be near Honor to relive the heartbreak. It's something I do daily, with or without her presence near me.

When the maître d' grabs Tamlin's ear, Honor, Shelby and I take a walk around the ship. As we ascend the stairs to the upper deck, a mix of reverberating guitars and rhythmic drum beats thrums through the air, lighting up Honor's face with a gigantic smile. "I can't believe Two-Way Street is here. I thought they were on tour." Honor beams.

"They are," Shelby says. "They came back to town for you." Shelby takes hold of Honor's hand. "C'mon, let's say hi."

Honor's hand flies to her mouth. "Oh my God, I can't. I've never met them before."

"Really?" Shelby's shocked.

"Well, she *was* homeschooled most of her life." I add. Not that I know the band either. Having just moved here this year, I've only heard everyone talking about them at school. I don't even have any of their CDs, but apparently Honor does, because she's star-struck.

"Keith, Matt," Shelby calls, "bring over the band." They come for Shelby, and I get a glimpse of that bully I saw in the beginning of the year. Not that she is being fresh, but she has her commanding personality on. It's just another part of Shelby that somehow intrigues me.

"Keith, Matt, Jenn, Tyler, Liam, this is Honor. Honor, this is Two-Way Street."

Honor blushes. "Hi." She addresses them collectively.

"Hi, Honor. Happy Birthday," the one Shelby introduced as Matt says.

"Yeah, Happy Birthday," Jenn and Keith say.

"We hear you're something special," Liam says. "You're all Tamlin talks about."

Honor laughs.

"How come we've never seen you around," Tyler says. "We only graduated two years ago, but I don't think I've ever seen you before."

"I, uh, just started going to Jefferson this year, so...yeah. I love your music though. I have both your CDs. You're awesome." Her smile could light up New York City it's so big. It's good. She's happy. She's ecstatic. Honor needs ecstatic.

"Hey," Keith says. "We need to finish setting up. We'll talk to you in a bit?"

"Sure," all three of us say.

"See ya later, Shel," Matt says.

"That was so cool." Honor reaches the side rail first. Then Shelby. I stand back, appreciating the silver sight in front of me. With the orange setting sun and the gray rippling water, tiny shimmers of different colors dance up and down Honor's dress as she leans over the railing—just enough to slide the silver hem a teensy bit higher. Again, my heart stops.

Tonight will not be easy for me.

"Honor," Tamlin hollers running up the stairs. "You gotta taste the shrimp." Holding a shrimp in her hand, Tamlin feeds it to Honor. "C'mon, there's more." Tamlin grabs Honor by the arm and drags her down the stairs. All night Tamlin will be doing that, I'm sure.

I walk up to the rail to stand by Shelby. "No shrimp for you?" I ask her.

"Nah. I'll let Tamlin spend some time with her. I'm new in this group. Remember?"

"Whoa." The ship jolts. "Looks like we're leaving port."

"The party's starting," Hunter shouts behind us.

"When did you get here?" I ask. I hadn't seen him come up the stairs.

"There's another set of stairs." He points to the spot around the bar. "Eli's downstairs trying to get Tam back."

"Why'd they break up anyway?" I ask, not really giving a crap.

"Tamlin caught Eli flirting with a freshman," Shelby chuckles.

"Guess that didn't sit well with the old lady?" I joke.

Shelby laughs. "I think it was more the fact that he was flirting than that she was upset that the girl was younger."

"See ya later," Hunter says. "I'm going to get some food."

"You hungry?" I ask Shelby.

Shaking her head, she tells me, "Not yet. Don't feel obligated to stay. Go. Go eat, Eeth."

"Not really hungry." A row of white folding chairs lines up behind us. "Sit?"

Shelby and I pull up a couple of chairs and sit, throwing our feet up on the lower railing.

"You know," Shelby says after a couple of minutes of silence, "sometimes girls just want the bad boy."

"What?" I ask, wondering why she decided to say that.

"I'm talking about Honor. It's probably just the bad boy thing she's after...you know, 'cause she's so nice. He probably represents what she isn't."

Not really in the mood to talk about Storm and Honor, I take another approach. "Is that what you want? The bad guy?"

She takes her time in responding. "No. Not anymore."

I don't know how to take this. Is she not into bad guys because she's been there done that? Or is she not into them because she's into me? If it's the latter, I don't know whether to be happy about that, or upset because I'm in love with somebody else. We let her answer blow away with the wind. She's staring at the skyline in front of us. It's such a peaceful view. Manhattan. Such an irony really. From the river it looks so calm and serene. But enter the city and it's anything but. For a person who *feels* as part of who he is, Manhattan is not the place to be. But sitting here watching her light up the sky, it's so enticing. Too bad I'll probably never set foot in the Big Apple.

"Penny for your thoughts?" Shelby asks.

"Just amazed at the skyline," I offer quietly.

"It *is* beautiful, isn't it? I've always wanted to live there." There's a sad smile on her face.

"Really? Is that where you plan to live one day?"

"I'm not sure. Maybe if the children's hospital in Morristown doesn't work out, I can apply to a hospital in New York. I mean Sloane Kettering would be a wonderful place to work."

Shelby is remarkable. She has dreams. Aspirations. In such a short time, she's made such a turnaround from who she was. Not everyone would have done that. And for some reason, I need to tell her so. "You are amazing, you know that?"

She looks like I said something in a foreign language. "Where did *that* come from?"

"I just think you're kinda courageous. Not everyone would own up to their mistakes and then become a better person because of it. Most people find it's easier to stay the way people see them."

Her eyes narrow. "Thank you, Ethan, but I don't feel too courageous...or good about myself. I'm still ashamed at my behavior. It was no excuse." Shelby turns to look out at the passing skyline.

"No. There is no excuse. But you made good of it. That alone gets my respect." With my fingertips on her jaw, I gently turn her to face me. "You need to own it. You're a good person."

Though her hand feels cool when she touches my arm, the vibration it sends through me is warm and electric. It's so odd to feel this way about her, especially when I know damn well I love Honor, but I like her arm on me, and so I place my other hand on top of hers to keep it in place. Her eyes soften, and her face relaxes. When her mouth breaks into a smile, I can't help myself. I lean in and press a soft kiss to her lips. It only lasts a second, but we stare into each other's eyes for what seems like hours.

Just as Shelby is about to say something, Honor, Tamlin, Hunter, and Eli come barreling up the stairs in laughter. Behind them, the band is in hysterics as well.

"Oh, Ethan," Honor calls. "You should have been downstairs. Eli tried to help the waitress by taking a tray of stuffed mushrooms from her." She pauses to laugh, so I turn to look at Elijah, who apparently wasn't laughing as I'd originally thought. The scowl on his face is humorous, though, because it's accompanied by a swelling black eye and bloody nose. Honor looks at him. "I'm sorry for laughing, Elijah." She stops her chuckle mid-laugh. "I shouldn't be laughing at your expense." Honor reaches up and gives him a hug.

"*What* was funny?" I ask. "You didn't finish."

Honor looks to Eli for permission. "Go 'head," he tells her.

"He went to take the tray from her, thinking he was helping. But the waitress said, 'No. I got it.' Then she turned to avoid him. But," Honor chuckles all over again, "Eli reached for it, his hand landing right on her boob." Everyone starts laughing along with her. "The waitress shouts, 'Ooh.' She elbows Eli with the tray still in her hands. He slips. His foot catches the waitress's ankle. Eli falls flat on his back. The waitress falls face first, the back of her tray catching her fall…right on Eli's face. The girl was covered in mushrooms. Eli in blood." Honor shakes her head, clutching at her heart. "Oh, Eli. It really isn't funny." She stops laughing again, but everyone else continues. The band heads for the stage area.

"Honor. It's fine. It *was* funny. And hey, I got to second base." Elijah laughs, easing Honor's conflicting feelings.

Shelby gets up to follow everyone to the stage. Honor sits in her seat, but when the sound of the drums start, I reach for Honor's hand and say, "Come on, birthday girl. Let's go watch this band that's here just for you."

We're moving toward the stage, still hand in hand, when Keith, the lead singer, calls into his microphone, "Honor Stevens, are you ready to rock?"

Honor smiles and holds our hands up in the air. The rest of us shout a loud, "Hell yeah."

The private concert is a nice touch and Honor is blushing for the whole forty-five minutes, because before each song, Keith says something flirty to her. Like how beautiful the birthday girl is. How stunning she is in silver. How long and luscious her legs look in that short dress. By the end of the concert, I'm ready to jump on stage and knock the guy out. But then Shelby gives me this look that makes me cringe. Her mouth is set in a straight line, and she's shaking her head. I realize that she must know why I look like I'm about to kill someone—she knows I'm jealous over Honor. This, after just kissing Shelby.

Sending Shelby an apology with my eyes, I receive a smile full of pity in return. In a perfect world, what the heart wants, the heart would get. But the world isn't perfect, and the heart ends up longing for what it can't have. And so we learn to live with the broken heart. And Shelby seems to be able to see right through me.

Chapter Eighteen

When the band is finished with their first set, Keith heads right for Honor, even though she's holding my hand. She lets it go to give him a big thank you hug.

"You were awesome," she gushes. "Thank you so much. This was the best birthday ever. Thank you."

"You're welcome," he says seductively, which pisses me off. "Can I get you a drink?" he asks, despite the fact that he sees me standing with her.

"Oh. No thank you, I'm good."

He shrugs and walks away. Asshole.

"Let's go by Tam and Shel," Honor suggests.

"'kay."

Tyler comes up to us while we're talking with Tamlin, Shelby, and Jennifer, the guitarist. "Hey, guys." He addresses all of us. "How's it going?"

"Good," we all kind of say together.

"You guys were great. Thank you," Honor tells him and Jennifer.

"Thanks," Jennifer answers.

"You should come to one of our concerts," Tyler says, but Jennifer elbows him in the ribs.

"Ow." He looks at her. Her eyes are bulging, and she's trying to silently tell him Honor can't go to concerts.

Honor gets it. "It's fine. Maybe one day," she says, though I know she's just trying to be nice.

"So," Tyler starts, in an attempt to change the subject, "where's that big guy you were sometimes with, Tam."

Now Tamlin widens her eyes to shut Tyler up. Poor Tyler. He can't seem to say anything right. I know the feeling.

"I mean that guy with the orange Challenger. Why are you looking at me like that?" Tyler asks all frustrated.

Tamlin sighs and drops her shoulders. "He left town. Haven't seen him." Tamlin grabs Tyler by the arm and pulls him away from us.

"So...awkward," Jennifer lends.

"Yeah, this whole night has been awkward," Shelby adds, intentionally not looking in my direction.

"Oh, you gotta see this," Jennifer says to Shelby before pulling her over to the stage.

"What was that all about?" Honor asks me.

I take her hand again and walk her back to our seats. "About Storm?"

"No, I mean with Shelby. Why did she say this whole night has been awkward?"

Crap. "I have no idea. Come on, let's go sit." I place my hand at the small of her back to lead her to the chairs. My hand is on fire. I want to take her in my arms so damn bad.

"It's just odd that she'd say that. I think tonight has been amazing." Instead of sitting, Honor chooses to lean against the railing. "Look at the Statue of Liberty. I remember when my mom took me there when I was little...hmm...come to think of it, we had to leave as soon as we went inside. I wasn't feeling well...wow...now I know why. Now I know why I got sick every time my parents took me anywhere there was a crowd." Honor sits down.

The ship seems to have gotten darker—Honor has lost her smile.

"What is it?" I ask, sitting and putting my hand on her arm.

"Being an empath sucks, Ethan."

"Yeah, it does. It's finally gotten to you, huh?" My hand moves to clasp hers.

"Yeah. I mean, don't get me wrong. I love that I can help people. But I hate that it hurts so much."

"I'm surprised it took you this long to admit it. But it'll be okay. Maybe after you get your new heart, you'll feel a little better." When she responds with a frown, I feel compelled to say, "Hey, Honor. You're gonna get a heart. I know it.."

"I don't doubt it. I just...how different is it going to be? I mean...I'm still going to hurt. I still have to live in solitude. I don't want that anymore, Ethan. And how am I going to stop myself from saving someone that hurts? That goes against everything I believe."

I let go of her arm and take her hand. "I think the first thing you have to do is learn to love yourself enough to say, 'I'm too important to risk my life. My family is too important to me to put them through this again.' I think it's time to practice saying no." I close my eyes and ignore the need to hold her. "It won't be easy, but, Honor, you come first now. You have to start thinking that way...eventually, it'll become second nature to you."

Honor squeezes my hand. "What about you, though? You stopped blocking everyone out. It can't be that easy."

"I only opened up because of you. I can easily close my-self off again. Don't worry about me. Try not to worry at all...about anything."

"Thanks, Eeth." Honor's hand loosens, so I let it go.

"Listen, Honor, I'm starving. I haven't eaten yet. Do you want to come with me, or can I get you something?"

"No, I'm good. If you don't mind, I'm just going to stay here. Is that all right?"

"Of course it is. Be right back."

**

After several minutes of choosing food from the buffet, Honor comes running down the stairs from the upper deck. Out of breath, she shouts, "Ethan, come..." she grabs my elbow and yanks me forward. "You need to heal her. Hurry."

I drop my plate on a table and follow her up. "What? Who?"

A bunch of the ship's employees fly by us with first aid equipment and what looks like a defibrillator.

"What the heck is going on, Honor?" I ask, grabbing the handrail for fear we'll be knocked down by the passing employees.

"Jennifer. She hit her head."

We reach the top of the ship, where everyone who is on the ship is convened near the stage.

"She's unconscious," Honor cries. "Come on." She pushes us through our little group.

"Please let us work on her. We're turning the ship around. We've called an ambulance to meet us," one of the ship's workers informs us.

"But Ethan can help." Honor looks at me. "I should have done it already, Eeth, but...but I was doing what you said. I was saying no. Now...now they're not going to let you help."

I place my hand on Honor's shoulder. "You did the right thing, Honor." I drop in front of Jennifer, who I've only just met tonight, and put my hand on her unconscious head. I look to the woman with the first aid kit. "Just give me two minutes. If I can't help, you can take over."

I don't wait for her response. With both my hands on either side of Jennifer's temples, I close my eyes and concentrate on her injury. Breathing deeply, I shut out everything around me and force my energy into her. The weaker I begin to feel, the stronger I know she's becoming. I'm just about to pass out when I hear, "Oh my god, she's up. Oh my god, Jenn."

When I lean back, I fall into Honor's arms but remain conscious. "Thank you, Ethan," she whispers.

"What the hell?" I hear one of the band members say. "How the hell did you do that?"

"It was probably just a slight injury," Hunter says. "She was probably coming out of it anyway."

"No way, man," another band member insists. "She was out. She fell off that stage backwards. Hit her head hard."

"I'm fine," Jennifer says, sitting up. "Really...but...was I unconscious?" She's rubbing her head, confusion apparent on her face.

"Uh, yeah," Keith says. "Ethan, here, just made you un-unconscious."

"It was no big deal, really," I insist, trying my best to avoid too many questions. "I just rubbed her head. She was probably ready to come to anyway."

The women who work on the ship are staring at me. "What *are* you?" one of them asks.

Honor is rubbing my head. "Are you okay, Eeth?"

"I'm fine." I stand and pull Honor up with me.

We walk away from the mumbling group and go sit on the side.

"How come you're not all drained and stuff? You looked like you were going to pass out and then you were fine." Honor is grasping my hand.

"Probably 'cause of that immortal thing," I say softly. "My heart must be stronger. I don't really know." I caress her hand with my thumb.

"So, all I have to do is kill a person or two and I'll be fine." She chuckles.

"Kill an empath and you'll be golden." I laugh along with her.

She shakes her head.

"I should have let *you* kill those guys who shot Storm. Then you wouldn't be going through this." I run my other hand up her arm. The fight within myself is damning. I want to hold onto her forever; it kills me that she doesn't want the same thing.

"Yeah. Like I could've pulled the trigger." When Honor leans her head on my shoulder, I pretend for the moment that she's mine.

Until she whispers, "I wonder where Storm is. I hope he's okay."

Chapter Nineteen

By the end of the night, the atmosphere is back to normal and the band's second set consists of some dance covers. Though I'm not one for making a spectacle of myself, Honor insists I join them on the dance floor. We all spend more time singing along than dancing, but it's exactly what we need to end Honor's birthday bash on a happy note.

"Thank you for tonight, Ethan. I needed you. Thank you," Honor tells me as I'm hugging her goodbye at Tamlin's father's limousine. "You really should have taken Tam up on her offer to drive you in. Then you wouldn't have to drive home alone," she adds, while her arms are still slung around my neck.

"Yeah, well, because of how we left things the other night, I wasn't sure you wanted me driving in with you." I glide my hand down her silky hair.

"I always want you around, Ethan. You have to know that." I'm rewarded with a chaste kiss on the cheek. Not really what I want, but it'll have to do.

"Yeah. I do." I grasp her wrists behind my neck and hold her hands out in front of us. "I'm glad you had a good time tonight, sweetheart. You needed this."

"Yeah."

I leave her with a kiss on her forehead and watch her get into the car, wishing like hell I could spend all night with her.

**

Since school is out and I don't have a job, I lazily sleep until noon the next day—waking up only because my cell rings. It's Honor. "Good morning, beautiful."

"Ethan," she whispers, and it sounds like she's crying. "I'm hiding in the bathroom. The CIA is here. They're asking my mom a lot of questions. Can you come over right away?"

"The CIA? What for?" I scratch my head, yawning and not quite awake.

"About me. Healing all those people. Please, Ethan. Storm's not here. I don't know who else to call."

Fuck. Storm. Her first choice. "Yeah, of course, I'll be right over. Just stay in the bathroom. Let your parents handle it."

"Hurry. Dad's not here. He's working."

"Just stay where you are." I hang up, grab my keys, and head right over.

I don't even knock. Mrs. Stevens is sitting on the couch biting her lip and looking nervous as hell. "Oh, Ethan," she says surprised. "Um, this is Mr—"

"Frank Burke," he says, offering a hand to shake.

"Ethan." Shaking his hand, I'm suddenly afraid. The fear is not emanating from him. It's my own emotion—brought on by the fact that this man is cocksure and presumptuous. And he's only offered his name. Wiping my sweating hands on my jeans, I risk offending him by wiping off his handshake.

"Um, Mr. Burke was asking about Honor. I told him she's in the shower. He said he'll wait." Mrs. Stevens' attempt to be cryptic is weak at best. Her wide eyes give her away.

"Sure. Is Mr. Stevens home, ma'am? I came to ask him for his help on my car." I rub my neck and hope the man doesn't seem to notice my panic.

"He's due home any minute." Taking that to mean she's already alerted him, I head up to Honor's room, letting Mrs. Stevens know I'll wait upstairs to leave them to their conversation.

"Honor," I whisper, turning the knob on the bathroom door.

"Oh my God, Ethan." She gives me such a tight hug, she leaves me breathless. "What are we gonna do? He's gonna take me away. I'm so scared." Her tears are warm and wet on my shoulder.

"No," I assure her, rubbing her back. "No. He can't just take you away."

"He's the government. They can do anything they want," she cries.

"Not without your parent's consent, Honor. You're still a—"

"I'll be eighteen a week from today, Ethan. What am I gonna do? They can take me." She paces the bathroom floor, wiping her eyes with ripped-up tissue that she's probably been using since the man got here.

I rip her some fresh toilet paper and hand it to her. "No. They can't just do that, so calm down. We'll get a lawyer. I'm sure your dad is thinking about that right now. Please, Honor, you gotta stay calm. You need to protect your heart." I close the lid on the toilet, sit down on it, and pull Honor onto my lap. "Breathe." Holding her face in my hands, I look her in the eyes and breathe, silently asking her to follow after me. "You need to breathe. Calm." She inhales. Then exhales. "Again, sweetheart." Honor does as I say. "We'll get through this. I promise."

Tired to the point of exhaustion, Honor closes her eyes and rests her head on my shoulder. Taking my own deep breaths, I try to take my own advice to calm down.

Sometime later, there's a knock on the door. "Honor. It's Dad." He lets himself in.

"Oh, Daddy." She goes running to him.

"Shh. It's okay, sweetheart. You don't have to talk to him. I told him we're getting a lawyer. He's gone."

Honor clutches her chest and goes down.

I catch her before her head hits the counter.

"Honor. Honor." Looking directly into Mr. Stevens eyes, I cry. "I...I...I don't think she's breathing."

He grabs his phone and calls 911. "I need an ambulance now." He looks at me. "Go get my wife."

When Mrs. Stevens and I get back upstairs, Mr. Stevens is giving her chest compressions.

"Oh my god, Honor." Mrs. Stevens cries.

"Leanne," he says calmly. "Go outside and wait for the EMT. Just go outside," he directs. She listens.

I watch as he gives compression after compression, stopping every so often to breathe into her mouth. My heart feels like it's about to stop, and I'm not so sure it's just because I'm taking on Honor's symptoms. I'm afraid I'm going to lose her.

"Let me try, Mr. Stevens. Please."

He backs away and allows me to take over. I place my hands on her heart, concentrating harder than ever to bring her heart back to life. I don't continue the compressions. I just press my palms against her unmoving chest. Leaning down, I kiss her mouth and breathe in the words, "You got this, Honor. Breathe, baby." With my hands on her chest and my lips on her mouth, I will her heart to start beating. And as if I'd just performed a miracle, which on some level, you can say I did, her chest rises and her mouth spits out a warm breathe.

I collapse on top of her on the floor.

I don't pass out. My body is just exhausted from seeing Honor's lifeless form on the floor. I thought that was it. I'd never see her again. My arms and legs are trembling, and I am still lying with my upper body wrapped around Honor—her warm breath rhythmically blowing into my ear.

"Ethan." Mr. Stevens interrupts the moment by pulling me off of her. His hand attaches to her chest and he closes his eyes. "Oh thank God," he utters, his voice shaky and hoarse.

Both of us are kneeling at her side when the paramedics come running up the stairs. We jump up off our knees and get out of their way. "Her heart gave out," Mr. Stevens informs them. "She's on the waiting list for a new one. It's beating now, but it wasn't..."

"Her heart was stopped?" the one man asked.

"Yes. She had no pulse," Mr. Stevens answered.

"It started beating on its own?"

Mr. Stevens and I look at each other. "No," Mr. Stevens lies. "I gave her CPR."

"Good," the man says, hooking Honor up to some portable machines.

Watching them pull her up on the gurney makes me sick to my stomach. Her eyes are only fluttering open, she's still not fully conscious, and I want to throw up. Where the fuck is Storm?

And where that thought comes from, I've no idea, but I feel if he were here, Honor would be okay. If Storm were here when the CIA had shown up, Honor wouldn't have collapsed in the bathroom; he'd have known what to do to calm her enough to subdue her heart.

But he went and ran away.

And I'm at a loss for what to do to keep Honor safe.

Chapter Twenty

Honor is stabilized but needs her rest. That's what I'm told after sitting in the waiting room for three hours without being able to see her. Though Mr. and Mrs. Stevens give their permission for me to peek in, the doctors slam the door in my face. Not literally, but it's the same result—I'm not family, I'm not allowed to see her. I understand her heart is in jeopardy, and it needs to last until she has a donor, but honestly, is peeking in to say hi going to hurt?

Too tense to go home, too anxious to sit any longer in the waiting room, I pull out my cell and dial Shelby.

"Hey. It's me," I tell her when she answers.

"Hey." She doesn't sound too pleased.

"Honor's in the hospital again."

"Damn. Her heart?"

"Yup." I have no idea why I called Shelby instead of Tamlin or one of my brothers, but I went with my instincts. Now I'm wondering if calling her is fair. Especially after kissing her last night then spending the rest of the cruise with Honor.

"Ethan," she says after several seconds of silence. "Tell me...what the heck? Is she gonna be all right?"

Taking a deep breath to stop myself from screaming, I finally say, "Yeah. I think. They're keeping her in until they find a heart."

I hear Shelby gasp. "Oh my God, that could be a long time."

"I hope not." I am so at a loss for words, regretting now that I even called. I'm making such a fool of myself.

"Ethan," she calls out again. "Listen. You sound weird. Should I come get you?"

"No."

"Ethan. Where are you?"

"I'm at the hospital...I'm sorry...my mind is on everything all at once. Plus, all these people in here. I'm feeling everything." I pace the hallway.

"Okay. Then get the hell out of the hospital."

"Can I pick you up?"

"Sure."

In forty minutes, I'm parked in front of Shelby's house, where I find her sitting on her front step tapping away on her phone. The chunky silver medallion that hangs against her black tank top lends a biker chick look to Shelby's dark hair, which today is pulled back in a ponytail. When she stands to greet me, I can't help but notice her tan legs beneath her denim cutoffs. "Nice boots," I tell her, commenting on the Doc Martens she's wearing on her feet. "Purple. It's different."

"Yeah. I like to be different." She steps forward and reaches for my arm. I think I'm going to be getting a hug, but she rubs my arm instead. "You doing all right?"

I nod. "Better. Thanks. Wanna go for pizza or something?" I ask, peering into her eyes. I'd never noticed they were green. Not girly bright green but a dark army-type green.

"What?" she asks about my staring.

"Your eyes. I hadn't noticed them before. They're nice."

I get half a smile from her, like she's suspicious of my compliment. "Thanks?"

"Come on." I tap her arm and we walk to the car.

"So, about Honor. They're really keeping her there until they find her a heart?" Shelby's thumbs twirl around each other while her hands are set on her lap.

"Yeah. It sucks." My head is one conflicting mess—worrying about Honor while lusting after Shelby who's sitting so close to me that I can smell the pears wafting off of her. Guilt is not a fun thing to feel, especially while my heart is hurting over Honor.

"Did they say when?" I see her hands tensing. She must be nervous too.

"No. They didn't." I grip the steering wheel tight and focus on the road ahead of me. "Listen, Shel. I'm sorry about last night." I turn in her direction for a fraction of a section. "Kissing you and then...sitting with Honor the rest of the night...I'm sorry."

I wait for her to say something, but she doesn't.

"Penny for your thoughts?" I ask her.

A chuckle forms under her breath. "It *was* kinda shitty. But I understand."

"What do you understand?" I ask, taking my eyes off the road for a little too long. "'Cause I sure as hell don't."

"You're in love with Honor. I get it."

Since we've made it to the pizza place, I wait to pull in to say anything. "That's just it. If I'm so in love with Honor, why do I have feelings for you?"

Sucking in her lower lip, Shelby shrugs. "I don't know, Ethan. You tell me."

All I can do is sigh.

"C'mon. Let's get that pizza," she says, getting out of the car.

We bring our slices and soda to a table.

"I *am* sorry, Shelby. I'm just...I don't know what I'm feeling lately. There's just so much on my mind—"

"I get it. No big deal. You're cute, Ethan. I like you. But if you're into Honor, it's not gonna break my heart. I hardly know you." She shrugs before taking a bite of her pizza. She's cool. Probably too cool for me.

After taking several bites of my pizza, I finally say, "The government came for her today."

She dropped the slice that was on her way into her mouth. "You're kidding, right?"

Shaking my head, I tell her that I don't joke. Anyone who has spent any time with me should know that.

"What the heck? What do they want?" Shelby pushes her food away, suddenly too disgusted to eat I guess.

"They want her for what she can do." Though I haven't eaten since yesterday sometime, I find it difficult to eat right now.

"They said that? They can do that?"

Slouching back in my chair, with a defeated sigh, I say, "They were there to ask her questions. They never got to. She hid out in her bathroom." I start ripping a napkin into little pieces. "Her dad told them he would get a lawyer, and they left. Honor's heart stopped when her dad told her."

"Holy shit, Ethan. Can they just take her and use her like that?"

"I don't know. That's been my fear all along. She healed a whole plane that went down. They'll find a reason to take her, I'm sure. I don't trust them at all."

"Damn. Now what?" Shelby asks, slinking down in her chair.

"Hopefully, Mr. Stevens will find a good lawyer, but the government sucks. They do what they want."

"I wish there was something we could do." She wraps her arms in front of her chest, shivering as if she just got a chill.

"You okay?"

"Yeah. Just freaked out by all this." She squeezes herself tighter.

"You wanna get out of here?" I ask, not into finishing my pizza at all.

"I'd like to go to the hospital. Can we see her?" Shelby leans forward, placing her elbows on the table, she clasps her hands together.

"No. Not unless you're family." I lean forward myself.

"I'd like to be there anyway. Wanna take me, or should I get my own car?"

"I'll take you." I stand and fish in my pocket for my keys.

"Let me just give Tam a call. She'll probably want to know this...unless," she stands and looks at me, "did you tell her?"

"Dammit, no. You were the only one I called."

Shelby's eyebrows shoot up in surprise. A cute dimple highlights her cheek when she tries to subdue her smile.

Which makes me smile back at her.

And makes me more confused than ever.

Chapter Twenty-One

Tamlin shows up at the hospital, barely minutes after we do, in hysterics. "Tell me she's going to be all right, Ethan. Tell me she's okay."

What am I going to say? I have no idea if she's going to be all right. "I'm sure she'll be fine once they get that heart." Of course this is a lie. Once she gets her new heart, the government is going to come back and claim her.

After an hour or so, the hospital smell is finally getting to me. I need to get some fresh air. "You guys want anything downstairs? I'm going to take a walk."

Shelby and Tamlin shake their heads. "No thanks," they both say.

When I'm halfway out the door, I hear Tamlin say, "I saw Storm today."

Spinning around and grabbing the door jam, I shout, "Storm is back?" For some reason this gives me a sense of relief. I don't know why. I can't stand the guy, but if he is here, I am certain he'll make things better.

"I saw him driving down Berkshire Valley. I'm not sure if he saw me. I turned around and went to his apartment, but he wasn't there." Tam said, sitting cross-legged on the waiting room chair.

"Was he alone?" I was curious. Why the hell would he leave? And if he's back, why wouldn't he let us know?

"He was alone. I was honking and beeping, but he didn't turn his head at all. I think he has a beard now."

My tension is back. "I'm going for that walk."

The reality of Honor's fate slaps me in the face as I step out onto the pavement. Even if she survives this, the government is going to control her life. Honor will never be free. Not only will she keep absorbing the world's pain, she'll be made a guinea pig to see just how much she can endure, and just how far her healing abilities will go. What kind of life is that? Honor doesn't deserve it.

Then I realize—this is all happening to her because I came looking for her. My stupid ass curiosity about Honor Robinson got the best of me, and now she's paying the ultimate price.

My mind starts working overtime. I have to find a solution - a way to fix this mess I made of Honor's life.

"Ethan," Mr. Stevens calls from the hospital doorway.

"Mr. Stevens?" I ask, apprehensive to feel what I'm feeling, because suddenly I am overwhelmed with hope. "Everything okay?"

He laughs and cries at the same time. "A heart is on its way." He hugs me so tight I can't breathe.

"Oh thank God." I cry onto his shoulder.

"They're going to start prepping her for surgery in an hour. I can't believe this," he says, gasping, smiling, laughing, and crying. His emotions are everywhere. I feel them deep in my soul.

I involuntarily bring my hands to my mouth, overwhelmed with gratitude. "Can I see her?"

Shaking his head, he tells me no. "They need to keep her sterile. Her mom and I aren't allowed in either. But it's okay. It's good." His smile reaches across his entire face.

Patting him on the back, I say, "Come on. Let me buy you a cup of coffee."

"I could use something stronger, but coffee'll do." His hand slaps across my back. "The girls are upstairs screaming, they're so happy."

I roll my eyes. I can only imagine Tamlin's reaction. She must be bouncing off the walls.

As suspected, Tamlin is beaming and barely staying still when I get back upstairs. "Oh, Ethan, you heard? Isn't it awesome? Oh my God, I can't believe they have a heart for her already. Oh, Ethan." She hugs me almost as hard as Mr. Stevens did.

"It's awesome, Tamlin," I say, much more collectedly than my inner-emotions reveal.

After several highly emotional minutes, we sit waiting, much more relaxed than we were a while ago.

"I can't wait until this is all over with," Tamlin muses.

"Me neither," Shelby agrees.

With a sigh, I sit back, my head against the wall, and silently disagree with them. When this part is all over, the CIA is going to come back looking for her. They're going to use her for all she's worth. Something tells me getting this new heart may not be the best thing for Honor.

"Where the fuck is room 433?" we hear out in the hallway. "Where the fuck is she?"

"Sir, calm down," a female voice says. "Who are you looking for?"

"Oh my God," Tamlin shouts. "That's Storm." She goes running out of the waiting room.

"Holy shit, it is," Shelby says after her.

"Storm?" I ask when I get into the hall. "Where've you been?

"Where's room 433, Eeth?" His voice is shaky. He's scared. Tamlin was right, he does have a beard. And he looks like he hasn't showered since before he left town.

"It's right over there," I say, pointing across the wide hall.

"Sir. You need to lower your voice," the nurse says to Storm.

"Honor Stevens is in that room?" His voice is still loud and very hoarse. He's frightened. I feel it.

"Storm. It's okay..."

"Shut up," he demands of me before looking at everyone else. "I have something to say." He's still shouting. "You," he says, pointing to the nurse. "You listen to me. Ethan." Now he looks to me. "Record what I have to say."

"Storm..."

"Record it," he yells.

I pull out my phone. God knows what he's about to say, but I press the record button on my phone.

"This heart," he says pointing to his chest. "It's hers." His other hand points to Honor's room. "This heart is Honor's. You hear me?"

The nurse shakes her head, but a grin is forming on her face. She must think he's a drunk professing his love for her.

"This heart doesn't go to anyone else. You got that?"

I look around and everyone else is as confused as I am.

"Okay. Ethan, you got that?"

I chuckle. "Yeah. I got that." Storm must be saying all this for my benefit. He's finally claiming Honor as his own. He's fighting for her, and I have to back off.

"I got it, Storm. You want Honor. I got it." I stand there shaking my head.

"NO. YOU DON'T GOT IT," he screams as loud as he can. "*MY* HEART IS TO BE PUT INSIDE *HER* HEART."

Oh my God. "Storm. No. Don't. You got it wrong." I try to tell him, but I'm too late.

He pulls a gun out from his back pocket and shoots himself right in the temple.

"Oh my God, nooooo," somebody, or everybody, yells.

"Help, we need help," someone else yells.

So many people surround us that I'm pushed out of the way.

Security guards. They're pushing at us.

"No. You don't...you can't," I try to say, but I'm in shock. I can't form a coherent sentence.

"Please get back." The guards have their hands on us, pushing us down the hall.

More hospital people show up. Racing to get to Storm. Squeezing us out of the way.

I try to push my way back, but they won't let me.

"Oh my God," Tamlin cries next to me. "He's dead. Oh my God, he's dead. Oh my God, oh my God, Oh my—"

"Shut the fuck up. Shut up," I yell.

"He's dead. Storm is dead."

PART FOUR

HONOR

Chapter One

This has to be a dream.

Or a nightmare.

How else could I explain being able to stare at the lifeless form in front of me? The lifeless form being me—asleep on some hospital bed.

The ironic part is, I don't want to wake up. That would be the real nightmare.

It's been several hours since Ethan held me in his arms on my bathroom toilet. Several hours since I'd learned that my life from here on out would not be my own. Once the government gets hold of me, I will belong to them. My dad says he's hiring a lawyer, but everyone knows that what the government wants, the government gets. And they want me.

So why would I want to wake up?

I just wish I didn't have to stare down at my own body being kept alive by a machine. But I don't know how to get back into my body, so, I sit on the chair next to my bed. And though I try to close my eyes to sleep, it's senseless, because the commotion outside my door keeps jarring me awake. The good thing about being in this ghostly state, though, is that I feel no pain. Not mine. Not anyone else's. It's not that I'm not grateful for being given the ability to heal people, but it's a twenty-four hours a day painful existence. An existence that I'm not so sure I can live with anymore—even if the men from the CIA *weren't* looking to use me as their guinea pig.

I'm not quite sure *when* I separated from my physical body, but it was definitely sometime in this room. The last thing I remember before passing out is hearing my daddy say he's getting a lawyer. Then all of sudden, I was here, standing next to this hospital bed...with me in it...and my parents crying alongside of me. For some reason though, Ethan hasn't been here. I haven't seen him all day, which surprises me, because he's always so protective and worried about me. Maybe they wouldn't let him in, or maybe he just couldn't bear to see me like this. Since he's been feeling his empathic emotions again, it must be getting hard for him to deal with everything. I know how tormenting it can be.

Thinking about Ethan, I realize how I've hurt him lately. I'm sure he knows that it wasn't my intention to do so, but I hurt him nonetheless. If only I could apologize to him before I...I can't even say the word. A new heart is coming, I heard them talking about it before, but I'm not sure I want it anymore. But then I think about my parents and how they would have to live without me and I can't do that to them. A seventeen, wait, almost eighteen-year-old girl should not have to be burdened with this type of decision. *Do I get back inside that body, if I can figure out how, and take the new heart, returning to a life of feeling what everybody else is feeling? Or do I stay here, outside my real body, living pain-free every day...and hopefully finding my way to heaven?* It's tempting to stay here like this. The isolation wouldn't be anything new. If it weren't for my parents, my answer would be easy—I wouldn't go back. I know that a teenager wishing her life to be over sounds so sad and desperate. Under normal circumstances, I would agree. It's a terrible thing for someone so young to feel so hopeless, but I see no way out of the pain and no way to live with it. Even going back into isolation, crocheting in my bedroom alone, would cause me too much pain, because now I have friends. I don't want to exist without them. And hanging with them causes me just as much hurt, because I know when their hearts are breaking, and I'd want to help them. Where does it end?

Then there's the whole matter of Storm. He broke my heart the day he left and never called. That was a whole different kind of pain. I knew instantly that I owned the crushing in my chest the day he swam away. And when I noticed later that he'd left his phone behind, leaving no way for me to contact him, that's when I knew I'd fallen in love with Storm Sutherland.

That's when I knew my heart never stood a chance.

Chapter Two

The commotion outside has now settled into a mild disturbance. The voice levels have sunk to just above a whisper, and I'm finally able to close my eyes again, hoping for a temporary reprieve from this next bit of paranormal in my life. I'd have never guessed that I would be a ghost on top of being an empath, but behind my closed eyes, the darkness is welcoming. A peace washes over me, and I'm okay with being in this state—all right with floating in the pain-free air.

A fussing with something on my end table forces me to open my eyes. The heart that doesn't exist in my chest suddenly bursts with excitement.

He's here.

And he's standing next to my hospital bed playing with the nurses' call button remote.

Oh my gosh. He came back to see me.

Though I don't have a heart, I can almost feel it skip a beat.

Storm Sutherland is beautiful. And he's here. With me.

The smirk sliding across his face puzzles me though. He isn't sad. In fact, he looks pretty proud of himself. Grasping the remote in his hand, he nods his head. "I knew I could do it, princess. It just takes a hell of a lot of concentration."

I chuckle, because he probably can't think of anything else to say to my comatose body.

"You find this funny?" he asks with a smirk.

Why would he ask if I find this funny? *Did he hear me laugh?*

When he turns his attention away from the remote, he doesn't look at the bed.

He looks at me.

"What's the matter, princess? You surprised I can see you?" When he walks toward me, he runs his hand over my arm—the arm of the me in bed.

I stand from my chair. Something's not right.

"There has to be *something* you want to say right now." As he passes the bottom of the bed, he runs his hand over my blanket-covered feet. His hand disappears inside the blanket.

When he finally reaches me, he is looking right into my eyes. His grin is replaced by a frown. "I am so so sorry I took off, princess."

I'm kind of freaking out right now, because when Storm takes my hands in his, I notice that his hands are as translucent as mine.

"Wow, princess. Put your eyes back in your head. You act like you've never seen a ghost before."

I blink these fake eyes of mine and open my mouth to speak. I'm surprised when a sound comes out of my throat. I wasn't expecting that.

"Are you more surprised that I can *see* you?" he asks. "Or are you surprised I'm here in the same form as you?"

"Why?" I eke out. But that's all I can get out. I can't form my thoughts into words.

"Why am I a ghost? Why am I here? Why did I leave?" His eyes peer deeper into mine. "There are a lot of *whys* you can be asking about. Care to clarify?"

Yes, there are many questions I have for him, but the first one is the most obvious. "Why...why..." I concentrate on spitting out the words. "Why...are you...transparent?"

"Why am I a ghost?" He continues to hold my hands.

It's odd. I know he's holding my hands, and I like the feeling it gives me to have him holding them, but I can't really *feel* his hands on mine. I nod in response to his question.

"How about I fill you in on why I left first," he says seriously. "Maybe that'll help me to explain it."

He sits down on the edge of the bed, and I sit on the edge of the chair, reminding me of the last time I was in the hospital and he kissed me.

"I'm sorry I kissed you and left that day." He presses his lips in a firm line. "My emotions just took over and I panicked." Shaking his head, he continues. "I don't like to feel helpless, Honor. And you being so sick and needing a heart, well, it left me feeling out of control. You needed help. I wanted to be the one to help you, and I couldn't. Unless...well there was one way I knew I could help, but if I did it, I'd piss you off. And if I didn't do it, you wouldn't be around much longer. So I made the decision to piss you off."

Because I'm thoroughly confused, I say nothing.

"Honor, I'm not sure if you realize this," he says, taking hold of my hands again, "but you are the single most important person in my life. Since the first time I saw you in

Math class, you took hold of my heart." There's a quick fluttering where my heart should be. "You've owned my heart ever since." Storm stands, bringing me up with him. His transparent hands wrap around my face and neck. "So you see," he kisses me on the lips, sending a tingle through my phantom limbs, "there really was no choice for me. I had to leave for a while, not to decide if I could actually do it, but to decide if I could let you live the rest of your life with the decision I made without your consent."

Storm pulls me under his chin. His words are so cryptic that I can't figure out the puzzle he's throwing at me.

"I hope one day you'll understand why I did what I did and you'll forgive me. But it's only because of how deep my love is for you that I did it." He kisses the top of my head and leaves his lips there.

Concentrating really hard to speak, because it's hard for me in this form, I open my mouth. "I don't understand." I speak into his neck.

"You'll understand soon, my love." Though it seems unlikely he could do it, he squeezes me tighter.

"Storm?"

"Yeah, princess?" he says above my head.

"Why are you here...like this?" I pull away, running my disappearing hand slowly through his body. "Like my grandfather and parents were when I saw their souls release."

After a long silence, he speaks. "I gave you my heart, princess," he says, looking like he wants to cry. "Because I know you'll take good care of it."

"Storm?"

"It's time to go, angel. I'm fading."

He is. His transparent form is disappearing.

"No, Storm. Please."

"I gotta go." He moves his hand back and forth. "Look, I'm fading."

Then he starts moving backwards toward the door.

Confused, he looks up at the ceiling. "It's up or down, Old Man. Backwards is not an option."

What is going on?

Storm drops his head and turns toward the door. "I gotta go fight whatever they're doing out there, princess." He turns his head to look at me. "I love you, you know?"

I nod, still puzzled. "I know."

Chapter Three

Since it's finally sinking in what Storm has done, I race to the door, struggling to turn the knob. Then it occurs to me. I'm a ghost. I can probably walk *through* the door. When I do, there is a whole mass of people huddled around something on the floor. I realize that it must be Storm, so I move closer. No one sees me.

It *is* Storm.

Lying dead and bloodied on the floor.

My hand immediately covers my mouth. *Oh my God, what has he done?*

His face is covered in blood, and the paramedics are working vigilantly to start his heart and stop the blood. The one side of his face is completely gone.

In front of his dead body, Storm's soul is kneeling. When he catches me standing over him, he blows me a kiss, but I want to look away. Seeing him lying on the floor in his own pool of blood is making me hurt all over. I don't have a body, how can I hurt? But it does, deep inside my chest. If only I could heal him again and make it all better.

From the corner of my eye, I see a ruckus. Ethan is shouting and pushing his way through three security guards who are keeping him from getting close.

"No. No," I scream. "Let him in. Let him through. He can save him."

But nobody hears me. No one except Storm. "Stop it, princess," he says from the floor. "This is the only way you can survive."

A few moments ago, before Storm showed up in my room, I had no desire to survive. But now, now that I know he loves me. I have every desire to live. "Storm, you don't understand," I shout, trying to be heard over the crowd. "I don't need your heart—"

"Yes you do," he interrupts. "You need to live, Honor. I won't let you die." He stands to be at eye level with me.

"They have a heart for me, Storm. I don't need yours." I cry, because I realize it might be too late for him. Even if Ethan got to him, he couldn't bring him back from the dead. Storm had said I was the only one that could do that.

I fall to my knees and sob. No tears spill, but my body convulses on the floor. If Storm can't be brought back to life, then I don't want that new heart. "Storm," I call through my sobs, "I'll stay here with you. I won't take the heart. I'll fight them. We can be together, just you and me...no more pain, no more games, no more anything to keep us apart," I cry out loud.

He floats over his dead body, stepping on air. His lip quirks as he heads straight for me, not dropping eye contact. Again, his hands reach for mine, and he pulls them to his chest. "They found a heart?"

I nod. "Yes."

"You didn't need mine?"

I shake my head. "No."

His head drops in regret. He killed himself for me unnecessarily. And now we can't be together.

Looking back up at me, his face pained, he says, "It's not your time to die, beautiful. There's so much more out there for you." He's practically crying. "You need to accept that heart. Your parents need you."

My parents. The whole reason my decision is a challenge. But I love Storm more. I don't want to live a life without him in it. "But I need *you*." I reach up to kiss his mouth.

"And I need *you* to stay here on Earth, baby. Live. You have a second chance."

"But it hurts too much," I cry.

Storm sighs. "And you've had enough?"

"I've had enough."

He nods his head and envelopes me in his arms, where I feel safer than I've ever been.

"I love you, princess."

"I love you too, Storm."

A loud crash cuts off our hug. We turn to see a metal cart turned on its side and Ethan scurrying through the parted crowd. "I need to get to my brother," he demands in a voice so deep, it's frightening. He spares no one as he pushes through every medical person in his way.

"You need to let him touch him," I hear Shelby yell. "He can heal him. He really can. He can get his heart started again. If there's a pulse, if there's any beat at all, he can do it. You have to let—"

Everyone stops what they're doing to look at her. "Really. He can," she repeats.

A security guard comes barreling at Ethan, but Shelby blocks him and Tamlin takes him down. Holy crow. Tamlin just took down a two-hundred pound man. She's actually straddling him and punching him in the chest. This causes enough disturbance to free up Storm for Ethan.

"What are you doing, loser?" Storm asks, moving away from me. But of course, Ethan can't hear him.

Ethan leans over Storm and puts both his hands on either side of Storm's face. He pulls his body over Storm and straddles him much like Tamlin is straddling the guard. If this weren't such a sad and disturbed scene, it would be quite comical. Ethan squeezes his eyes shut. "Come on, Storm," he chants. "Come back to me, brother. Honor needs you."

Storm looks at me. I shrug.

"Come on. Come on," Ethan continues, while running one of his hands over the wound and bringing the other to Storm's heart.

"Dammit," Storm says to me. "I'm fading again. He's doing it, Honor." Storm comes back and holds my hands. "Fight it, baby. Don't let me go."

"But...but if he can save you...then maybe...when I get that new heart...I can still be with you," I say hopefully.

"You want to go back?" Storm shakes his head. "You wanna live with all that pain again?" He holds my neck and runs his thumb over my lips.

I nod. "I do. If it means being with you. I do. And then I don't have to break my parents' hearts."

His lips touch my mouth and then he backs away. Storm's image fades in front of me as he slinks back into his physical body. "Don't let me down, princess," he calls out, though I can no longer see him. "Don't fight that heart, baby."

The disfigured side of Storm's face begins to form together, almost as if by magic. With my hands over my mouth, I watch Ethan struggle to start Storm's heart. The medical people stand with mouths dropped, in awe of the miracle taking place in front of them.

And then it hits me...the government. With everything going on with Storm, I completely forgot that I may not have a life to go back to. And when the government hears about *this*, Ethan will be taken away with me. Oh my God.

I float over to Storm's body and try to push at Ethan. Storm said you just have to concentrate, so I do. I close my eyes hard and will myself to push Ethan away from Storm. But another commotion behind me breaks my concentration. Again, I close my eyes and force my will on Ethan with my transparent hands. "Ethan, leave him alone," I yell.

It must be too late, because Storm's soul is not returning.

"Storm...Storm...," I yell. "Don't let him heal you. No. I'll stay here. I won't take the heart. You can't let him heal you." I'm screaming in vain. Storm can't hear me. But I can't let Ethan bring him back to life. I wouldn't be able to be with him anyway. Not if the CIA is going to take me away. "Storm. Please. I DON'T WANT TO LIVE!"

I push at Ethan one last time before I hear what's going on behind me. Turning toward my hospital room door, I see them wheeling me out of the room.

I'm getting my new heart.

Chapter Four

Strong.

I have to be strong.

Accepting that heart will leave me vulnerable and not in control of my own life. If I am strong and do not surrender, I can stay here in limbo. If Ethan doesn't save Storm, Ethan can live a normal life and Storm can stay here in limbo with me. I have to stop him.

"Ethan, please," I yell again, wrapping my whole ghost of a body around Ethan.

He flinches.

He can *feel* me. I'm sure of it.

"Stop, Ethan. You can't do this," I scream into his ear.

He pulls his hands off of Storm and looks around the hall. His eyes narrow as he scans the crowd, but he shrugs it off and looks at Storm. Ethan feels something, but he doesn't know what it is. He takes a while to return to Storm, but when he does, he rests his hands, one on Storm's head, the other on his chest.

When Ethan closes his eyes, I lose hope.

Storm will survive and Ethan will be left susceptible to the government's whims.

Now I need to decide if *I* should live.

Police officers have now entered the hallway, but as soon as they get close to Ethan and Storm, they stop. There is no way they'd interrupt the scene in front of them now. Before our eyes, Storm's open face begins closing. As if the healing were displayed on a time-lapsed video, his facial wounds close completely within seconds. When Ethan moves his hand to Storm's temple, a lone bullet flies out and hits Ethan in his Adam's apple before the wound fills up and covers with skin. Aside from the mess of blood glued to Storm's hair and face, there is no sign of a bullet ever entering his temple.

Even though seeing the bullet with my own eyes is proof, I am in a state of disbelief that Storm put a bullet to his head to save my life. He sacrificed everything for me. Suddenly, I feel so unworthy of the commitment that took. Would I have done the same for him? A smile spreads across my face. *In a heartbeat, I would.*

Storm's eyes flash open. Still on his back, he seems stunned to be lying there. He inhales loudly then turns his head to look around him. He places his hands on the floor and sits up. Shaking his head, he mumbles something that sounds like "What the fuck?" under his breath.

Ethan, still on his knees, inches his way beneath Shelby, and I notice that she pushes Tamlin on top of Storm. Once again, Storm's on his back, but this time the cops rush over toward him. In the time it takes to watch Tamlin fall onto Storm and the cops running to him, Ethan and Shelby have disappeared. Ethan must have realized what saving Storm would mean for him. The cops would have questions, and Ethan's powers would no longer be private. Just like I had assumed, Ethan will be wanted by the CIA, just like I am.

But I can no longer choose death over life. Not after the courage the people in my life have shown. Not only had Storm tried to give me his heart, but Ethan, knowing the government was already on to me, still risked his secret to save his brother. Leaving friends like that would be cowardly. I need my body to accept that heart. I won't let it reject it. The people in my life are too important.

One of the cops pulls Tamlin off of Storm while the other helps Storm to his feet. After the shock of seeing a bloodied dead man come back to life completely healed from the touch of a teenager, the nurses run back to him.

"Ma'am," one cop says, "we need to question him."

The nurse's eyes pop up and she takes Storm by the upper arm. "Excuse me, but this is a medical emergency. We need to see to him first."

The cop opens his mouth to speak, but Storm yanks his arm from the nurse's grip and says, "Get the fuck away from me, all of you."

He begins walking toward me, but the cop grabs him. "I'm sorry, but you committed a crime, we need to take you in."

Storm stops in his tracks and turns slowly to look the cop in the face. "A crime? Exactly what crime did I commit?"

"You attempted to kill yourself—"

"Yeah, well, I won't press charges." Storm turns and heads right towards me, but he actually walks *through* me.

He stops. Turning his head from side to side, "Princess?" he whispers.

He knows I'm here. Maybe I'm invisible to him now, but he can feel me. "I'm here, Storm," I say, though I know he can't hear me.

The cop grabs Storm, pulls his arms behind his back, and slaps handcuffs around his wrists.

"Princess, if you're here, you promised. I'm alive. Now *you* need to be. Don't let me down," he says as the cops pull him backwards down the hall.

"He didn't do anything," Tamlin cries. "Why are you taking him?" She jumps on Storm's back in an attempt to slow down the cops. "He's not a criminal. He was trying to save his girlfriend's life. You can't arrest him for that."

The cop holding on to Storm gives Tamlin a smug expression, but the cop that had helped Storm up gives Tamlin a sympathetic, head-tilt. "We just have to see what's going on. We're not arresting him."

"Then why the cuffs?" a nurse asks in Storm's defense.

"Honor," Storm yells. "I'm coming right back. These fucking cops can't keep me."

Both cops look at Storm. "Taking a guess here," the nice cop says, "but he doesn't seem like he'll be giving us tons of cooperation."

Tamlin follows them to the elevator and puts her hand on Storm's bent elbow. "Well, I'm coming with you."

When the elevator doors shuts, Storm hollers, "I'll be back, princess. I'm coming right back."

I hear Storm's words and I close my eyes. Making a vow to fight hard, I finally decide to fight for my life. Fight for Storm. Fight the government. Ethan and I *will* live a normal life free of being lab rats. I'm at last content with a decision, and I know I'm sure of it. There is no doubt in my mind that I want to live amongst some amazing people. People I'm proud to call my friends.

In an effort to get back to my body, I turn and head in the direction I saw them wheeling me. At the farthest end of the hall, a sign on one of the double doors says *Operating Room One*. Through the doors, I see at least ten people in turquoise scrubs standing in a circle. Upon walking further into the room, I see the operating table they are all standing around. Under a ton of bright lights, my body lies open and motionless. I gasp. The sight makes me want to run. A person should not see their own organs spread out like slabs of meat on display across a cold metal tray. My heartless body lays dead and vulnerable, and it scares me to death to see it like that. Fear seeps through every part of me as I think about my heart sitting on that table, tossed aside and left never to beat again.

The room starts to dim as it gets smaller and farther away from me. Reaching out my hand to grab something, anything, I feel the room get hot. I'm burning up. Sweat pours from my brow, but I have no brow for it to fall from. *A ghost can't sweat.*

Suddenly I think, *I'm going to hell.* That's the only explanation. But I know I've done nothing wrong.

Unless—

Can loving two boys at the same time earn me a lifetime spot in hell?

I hope not.

Suddenly, the room goes pitch black.

My ability to think coherently is quickly diminishing, and I'm panicked.

Out of breath.

Confused.

Gone.

Chapter Five

"It's me, princess." His hand is warm. "I made it back." His voice is hoarse. "Thought I was gonna have to *kill* someone." His laughter...forced.

Storm is near, but I can't see him. "Storm," I say, but no words come out.

"Those cops certainly made it difficult for me to get back to you." He stops talking. "It's done with now." He coughs. "I'm here." Again I hear him cough, but it sounds more like he's clearing phlegm out of his throat. "Anyway, I'm here." There's silence for a while. "You promised..." It sounds like he's choking back tears.

"You made a promise to me, sweetheart." I know his thumb is caressing my hand, but I can't see it. "Please don't let me down." His voice hitches, and I hear him sniffle.

"Honor, I know I usually call you princess, but I need to be serious here for a minute. You need to recover, Honor. You need to allow your body to accept this new heart." I hear the congestion in his nose and throat. He *has* been crying.

"I don't exactly know what's going on in that mind of yours, but I hope it's that you want to live." It feels like both of his hands are on my hand. Maybe his head too, because I feel hair tickling it.

"You have to be strong, angel." His voice is muffled, probably because he's talking into my hand. "You need to be brave and courageous and pull through this." My hands are wet. His tears are hot. "I promise, when you get through this, I'll take good care of you. I'll take you away from everyone if you need to be alone, if the pain of others is too much. I promise I won't run away again, darling." He must have sat up, because his words are clear and my hand doesn't tickle anymore. "I just...I knew what I needed to do...y'know...about killing myself so you could have my heart, but...but I also knew that once you found out that it was my heart inside you...well...I know you, and you would have felt guilty the rest of your life." When he starts sobbing, I want to cry with him. I want to rub the back of his head and tell him it's all going to be okay. "But I chose to do it anyway, Honor, because I needed you to live.

"I don't know if you remember being a ghost yesterday or not." He chuckles underneath his crying. "But I remember. I would have stayed there with you, angel. I would have lived in limbo or in Heaven or in Hell...wherever you were, I'd have gone. But now," I hear him swallow, "you told me you were getting a heart. So, I decided to come back...it's funny...how many other people could say they were brought back to life not once, but twice? I think I got Jesus beat, don't you?" I love the sound of his laugh, even if it *is* laced with sadness. "Anyway," he sniffs, "I'm here to take care of you, but you need to survive in order for me to do that. You need to live, Honor. I need you, princess. I need you real bad." The sobbing begins again and I just can't take it. I need to tell him I'm here. *Why can't I?* "Oh, baby, please," he says through a rainfall of tears. "Please."

Storm's head is back on my hand. I feel his hair. If I could only run my hand through it and comfort him, I could make him feel better. Ease his sorrow. *Why can't I do that? Why can't I open my eyes?*

A warm tingle creeps up my limbs. Storm is no longer talking. No longer crying. But I feel his hands and head on my hand. He's still here. Though the room is silent, my mind is screaming to let my body out. I can't move, but I try anyway. My body feels heavy, like a thousand-pound blanket is covering me. "Storm," I want to say out loud. "I'm here. I'm trying. Don't give up on me. I'm coming."

But no matter how much I try, I can't get there. My eyes just won't open. "I'm so sorry, Storm. I'm so sorry," I say, wishing he could hear me.

I'm not sure how much time has passed, but when Storm lifts his head from my hand, other voices come into play.

"Nothing yet?" my mother asks.

"No." Storm answers.

"They said it may take up to twenty-four hours for her to wake up." Dad's voice is hopeful.

Wake up? So I'm sleeping? If I'm sleeping, why can I hear them?

"So, Storm." My father speaks. "Thank you. For what you did. I...I can't believe you did it...and I can't believe you are standing here in front of me...but I know you did it for Honor...and well, not many people would have done that." My dad chuckles. "But, really, don't do that again. I...I don't know how Ethan brought you back, but thank goodness he did. I mean, what a mess. I don't know how we're going to get around this with the government though."

"Yeah, I'm sorry about that. The cops had a lot of questions. I...I didn't say anything, but they're not done questioning me."

"I'm sure they're not," my dad clears his throat. "I have no idea where Ethan ran off to, though. Tamlin hasn't seen him. He and Shelby aren't returning any of her calls."

"I'm sure he's okay. He's used to running...hiding...it's what we were raised to do. Don't worry about him, though. He'll be okay."

"Yeah, but Shelby's parents are concerned. I explained that Ethan is a nice guy, but they're really worried. After what they've been through with their daughter, I don't blame them."

"Sorry we messed up your world, Mr. Stevens. We should have never come to Jefferson." Storm sounds sad.

"I'm glad you came," I say to myself.

"Well," my dad says, "I'm glad you came. Honor needed good friends. She's lived a lonely life prior to you guys being a part of it."

"Some friends," Storm says sarcastically. "We've only brought her trouble." Storm lets go of my hand. "Mrs. Stevens, you should be here," he tells her.

A smaller, cooler hand picks up mine. Mom. I'd know her touch anywhere. Strong, yet gentle. I wish I didn't have to put her through this, especially after her recent heart attack. Once again, I try to will myself to move my hand or open my eyes.

Why won't my brain work? Why won't it send the signals to my body?

I'm sad all over again for my mom. But not because *she's* feeling sad. Yes, she is feeling sad, I'm sure, but I don't feel it. Maybe while I'm *asleep*, I can't tune into my empathic side. Maybe this is a good thing.

But really not. I want to see my family. I want to hug them. Who I'm really sad for is me, because I am unable to do these things right now. I just wish I were strong enough to force myself awake already.

Chapter Six

"How is she?" This is not Storm's voice. It's Ethan's. Oh my God, he's here. What if the government comes after him? I remember the looks on everyone's face when he healed Storm out in that hallway. They'll think he's a freak. The CIA will come after him next. I can't let them do that.

"The same," Storm answers. "Her heart's beating, but she hasn't woken up yet."

No one's holding my hand right now. I haven't heard my parents' voices in a while. The last I heard them say was that they were going for tea. A cup of tea would be very comforting at the moment. Sweet. Hot. Creamy. Why can't I have a cup of tea right now? I'm aching to scream because I can't have a cup of tea. I can't hug my mother. I can't comfort Storm. And I can't save Ethan from the crazy government people. *LET ME OUT! Let me out.* Let me out. My command gets weaker as I chant it. It's no use. No one is letting me out of my mind.

"How's it going, Ethan? Anyone come after you yet?" Storm asks.

Ethan gives a throaty, humorless chuckle.

"Sorry I caused this," Storm says. "But I didn't think you'd go and save my ass."

"I knew they had a heart, though. She didn't need yours. It would have been a senseless death."

"You still shouldn't have done it. I wasn't worth the risk."

It's bothering me to hear them talk like this, as if I'm not here. I hate that all this...this drama is because of me.

"I didn't do it for you, asshole," Ethan says. "I did it for Honor. How do you think she'd feel if she knew what you did? You think she'd be able to live with herself knowing you killed yourself for her?"

"No. I know she wouldn't, but I didn't have a choice at the time. I was afraid she wouldn't get a heart in time, and I didn't want her to die."

"Well I didn't want her to live *knowing* you died to save her."

There's silence for a few seconds.

"She loves you, Storm," Ethan says quietly. "I couldn't do that to her."

"Now what's gonna happen though? All those people made quite a stink out there. The cops were hounding me like you wouldn't believe. I played it off all innocent, but Ethan, man, they're gonna come after you." Storm sounds scared.

"Yeah, well better me than Honor," Ethan says.

"What do you mean?"

"The government came after Honor the other day."

"What?!" Storm shouts.

"Her father kept them from seeing her, but he needs to get a lawyer. They want to question her about saving those people on the plane."

"Oh my God. What do you think they'll do?"

"I don't know. I guess we're afraid they'll take her for their own use. I...I don't know."

"Damn it." Storm's voice gets closer. "I need to take her." My hand feels warm again. Storm is holding it.

"You mean take her away?" Ethan asks, astounded.

"Yes, take her away. What else *can* we do?" Storm is caressing my thumb knuckle. "Maybe you should disappear too, Eeth. Maybe we should just go into hiding like our parents did. Getting out in public…it was all wrong." Storm lifts my hand and runs his fingers along my palm.

"Yeah. My fault. I shouldn't have followed her—"

"It's too late now," Storm interrupts Ethan. "Let's just figure out where to go next."

"I hate to think of Honor living underground, Storm. She's too good for that. And her parents—"

"Her parents would want her safe. You know that."

"Yes, but it would break their heart to have her taken from them like that."

This conversation is getting way too much for me. I'm screaming. At the top of my lungs I'm screaming, but the sound is stuck somewhere inside my head. I need to get out. Stop this talk. I can't take it any longer. It's all too much—

"No," I eke out, though to me it's a scream.

Storm squeezes my hand. "Honor? Get the nurse. I heard you. Open your eyes, baby, I heard you."

Once again, I try to scream, but I can't. Instead, forcing my eyes open, I see light. My eyes aren't really open though. They're slits, because all I see is a line of brightness.

"Honor, you can do it, babe." Storm sounds like he's trying to laugh. He strokes my whole arm now.

The brightness flickers.

"That's it, darling. Keep opening them."

"She's up?" a female voice asks.

"Not yet, but her eyelids are moving, and she said no."

Somebody picks up my other hand and touches my wrist.

"She said no?"

"Yeah. She said no. I don't know why, but she said no." Storm is chuckling.

"Her pulse is strong. Her numbers are rising," the female remarks.

I need to do this.

With all my might, I push my eyelids open and finally I see the light on the ceiling.

"Honor," Storm shouts, and I've never heard him sound happy like this. "Oh, Honor, princess. Your eyes are the most gorgeous thing I've ever seen."

I'm still looking at the ceiling, because I'm having trouble moving my eyes in Storm's direction. But I really want to look at him.

"Honor?" I hear Ethan walk towards me, speaking quietly.

With as much concentration as I can muster, I shift my eyes a tiny bit.

"Hey there, girl," Ethan says, smiling that beautiful smile. Hopefully, he can tell I'm smiling back, though I'm pretty sure my lips haven't moved.

"Storm's right, those are some gorgeous eyes you got there. Darker than I remember," Ethan observes.

My new heart does a bit of a flip when Storm runs the back of his fingers along my cheek. I feel myself lean into him, though it's only performed in my mind. The heart. It's different. It's strong, there's no mistaking that. But it's something else. *I feel different.*

"Oh, Honor," I hear my mother cry. The next minute Storm is gone and she's standing over me. For my mother's sake, I try really hard to smile. It feels like my lip twitched, but I don't know.

"Look, Lea," Dad says, "she just smiled."

I did it. I smiled at my mom.

I got this.

"Hey, pumpkin." Dad's words are smiling, if that's possible. "I am so proud of you."

Again, I try really hard to smile.

"What a beautiful smile you got there, pumpkin."

"Okay," that female voice returns and I realize it belongs to the nurse. "I'm going to have to ask you all to leave for a bit. Doctor's on his way to run some tests. You can come back in about an hour or so."

I finally get to see my family and they have to leave?

"No," I force out again.

Storm laughs. "See. I told ya she said no."

Storm takes my hand after Mom let it go when the nurse said they had to leave.

"What is it, princess?" he asks, smiling.

"Th..tha..." I take a deep breath. Storm's smile is replaced with a furrowed brow. "Than...k..you," I barely breath out.

His hands cup my face while his nose touches my nose. "Don't. I don't ever need a thank you from you, princess. All I need is you."

I know I'm smiling now, because it hurts my cheeks to do so. My eyes flicker, and I feel his forehead with my lashes.

"I gotta go now, but don't you doubt that I'll be back. You hear me? You're stuck with me for life now, kiddo."

I haven't let my smile fall. He needs to know how happy I am to see him.

Storm closes his eyes and kisses my lips, making that new heart of mine beat way faster than it probably should right now. Though I don't move my lips to kiss him back, I hope he knows that I want to. I hope he knows that he is the one I finally chose...

If only the government doesn't take me away before I can tell him.

Chapter Seven

After two and a half long boring weeks in the hospital, I'm finally allowed to go home, though it won't be much different. Mom said she bought me a hospital bed to put in our living room. Lord help me, I feel like an old lady.

Ethan hasn't come around much, but Storm has been spending every day with me. He seems like he's back to his old self. Before he'd taken off that day on the boat, he was acting so strangely—pensive and distant. Lately, he's been acting like his usual sarcastic but sweet self. Although, he has been a little afraid to touch me. He's always holding my hand, and I'm always getting little kisses on my lips, cheeks, nose, or forehead, but that's it. No hugs or anything. I know he's probably afraid of hurting me, but, come on, I'm still an eighteen-year-old girl. Yeah, I turned eighteen in the hospital. Fun. Mom and Dad bought me a car I can't even drive. They said it was for when I recover, but just seeing my little red Mini Cooper today in my driveway, I am dying to drive it. They are so great for buying it for me. Maybe it was an incentive to stay positive and recover quickly.

Soon. I'll be driving it soon.

The massive hospital bed sits front and center in the living room. This won't embarrass me at all. What were they thinking? I could have just spent my days on the couch like a normal person. Then again, mom wouldn't be mom if she didn't go overboard.

Settling myself, with the help of Dad, into my new bed, I attempt to get comfortable. I finally find an upright position I am happy with when Mom brings me a cup of tea in my toaster mug. Chuckling to myself, I recall wanting a cup of tea so badly I could scream. But I can't remember when that was. Was it before I went into the hospital? No. *When did I want that darn cup of tea? And why did I want it so badly?*

"Hey, princess," Storm greets me after Dad let him in. "Got you a banana chocolate chip muffin." He holds up the white bag. "Can you have it? I forgot to ask."

"Yes." I laugh. "I can have it. Thank you." I pat the side of the bed for him to sit. "Mom can get you a chair if you'd like."

He kisses me on the nose. "Nah. I like the bed."

When he winks at me, my whole body grows warm. I like having Storm here. It feels good to have him back.

"Storm," Mom says when she walks out of the kitchen, "would you like a cup of tea or coffee? Soda?"

"Coffee sounds good. Thanks, Mrs. S." Storm brings his attention back to me. "Does it feel good to be home?"

"Yes. I just wish I could get out of bed. I want to drive my car," I say wistfully.

Storm finds this funny. "Soon, princess. You can take me out on a date." His smile is so genuine and comforting. "By the way, I still owe you a birthday present."

"No you don't. I never got you anything."

"That's 'cause I haven't celebrated a birthday with you yet. I came to town *after* my birthday."

"When is your birthday?"

"September thirtieth." Storm caresses my wrist, sending little chills up my arm.

"That's when you'll be twenty-three?" I ask, trying to talk while ignoring the growing tingles taking over my body.

"Yup. You don't think I'm too old for you?" The hesitation in his voice and the knitting of his eyebrows leads me to believe he's concerned about my answer.

"No. Not at all."

"And your parents? They're okay with it?" He's still rubbing his fingers up and down the inside of my forearm, and I'm still trying to ignore how wonderful it feels.

"I think so." Hmmm. I'll have to talk to them about it. "They never said otherwise."

"But...maybe they think we're still just friends...um..." Storm bites his bottom lip. "*Are* we still just friends or..." Storm doesn't finish the sentence, and he stops running his fingers along my wrist. Instead his thumb presses into it, causing me to feel deeper sensations than just chills and tingles. It's not a forceful press, but it's firm and powerful.

"What do you think we are?" I ask, suddenly afraid to broach the subject.

His fingers return to stroking my arm while he says, "I was hoping we were more?" he asks, apprehensive to just state his wish.

I can't help but smile. "Me too."

Storm closes his eyes momentarily, and when he opens them, his dark purple eyes are serious. "So, you chose me?"

I nod. "I chose you."

"Thank you," he whispers.

"I think," I say slowly, "it was always you. I was just getting confused with, you know, taking on Eeth's feelings and all, but whenever I wasn't with him...it was always you I thought about. I know it makes me a bad person, for leading Ethan on and all, but—"

"Hey. Princess. You're not a bad person. You can't help who you fall for. You just fall. Sometimes, the one you fall for, falls for you; sometimes...she doesn't. I can't say I'm not ecstatic that you fell for me, though. Because I fell for you the day you dropped your books all over the classroom floor."

We stare into each other's eyes for I don't know how long until we are interrupted by the doorbell.

Storm pushes back and sits at the other end of the bed, leaning against the footboard. His leg butts up against mine, and since I, too, am lying atop the blanket, it feels quite intimate to be touching his leg.

"Ethan," I say when I see him walk into the living room. I lean up to give him a kiss hello.

"How are you, Honor?" he asks with a tentative smile.

"I'm good, Eeth. Thanks."

"Here's a chair, Ethan." Mom pushes it up behind him. "Would you like something to drink?"

"Oh, no thanks, Mrs. Stevens." Ethan sounds sad.

He nods to Storm.

"Ethan. You good?"

Ethan nods again, and puts his hand on my leg. "What about you, Honor. You good? You feeling okay?"

"I am. I feel wonderful really. Almost back to myself."

Ethan forms a smile, but it doesn't quite make it to his eyes. "What's the matter? Something wrong?"

"Nope. Just worried you weren't going to be all right. I'm glad to hear you are." He rubs my thigh in a petting like manner. As if I were his dog.

"Ethan. Don't lie. I can—" About to tell him I can *feel* what he's feeling, I stop. *I can't feel what he's feeling.* I know he's sad because of his demeanor, but I don't feel anything for him. I mean, I'm sad if he is, but I'm *not sad too.* Hmm.

"Honor, I'm fine. Really." His smile is still half-hearted, but it's better.

"Ethan...you good?" Storm says again.

"Storm," Ethan says firmly, shaking his head and giving him this strange look with his eyes.

"I'm right here. I can see, Ethan. What's going on?" I have to know. Ethan is always serious, but the only time he ever looks this grave is when something is seriously wrong—like when the government came here that day. Oh my God. "The government? Are they coming back?" I ask anxiously.

Storm slinks back against the footboard and sighs.

Ethan looks up towards the ceiling then shakes his head. "Not for you, sweetheart. There's no need to worry."

"Not for me? What's that mean?"

Storm and Ethan give each other a knowing look.

"What?!" I am so frustrated right now, and this can't be good for my new heart. Taking a couple deep breaths I calm myself down. "Please, guys. You need to fill me in here."

When Ethan looks at Storm, Storm nods his head once.

"They're questioning me right now, Honor. The CIA." Ethan informs me.

"You? Why? How do they know you're an—" It all comes flooding back to me. That's right. I was a ghost. I saw it all. Storm shot himself in the head and Ethan healed him, brought him back to life in front of a whole hospital floor full of people. Oh my God. "You brought Storm back to life!" I shout.

They look at each other. "You told her?" Ethan asks Storm.

"No," Storm says wide-eyed, sitting up and moving closer to me on the bed.

"But how...how did you know that?" Ethan asks me.

I tilt my head and look at Storm. "You remember? Do you remember?" I ask him.

A small smile plays on his face. "Yeah." He nods. "I do."

"I'm lost," Ethan says.

I'm still looking at Storm, unable to tear my eyes from his, when I speak to Ethan. "Eeth...when I was...out...before my new heart, I, uh, kind of saw things." How do I explain this?

"When we were both on our way out," Storm says, still looking at me, "our souls kind of met up." He shrugs. "We were ghosts for a little while...and...we were able to talk to each other."

"You're kidding, right?" Ethan asks.

I shake my head, still staring at Storm. "As supernatural as it sounds, I had an out-of-body experience. It was weird," I say, "but nice." I can't help but smile at Storm, who smiles back.

Storm breaks the stare, finally, and turns to Ethan. "When all the commotion was going on out in the hallway, when you were...*healing* me...she followed me out." Storm sighs. "She had seen what I had done." Storm looks back at me. "I had no idea if you'd remembered that or not. I was afraid to ask."

"I didn't remember it. Not until a few minutes ago. I do remember something though. I think when I first woke up, I must have recalled something, because I said thank you to you. I kept wondering the past two weeks why I said thank you to you...now I remember...for trying to offer me your heart."

Swallowing something that may have gotten caught in his throat, Storm leans forward, taking both my hands. "It's still your heart, darling." He taps at his chest while bringing my hand along. "You *own* it. I'm just keeping it warm for you."

He brings his forehead to mine and closes his eyes. "You will always have my heart...in whatever capacity you need it."

I swallow back a lump in my throat, holding back tears as well. Who'd have ever thought when the callous whirlwind that is Storm Sutherland first set foot in Jefferson that he'd end up as sweet and sentimental as this? Like his name insinuates, Storm came in, forcefully disturbing the environment around him, only to leave it calm and peaceful and more beautiful in the end.

How could I not have fallen for him?

Chapter Eight

"Ahem." Ethan clears his throat, reminding us that he is still there.

Storm backs away with a smug expression on his face.

"I'm sorry, Eeth. I didn't—"

"Don't apologize. I just didn't want to watch this sappy display of affection."

I realize it was probably inconsiderate of me to display my affections for Storm in front of Ethan, so I apologize again. "I am sorry though, Ethan."

"It's fine," he says standing from his chair. "I should be going anyway."

"Nooo. You can't. We didn't even talk about what happened when everyone saw you heal Storm. The government. What about the media? They had to be after you. Tell me, Ethan. What happened?"

Sitting back down, Ethan looks at Storm. "It ain't good," he says. Looking at me, he says, "But it'll be okay. I'm working things out."

"Really?" I ask, hopeful. Only because I don't want to lose hope do I believe him when he says he's working things out.

"Really. And as for the media, well, the government put an end to that right away."

"The government? So they've already talked to you?"

"Yeah. They have." His voice sounds so serious now.

"Are they going to take you away?"

Shaking his head, Ethan answers, "Not the way you think, Honor. I promise. I'm going to be okay. I'm just glad they got to me before they came back for you."

"Why? They came to me first. You shouldn't have to be involved."

"Honor," Storm cuts in. "You're too weak for them right now. And Ethan's a good alternative. Besides, he can bring people back to life now too. Probably, 'cause he killed Asa, who killed Moore, who killed Seth, but you get the picture. Anyway...he can bring people back from the dead. Everyone saw it, so now the government has their sights on Ethan instead of you. And they have know idea that you can raise the dead, so let's just keep it that way. Okay?"

"No. It's not okay," I say. "Why should Ethan pay for something that I started?"

"*You* did not start this, Honor. I did. By coming here and alerting them to the fact that you existed. Your parents...Hanna and Daniel...did what they thought would be the best way for you to stay hidden. And Mr. and Mrs. Stevens continued that privacy. I'm just trying to correct a wrong that I made. I wronged you, Honor, and now I'm trying to make it right." Ethan stands again, this time more abruptly. "I gotta go." He covers his face with his whole hand. I think he's trying to hide the fact that he's crying. But I know better. And it's not because I can *feel* it. I just know Ethan well. He's too proud to let me know this bothers him.

Storm gets up to walk him out. I can't help but feel sad for Ethan. His life is going to change, especially with the government on his back. I wish I could do something for him, but I can barely do anything for myself right now.

"He'll be fine, Honor. Don't let this hurt you." Storm sits back down on the bed, this time up at the headboard. "You can't start straining your heart feeling other people's pain anymore."

"Storm?"

"Yeah?" He drapes his arm around me, and I lean my head into his shoulder.

"I don't think I *can* feel other people's pain anymore."

Pulling away from me to look at my face, Storm says, "What? Really? Like, you're not an empath anymore?"

I shrug. "I don't think so," I say quietly. I think back to when I'd first woken up after the surgery. I remember feeling different. Not as burdened.

"Hmmm. Just like what happened to me," Storm muses. "I wonder if it has to do with your new heart or the fact that you were actually...dead...on the operating table."

"Dead?" I cringe when I say that word.

"Sorry, princess, I meant...well, shoot, that's exactly what I meant. I died and when you brought me back, my empath stuff was gone. I thought you healed it out of me, but maybe once I died, it just died along with me." Storm shrugs. "Maybe that's what happened to you."

"So.., all we have to do to get rid of our abilities is die?"

"Maybe. And as long as there's someone there to bring us back to life."

Leaning my head back down on Storm's shoulder, he squeezes me tight. "I'm glad you're alive, princess. So glad."

The kiss he plants on the top of my head is just sweet enough to put me to sleep.

During my slumber, my heart grows warm and I get this overwhelming urge to eat a cinnamon roll. The kind you pop out of a can and bake in the oven. I don't think I've ever had them in my life, yet I can taste the sticky sweetness on my tongue. My mouth waters and I wake up ravenous.

"Good nap, princess?" Storm's warm breath blows at the top of my head.

"Yes, but I'd really like those cinnamon rolls right now."

"What? You never eat sweets."

I push my hair out of my face and shift to face Storm. "I know. Isn't that crazy? I, like, dreamed about them."

Shaking his head and laughing, he stands from the bed. "Well if that's what you want, that's what you'll get. Besides, your mother said when you woke up, she needed to take your blood pressure and give you your medicine, so I'll run to the store while she does that. Want anything else?"

"Yeah. A bottle of cream soda." Surprising myself, I blurt out, "Geez, why all the cravings for sugar?" before I adjust myself to lean back against the headboard.

"I don't know, princess. You're sweet enough, though."

I laugh and grab the People magazine that mom had put on the end table.

Flipping through the pages, I learn that yet another celebrity is vacationing on some exotic island. Naturally, this brings me back to *my* island vacation and the plane crash. Although I haven't thought of that crash in a while, I'm suddenly drawn to the image of the devastated mother who was screaming for her burning daughter. My instinct is to reach out and hug her and tell her it will all be all right. But it *is* all right. I *saved* her daughter. My eyes were witness to the restoring of each and every burn on her body. Her eyes opened white and healthy.

So, why do I want to cry for this mother? After feeling no one's pain since my surgery, why am I suddenly suffering inside for this mother?

Mom enters the room with our new portable blood pressure machine.

"Mom. Do you remember that mother and daughter from the plane crash? The daughter who was burned from the engine that caught fire?"

"Yes. What about her?" Mom's cool hand touches my skin as she wraps the band around my upper arm.

"I don't know. I just...I'm thinking about the mother. I'm feeling something." My heart sinks into my stomach a little. "I guess my empath stuff's coming back." My words taper off, because my disappointment heightens. I liked being free of those feelings. I do not want them back.

"Oh, Honor. You need to fight those feelings." Mom stops taking my blood pressure. Her expression takes on that of someone very exhausted from worry. "Please, honey. Please try to ignore them."

Nodding, I appease her. "I will, Mom. I'll try."

Chapter Nine

Ignoring that mother's suffering is not an option. Three days have passed since she and her daughter entered my consciousness, and the heaviness in my heart is overwhelming. I thought my body was growing stronger; why my heart feels strained again is beyond me. These symptoms—they're different than before. Before the transplant, if I was healing someone, my heart and body would both deteriorate at the same time. Now, I'm not even healing anyone, yet my heart is draining...but my body feels strong. Of course, explaining any of this to my mom would just gnaw at her sanity, so I talk to Storm instead.

"And you don't *feel* anyone else's emotions? Not mine or your mom's or dad's?" Storm is trying to help me sort through this.

"No. Not like that. It's so strange. I just keep getting these flashes of the two of them. Like an accident, but they are not on a plane." I pause to collect my thoughts. "Actually, the accident only involved the girl. I keep seeing the mom at her side in the hospital." I run my finger over my bottom lip. "I see her like I saw my own mom sitting next to me when I was lying in the hospital bed...back when I, you know, came out of my body."

"Hmm." He scratches his temple. "It could be—"

I interrupt him. "Maybe I'm just hallucinating from these drugs I have to take."

Storm nods. "Or...did they give you any information about whose heart they gave you?"

Widening my eyes, I say, "No. I don't want to know." The thought of knowing whose heart is beating inside me scares me. If my empath abilities come back, and I know the name of the person who lost their life so I could live, I don't think I could live with that. I'd carry that around with me forever. My chest burns thinking about it.

"Honor. I know this may be hard to hear, but I think you should find out about the donor. It may hold the clue to why you're feeling this way." Storm pulls me up from the chair I've been sitting in all morning and hugs me, holding my head against his shoulder. "It may be scary, but I really think you need to find out...so you can move on."

Because I love and respect Storm so much, I reluctantly agree.

A week later, with the hospital bed finally returned to the medical supply place, my foot twitches repetitively against the couch. Mrs. Cooper is expected any minute.

"You okay?" Mom asks, absentmindedly rearranging the fancy teacups she purposely puts out for company.

"Yeah," I say quickly, because I'm really not okay.

"It'll be fine, sweetheart," my dad tells me.

"He's right, princess. You'll see. This will be good for all of you." Though I usually take pleasure in one of Storm's back rubs, his hand running up and down my back at the moment is stifling. Shifting to get comfortable is a wasted attempt. When the doorbell rings, I jump to my feet, crossing and uncrossing my arms. I don't know how to stand when she comes in. Do I walk up to the door and shake her hand? Do I wait for her to come to me? Do I stand? Do

I sit? Oh my God, I wish it were tomorrow already. This would all be over with by then.

"Mrs. Cooper, this is my daughter Honor." My mom's introduction is stilted.

Mrs. Cooper smiles at me with the side of her bottom lip caught between her teeth. She moves to speak, but no sound comes out. Her hand flies to cover her mouth and tears well up in her eyes. Seeing her again brings back all of my emotions from the plane crash in the Bahamas. But I also get images of the car accident that caused her daughter's death three weeks ago.

"I can't believe it's you," she says through her tears. "When they told me it was you, I had to sit down. I almost passed out."

My hand covers my mouth now. It is so hard to hold back my tears. Looking in her eyes, I see the same desperation that was there the day she was screaming for her burning daughter.

"What are the chances," Mrs. Cooper asks, "that you would save Trisha only for her to save you a few months later?" I know there are two ways to take this, but I choose to hear the sincerity in her statement and not the resentment.

"I'm sorry, Mrs. Cooper," I say quietly, a large sob threatening to escape. I have this urge to hug her, but I don't even know her. "I'm so so sorry." Unable to keep them reigned in, my tears rush out. To me, this feels like her daughter's episode. It's distant like my empathic sufferings, but it also feels so personal.

Unable to restrain her own emotions, Mrs. Cooper takes both my hands, looks me in the eyes, and pulls me into a strong bear hug. In two seconds, my shoulders are wet with her many tears. "Oh Trisha. I miss her so much." The pain in my chest is unbearable. The regret I feel is unexplainable.

"Mrs. Cooper?" I ask apprehensively into her shoulder. "I think your daughter is sorry for leaving you."

Holding me at arm's length, she widens her eyes. "What?"

I shrug and Storm, standing next to me the whole time, pushes my hair behind my shoulders. "I just think some of these feelings I'm getting are from her."

Mrs. Copper closes her eyes and smiles. "She still exists," she says mostly to herself.

I nod. "I feel her." With a hand to my chest, I say, "Right here. I feel her. I feel her love for you." Which is the truth. Deep in my new heart, there is a place set aside for Trisha Cooper's mother. Their bond must have been close.

"Thank you, Honor," Mrs. Cooper says. "I needed to hear that."

After a few silent seconds, Mom dries her own tears and offers refreshments.

"A cup of tea is fine, Mrs. Stevens," Mrs. Cooper answers.

"Oh please, call me Lea."

"And call me Terry."

"I'll help you," Storm says.

"I'll have a glass of cream soda, Mom."

I sit down at the dining room table when Mrs. Cooper announces, "Cream soda? My Trisha *loved* cream soda. Drank a glass every morning before school."

"With a cinnamon roll?" Storm asks innocently.

As her mouth drops open, Mrs. Cooper's skin fades to white. "How did you know?"

Storm answers apologetically, "Honor's been craving them."

"Really?" she mumbles through her hand, holding back more tears.

As difficult as meeting Mrs. Cooper is for me, I realize it must be one hundred percent harder for her. This thought impels me to say, "I'm sorry, Mrs. Cooper. I'm so sorry you had to lose your daughter." My own eyes fill up again. "So sorry."

"Thank you," is all she could manage to reply through her tears.

Chapter Ten

My new red Mini Cooper. Yes! Today I get to drive it.

Storm laughs at me because I touch every inch of the dashboard before I even start the car.

"If you don't want to be late for orientation, you better stop making love to your car and start the ignition."

Giggling, I apologize half-heartedly. "Sorry. I just love this car." Running my hand over the huge round speedometer, I add, "Just look at this. It's so retro. So...awesome."

"Yeah. It is," Storm resigns. "And you deserve it," he says sincerely. "But can we get our asses moving, because I'm pretty sure you're going to be late for your first day of college."

I turn to him and smile. "Thanks for coming with me."

"Get used to it."

Flashing him another huge smile, I return my attention to the dashboard and press the ignition button. I still can't get over how I don't even have to take the key out of my purse to start the car. It just adds another toy quality to my already awesome toy car.

"You nervous?" Because of the fortunate miniscule size of the car, Storm is able to keep his hand on the top of my thigh while I drive.

"A little. I'm glad Shelby's going to be there. Too bad we don't have any classes together."

"You'll meet new people, princess. And it'll be good for you too." His large hand squeezes my thigh. "Just think, you can finally get to know people without it causing pain."

Tapping my fingers on the steering wheel, I think about what Storm says. This is the first time I will be around people where I don't have to worry about what they're feeling. The only emotions I'd picked up from someone else since I got my new heart were Mrs. Cooper's, and I'm sure that was because of the close bond that Trisha and she had shared.

"Princess? You okay?"

I nod. "I think. I just...I keep waiting for it to come back. Like it's not real."

"It's been two months, sweetness. I don't think it's coming back. Besides," he says, stroking a few strands of my hair, "you're hair's almost the color of honey already. That's a far cry from the platinum blond you used to be. You're looking healthier every day, babe."

The tan hands on the steering wheel confirm his remark. "I guess." I glance in the rearview mirror. "My eyes have gotten darker too, haven't they?"

"Yup. A beautiful, rich dark purple." He runs his hand down my arm and returns it to my thigh. "You're still the most beautiful girl walking this earth."

I feel the skin on my face grow warm.

"I have a surprise for you." Storm's index finger draws circles over my leg.

"Oh yeah?"

"Yeah." His finger starts moving more quickly. "This is *my* college orientation too."

My head snaps in his direction.

"Eyes on the road, princess. No need to crash your new car just yet."

"You registered for college?" I don't hide my surprise. Suddenly, I get little flutters in my stomach. "Really? *You're* going to college?"

"Uh...you find that hard to believe?" Storm really seems offended.

"No, no, no, I meant—"

"I know what you meant. I was just teasing. But seriously, I did register."

"Oh my God, Storm. Why didn't you tell me?"

"I'm telling you now."

"No, I mean. When? You're with me every day. I didn't see you—"

"When I go home at night. I've been thinking about it for a while, and I just decided to register."

"Do you have a major?"

"This semester I'm just taking some core requirements. I'm waiting to see if I get into Sanford Brown for spring semester."

"Sanford...where's that?"

"Iselin...New Jersey. I didn't want to go far from you."

Because Storm had never mentioned going to college before, I'm so taken back that I miss the exit for school.

"You can make a U-Turn at the next exit. Why are you so upset about this?"

I wish I wasn't driving right now, so I could look at him. "I'm not upset. I'm really not. Just surprised. You never talked about it."

He shrugs. "I'd rather talk about *you*, sweetness."

"Storm, stop. Why won't you talk to me about it?"

"Honor. I *am* talking to you about it. Right now. I hadn't made the commitment until a couple weeks ago, so I really...I really wanted to wait to get my acceptance from Sanford first, but...well, I thought I'd register now for some basic courses. To be with you."

"Sweet-talker," I say with a smile.

"I'm not sweet talking. It's the truth." Now he's running his thumb *and* his index finger on my thigh, and I'm finding it hard to concentrate.

"Why Sanford-Brown?"

"They're the only college close enough that offers Medical Perfusionist as a major."

Another surprise. "What's the heck's a Perfusionist?"

"How 'bout we go to orientation, and we'll talk about it later," Storm suggests, since I just pulled into the county college parking lot.

My heart is racing. I hadn't realized until I pulled into the lot that I am a nervous wreck. My short stint in public school was not enough to prepare me for the amount of people I would encounter in college. Until recently, I didn't even think I'd be going to college, yet here I am.

Storm's hand presses on my lower back when he meets me on my side of the car. "You okay? You look a little pasty right now."

"Just a little anxiety attack. No biggie," I joke.

"No biggie," he mimics, throwing his arm around my shoulder. "You'll be fine."

That's what he thinks.

"C'mon," Storm takes my hand. "Orientation's this way."

In the student center, while I had expected to see Shelby, I had not counted on seeing Ethan with her.

"Ethan?!" I practically cry in excitement. "What are you doing here? Are coming here?" He never spoke of college before, so this is such a surprise.

He shakes his head. Yes, I'm disappointed. With a noticeable sigh, I'm sure, I say, "Oh." Then I look from him to Shelby. Oh. Maybe he's just here with Shelby.

"I came with Shel. For moral support."

"Oh." Then I think—maybe he has just been quiet around me because of me, and not because something else is going on his life. Maybe he isn't interested in being my friend anymore. "Hmm. Well," I shrug, my hair annoying my neck as I do so, "it's nice seeing you here anyway." Though I don't look at Storm, I feel him notice my change in demeanor. I can't help it. I love Ethan. I miss him. I just wish Ethan hadn't expected me to love him more than I do. I know that it's my fault. If Storm hadn't entered the picture, I might have still been with Ethan and not have questioned my feelings for him. But Storm *did* walk into my life. And though I wanted to ignore my increasing attraction to him, he aroused a craving inside me I never knew I could feel. Where Ethan was beautiful, dependable, safe, Storm was unpredictable, hardened, and so dangerous. But the more I got to know each of them, I found so many more layers to Storm. And they really weren't even layers—underneath his very thin veil of apathy was a sensitive, passionate, and all too vulnerable man who just needed to love and be loved.

I'm sorry for Ethan that I fell for Storm in the midst of falling for Ethan, but once Storm grabbed hold of my heart—both of them—there was no turning back. Now, of course, I have to pay the price of losing a good friend in Ethan.

"Honor," Shelby flails her schedule in front of me, interrupting my sad moment. "Let me see your schedule. I know we have no classes together, but let's see if we have any breaks at the same time."

"Oh, sure." While Shelby and I compare schedules, Storm and Ethan are whispering something a few feet away from us.

"Ooh, we have from eleven thirty to one o'clock on Mondays and Thursdays. We can do lunch together." Shelby's excitement is reminiscent of Tamlin's, who is at her own orientation at Seton Hall. I wish I could experience college with my very first friend, but of course her parents wanted her to go to a private college. But I do look forward to visiting her. Since Seton Hall is less than an hour away, Tam and I figured I could bunk in her dorm every other weekend.

"Oh," Shelby interrupts again. "We also have a break on Wednesday from two to three."

"Great," I respond, though my eyes are glued on Storm and Ethan's conversation. I wish I could hear them.

"So, is Storm going to hang with Ethan while we go to orientation?"

"Uh, no, actually. Storm is here as a registered student." I push my bangs behind my ear and try to turn my attention from the boys. "He surprised me this morning."

"Wow. Cool. I had no idea Storm was interested in college. I mean with all the money he and his brothers inherited, I thought he'd just sort of traipse through life untethered."

"No. Not Storm," I tell her, realizing that Shelby knows nothing about Storm if she thinks he intends to go through life untethered. He did that his whole childhood. What Storm wants is security and commitment. A sense of purpose. All the money in the world can't buy that for Storm, unless he himself puts roots down in an attempt to grow. She doesn't know the Storm I know *at all.*

"Well, cool." She shrugs. "We should get over to the auditorium. It's almost nine."

Storm must have heard her, because I see him look at his phone and pat Ethan on the shoulder.

"Ready, princess?" he asks, running his hand down my arm then stopping when he takes my hand.

"I'll be hanging in here," Ethan says to all of us. "I have some work to do on my computer, so I'll see you in a bit." He turns to Shelby and kisses her softly on the lips.

Hmmm. Two things—when did he start seeing Shelby? And when did he ever have *work to do*? I may not be able to feel what's going on, but I certainly have good instincts still, and my instincts tell me this work he's doing is *not* good.

Chapter Eleven

When orientation is over, Ethan is right where he said he'd be. Only he's pacing the lobby, his phone at his ear. A shaky free hand runs through his hair repeatedly. My instincts are proving me correct—this is bad.

"Is everything okay with Ethan?" I ask Shelby.

"I guess. He's been kind of secretive lately, but I think he's okay." Shelby doesn't seem too concerned, so maybe I shouldn't be.

Yet something inside me disagrees.

"Everything cool?" Storm asks Ethan when he returns his phone to his back pocket.

Ethan's eyes roll up to his brow, but he quickly nods his head and says, "Yeah, everything's good. How'd orientation go?"

"Good," Shelby answers.

"Okay," Storm says at the same time.

I just stand here numb, worried about whatever has Ethan so troubled.

"Honor, you have a good time too?" Ethan asks quietly.

I nod. "Yeah. It was good."

There's a brief visual exchange between Storm and Ethan, that if I hadn't been paying close attention to Ethan's facial expressions, I would have missed.

"Shelby." Storm taps her arm with the back of his fingers. "I wanted to talk to you about the nursing program here. In case I don't get into Sanford-Brown, I may try nursing. You got a minute?"

Something's up. Ethan nods when Shelby looks to him for an answer to Storm's question. *Is Shelby in on this too? And since when have they gotten so close?*

"Come on, Honor, I'll buy you a cup of tea."

When Storm kisses me goodbye, I feel dread in his kiss. Maybe not all of my empathic abilities have disappeared, or maybe I'm just extra sensitive to Storm's and Ethan's emotions. Either way, my stomach feels like it's being gnawed at from the inside out.

"So how've you been?" Ethan asks, as he sets my tea in front of me.

Blowing on the opening of the cup's lid, I shrug, "Okay."

"You don't seem it." Ethan sips his coffee then sits forward, leaning his elbows on the table.

"I miss you." Running my finger along my cup lid, I wonder why I just said that. I want to kick myself, because I don't want him to think I'm leading him on. But I really do miss him.

"I miss you too." A tiny clamp squeezes at my heart when Ethan flashes me a sad smile. "But we know who your heart belongs to," he says with a tilt of his head. "How *is* your new heart, by the way?"

"It's good. Strong." Then quietly I say, "I'm not an empath anymore."

Ethan runs his fingers along my almost tan hand. "I can tell." He smiles. "But Storm already told me. I'm happy for you. You didn't need that anymore. You've been through too much already."

"I guess." He abruptly stops stroking my hand.

"Now you can finally enjoy life without the burden of everyone else inside you."

When Ethan sips his coffee again, I realize he's stalling. There's a reason why Storm took Shelby away and Ethan took me for tea. "What's going on, Eeth? I know you're hiding something."

Bringing his hands together and to his lips, he looks like he's readying himself for prayer. In reality, he's readying himself to tell me whatever bad news it is he needs to divulge. Seconds pass, though they feel like minutes, as he takes several clearing breaths, before finally uttering, "I'm going away tonight."

"Vacation?" I ask, knowing damn well he wouldn't be taking me for tea if that were the case.

"No. Not vacation." His words are clipped, but he doesn't seem angry. Just sad. "I'll be gone for some time." I watch as his eyes glisten with sadness.

Biting the inside of my lip, I taste blood. I'm so nervous that the pain of drawing blood is more pleasant than the cluster of rope that has formed inside my stomach.

"I'm going to Virginia." He states as a matter of fact.

I was *not* expecting *that*. "What's in Virginia?"

The casting of his eyes on his paper coffee cup lends me to believe Virginia is not his location of choice.

The corner of his lip quirks. Then his bottom lip trembles a hair. "The CIA."

I am inundated with fear—the same fear I felt in the bathroom that day with Ethan. Clasping my heart with one hand, and covering my mouth with the other, I panic. "Ethan. No." I cry. My body shakes involuntarily. "No.

They can't—" I am so distraught that I can't complete my sentence. My biggest fear has come true. The government wants to take us apart piece by piece to see what makes us what we are. "You...you...can't...you can't go."

"Honor." He pulls my hand from my mouth. "They're not taking me. I volunteered."

"What?" The word comes out of my mouth, but I don't hear it. How could he volunteer to let the CIA have their way with them?

"I volunteered." The intensity at which he stares me in the eyes is frightening.

"Why?" I barely breathe the word out. My heart is straining to beat.

"If I go voluntarily," he swallows hard, "they'll work with me on my terms instead of theirs." His hand still holds mine and I feel it tremble. He's scared.

"You believe that?" There's no way he really believes that the government will work on his terms.

Ethan shrugs. "I gotta believe it, Honor. I got no choice."

I start tapping at my chest with my knuckles. "There has to be a way out, Ethan. Maybe—" I'm about to say, "Maybe you can run," but he shouldn't have to. Not alone anyway. "Maybe we can all run away together. You, me, Storm, your brothers, and Uncle Tom. My parents will understand. As long as we're all together."

Releasing my hand from my chest, Ethan takes my other hand as well. "We're not running away. That's no life for you. I won't let that happen."

"But—"

"But nothing. Your parents may understand, but they'll never get over the fact they'd never see their daughter again."

I drop my head in defeat. "Oh, Ethan." Lifting my gaze to meet his eyes again, I see him through thick liquid, distorted and blurry. "What if...what if you run? With your brothers, so you're not alone."

Ethan blinks away the pooling gel in his eyes. "I can't do that."

"Why not?" I squeeze his hands so hard he flinches. "I'm sorry."

"I'm impressed. You've gotten your strength back." He laughs, though mirthlessly.

"It's not funny, Ethan. Why can't you just run? Hide out or something?"

"I can't."

"Why?"

His face frozen in terror, he stares at me motionless.

"Why, Ethan?" I yank my hands from his grasp. "What aren't you telling me?" I push the table at him to stir a response. "Tell me," I shout then look around to see everyone in the cafeteria looking at me.

Pushing the table out from his stomach, Ethan stands. "Let's go, Honor. Not here."

I let him take my hand and walk me out of the building. Down the side stairs sits an isolated tree. Ethan coaxes me up against the tree and sets his hands around my upper arms. "I can't run, Honor." His voice is stern yet quiet.

"Why?" I choke out.

Again he stares right into my eyes. His bright violet irises pierce through mine. "Because they'll come after you." The words are spoken so low that it takes an extra second to register them.

I'm silent.

"They want you, Honor. But I won't let them have you." He lowers his hands down my arm and takes my wrists. "They said if I come willingly, and they get what they need, they'll reconsider coming to get you."

Everything clenches. My stomach, my heart, my lungs. I can't breathe. I ball up my fists and want to punch something. *This is all my fault. Everything Ethan has to go through is my fault.* I fight to remove my wrists from Ethan's hold, but he hangs on to them. I want to thrash at something, but he won't let me. I am angry. Angry at myself for being what I am. What I was. When my sobs get stronger than my will to throw a punch, I slide down the tree, taking Ethan with me.

"I'm sorry," I'm finally able to say.

He lifts me onto his lap and strokes my hair as I lean into his chest. "Don't be sorry, Honor. It's not your fault, it's mine, for coming here in the first place. I owe you this." His breath in my hair feels comfortable.

Into his chest, I mumble, "I'm sorry I broke up with you, Ethan. I really do love you, it's just—"

"Shh." His fingers twist a few strands of my hair. "I know where your heart lies. I'm okay with being your friend."

My throat catches another of my sobs. "But now...why do you have to go? I'm not an empath anymore. Let them take me. They'll see they'll get nowhere and send me back." I pull away so I can look at him.

His sad smile is back. "I'm afraid it won't work that way. What if they think you're faking it and decide to cut you open to check for real?"

Oh my God.

"They're ruthless. They want our DNA. They're going to do what they can to get it." When his hand drops to my knee, that familiar feeling for Ethan returns.

"But what if they do that to you?" I lay my hand on top of his.

"I'm cooperating with them. They won't." When his hand turns upside down, he wraps it around mine. The tingles that shoot through my limbs may not be electric like when I feel Storm's touch, but they're still there, and I still miss the days when I was Ethan's girlfriend.

"How long will they keep you?"

He shrugs. "A while. They want me working for them. You know, if someone important, like the President, gets shot, he doesn't have to die."

"Oh my goodness, so they're going to make you heal whomever they want? Whenever they want?"

"Pretty much. Otherwise they'll try to clone my DNA...make another empath."

"Oh my God. You have to do this *forever?*"

"I hope not. But I am immortal, remember."

"Do they know that?"

Nodding his head, he tells me, "I thought it'd be another reason for them to leave you alone. Of course, they don't believe me, but they'll figure it out soon enough."

"Did you tell them everything? Like how when empaths kill, they become—"

"I felt I had no choice but to tell them everything, Honor. The more I divulged, the less interested in you they became."

I want to cry all over again. I hate that this new heart is so strong, because to me it feels like it hurts worse than my other heart, because *this pain* that I'm feeling is all my own. An intense and unpleasant sensation spreads from my heart, like tentacles, crawling through every vein and nerve ending in my body. This is the end for Ethan. He will never be a free man again. "Oh my God, Ethan, what kind of life will you have? You'll be a slave to them—"

"It's not that bad, Honor. They're actually paying me. They've even set up a nice apartment for me in Langley."

"Langley?"

"Virginia. It's where their headquarters are. I'm free to come and go as I please. Like a regular employee, but...if I quit...well, I'm not sure what'll happen to you, so I just. Won't. Quit."

The urge to hug him takes over, so with both my arms, I pull him tight against me and hug him like there's no tomorrow. 'Cause essentially, where Ethan and I are concerned, there *is* no tomorrow.

While wrapped in our embrace, I ask into his neck, "Can I visit you?"

He sighs into my ear. "I don't think that's a good idea, angel. They'll be watching my apartment. If they see *you*, it just may be incentive enough for them to take you anyway."

"I'm so sorry it didn't work out between us, Ethan." I whisper. "I really am."

He holds me tighter and I feel something drip onto my hair.

Ethan's crying.

And again, *I* cry.

And slink into Ethan's arms for what may be the very last time.

Chapter Twelve

Many moments have passed before Storm and Shelby find us under the tree.

"You guys all right?" Storm asks, walking slowly toward us.

With Ethan still holding me, I feel kind of guilty, but I have a feeling Storm doesn't mind. At least it doesn't appear so on his face.

Then the thought hits me. "Does Shelby know?" I whisper to Ethan.

He nods. "Yeah."

Why was I the last to know? Wiping my face with my palms, I climb out of Ethan's lap and stand. Ethan follows.

"Do you need more time?" Storm's looking at me as if gauging my reaction.

Ethan shrugs. "I told her."

"He can't go," I cry to Storm, as if he can do anything about it.

"It's either him or you, Honor." He shakes his head. "Ethan insists it's him."

"It's all my fault," I declare over the gigantic mass in my throat. "It *should* be me."

"But you're not an empath anymore, Honor," Shelby says innocently.

"But...it's just—"

"Honor," Ethan puts his arm around me and pulls me to his side. "Stop. It's something I *want* to do." He pulls me away from Shelby and Storm. "I couldn't live with myself if I declined them and they came after you. Empath or not, they know you healed more than a dozen people on the flight."

I hiccup, trying to keep my crying to myself.

"They're not going to just accept that you're no longer an empath. And that's another thing I don't want to explain—you have to die and be brought back to life in order to lose your abilities? I dread it if they find that out. What they wouldn't try, knowing that. For now they think it's the heart transplant that did it." He tilts his head and grazes my chin with his fingertips. "I led them to believe the abilities stem from the heart...one day they may find out the truth...but I'll worry about it then." He laughs, but not a real laugh. "If they don't have another empath to heal me, I figure they won't kill me, right?"

"Oh, Ethan." He pulls me into his arms and I squeeze him tight.

"Uncle Tom and my brothers left this morning."

I pull my head back. "What?"

"They're going to start over somewhere else." Ethan shakes his head. "We didn't want the government looking into them. Right now they don't know they exist...well, hopefully."

"This is just horrible." I close my eyes and sink into his chest. "I'm gonna miss you so much."

"Me too, angel." His voice catches and I know he's crying too. "But I'll always be here." He taps my heart. "You know that, don't you? I will always be in your heart and you'll always be in mine."

His words make me convulse in his arms. "Oh, Ethan." My heart squeezes underneath my chest. Through the pain,

I finally say, "You'll always be in my heart. Always. Always." Pausing to catch my breath, I try to inhale his scent and remember it always. "You were my first love, Ethan. I could never forget you. Ever."

The top of my head feels damp. "You were mine too, Honor. Thank you for opening up *my* heart. I—" He doesn't finish, he's crying too hard. "Oh my God, Honor—" His hand moves from my back, to his mouth. "Oh my God, I...I—"

I want to wrap him up and never let him go. "I'm so sorry. So. Sorr—" Words just won't come out, the pain hurts too much. This new heart is different than my old one. Its capacity to hurt is much greater than my own. My old one would have drained all my emotions and shut down. This one catches fire and ignites tiny embers throughout my entire body. There is no escaping this kind of hurt. Unlike before, my body doesn't just drop to the floor and pass out. But right now, I want to die. Because of me, a boy I love is sacrificing his life.

Then it occurs to me. Storm had sacrificed his life too.

I am a monster to allow this. To allow everyone I love to die for me. It's...it's...inexcusable.

Finally, I get out what I need to say. "No. You can't go, Ethan. You can't. Let them come after me. I don't care. If it's me they want, then it's me they'll get. I'm not worth this, Ethan."

Holding me at arm's length, he tilts his head and smiles. "I've made my decision, Honor." He wipes at his face. "And I'm okay with it. Aside from missing you, I'm really okay with it."

Into his arms, I fall again.

"No. This isn't the life you chose. You shouldn't have to—"

"Stop." He interrupts me. "I can't just not show up in Virginia, Honor. It's too late to run. Too late to turn back now. But..." He kisses the top of my head and looks in my eyes again. "But I'll always love you. Remember that. Please."

One last hug and he steps away. "It's time to go now, babe. I have a long drive tonight." He swallows hard and looks down at the ground, turning silently and walking away.

Before the sight of him disappears behind my tears, Shelby runs to him, takes his hand, and walks with him the rest of the way, leaving me to watch, heartbroken, as the first boy I ever loved walks out of my life forever.

"Come on, sweetness," Storm's suddenly beside me, wrapping his strong arms around my shoulder. "Let's get you home."

I feel so guilty...for everything. For loving Ethan, but falling *in love* with his brother. For leading Ethan on. For taking a young girl's barely used heart. For allowing people to die in order to save me. For not deserving Ethan *or* Storm, both of whom committed such extreme sacrifices...for *me*. It doesn't make sense. And I don't think it ever will.

Hand in hand, Storm and I make our way back to my new red car, and I think how this moment should have been such a happy one—my first day at college, my boyfriend at my side—yet it is tinged with a sadness I'd

have never expected—my new heart will forever be dam-
aged by the scar left by Ethan's leaving. And knowing he
left, to save me from the same captive fate he now owns,
doesn't lessen the pain of his absence.

It makes it greater.

Chapter Thirteen

"I want to take you out tonight, princess," Storm's deep voice resonates through the tiny speaker of my cell phone, "so no studying tonight. You need a break."

"But we have finals next week," I whine.

"Yeah. *Next* week. Not *this* week. Plus, you study every night. I'm sure you're going to ace your exams."

I remove the text book from my lap and stand from my bed to look in my closet for something to wear. "But I really want to get into Seton Hall so I can go to school with Tamlin next year." I pull out a deep purple skater's dress, hoping it's perfect for wherever Storm is taking me.

"Babe, you're going to get in. There's no doubt. Stop worrying."

"I just really miss her. And I really want to get into their psychology department."

"Honor. You will. Now will you go out with me tonight?" Storm pleads.

I chuckle. "Yes, I'll go out with you tonight." I hang the dress on top of my closet so it's all set for later. "It's cold. We're not going for one of your hikes through the woods are we?"

"Nah, though I do love walking behind you when you're climbing those rocks."

"Pervert."

"Yeah, pervert. If I were a pervert, I'd have gotten past second base already."

Thank goodness he's on the other side of the phone, because I *know* I'm blushing. My cheeks actually feel hot when I touch them. It's not that I haven't *wanted* to go further with Storm, but I think he's afraid to make the first move. It would be the first time for both of us, and even though he's a guy, I know he's just as afraid as I am.

"Did I make you blush, princess? I think I did."

"Storm," I whisper, because I *am* still blushing. And I can't help thinking about what it would be like to finally be with Storm like that.

"Sorry, sweetness. I won't make you blush anymore, at least not when I'm not there to enjoy seeing your face get cherry red." His smirk is so big I can hear it over the phone.

I know he talks like that because he's ready.

So am I.

My body gets tingly just thinking about it.

**

A limousine showing up in my driveway was certainly not what I had in mind when Storm said he was taking me out. From my front window, I see Storm step out of the shiny black car. His newly bleached blonde hair and thrice unbuttoned crisp white shirt are striking against his black leather sports coat and black slacks. When he reaches my front door, I open it, looking down. His new black Doc Martens meet my gaze before my eyes travel slowly up to the black leather gunmetal warrior necklace he likes to wear. When my vision catches his mouth, I can't help but keep my eyes locked on his lips.

His Adam's apple bobs up and down as he swallows. His fingertips touch my chin, lifting my face to look him in the eyes. "You are so beautiful, princess."

Though he's used that term of endearment on me thousands of times, butterflies still insist on fluttering inside my stomach when he calls me princess.

"So. Do. You." I need to breathe between each word. I've practically come undone right in front of him. There has never been a more gorgeous sight than the man standing at my front door.

"I'm beautiful?" he asks with a raised brow.

"Most definitely," I say, licking my lips.

He laughs and takes my hand. "Your parents home?"

"No. They went out for the night."

The guttural sound that comes out of his throat signals to me that he has second thoughts about going out tonight.

"We gotta get outta here."

Storm's arm falls around my shoulders to slide me over to his side of the back seat. The limousine is so large that it'd take several steps just to knock on the partition window up by the driver. A rapid flapping of little wings swim around my insides as my limbs begin to quiver in anticipation of tonight. My eyes involuntarily close when he runs his free hand up my thigh and without warning, I can't breathe. When I lean my head on his shoulder, he leans forward and kisses my forehead, working slowly down my nose to my mouth. I open my eyes to see his deep purple eyes looking right into mine. "I love you, Honor. I love you *so* much."

A combination of warm and cold chills runs up and down my legs and arms. "I love you, too. More than you can imagine."

He takes my face in both his large hands. "And I am so grateful for that, sweetness. Every day of my life, I am so grateful that you fell in love with me. For the rest of my life, I want to earn that position." He swallows hard and brings his lower lip between his teeth. "I didn't think I would ever be deserving of anyone's love, never mind yours. When I think back to the man I used to be," Storm's thumb runs over the top of my ear, "it's staggering. When I first met you, my world turned around. I found a reason to live. A reason to smile. A reason to be a better person." My heart pounds listening to him. "Thank you, Honor. Thank you for making me who I am today."

His hands fall to my legs at the same time he drops to one knee on the floor of the limo. "I realize we're young, princess, and I intend for us to finish out college first, but," he reaches into his jacket pocket as he takes my left hand in his and holds it tight, "I was just wondering if when we graduate, you wouldn't mind becoming my wife." He holds up a solitary square diamond ring set on a white gold band. "Will you marry me, Honor? When we graduate, will you be my wife? Will you—"

"Storm," I interrupt. "You wanna give me a chance to answer?"

Sitting back on his leg, he nods once.

"Yes. YES," I say louder, "I *will* marry you. I would *love* to be your wife."

Sliding the ring on my left finger, Storm's hand trembles, reminding me that he may be big and strong, but he's sensitive and vulnerable too—the exact reasons I fell in love with him in the first place.

"Oh, baby," he cries, squeezing me between his arms. "Thank you...thank you, thank you, thank you," he says before kissing me on the mouth. Once I open my mouth just a little, his tongue claims mine and he tastes so good. A little sweet, a little salty. Just like him.

Just when Storm's hand finds my skin beneath my shirt, the limousine comes to a complete stop. "I guess we're here," he mumbles into my mouth.

"Mmmm," I utter back, unwilling to break our embrace.

"Mmmm, I know it's comfortable where we are." His lips are a breath away from mine now. "But we have reservations." He kisses me one more time. "We'll pick up where we left off later." Looking into my eyes and tapping my nose with his finger, he says, "Come with me."

We step out of the limousine into Manhattan. "New York City?" I ask.

Storm nods. "Hayden Planetarium."

"Oh my gosh. I've never been here." Looking up into this huge glass box with a big blue ball inside of it, I'm in awe. I never knew something like this ever existed.

"Look at you all bright-eyed," Storm remarks, pulling me by the hand closer into him.

"It's just so...so freaking awesome."

"I knew you'd love it," Storm says proudly. "I couldn't resist bringing you here."

"You've been here before?" I squeeze his hand and look up at him.

"Nope. I've only seen it online." Excitedly, he pulls me up the stairs into the building. "I thought to myself," he says, while he shows his identification to the hostess, "what would Honor like to see that she was never able to see before?"

I raise my eyebrows up at him.

"Yeah. Pretty much everything. So, I thought I'd start by showing you the Universe."

We settle inside the sphere to watch the most breathtaking images of the Universe I've ever seen. It's like being outside at midnight, only better. Though we are not the only ones in the theater, it feels like Storm and I are the only two people in the entire galaxy. The night is perfect. With Storm holding my hand under the stars and planets, there is nowhere else I'd rather be.

Until later that night...

Chapter Fourteen

The limousine pulls into the parking lot outside Storm's apartment building.

"We're not going to my house?"

With the back of his fingers, Storm gently strokes my cheek. "Yes, babe. We're going to your house, but I need a way to get home. I'm not paying the limo driver to wait around until I leave your house." Storm pecks my cheek then slides us out of the car, the limo driver holding the door for us.

Storm hands me the keys to his front door, and while I unlock it, he finishes talking with the driver. Two seconds later, he's at the door with me. When he sets his hand on my lower back, and I feel his skin through the lace of my dress, I can't help but want so much more.

"Let me just put some sweats on and we can leave," he says, kicking off his shoes and throwing his jacket over the sofa before he heads into his bedroom.

"Okay." My voice shakes.

Storm turns around. "You all right, princess?"

I nod.

"You sure?" he asks.

Again, I nod. "Yes." I speak so softly, I'm not even sure the word came out of my mouth.

When he turns to go into his room, I step slowly forward to follow him, my heart racing, my stomach twisting. I clutch my hand to my chest. When I get to his room, his back is bare and he's pulling down his black pants. Gasping as I grasp the doorpost with my free hand, I catch his attention as his one foot comes out of his pant leg.

The one side of his mouth turns up. "What's up, princess?" he asks slowly, now showing me a full grin.

Because I don't know what to do next, I stand there in his bedroom doorway, immovable.

He pulls the other pant leg over his foot and tosses them to the floor, his eyes never leaving mine. In just his dark gray boxers, Storm walks toward me, reaching me in three smooth steps. "Did you need something, sweetness?" he asks, though I can tell by his pompous expression that he knows what I need.

Words are caught in my throat while my body quivers. When his hands knead my upper arms, I turn to putty beneath them. The room around us turns black and the only three things I am aware of are Storm's hands on me, the thunderous beating of my heart, and my rapid breathing. In an effort to suppress my breathing, so as not to draw Storm's attention to it, I close my eyes, willing myself to calm down.

"You smell like vanilla tonight." Storm's right hand advances toward my neck. "No coconut?"

I shake my head.

"If I didn't tell you before, I like it." His hand passes my neck as he cups the back of my head. With his left hand, he fingers the side of my face, finally resting his hand on my neck. The breathing I had tried to calm picks up again when Storm takes my ear between his thumb and forefinger.

When he's done fondling my ear, his fingers move down my neck and across my right shoulder. His finger hitches beneath the neckline of my dress and he slides my sleeve and bra strap down my arm, exposing my shoulder for him to kiss.

Leaving a slow train of kisses from my shoulder to my neck, he finally finds my mouth and claims it with unreserved enthusiasm. His right hand moves down my back and, in one movement, he bends, scooping his left arm beneath my knees as he picks me up and brings me to his bed.

"We don't have to do this, Honor," he says seriously, his intense purple eyes intently searching mine.

Because I want him to know how much I *do* want this, I fix my eyes on his with the same intensity. "I *want* to do this," I tell him, finally finding my voice. Because though I'm fearful of what to expect, I know without a doubt that I am ready to give myself to Storm.

A groan escapes his throat before he lowers his mouth back on mine. While he tenderly kisses my mouth, his hands travel my body in an effort to release me of my dress. His kisses move down my body as they follow my dress. Once he's slid the dress off of me, he pulls back and kneels between my legs, his eyes appreciatively surveying my body. "God, you are beautiful."

His trail of kisses back up my stomach are followed by a path of warm tingles that once again leave me breathless and wanting. When he reaches behind to unclasp my bra, I am so aroused that I dig my fingernails into his back and let out a moan that reaches up from my abdomen. As he slides his hands back down my stomach, he slips his fingers under the elastic waist of my panties and slides them off.

I naturally open my legs as he climbs back up to kiss my mouth. "Open your eyes, princess," he says softly into my mouth. When our eyes meet, his mouth opens. "I want you to know that I will love you forever and always. There is nothing on this earth or beyond that will ever keep me away from you. Please know that it is your breath I breathe. *You* are my oxygen. *You* are what keeps me alive."

With a tender yet concentrated gaze, Storm slowly lowers his body on top of mine. And in one deliberate moment, I become his forever.

PART FIVE
SIX YEARS LATER

ETHAN

"You wanted to see me, Mr. President?"

"Oh yes, Ethan." The President of the United States stands from his chair, walks around his desk, and shakes my hand, covering it with both of his. "Yes. I did," he says excitedly, disengaging his hands from mine. "Please," he offers, pointing a hand to a deep burgundy leather armchair, "have a seat."

With a confident air, I sit as I thank the President for offering me a seat. "So, what can I do for you?" I ask him, my posture relaxed and composed.

"No. Today it's about what *I* can do for *you*." He sits in the chair beside me, instead of the one behind his desk.

I nod once to allow him to continue.

"I wanted to personally thank you, Ethan, for saving my life last week." The President is genuinely grateful.

With my elbows on the arms of the chair, my hands crossed in front of me, and my ankle leaning on my knee, I respond as I always do—with a single nod, and the acknowledgement that it's my job to save his life.

"It may be your job, but I need to be grateful that you are even able to do your job." He shakes his head in disbelief. "I still can't believe you extracted that bullet from my chest with your bare hands. And then proceeded to heal the wound it left. I'm still in awe."

"I would have healed you completely, but I was told not to," I say seriously.

"No, no, I would never expect you to. We can't let anyone figure out your *uniqueness*. We had to make it look like the bullet only grazed me. But, Ethan, in all seriousness, I died out there in front of the nation...and no one knew it."

"Well, I was trained to work inconspicuously, Mr. President."

"I'm aware of that, Ethan. Can I ask you something?" His fingertips rhythmically drum his own thigh.

"Of course," I say, still immobile, my fingers still laced together.

"Are you always this serious and reserved? I can't recall you ever breaking into anything that resembles a smile."

"I take my job very seriously, Mr. President. But I thank you for your gratitude. Please be assured I'd do it again in a heartbeat."

"I don't doubt that, Ethan. Now, I wanted to offer you something...anything. Of course, aside from a very generous bonus this year, is there anything personal I can offer you? Anything out of the ordinary?" He leans forward, looking intently into my eyes.

"I would like some time off to go to my brother's wedding next month. I haven't been home in six years."

"Of course. It's done. You want the whole month off?"

"A week is good, sir. The week leading up to the wedding would be perfect. Thank you."

"You haven't seen your brother in six years, and you only need one week off?"

"Yes, sir. We were never that close."

"Is he your only brother?"

"Yes, sir."

"Okay, Ethan," he says, standing from his chair.

As I rise with him, I hold out my hand. "Thank you, again, Mr. President. I appreciate the time off."

"Any time. Thank *you* for making it possible for me to actually be standing here to offer it to you." With a smile, he grabs my hand again with both of us.

Stoically, I nod again, and wish him well.

Grateful to be out of there.

I've certainly earned the reputation of stoicism, but I attribute that to my many years of practice in closing my heart. But the moment I requested off to go to Storm and Honor's wedding, an errant slice of my heart opened against my will.

Like the year I met Honor, and my hardened heart weakened its resolve. Unable any longer to protect myself from emotional attachment, specifically to Honor, I was left vulnerable and open. And nothing on Earth had prepared me for the pain my heart would endure the moment I realized I'd lost her to Storm.

**

"So, are you really up for going to New Jersey again?" Shelby asks me on the way up to my penthouse apartment.

"I think so," I tell her, stepping out of the elevator and into my stark white living room.

She kicks off her shoes and heads toward the dining room to grab a bottle of wine for the two of us. "Because, I'm not so sure that I'm ready to go back."

Though I've been in a monogamous relationship with Shelby for the past two years, we haven't spoken much of New Jersey since she transferred four years ago to Radians College to continue her nursing degree. "You don't have to come with me," I deadpan, reaching for the wine glasses from the wrought iron hanging rack.

As I open the six-hundred dollar bottle of red wine, Shelby hands me a glass one at a time. "I'm not sure I like the idea of you seeing Honor without me there." She sits down on my black leather sectional and curls her feet beneath her toned legs.

"Please. I don't even think about her anymore."

She stares at me with her eyebrows lifted and a smirk on her face. "Right."

"I don't." Which is the truth. I have become such a master at shutting out my emotions and closing down my heart, that I almost feel nothing—even for Shelby, regrettably. Loosening my tie and slipping off my shoes, I join her on the couch.

"Oh, and I'm supposed to believe that? Ethan Sutherland has finally stopped yearning for the perfect Honor Stevens? I don't think so."

"I'm with *you*, aren't I?" I cup my hand behind her neck and kiss her wine-stained lips.

"Don't patronize me, Ethan. She's the reason I didn't allow myself to date you for the first two years I was here. I didn't want to be second choice. Still don't." She licks her lips and sips her wine again.

I am even second choice to Honor—which is why I'm living this ridiculous life to begin with.

"Ok, that's reassuring." She puts her glass down on the glass coffee table. "You can't even respond to that, can you?"

"Shelby. This really is a non-issue. Either come with me or don't. I won't be offended if you don't. But please, don't make this about Honor." Just saying Honor's name causes those locked up emotions to beat their way through my heart. But I don't allow it. I can't. The pain was too great. And I will not go there again. Instead, I lean in to kiss Shelby again, but she pushes at my shoulders.

"No. I want to be sure." She pours herself another glass of wine, and I hold my glass up for more as well.

"Shelby. *You* are in my life now. Not Honor. I don't want her in my life. If I wanted her in my life, I would not have signed on to be the government's guinea pig, I would have run away with her somewhere. But I didn't. I know this conversation has been long overdue, but now that we've taken care of the elephant in the room, can we finally just drop it?" I look at her to see her reaction. She's thinking about what I've said. "I want to go to the wedding, because Storm asked. It will be nice seeing them again, now that I can be sure the government isn't after any more empaths." I lie to Shelby. Of course I wanted Honor in my life. But her life meant too much to me to hand her over to the CIA.

She rubs my leg and kisses my cheek. "I'm sorry, Ethan. You're right. This has been long overdue, but I'll take your word for it." She shrugs with a smile. "I have no choice."

Finishing my second glass and pouring myself another, I sit back and pull her stocking feet on top of my legs. "You have nothing to worry about."

I grab a bulk of her dark brown hair and yank her gently towards me, kissing her full on the lips before bringing up something else I have been wanting to talk to her about. "I've been wanting to talk to you about something." Another huge swallow of my wine and I think, *this probably calls for whiskey.* "Anyway." The words get stuck.

Moving closer into me, she touches her cheek to mine, her smile fading. "Ethan. Is this bad? I haven't known you to be flustered *since* New Jersey. What is it?"

"Before they put me in the Secret Service, as the President's *body guard,*" I say in air quotes, "they did some things to me."

Shelby leans in closer, her eyes curious. "What things?"

I rub her thigh. "Things. DNA type things. *Other* things...that they made me do to myself," I pause. I get up to pour myself that Glenfiddich I really need, down a glass, pour some more, and sit back down to a worried Shelby. "They wanted to *recreate* whatever it is I am. And I let them." Another gulp of the whiskey, and I'm starting to feel a little less tense. "I let them so they wouldn't go looking for...Honor...or my brothers or Uncle Tom. I had no choice."

Shelby squeezes my hand that rests upon her thigh. "It's okay, Eeth. You had to do what you had to do."

"Yeah, well, what I had to do...what I helped them to create, well, they're just about five years old now." I finish my scotch and slam it down on my glass coffee table.

"Oh my...you mean...they made...children?" Shelby looks horrified.

"Yup." Those familiar feelings are knocking again. This time with a sledgehammer. That time six years ago was one of my most frightening. The only thing I thought about while being poked and prodded was Honor. She was my motivation, because she was why I was there. She *is* why I exist—only I need to exist without her.

"Ethan?" Shelby kisses my ear, shaking me out of my painful memory.

I can't go there. I need to get back to my safe place. My black place. I close my eyes, toss all those thoughts into my mental closet, and lock the door. "There are children out there that have my DNA. Made from *my* sperm."

When Shelby's jaw drops to her chest, she's silent.

"Oh my God, Ethan. You're a father?" Shelby plops her feet on the floor and stands up. "And it took you this long to tell me?"

"Seriously, Shelby? *That's* what you get from this? Not the fact that the government reproduced empaths so they can use at their whim?" I stand to pour myself another huge glass of Glenfiddich. "And you know at some point they're going to train those kids to kill, right? So that they become immortal? And whoever they drugged to steal the eggs from, what'd they do to her? Some innocent. So get as mad as you want that my sperm fathered some innocent children. Because that's why I was telling you that." I storm into my office, pissed that Shelby seemed to blame me for this. Like I had any choice in the matter.

No.

No choice.

Not for me.

Unless I wanted them to go after Honor.

Sometime later, Shelby's standing at my office doorway.

"What is it?" I ask, giving her a blank stare.

She drops to the armchair next to the door. "I'm sorry, Ethan." Her words are said through a bucket load of tears, her eyes red and puffy as if she's been crying since I walked out of the room two hours ago.

"It's fine." I say, feeling absolutely nothing at this point.

She sits there, her black eyes as wide as quarters, and my heart is cold as ice. I know I'm an empath, and I should be feeling compassion naturally, but I don't. My only focus these days is keeping my eye on the President. If he's physically hurt, I'm there to heal him. I don't feel people's pain. I tune it out completely. Like I had before meeting Honor. Though it took me a while to close my heart, I'd successfully done it—filling any open cavity with the cement from my veins.

And then I went and opened a letter from Storm. I should have known better. Honor had been mailing me a letter every month since the day I left Jefferson. But I stuck them at the bottom of my underwear drawer, unread and unopened. Storm's handwriting on the front of the envelope should never have fooled me. Sure, the letter was from him, but it was written on Honor's behalf. *She's afraid I'm dead, because it's not like me to just ignore her letters.* Yes. It is like me. Especially since she is the reason I don't *feel* anymore.

"You know what, Ethan?" Shelby asks, after I picked up with my work where I left off when she interrupted. "You're an ass."

Dropping my pen, and crossing my fingers beneath my chin, I look at her.

"Anyone would have reacted that way to the news you just laid on me. Your being a father was not the only thing I was concerned about. It just happened to be the first thing that came out. Plus, after the whole conversation about Honor, I was in a mood."

"*You* brought up that conversation."

"Ethan. I saw your face when we were talking about her. You still love her."

With the alcohol doing its job, I have no desire to talk myself out of this anymore. I only have the energy to stare at her.

"I'm right, aren't I?" She moves herself to the edge of the chair. "You've never stopped loving her, have you?"

A drop of ice melts from my heart. "No." I say softly, yet firmly. "I haven't."

"Then I guess I'll be taking my things back to my apartment."

I feel just a tiny twinge of remorse when I watch her walk out of my office.

Maybe it's the guilt, maybe it's those darn emotions trying to tear down my resolve, but I am not expecting to feel sad when Shelby reaches my elevator with a bag filled with her belongings.

"Shelby. I'm sorry." I stand there defenseless, watching her hold back her tears. "Until tonight, and bringing her up, I had no idea that I still loved her. I mean, I guess I did, but...I hadn't realized how much those feelings were holding me back from giving my all to you."

Shelby laughs. "Really, Ethan? You didn't even give me close to your all. You were mentally checked out for most of the moments we shared together."

This actually surprises me. "Then why did you stay with me?"

"Convenience. It was nice to have someone to come home to after school and work. Plus, I've liked you since high school. I just thought," she pauses to chuckle again, "you'd somehow forget about her."

"I guess I thought I would too."

"Don't kid yourself. We were both blind. How could you *not* think of her, when your whole reality here is *because* of her?" Shelby reaches up to kiss me goodbye. "I know I'll get over you, Eeth. I can tell. But I feel bad for you, because, truthfully, I don't think you'll ever get over her. And forever, specifically for an immortal like you, is one hell of a long time."

When the door closes behind her, her words resonate throughout my entire body, sending chills and tremors from my neck to my toes. Forever is going to be one hell of a long time.

THE WEDDING

ETHAN

"Thanks for being my best man, Ethan. It means a lot to me."

Storm's changed *a lot* since I've seen him last. He's not afraid to show his feelings anymore. "No problem." I haven't changed. Not in my compassion for Storm anyway. Although somewhere deep inside I have respect for the guy, the only reason I'm serving as his best man is because Honor asked me to.

"Is my tie straight?" he asks, shaking his head and grinning. "Look at me. I'm a nervous wreck. Me. Nothing used to get me flustered, and here I am a fumbling mess. And you. Since when have you become so in command of yourself?" He runs his hand up and down in front of me. "You wear a tuxedo like it was made for you."

Smirking, I tell him that it *was* made for me.

"That's right. You thought it was a bring-your-own." He pauses. "What's with you, Ethan? All week you've been cool and distant. Is this the real you now, or is it an act?"

"The real me *is* an act, brother." I stick my hands into my expensive pockets and walk toward his dresser. "The real me died six years ago."

My comment is met with nothing but a sigh from Storm.

When I turn, he's sitting at the edge of his bed. "I'm sorry," he offers.

"Don't be. I would have made the same choice even if she *had* chosen me. There was no way in the world I would have let the government come after her. She'd have never been able to build a wall to protect herself. Even if they had realized she was no longer an empath, they would have poked and prodded her just to make sure. So, don't be sorry, Storm. It wouldn't have ended for me any differently."

Storm lets out a mirthless chuckle. "I don't think your life *does* end, does it, Eeth?"

My shoulders drop and I let out an involuntary emotional sigh. "Unfortunately...no. But it is what it is. I get to forever be eighteen years old, making more money than I know what to do with, and every twenty years or so, I'll get to start all over in a new relationship as my own son, or grandson, great-grandson."

I'm met with a pitying smile.

"Don't look at me like that. I don't need your pity."

"That's not why I'm looking at you like that." Storm stands and places his hands on my shoulders. "We could always find Tom and have him *take care of you*. You know what I mean? I mean he can heal you. You can come back to life free from this. Start over again. With us."

Now *I* laugh. And I haven't laughed in a long time. "You want Tom to kill me and bring me back to life, so I can watch you and Honor live happily ever after? No thank you. After tomorrow, I'll go back to my Secret Service life, watch out for the President, and worry about the future when it gets here." I give Storm a reassuring pat on his arm. "Really, guy. I'm comfortable where I am. My life may always be in a state of irony...healing people I have no feelings for...but it's a life I chose. I may not be good at showing it, but I'm content."

Storm takes my hand in both of his, much like the President did, and says, "You're a better man than I am, Ethan. Thank you. Thank you for sacrificing your life for her. I'll owe you for the rest of mine."

**

The dramatic timbre of the pipe organ announces Honor's arrival. The beating of my underactive heart stalls once or twice before it kicks over and converts its dormant dust into tiny fireworks awakening those emotions I'd tried hard to entomb. Standing at the altar, waiting for Honor to walk down the aisle, my mind replays the day, one week ago, when I saw Honor for the first time in six years.

She is beautiful.

Her long hair, no longer blonde, spills effortlessly over her shoulders and down her chest. The violet eyes I see every night in my dreams are now a dark blue. With a golden complexion, she's nothing like I remember.

Yet she's everything like I remember.

When she greets me with her dimpled smile, it takes all I have to not tell her I am still in love with her.

"Ethan," she cries, running up to me with her arms wide open. "Oh my gosh, I am so happy you came."

"Hey, angel," I say with a smile, trying to maintain my dignity when all I want to do is pick her up in my arms and run away with her. "It's been a long time." It's been a long time. What an asshole thing to say.

She stares at me with a reluctance to believe I am standing in front of her.

It's awkward. For both of us.

"I've missed you, Ethan," she says quietly.

I nod, afraid to admit out loud that I've missed her every second of every day. If I open up now, I'm afraid my heart would break in two. "So you're getting married?" Another asshole comment. Of course she's getting married. For someone so refined, I'm sure acting like an idiot.

She uses her hand to cover her smile.

"It's okay to be happy about it in front of me. That's why I'm here. To see you start the life you deserve."

Wrapping me in a big hug again, Honor tempts my resolve.

Setting her back down on her feet, I detour our conversation. "So I hear you're a school counselor?"

"Yeah." Her smile still hasn't left her face. She's genuinely happy that I'm here.

"I think that's terrific, Honor." I take her hand and lead her to her front steps. The front steps that adorn her new house. The house that she and Storm bought together. And though it's a modest home in a modest town, it is so much more than my penthouse apartment in Washington D.C. "You finally get to go to elementary school," I muse, sitting us down on the step.

"I know." She beams. "Plus, I get to help children. I've always liked that part of me," she says humbly, her shoulder coming up to meet her neck. "My desire to help others. I just hated how much it hurt." She shrugs again, smiles, and pats me on the knee. "Are you happy, Eeth?"

How do I answer that truthfully? Happy without Honor? No. I'll never be. But I am content with my decisions and the reason my life is what it is today. "Yes, Honor. I'm happy." Truthful? No. The right answer? Yes.

"You never responded to any of my letters," she whispers, removing her hand from my leg.

"No. I didn't. I'm sorry."

There's an awkward silence for several minutes.

Until I decide to break it.

"Honor." I clutch her hand in mine.. "I didn't even read your letters." When she attempts to take her hand away, I grasp it harder. "I couldn't."

A tiny gasp escapes her throat before revelation sets in.

"It was too painful for me, Honor. I'm sorry."

Her head drops to my shoulder. "I'm sorry, Ethan. I'm really sorry."

I lift her chin from my shoulder. "I still have them you know. I'd never get rid of them."

Nodding her head, she tries to smile. "Are you seeing anyone?"

"No." I pull her in and let her head drop to my shoulder. I don't think it's the right time to tell her about Shelby. With no explanation, Shelby stopped keeping in touch with Honor when she transferred to Washington. No reason to bring Honor down by talking about Shelby.

"Are you lonely?" Honor asks.

"I keep busy, angel. Some days, I'm working forty-eight hours straight. I'm too busy to be lonely."

She looks up at me through lidded eyes. "I'm so sorry it didn't work out between us, Ethan."

Holding her chin in my hand, I look into her eyes and re-member the day six years ago when she said the same exact thing to me. "It's okay, sweetheart. It wasn't meant to be."

A sad smile is offered as my consolation prize.

Patting her swiftly on the knee, to drop this entire subject, I say, "Let's go inside. I can't wait to see this house of yours."

She is every bit as beautiful as I'd imagined she'd be on her wedding day. Forgoing the traditional white for a pale pink taffeta gown, Honor is scintillating. Her hair, the color of butterscotch, sits high on her head, her bangs slicked back with a single pink pearl. The strapless neckline accentuates her long neck, while the pink gloves that reach her upper arms elongate her slim limbs. Honor is exquisite.

And she is Storm's.

That fact hits me once again like a brick to my chest.

The reason I never opened her letters.

The reason I've become a master of indifference.

Honor is not mine.

But my heart is hers.

Tiny fragments of my heart crumble with each step Honor takes toward him. The glimmer in her eyes is for him and him alone. As her hand reaches for his and he takes it, her smile invites him home. From this moment on...they are bonded for life.

I close my eyes to absorb the pain, tucking my emotions deep within my heart. Because this is the last time I will allow them to escape. From this point forward, I will no longer feel. As I have for the past six years, my only concern is to do the job I was hired to do, and no more. When I open my eyes, I turn toward the guests, zeroing in on all the couples. Something I'll never be a part of. Even if things had worked out with Shelby, in twenty years or so, she'd have aged, and I wouldn't have. The government would have me reintroducing myself to the Secret Service as Ethan Sutherland's son. And so will go my life until it meets an unnatural end. But as I'd said before, this would have been my fate whether Honor chose me to love or not. And with the understanding that I chose this life because I loved her *so* much, I am okay with it. I have found peace, because I had acted out of love. That is more than I could have ever expected of myself.

**

"Looking good, Eeth," a familiar voice says from behind where I'm sitting at my table at The Brownstone House. "Boy, Washington DC sure looks good on you."

"Cut it out, Tam." I stand to give her a hug. "How've you been? Honor said you were coming in from London."

Tamlin tosses her long honey blond hair behind her shoulder and nods. "Yeah, just got in this morning."

"Nice. So is that your natural color or another one of your concoctions?" I ask, referring to her many hair color choices from the past.

"It's natural. It's darkened over the years." She tugs at a couple strands. "Have to look professional in court. Could you see me with pink hair representing a client in front of the judge?" She laughs at her own joke.

"That's right. You're a big time lawyer now?"

"Not yet. When I'm finished with my degree I will be."

"Oh. What were you doing in London?"

"Visiting."

"Visiting?"

"Yeah. Your brother. Thank you," she says to the server who hands her a glass of wine.

"Can I get you anything, sir?" she asks me.

"A glass of Bordeaux red, please."

"Certainly, sir."

"What brother?"

"Eli," she says with a grin.

"Wait a minute," I say, grabbing her wrist. "I thought no one knew where they were."

Yanking her hand from me, she says, "Calm down, Ethan. It's not common knowledge, but *we* all know," she says, confused. "Why wouldn't we?"

I shake my head and stick my hands in my pockets. "I thought we didn't want the government finding them, so they don't end up puppets on a string, like I am."

"Yeah, well, you weren't around anymore and Tom took them out of the country, so what would be the harm, right?"

"Does Storm know?" Now I'm really annoyed.

"Yes, Storm knows. Geez, Eeth. You're the one that wanted them to go into hiding, so maybe Storm thought better of telling you. What the hell? You're just so...oh I don't know, maybe you are just like you used to be. You never did know how to chill."

I look at her straight-faced. "No. Chilling was never my strong suit."

Tamlin throws back her head in laughter. "No. Guess not." She pulls at my jacket sleeve until she's slid it all the way off my arm.

"Excuse me?"

Pulling the rest of my tuxedo jacket off, she throws it across my chair. "I think it's time you chill."

Next thing I know, she's yanked me onto the dance floor.

"I don't dance, Tamlin."

"Sure you do," a soft voice says to my right.

"Honor." As beautiful as she was when she first walked down the aisle, she's even more exquisite with her face aglow from dancing.

"You dance. I remember. The Wii game? My prom?"

So badly do I want to reach out and touch her. "Your prom." I remember it well. "If I recall, though, we only slow danced."

"That's not a problem," Tamlin says, running across the dance floor toward the deejay.

"In case no one has told you this today, you sure are beautiful, angel."

Honor takes my hand. "Thank you, Ethan. Thank you for coming today. It must not have been easy to get off of work." Now she takes my other hand. "I mean, I had no idea you actually worked for the President. When did you start doing that?"

As if by magic, or at Tamlin's request, "Your Song" by Elton John comes over the speakers.

"Remember this song, Eeth?" Honor asks innocently.

If she only knew. Though it wasn't Elton John's version, I picked this song for her prom playlist because of how much those words meant to me—back then as well as now. My gift may not have been a song like the man in the song gives to his girl. It's not the house or the potions or whatever else he wishes he could offer. It's what he is *able* to offer her that he gives to prove his love for her. My gift to Honor has always been my heart. Maybe not in the literal sense that Storm tried to give her. Or that poor Trisha unintentionally gave her. I handed my heart to Honor the only way I knew how—by keeping her safe. She may or may not know the torch I hold just for her, but she knows I'd give my life for her. She knows I *gave* my life for her. I may not get to hold her every night before she goes to sleep, but I can sleep peacefully, knowing she can sleep in peace.

As I hold Honor in my arms as the song comes to an end, I tighten my grasp, knowing that the next time I get to hold her will be in my dreams. When I kiss the top of her head and breathe in her scent one last time, I thank God that He put me in her life for me to love.

***

Before you go...would you mind leaving a review of Sacrifices on whichever site you purchased this book? Reviews, no matter how short, are the next best thing to word-of-mouth in helping a writer's book to get read. I would truly appreciate it. Please and thank you very much.

<u>Sign up at jpgrider.com to receive my newsletter and a free ebook.</u>[1]

<u>Books by J.P. Grider</u>
<u>YOUNG ADULT BOOKS</u>
<u>Love is Thicker than Blood Series</u>
Love Me Anyway
When Glass Shatters
Sacrifices

<u>NEW ADULT BOOKS</u>
Don't Look at Me
Unplugged (A Comeback Story)
Maybe This Life

---

1. https://landing.mailerlite.com/webforms/landing/e7v4a4

The Hunter Hill University Series
Calling California
Mending Michael
Reaching Rose

Don't miss out!

Click the button below and you can sign up to receive emails whenever J.P. Grider publishes a new book. There's no charge and no obligation.

https://books2read.com/r/B-A-BXUE-MVCR

Connecting independent readers to independent writers.

www.ingramcontent.com/pod-product-compliance
Lightning Source LLC
Chambersburg PA
CBHW030641120726
47905CB00001B/6